Kayla Miller

BESTIES

WORK IT OUT

BY KAYLA MILLER & JEFFREY CANINO
ART BY KRISTINA LUU

ETCH
HOUGHTON MIFFLIN HARCOURT
BOSTON   NEW YORK

Color by Damali Beatty
Lettering by Lauren Prescott
Illustrations & additional color by Kristina Luu

Based on the Click series, created by Kayla Miller

Etch is an imprint of Houghton Mifflin Harcourt Publishing Company.

hmhbooks.com

The illustrations in this book were done in Clip Studio Paint with digital brushes.
Cover and interior design by Andrea Miller and Stephanie Hays

ISBN 978-0-358-52115-0 hardcover
ISBN 978-0-358-56191-0 softcover
ISBN 978-0-358-61155-4 signed edition

Manufactured In China
SCP 10 9 8 7 6 5 4 3 2 1
4500824226

For every bestie I've made
along the way. —K.M.

For Mom. —J.C.

For Molly & Milo, my
four-legged besties. —K.L.

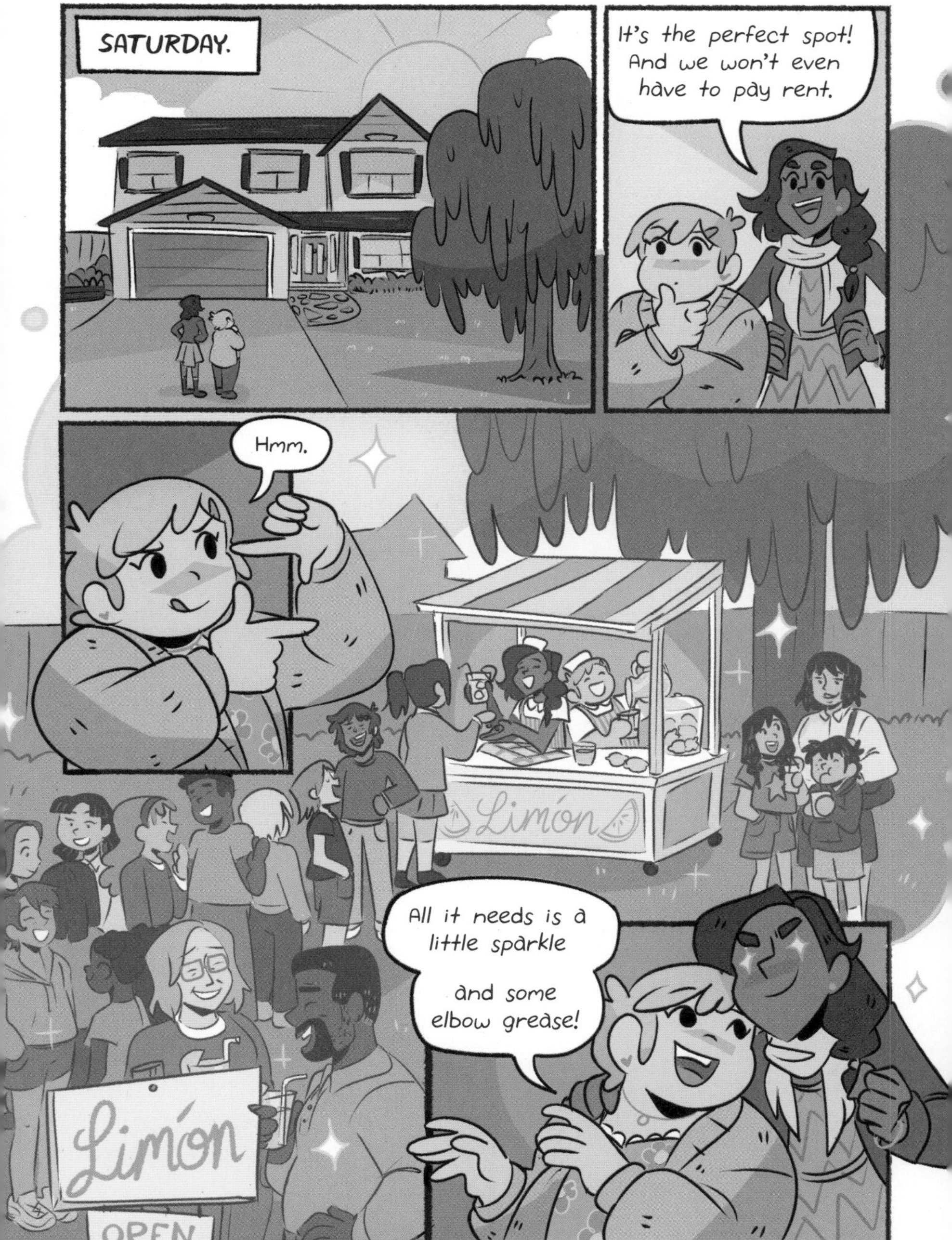
SATURDAY.
It's the perfect spot! And we won't even have to pay rent.
Hmm.
Limón
Limón
OPEN
All it needs is a little sparkle
and some elbow grease!

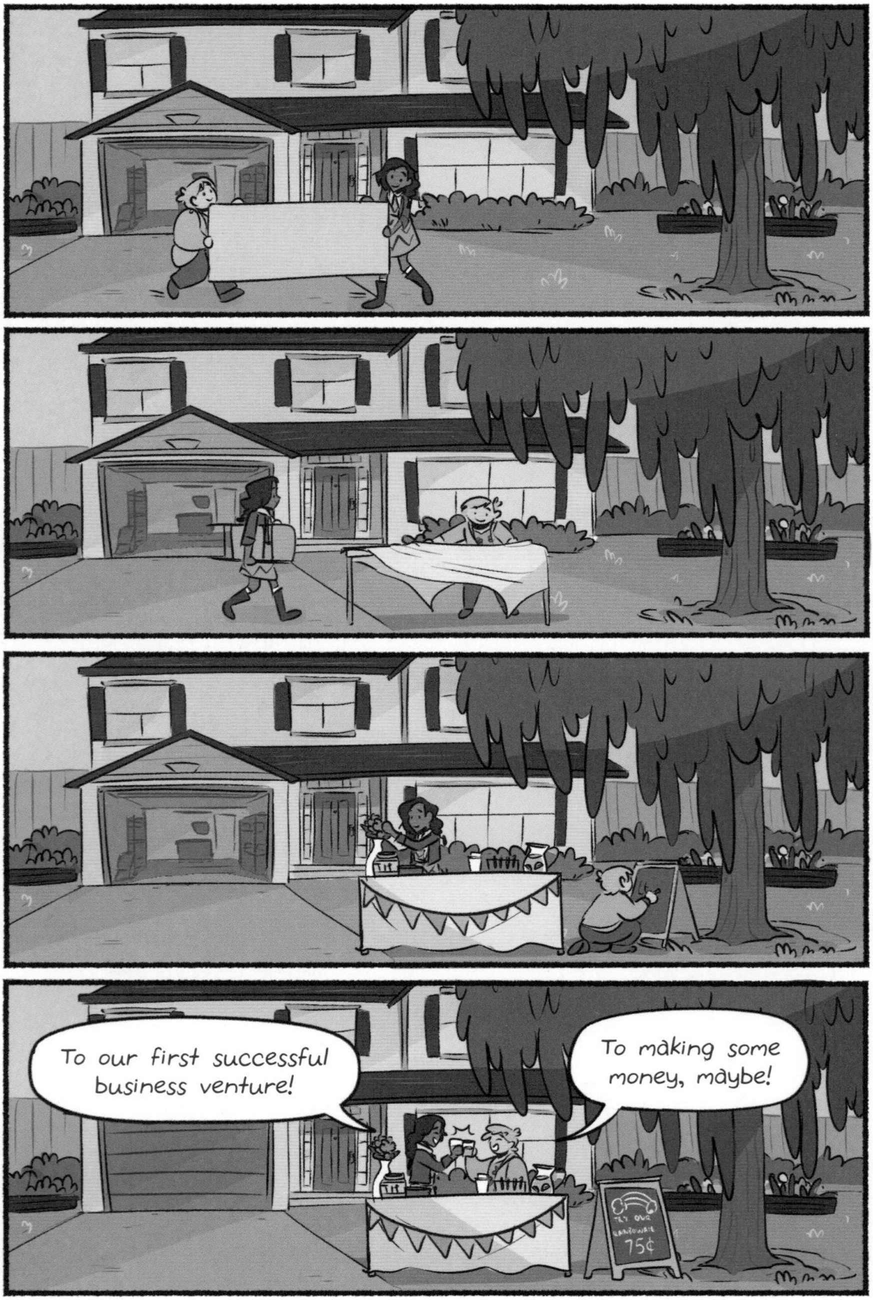
To our first successful business venture!
To making some money, maybe!
75¢

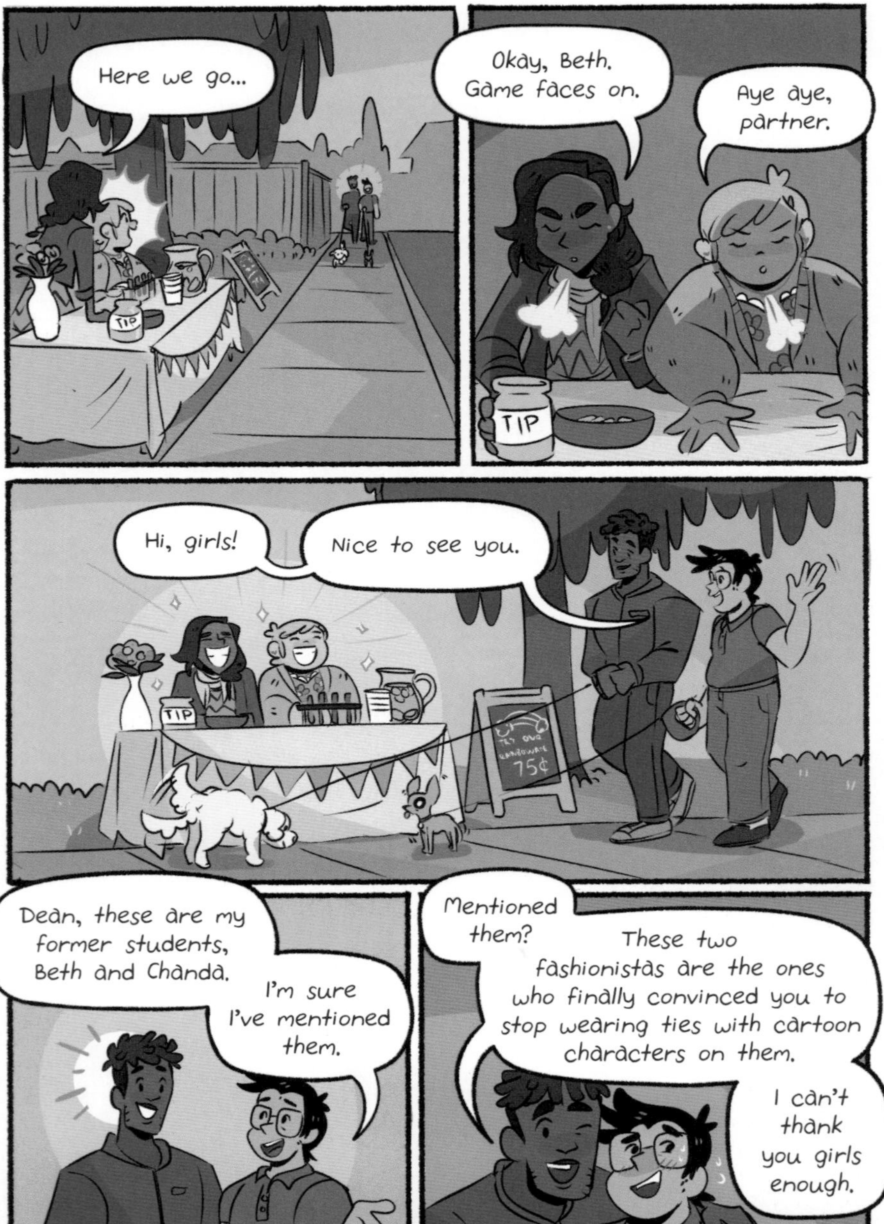
Here we go...
TIP
Okay, Beth. Game faces on.
Aye aye, partner.
TIP
Hi, girls!
Nice to see you.
TIP
75¢
Dean, these are my former students, Beth and Chanda.
I'm sure I've mentioned them.
Mentioned them?
These two fashionistas are the ones who finally convinced you to stop wearing ties with cartoon characters on them.
I can't thank you girls enough.

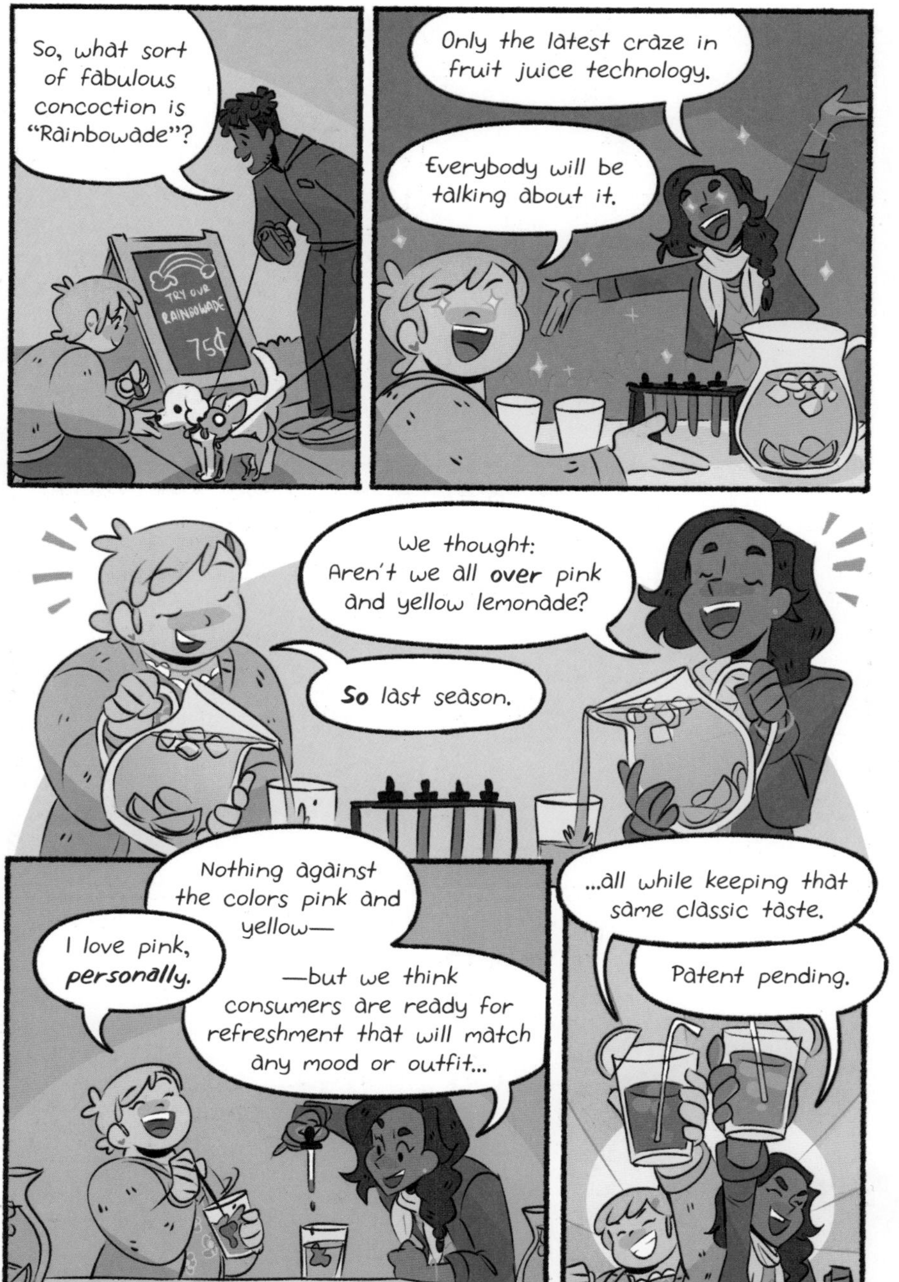
So, what sort of fabulous concoction is "Rainbowade"?
TRY OUR RAINBOWADE
75¢
Only the latest craze in fruit juice technology.
Everybody will be talking about it.
We thought: Aren't we all **over** pink and yellow lemonade?
So last season.
Nothing against the colors pink and yellow—
I love pink, ***personally.***
—but we think consumers are ready for refreshment that will match any mood or outfit...
...all while keeping that same classic taste.
Patent pending.

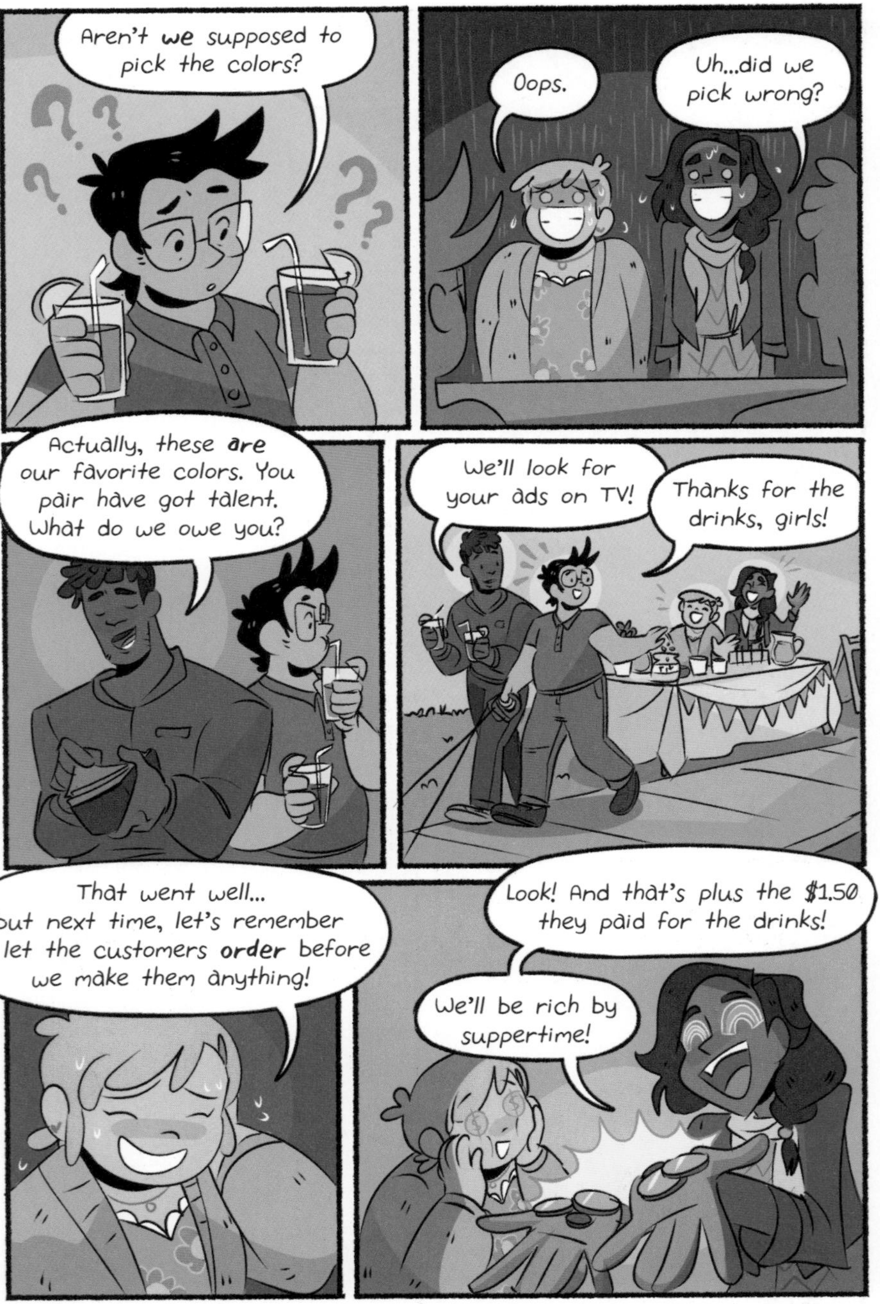
Aren't **we** supposed to pick the colors?
Oops.
Uh...did we pick wrong?
Actually, these **are** our favorite colors. You pair have got talent. What do we owe you?
We'll look for your ads on TV!
Thanks for the drinks, girls!
That went well... but next time, let's remember to let the customers **order** before we make them anything!
Look! And that's plus the $1.50 they paid for the drinks!
We'll be rich by suppertime!

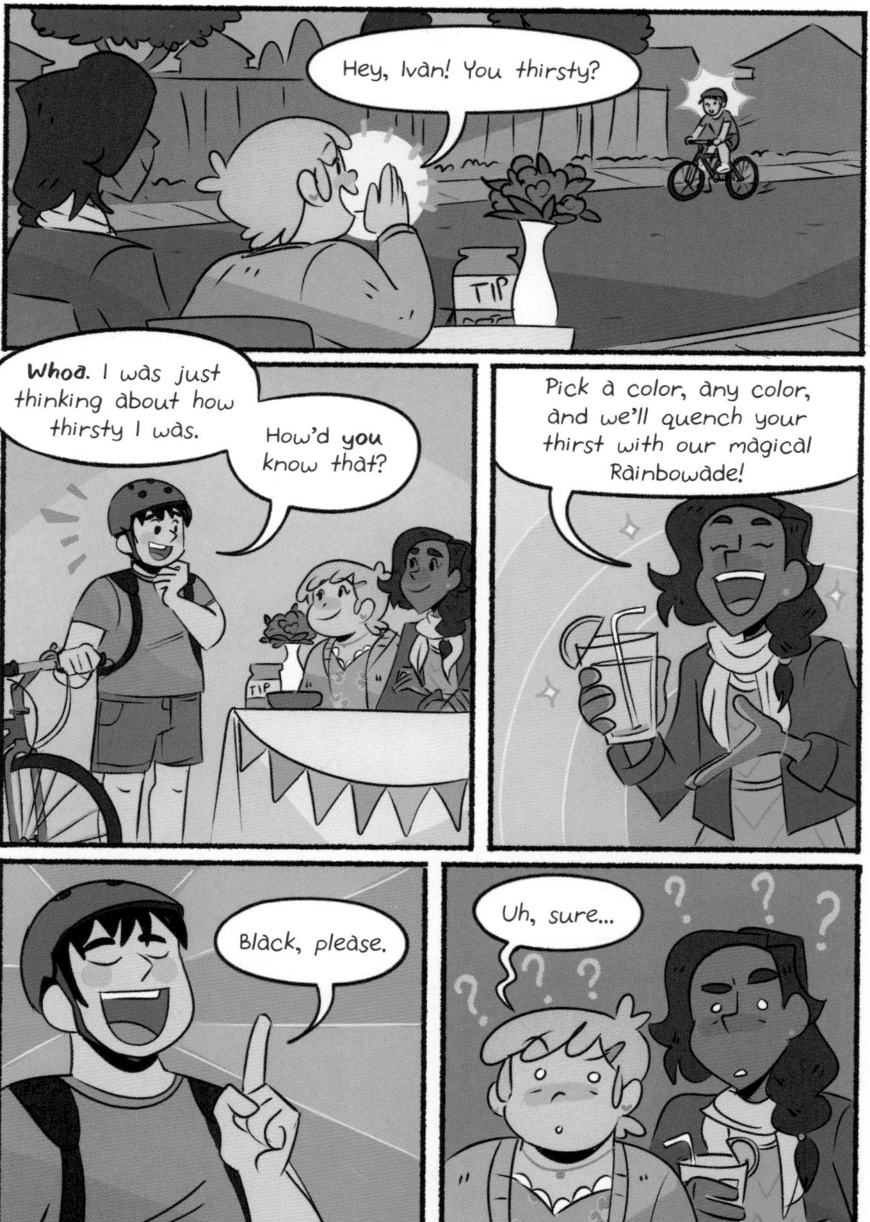
Hey, Ivan! You thirsty?
Whoa. I was just thinking about how thirsty I was.
How'd **you** know that?
Pick a color, any color, and we'll quench your thirst with our magical Rainbowade!
TIP
Black, please.
Uh, sure...

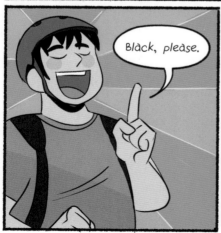

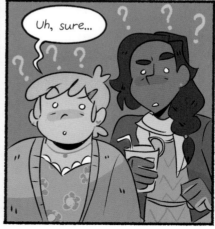

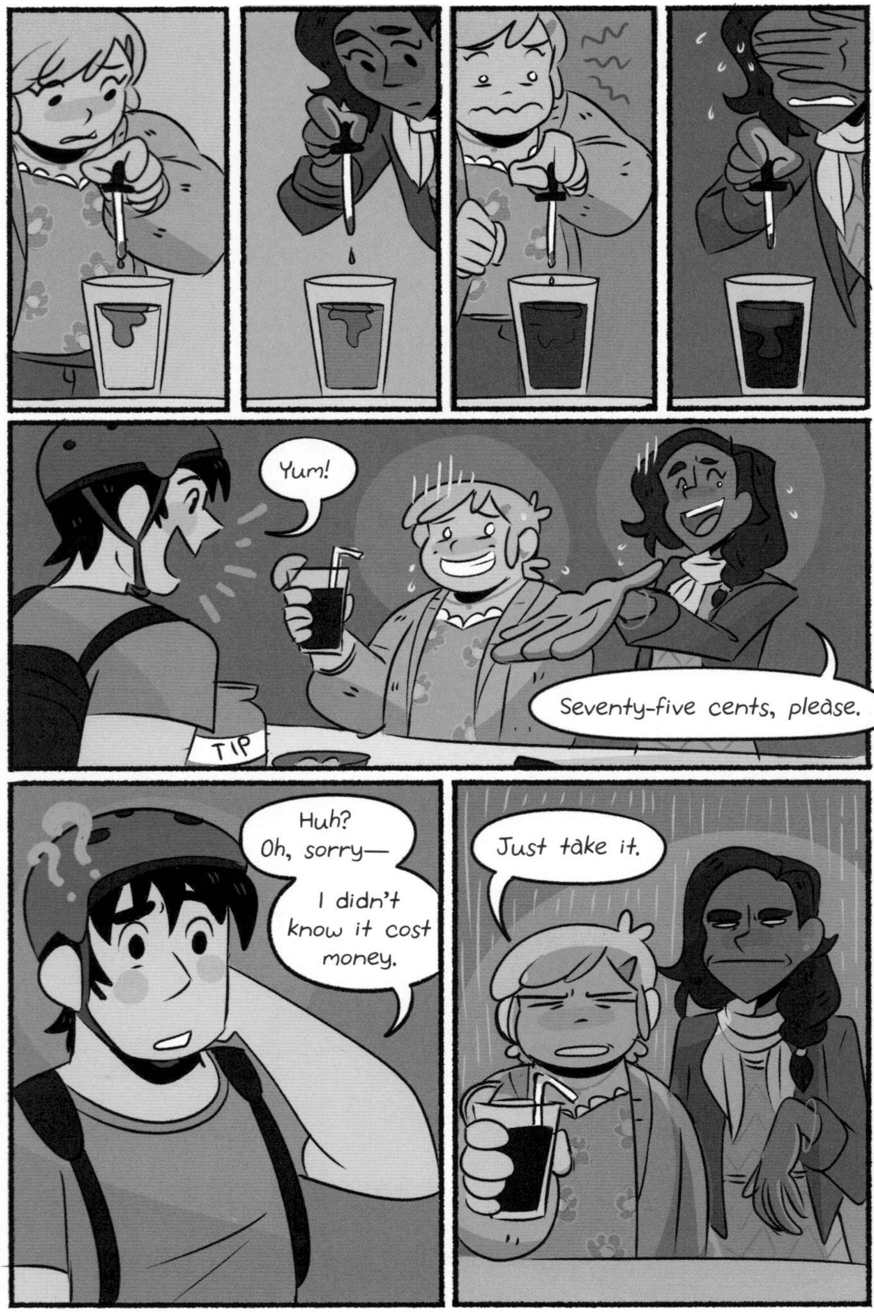

Yum!
Seventy-five cents, please.
Huh? Oh, sorry—
I didn't know it cost money.
Just take it.

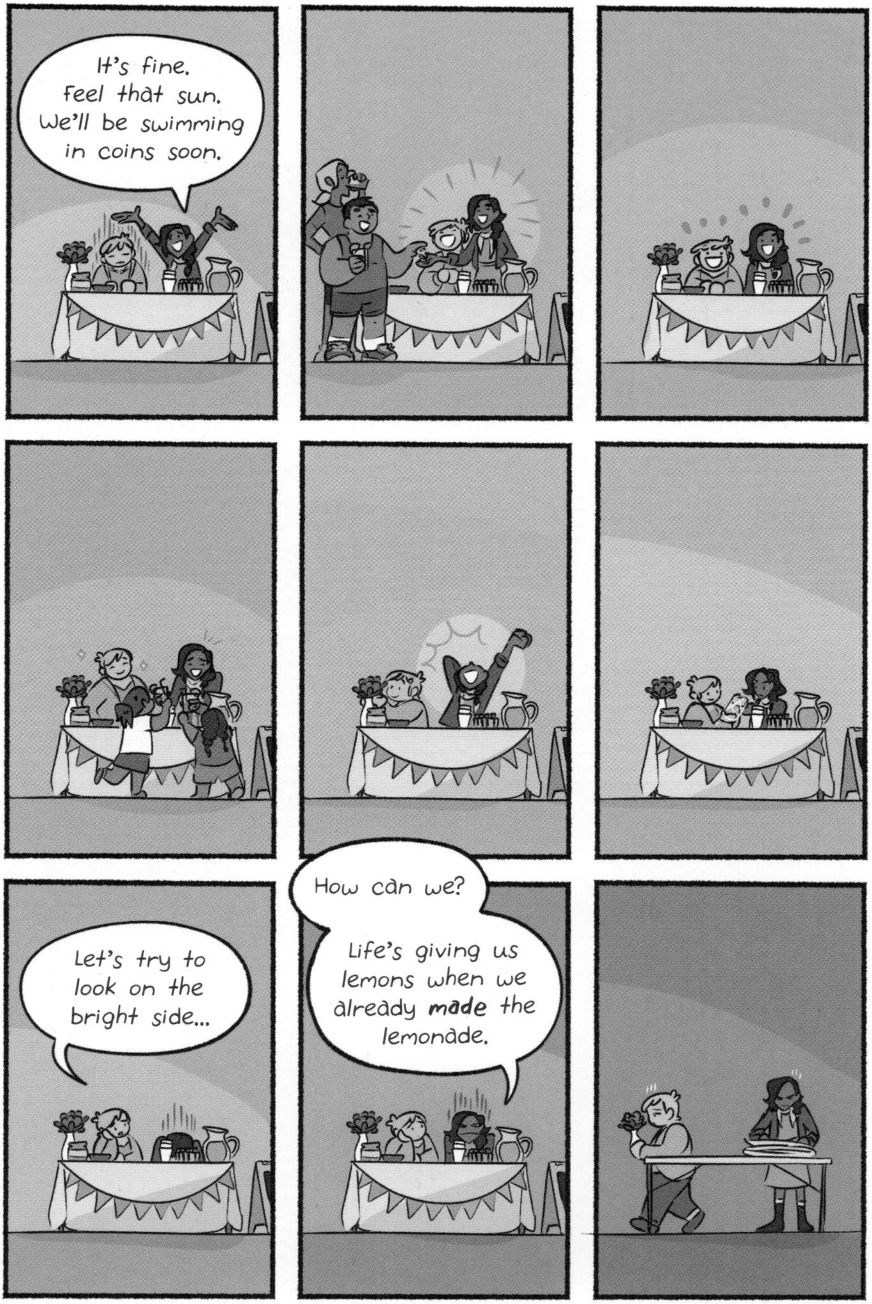
It's fine. Feel that sun. We'll be swimming in coins soon.
Let's try to look on the bright side...
How can we?
Life's giving us lemons when we already **made** the lemonade.

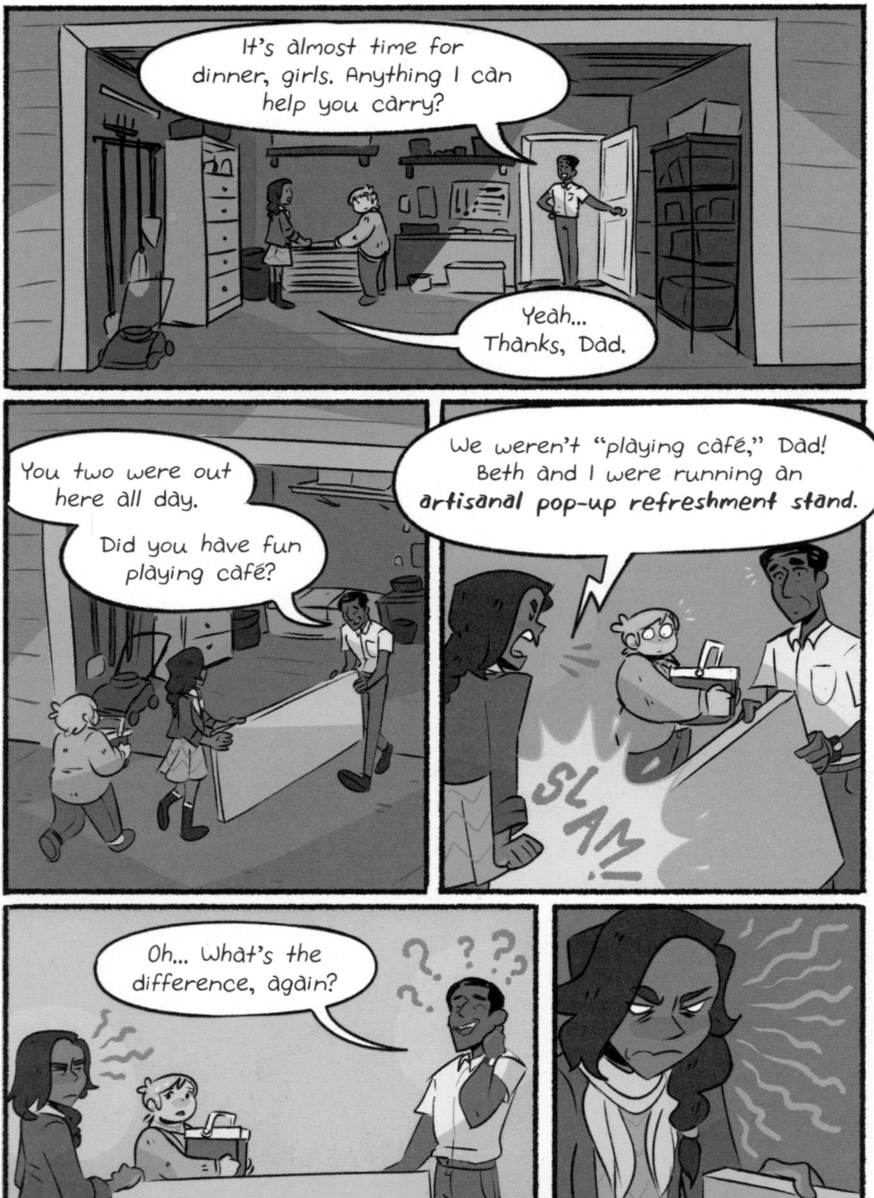
It's almost time for dinner, girls. Anything I can help you carry?
Yeah... Thanks, Dad.
You two were out here all day.
Did you have fun playing café?
We weren't "playing café," Dad! Beth and I were running an **artisanal pop-up refreshment stand.**
SLAM!
Oh... What's the difference, again?
? ? ? ? ?

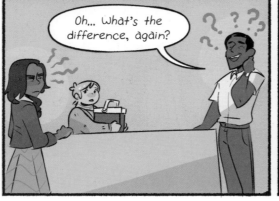

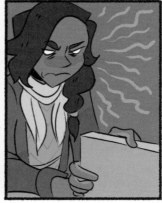

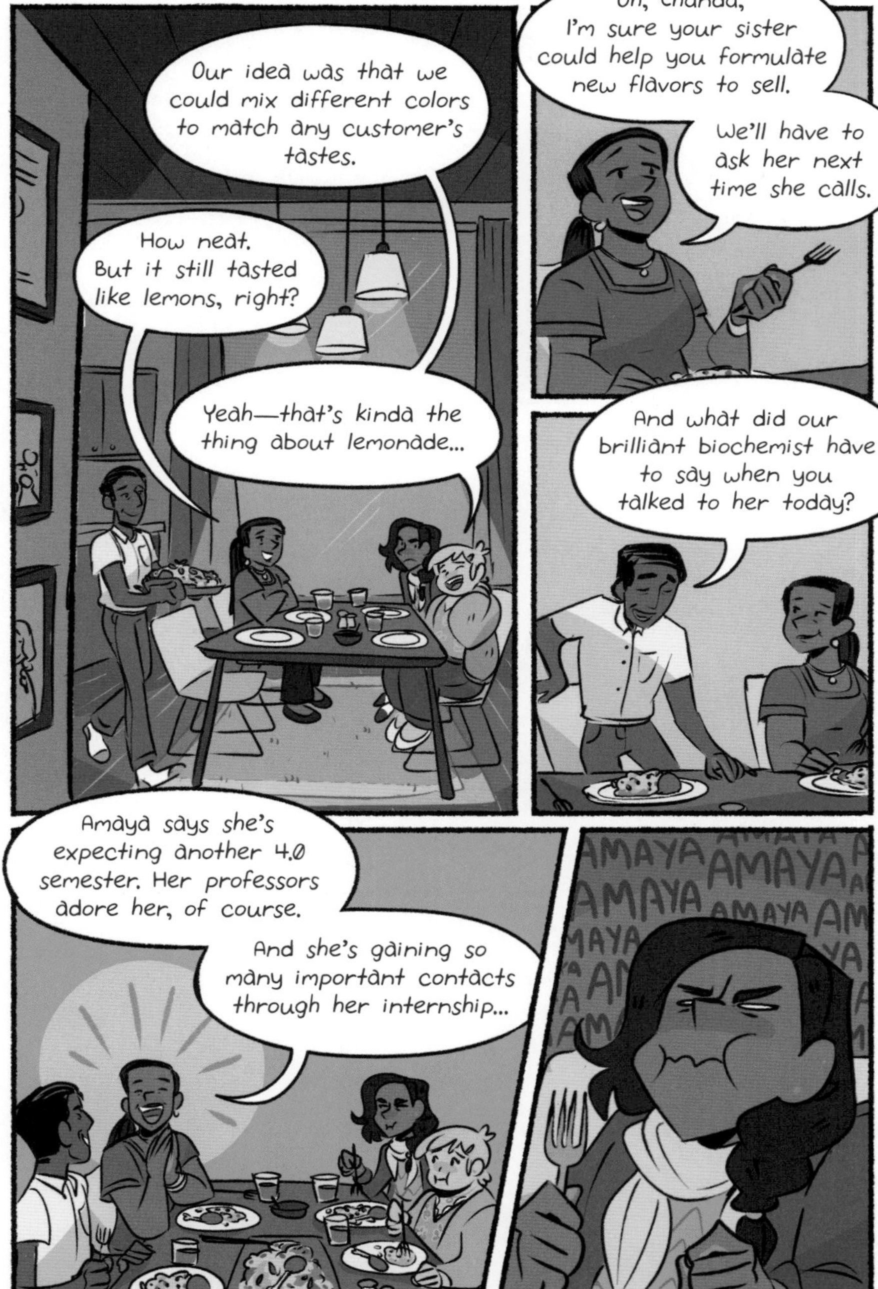
Our idea was that we could mix different colors to match any customer's tastes.
How neat. But it still tasted like lemons, right?
Yeah—that's kinda the thing about lemonade...
Oh, Chanda, I'm sure your sister could help you formulate new flavors to sell.
We'll have to ask her next time she calls.
And what did our brilliant biochemist have to say when you talked to her today?
Amaya says she's expecting another 4.0 semester. Her professors adore her, of course.
And she's gaining so many important contacts through her internship...
AMAYA AMAYA AMAYA AMAYA AMAYA

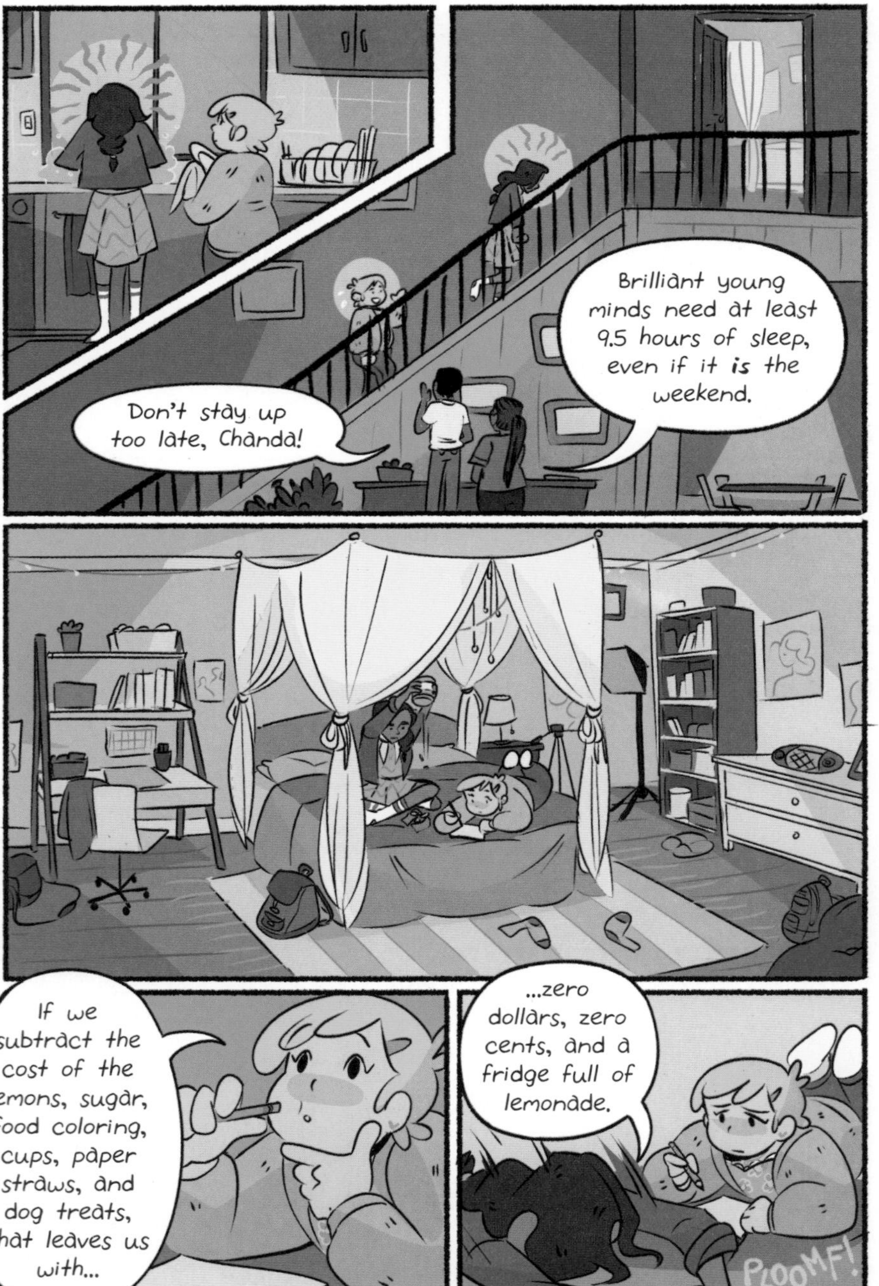
Don't stay up too late, Chanda!
Brilliant young minds need at least 9.5 hours of sleep, even if it **is** the weekend.
If we subtract the cost of the lemons, sugar, food coloring, cups, paper straws, and dog treats, that leaves us with...
...zero dollars, zero cents, and a fridge full of lemonade.
PLOOMF!

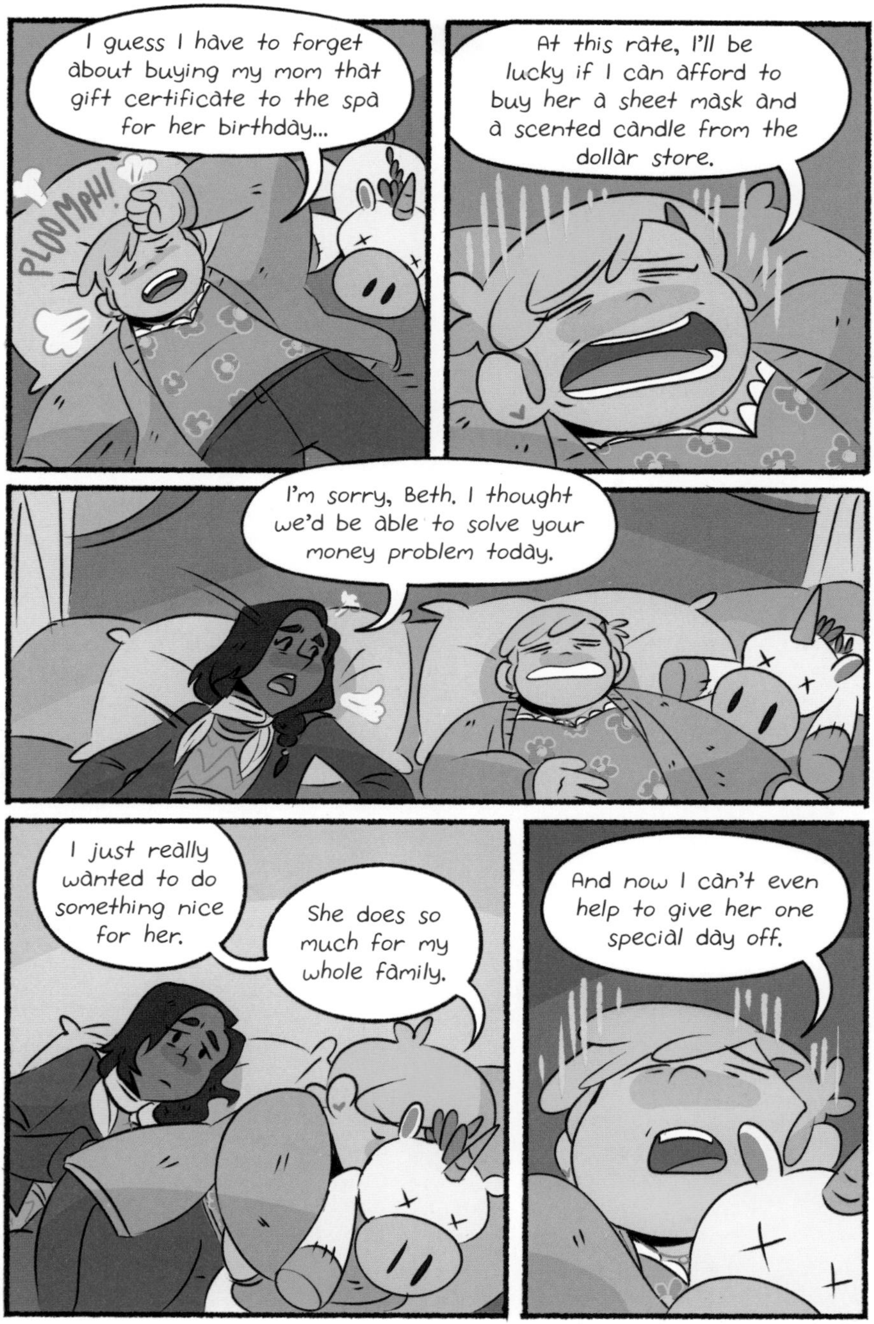
I guess I have to forget about buying my mom that gift certificate to the spa for her birthday...
PLOOMPH!
At this rate, I'll be lucky if I can afford to buy her a sheet mask and a scented candle from the dollar store.
I'm sorry, Beth. I thought we'd be able to solve your money problem today.
I just really wanted to do something nice for her.
She does so much for my whole family.
And now I can't even help to give her one special day off.

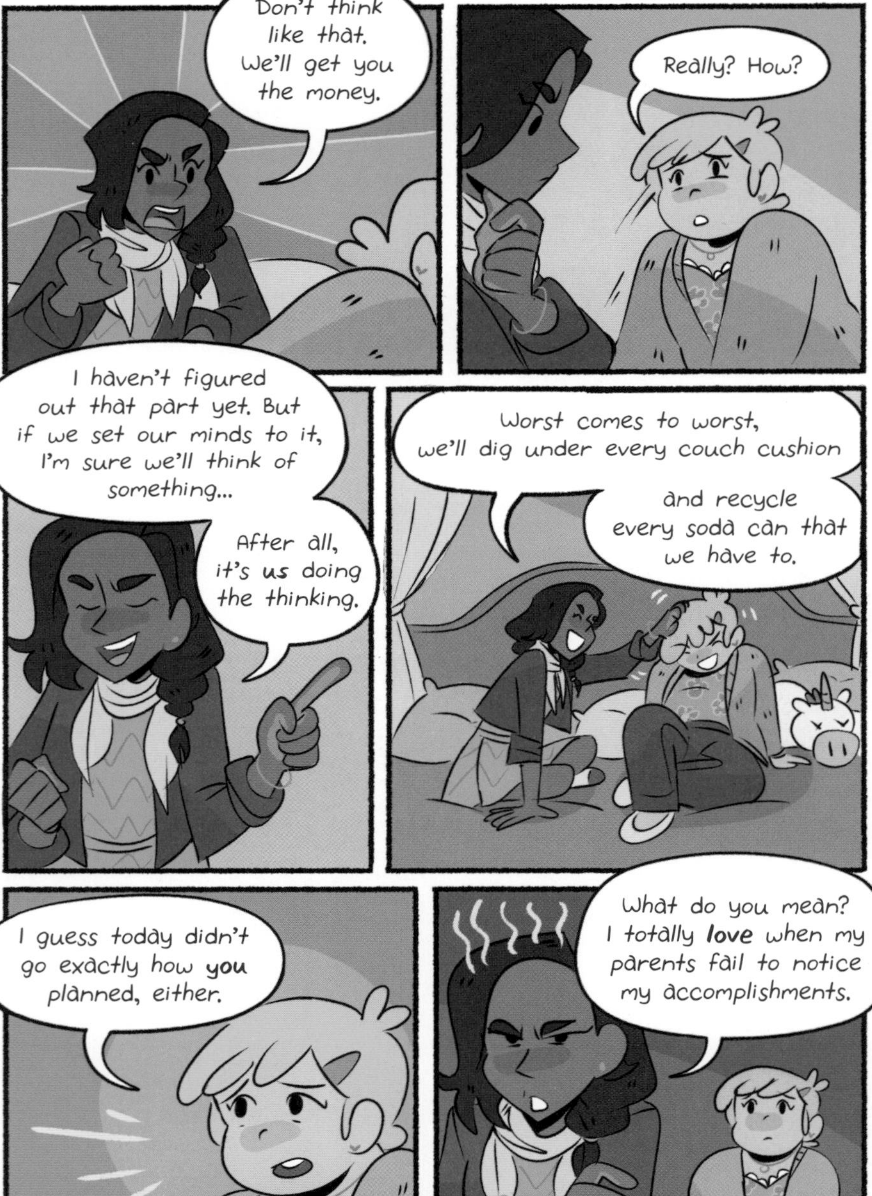
Don't think like that. We'll get you the money.
Really? How?
I haven't figured out that part yet. But if we set our minds to it, I'm sure we'll think of something...
After all, it's **us** doing the thinking.
Worst comes to worst, we'll dig under every couch cushion
and recycle every soda can that we have to.
I guess today didn't go exactly how **you** planned, either.
What do you mean? I totally **love** when my parents fail to notice my accomplishments.

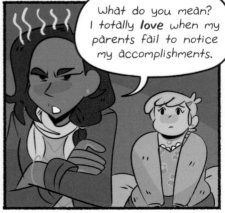

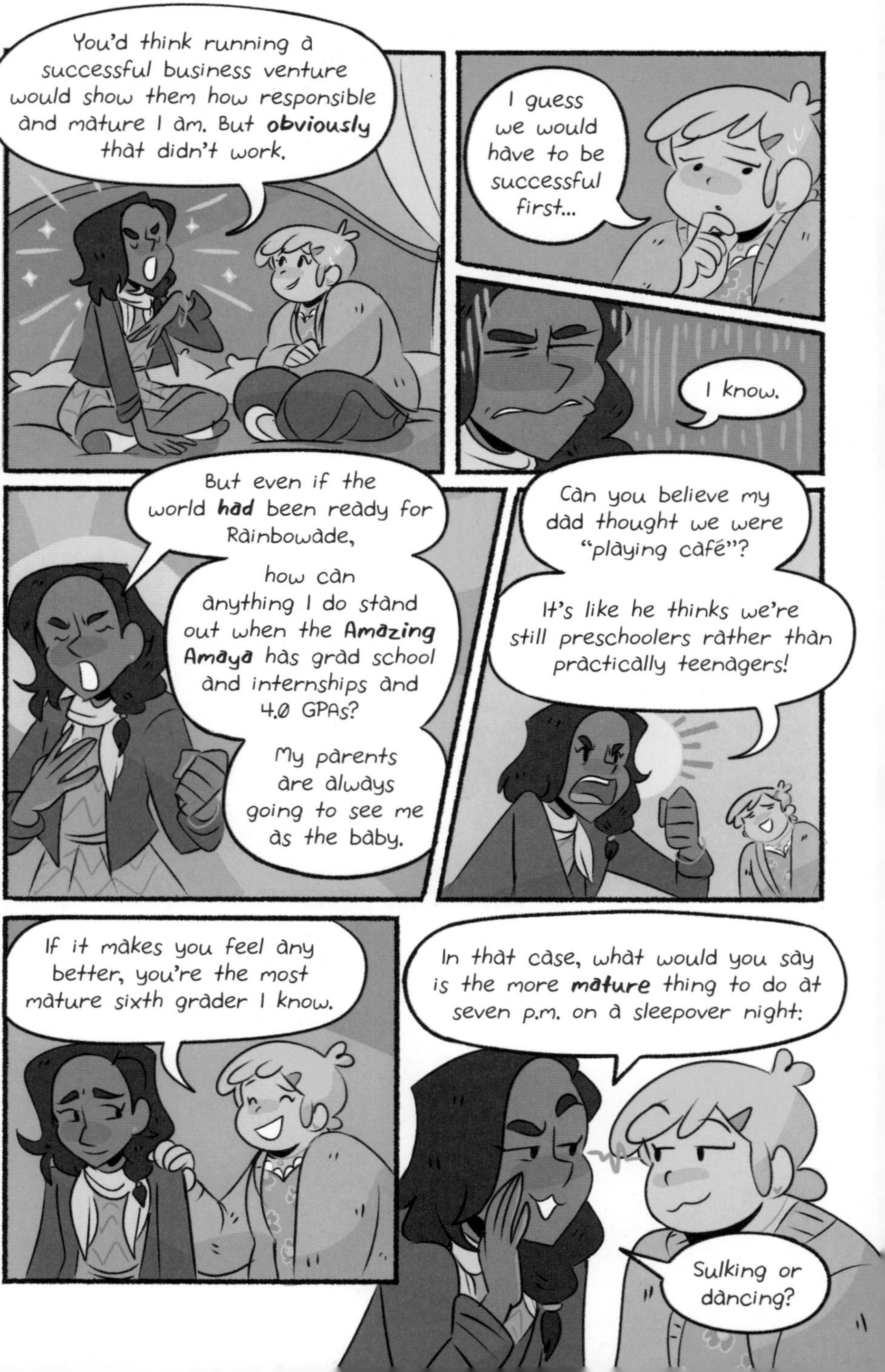
You'd think running a successful business venture would show them how responsible and mature I am. But **obviously** that didn't work.
I guess we would have to be successful first...
I know.
But even if the world **had** been ready for Rainbowade,
how can anything I do stand out when the **Amazing Amaya** has grad school and internships and 4.0 GPAs?
My parents are always going to see me as the baby.
Can you believe my dad thought we were "playing café"?
It's like he thinks we're still preschoolers rather than practically teenagers!
If it makes you feel any better, you're the most mature sixth grader I know.
In that case, what would you say is the more **mature** thing to do at seven p.m. on a sleepover night:
Sulking or dancing?

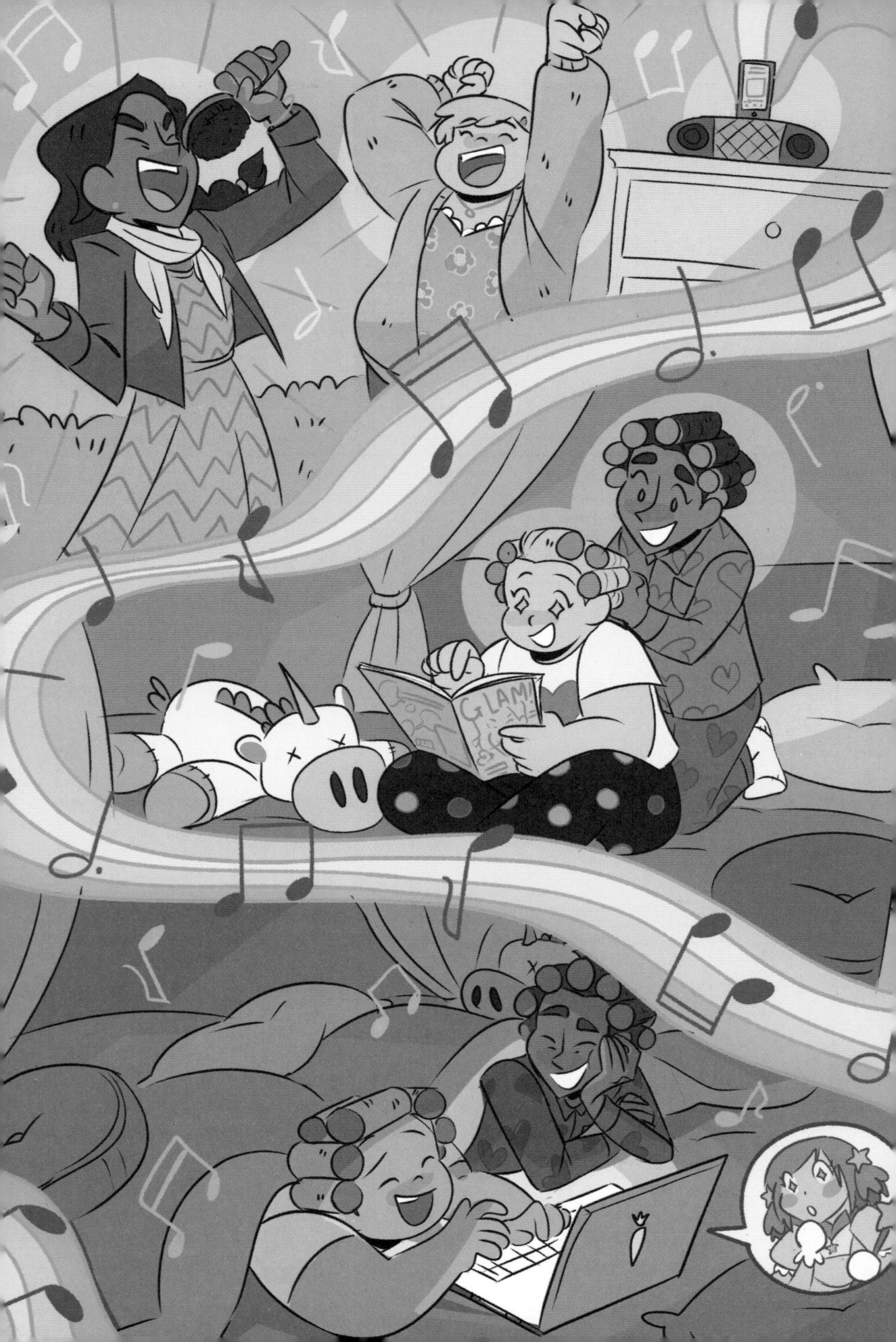
GLAM!

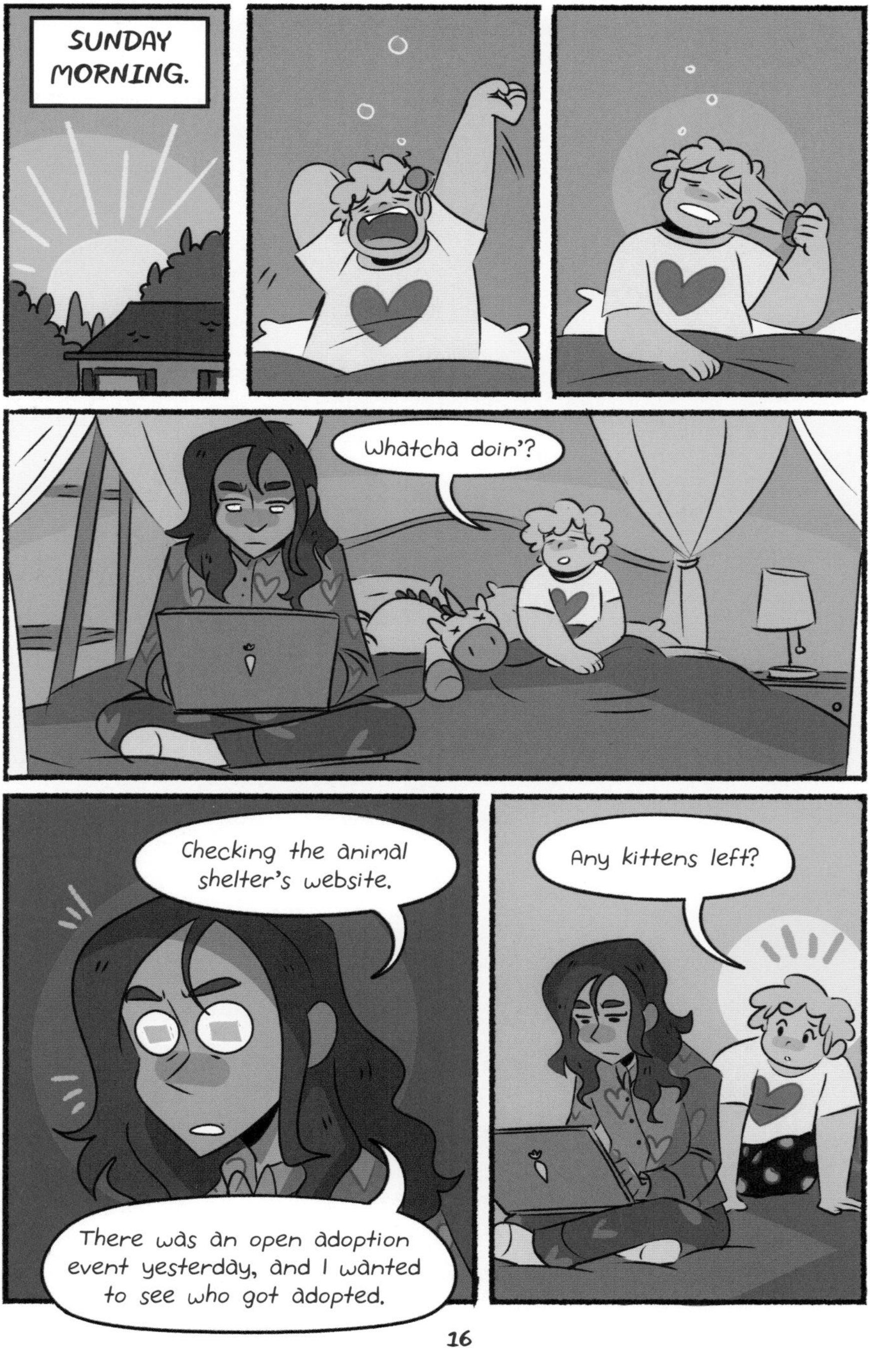
SUNDAY MORNING.
Whatcha doin'?
Checking the animal shelter's website.
There was an open adoption event yesterday, and I wanted to see who got adopted.
Any kittens left?

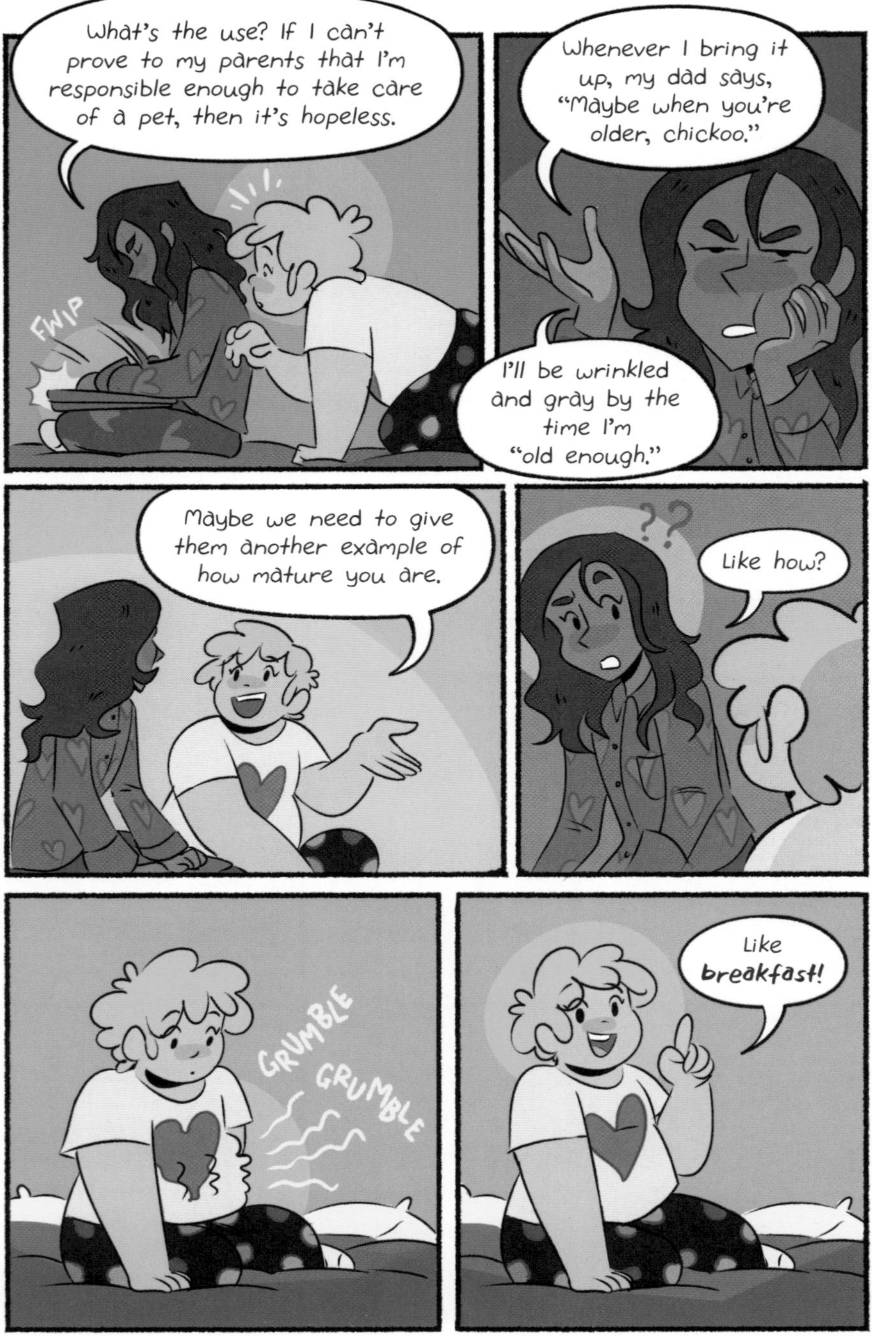
What's the use? If I can't prove to my parents that I'm responsible enough to take care of a pet, then it's hopeless.
FWIP
Whenever I bring it up, my dad says, "Maybe when you're older, chickoo."
I'll be wrinkled and gray by the time I'm "old enough."
Maybe we need to give them another example of how mature you are.
??
Like how?
GRUMBLE
GRUMBLE
Like **breakfast!**

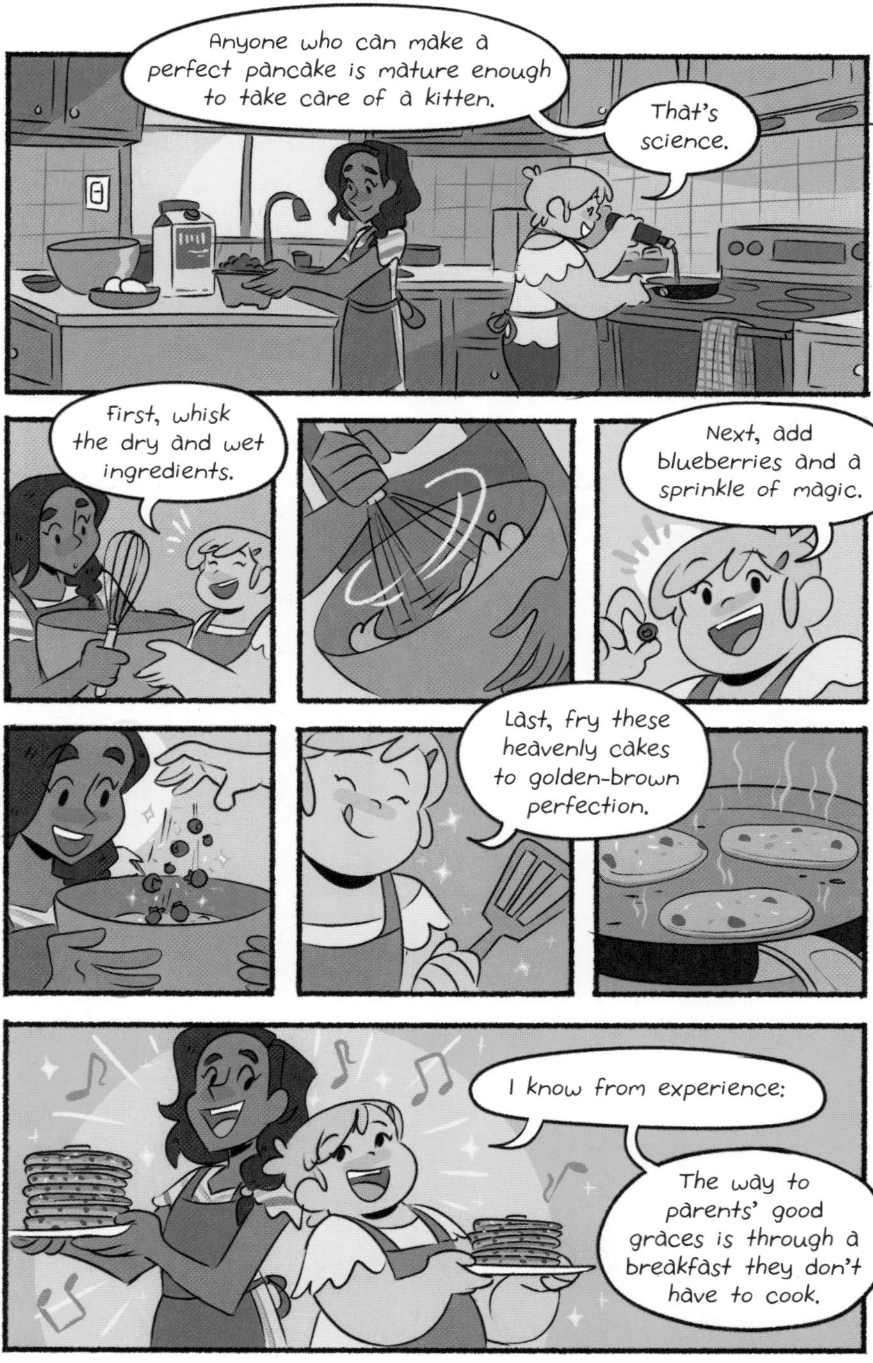
Anyone who can make a perfect pancake is mature enough to take care of a kitten.
That's science.
First, whisk the dry and wet ingredients.
Next, add blueberries and a sprinkle of magic.
Last, fry these heavenly cakes to golden-brown perfection.
I know from experience:
The way to parents' good graces is through a breakfast they don't have to cook.

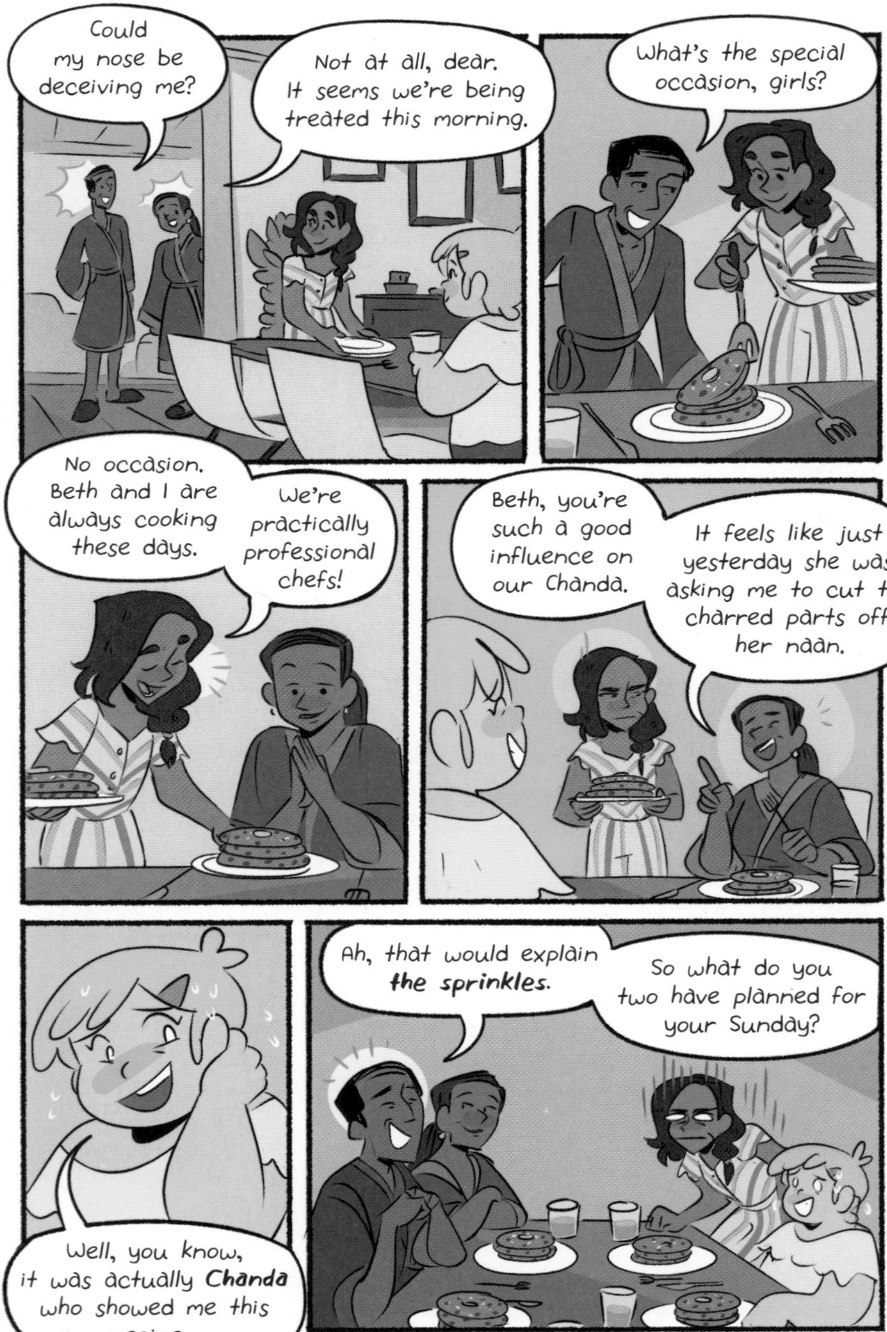

Could my nose be deceiving me?
Not at all, dear. It seems we're being treated this morning.
What's the special occasion, girls?
No occasion. Beth and I are always cooking these days.
We're practically professional chefs!
Beth, you're such a good influence on our Chanda.
It feels like just yesterday she was asking me to cut the charred parts off her naan.
Well, you know, it was actually **Chanda** who showed me this recipe...
Ah, that would explain **the sprinkles.**
So what do you two have planned for your Sunday?

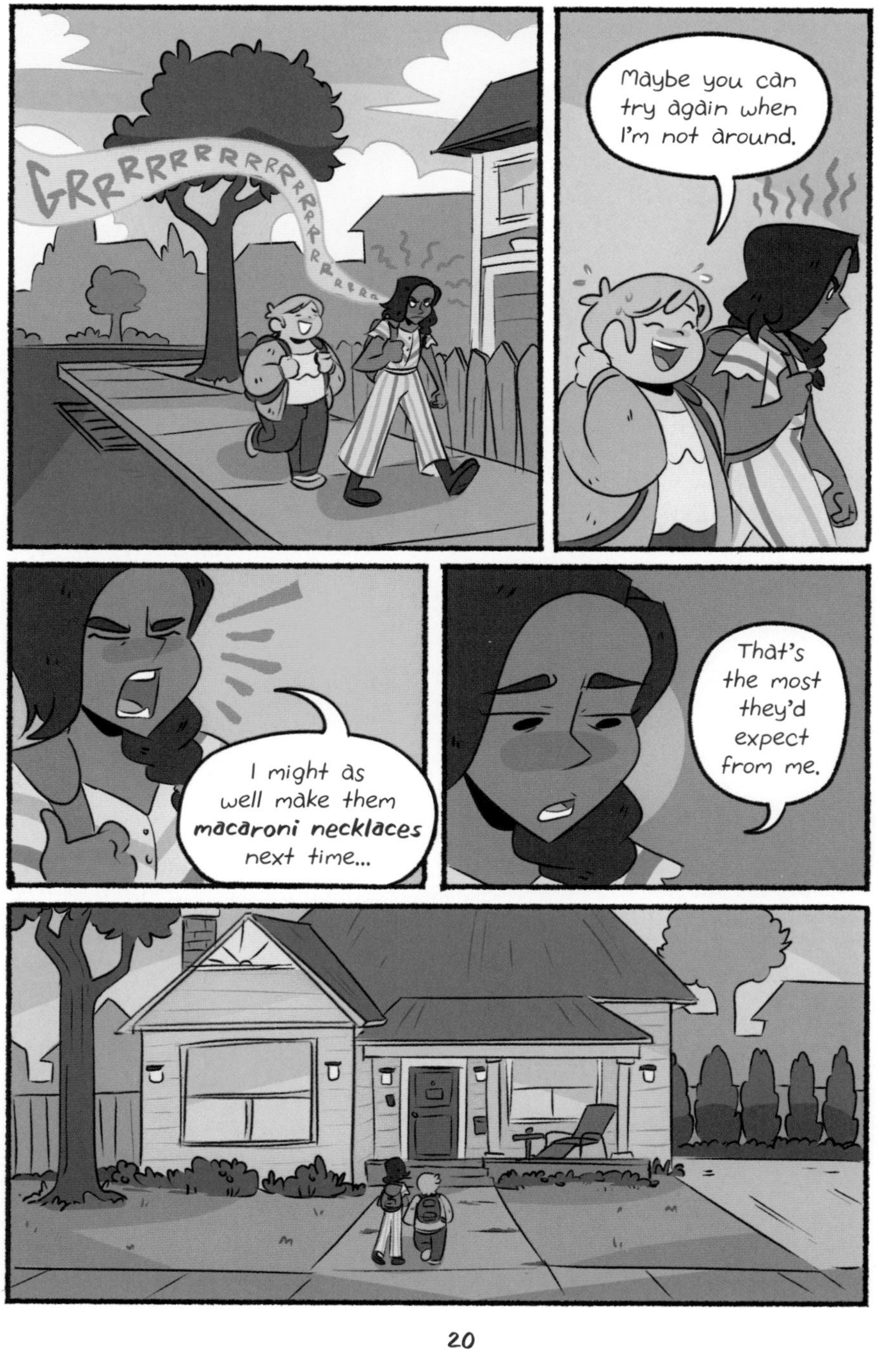
GRRRRRRRRRRRRRRRRRRR
Maybe you can try again when I'm not around.
I might as well make them **macaroni necklaces** next time...
That's the most they'd expect from me.

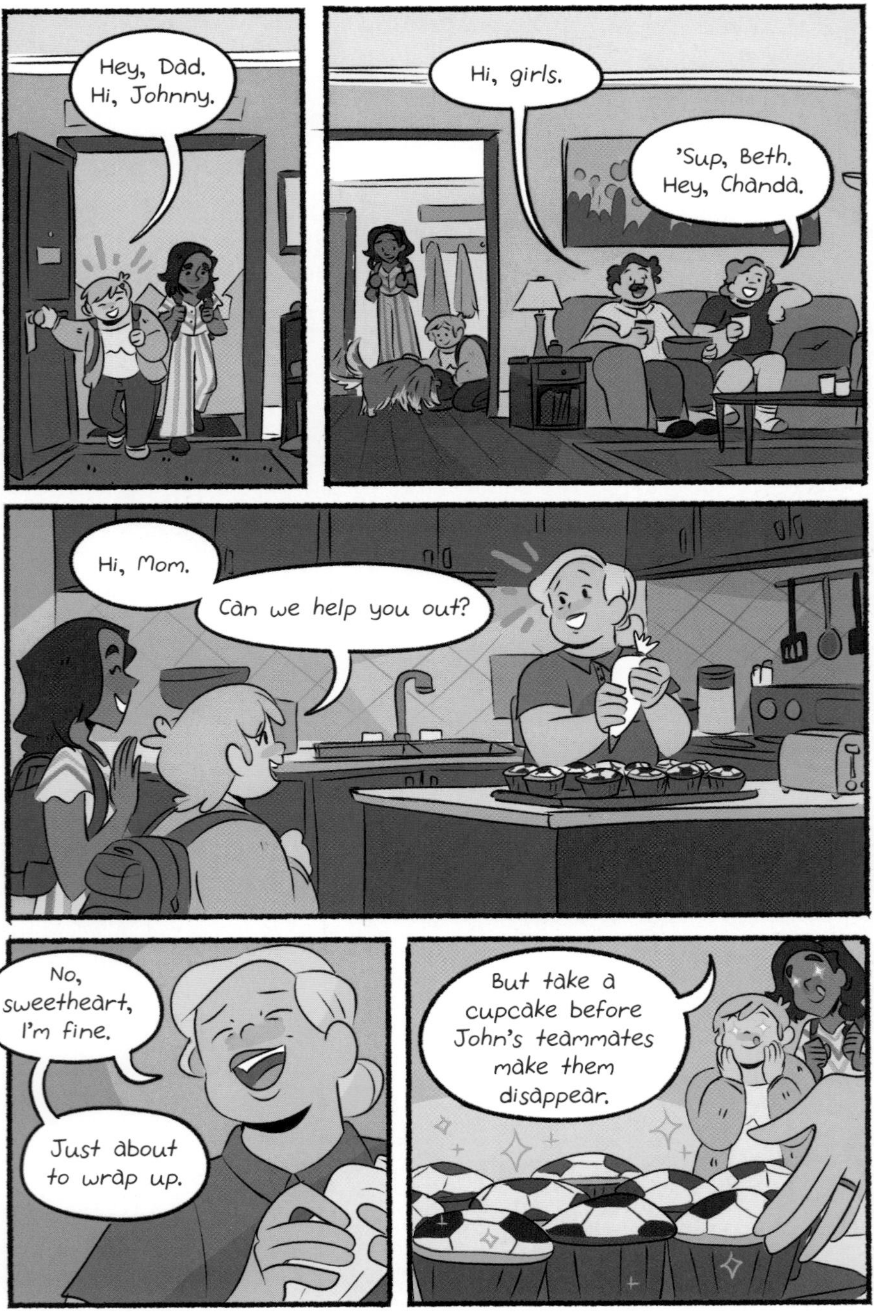
Hey, Dad.
Hi, Johnny.
Hi, girls.
'Sup, Beth.
Hey, Chanda.
Hi, Mom.
Can we help you out?
No, sweetheart, I'm fine.
Just about to wrap up.
But take a cupcake before John's teammates make them disappear.

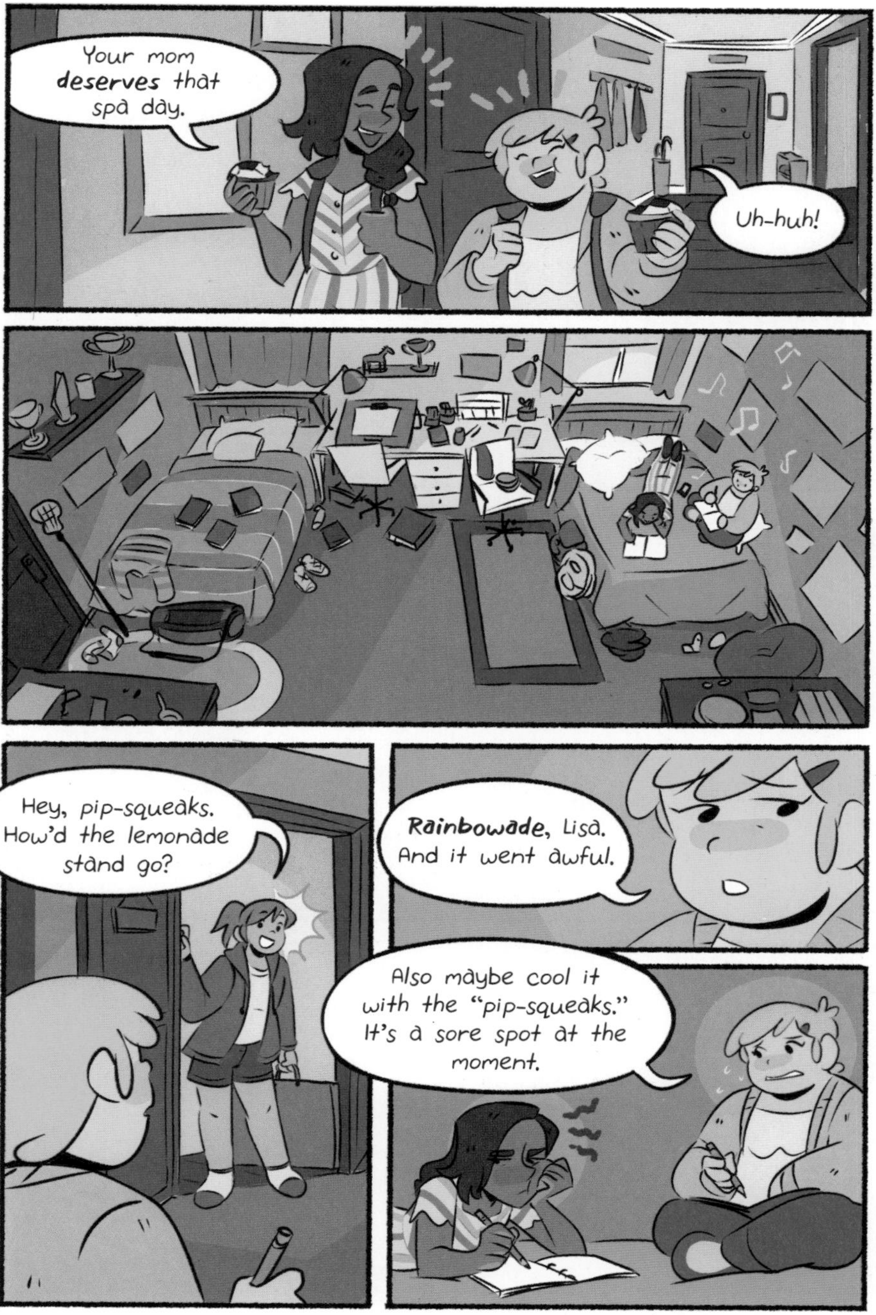
Your mom **deserves** that spa day.
Uh-huh!
Hey, pip-squeaks. How'd the lemonade stand go?
Rainbowade, Lisa. And it went awful.
Also maybe cool it with the "pip-squeaks." It's a sore spot at the moment.

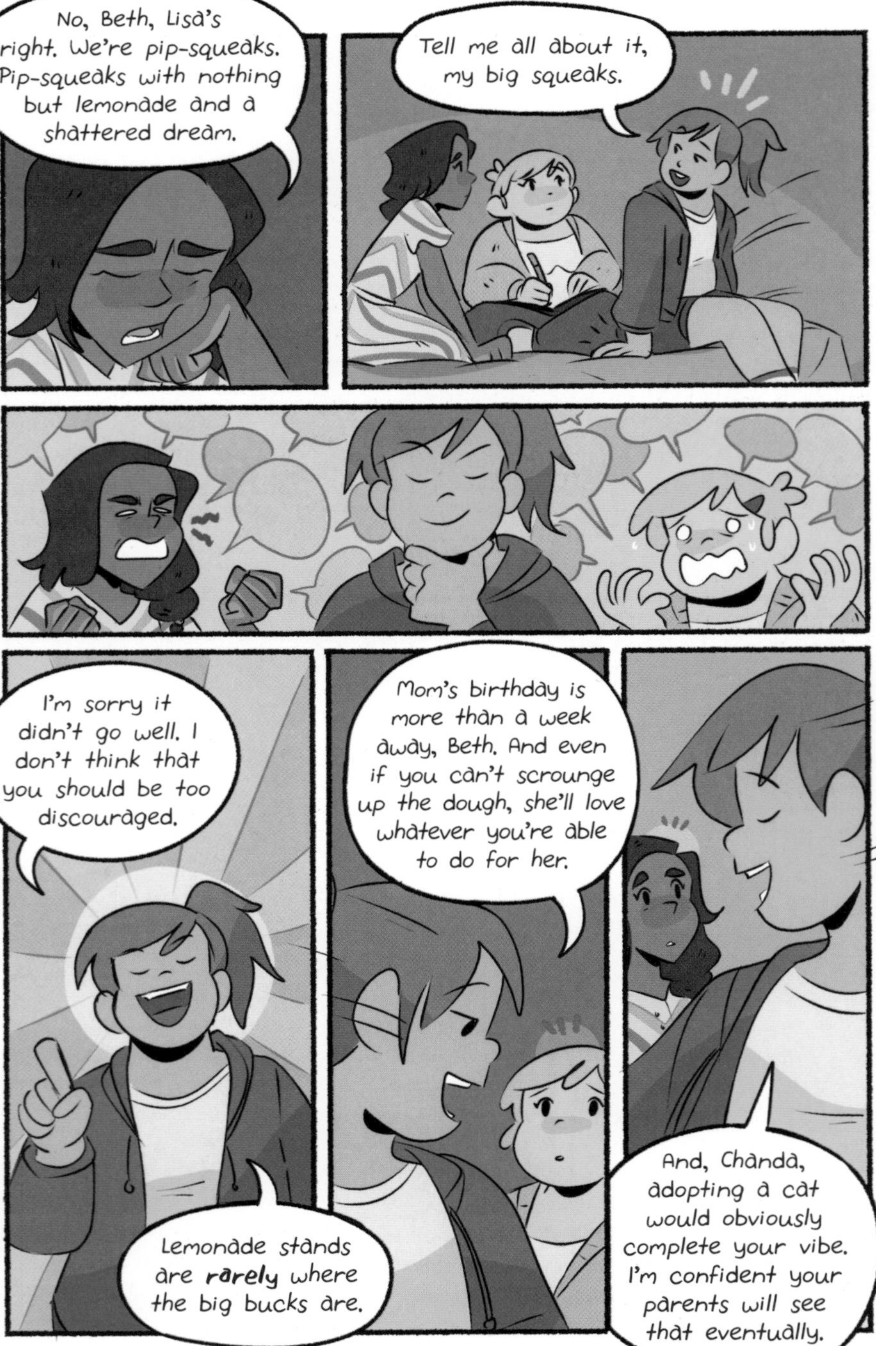
No, Beth, Lisa's right. We're pip-squeaks. Pip-squeaks with nothing but lemonade and a shattered dream.
Tell me all about it, my big squeaks.
I'm sorry it didn't go well. I don't think that you should be too discouraged.
Lemonade stands are **rarely** where the big bucks are.
Mom's birthday is more than a week away, Beth. And even if you can't scrounge up the dough, she'll love whatever you're able to do for her.
And, Chanda, adopting a cat would obviously complete your vibe. I'm confident your parents will see that eventually.

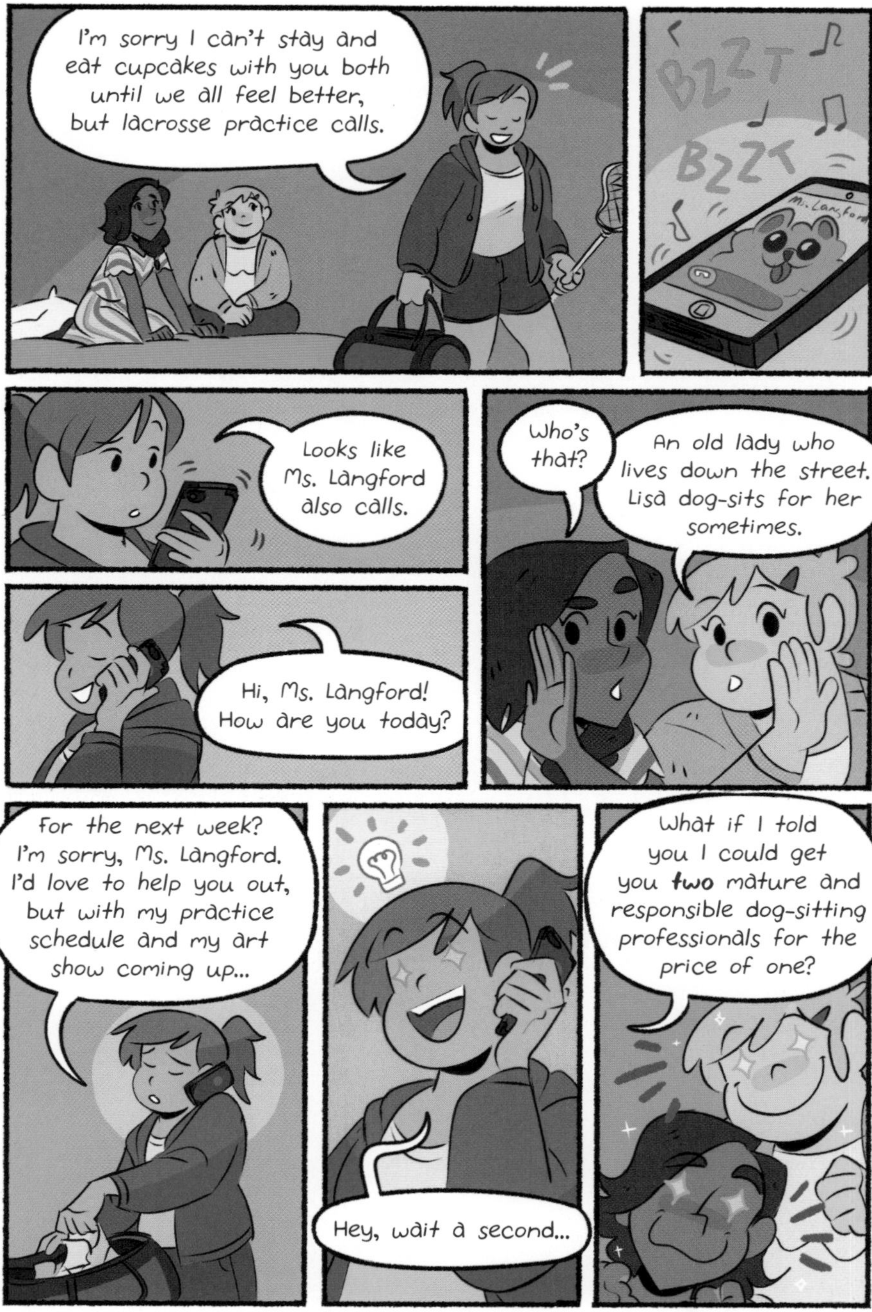
I'm sorry I can't stay and eat cupcakes with you both until we all feel better, but lacrosse practice calls.
BZZT BZZT
M. Langford
Looks like Ms. Langford also calls.
Who's that?
An old lady who lives down the street. Lisa dog-sits for her sometimes.
Hi, Ms. Langford! How are you today?
For the next week? I'm sorry, Ms. Langford. I'd love to help you out, but with my practice schedule and my art show coming up...
Hey, wait a second...
What if I told you I could get you **two** mature and responsible dog-sitting professionals for the price of one?

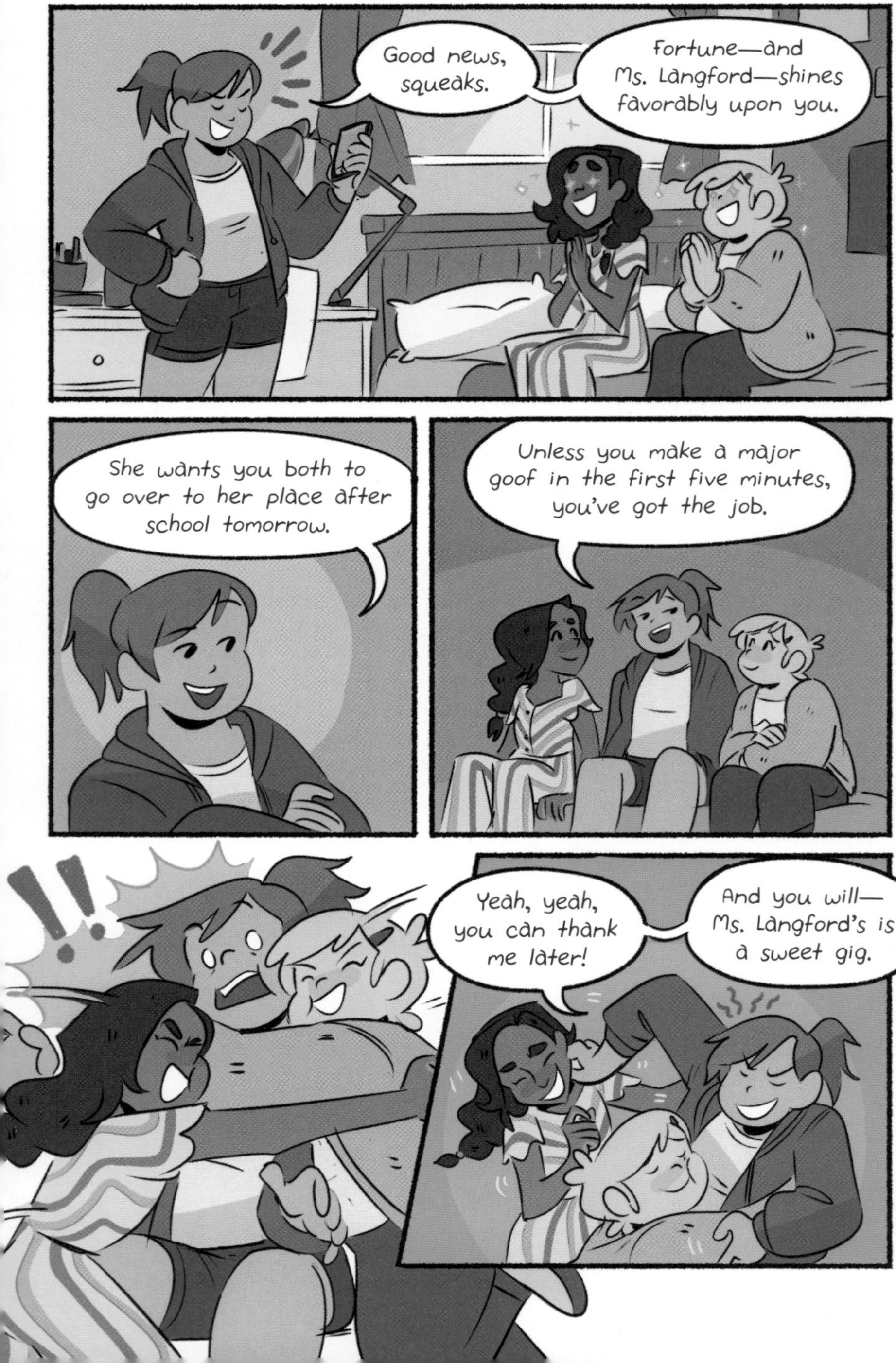
Good news, squeaks.
Fortune—and Ms. Langford—shines favorably upon you.
She wants you both to go over to her place after school tomorrow.
Unless you make a major goof in the first five minutes, you've got the job.
!!
Yeah, yeah, you can thank me later!
And you will—Ms. Langford's is a sweet gig.

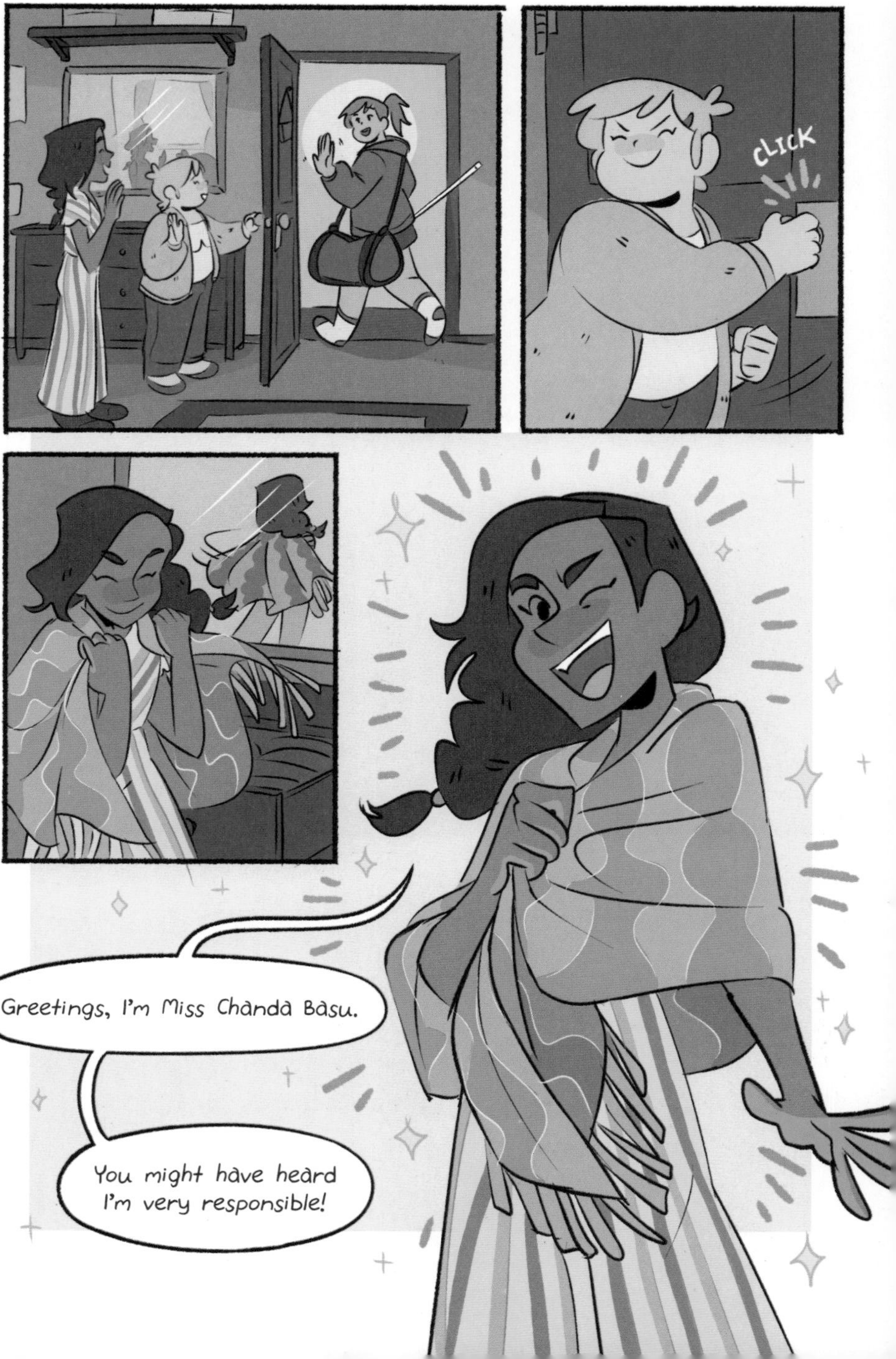
CLICK
Greetings, I'm Miss Chanda Basu.
You might have heard I'm very responsible!

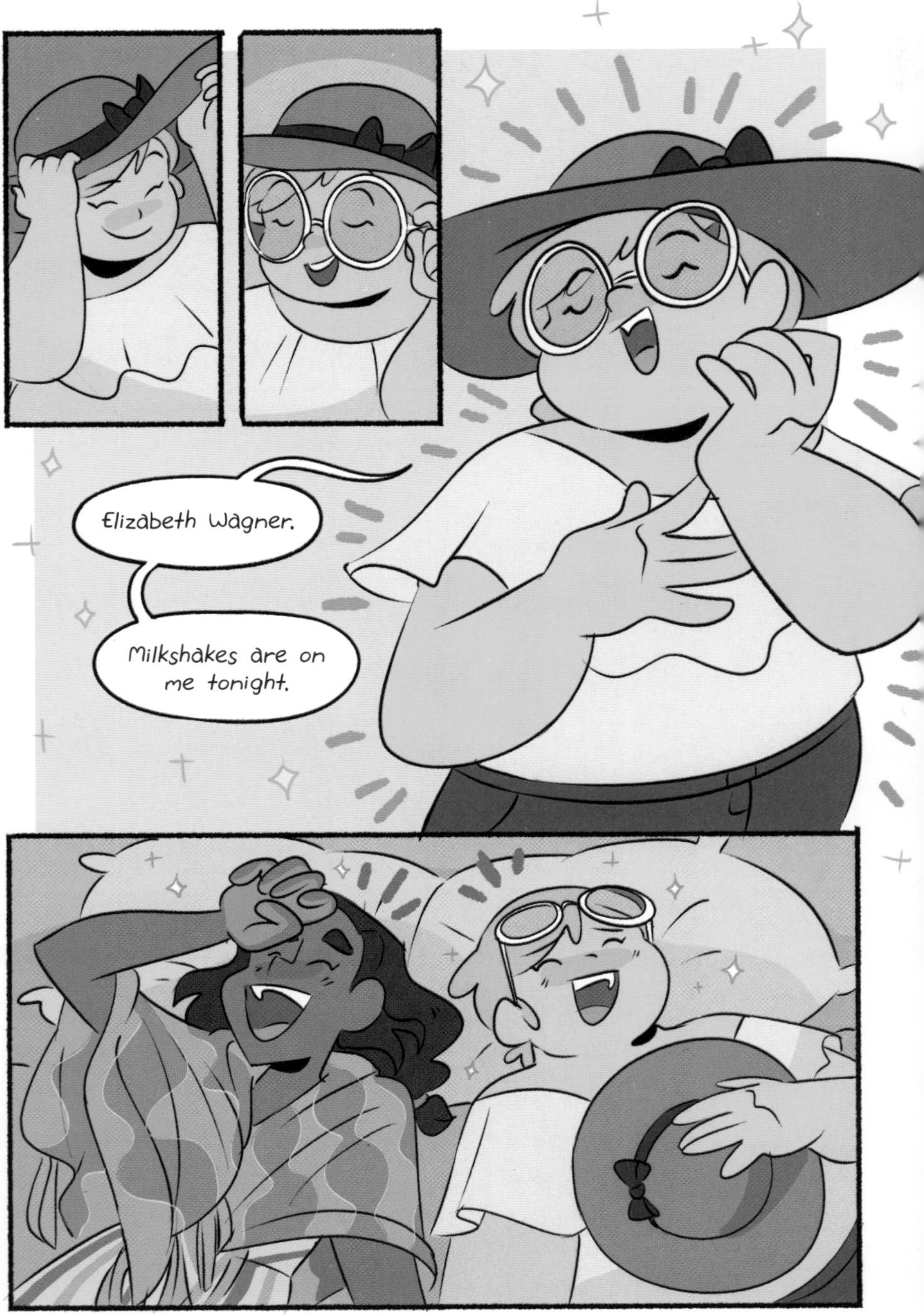
Elizabeth Wagner.
Milkshakes are on me tonight.

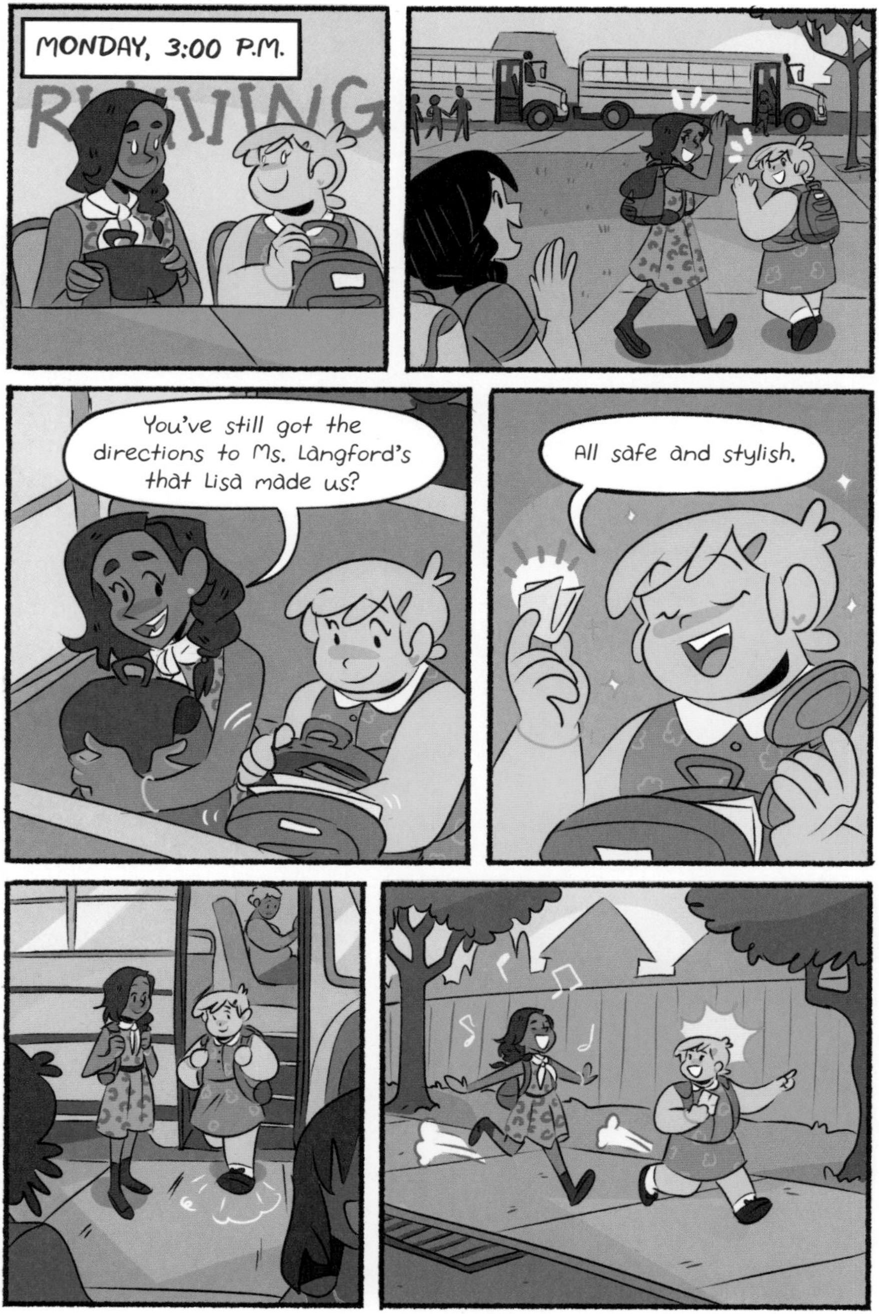
MONDAY, 3:00 P.M.
You've still got the directions to Ms. Langford's that Lisa made us?
All safe and stylish.

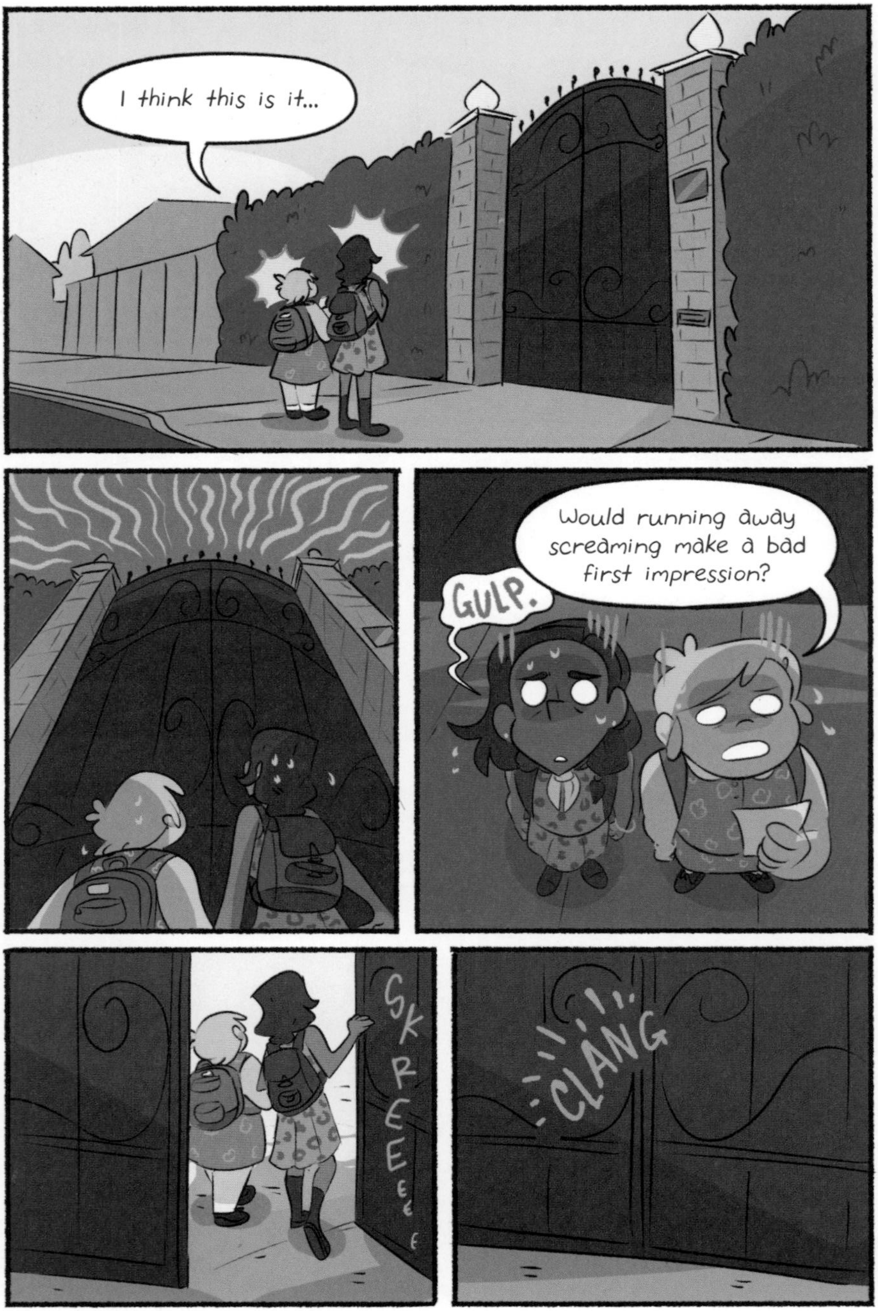

I think this is it...
GULP.
Would running away screaming make a bad first impression?
SKREEEEEE
CLANG

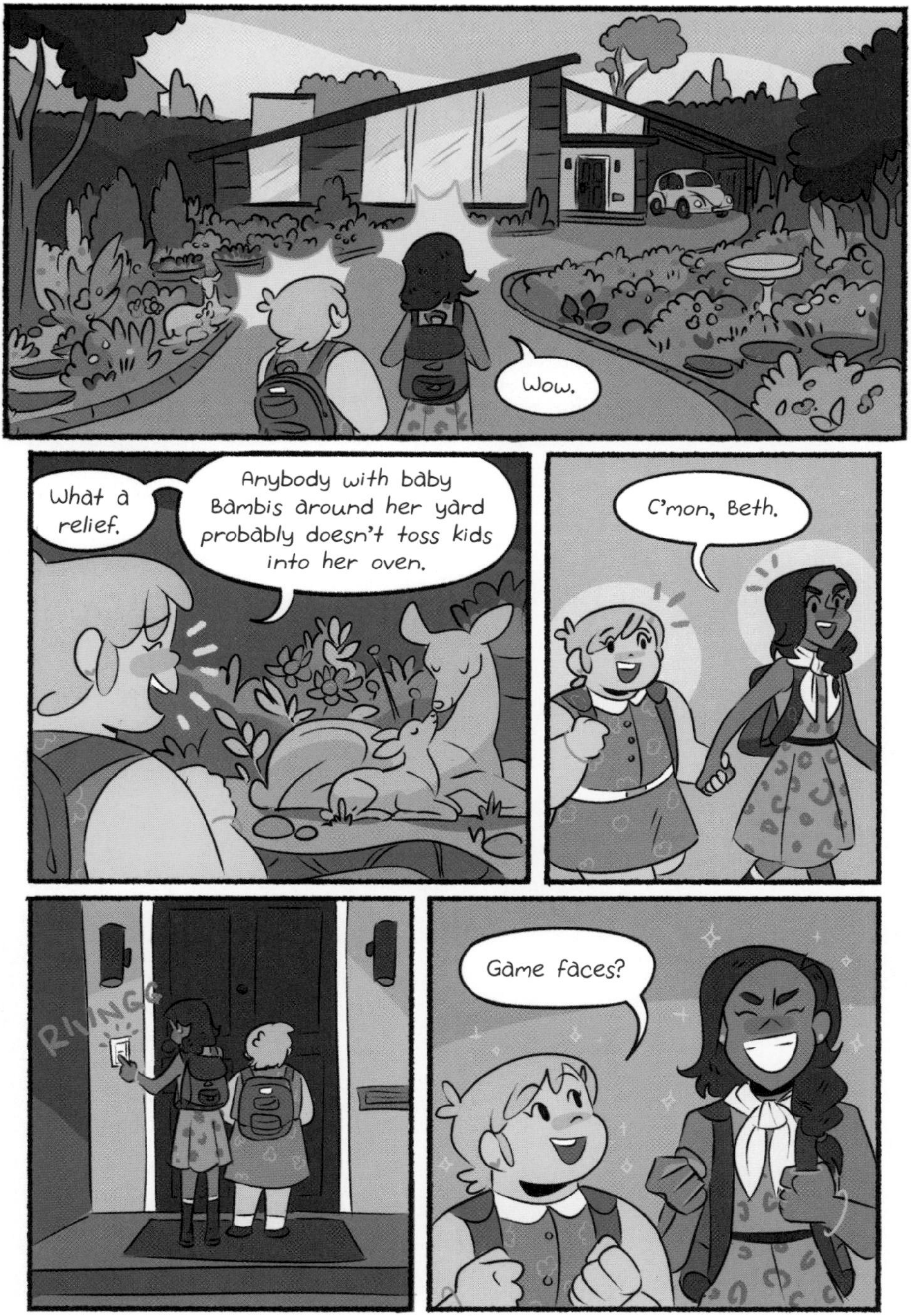
Wow.
What a relief.
Anybody with baby Bambis around her yard probably doesn't toss kids into her oven.
C'mon, Beth.
RIIINGG
Game faces?

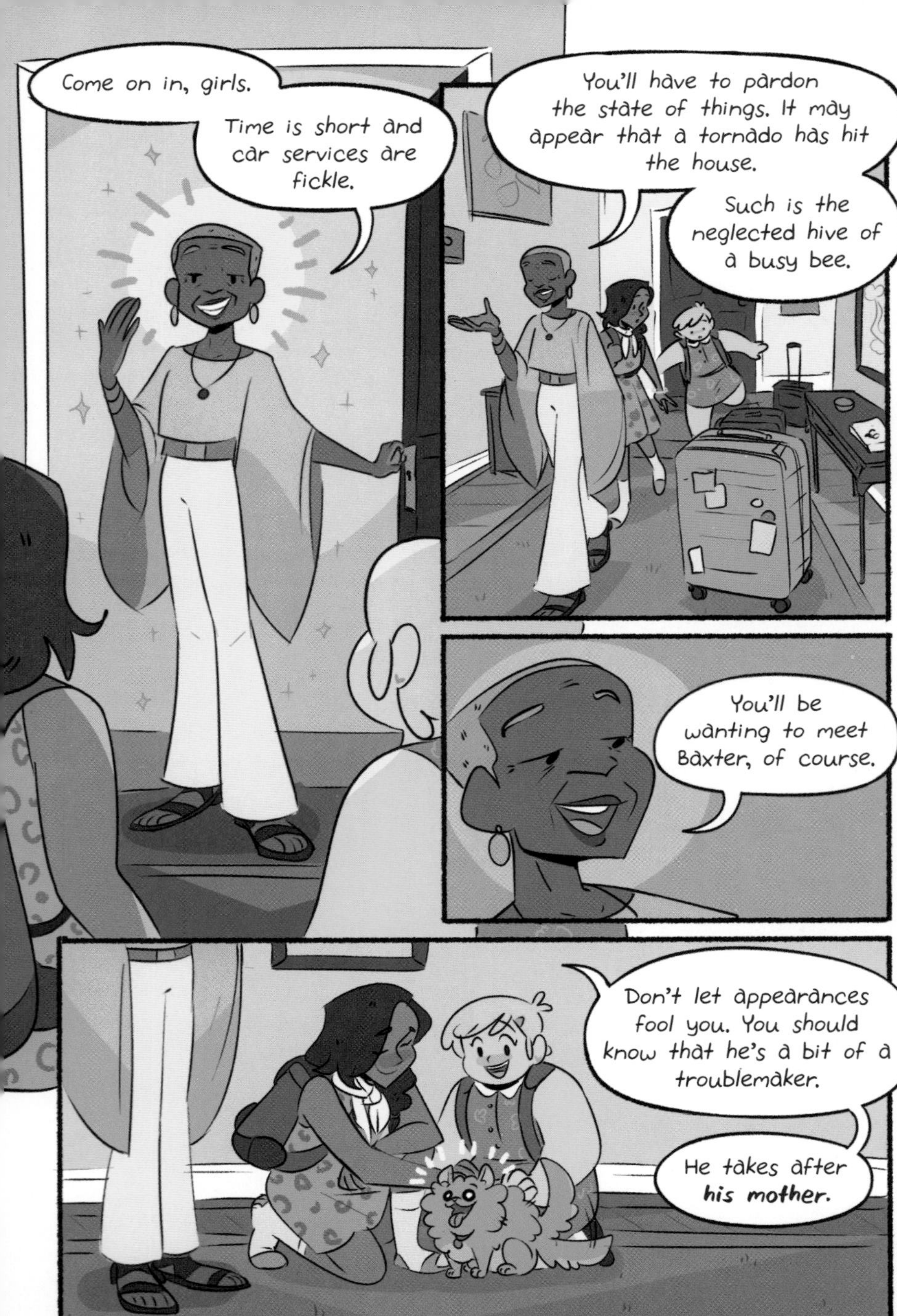
Come on in, girls.
Time is short and car services are fickle.
You'll have to pardon the state of things. It may appear that a tornado has hit the house.
Such is the neglected hive of a busy bee.
You'll be wanting to meet Baxter, of course.
Don't let appearances fool you. You should know that he's a bit of a troublemaker.
He takes after **his mother.**

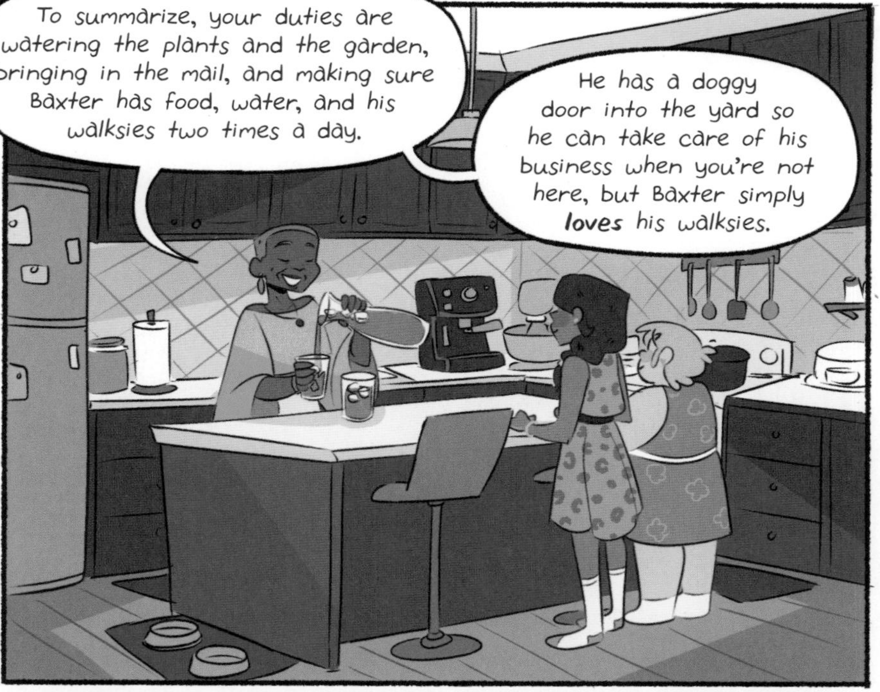
To summarize, your duties are watering the plants and the garden, bringing in the mail, and making sure Baxter has food, water, and his walksies two times a day.
He has a doggy door into the yard so he can take care of his business when you're not here, but Baxter simply **loves** his walksies.

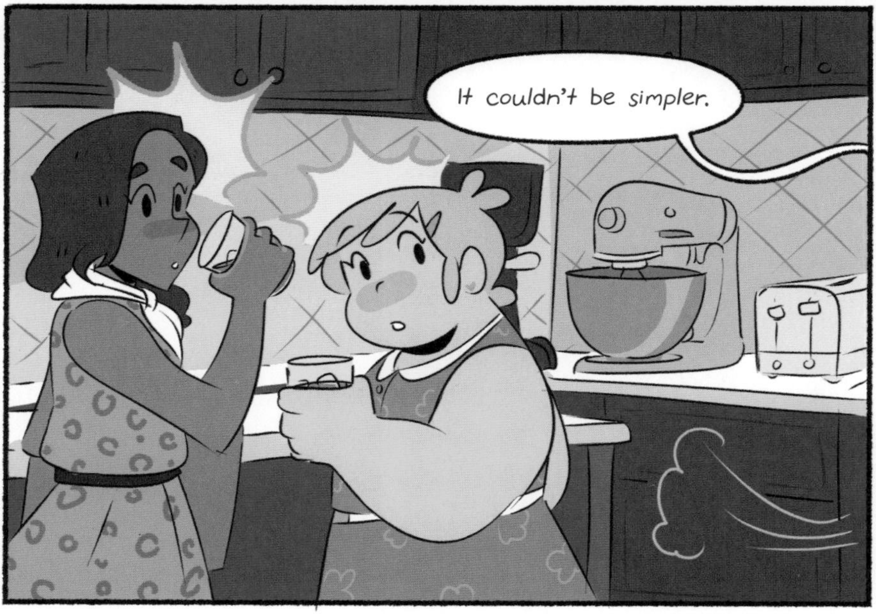
It couldn't be simpler.

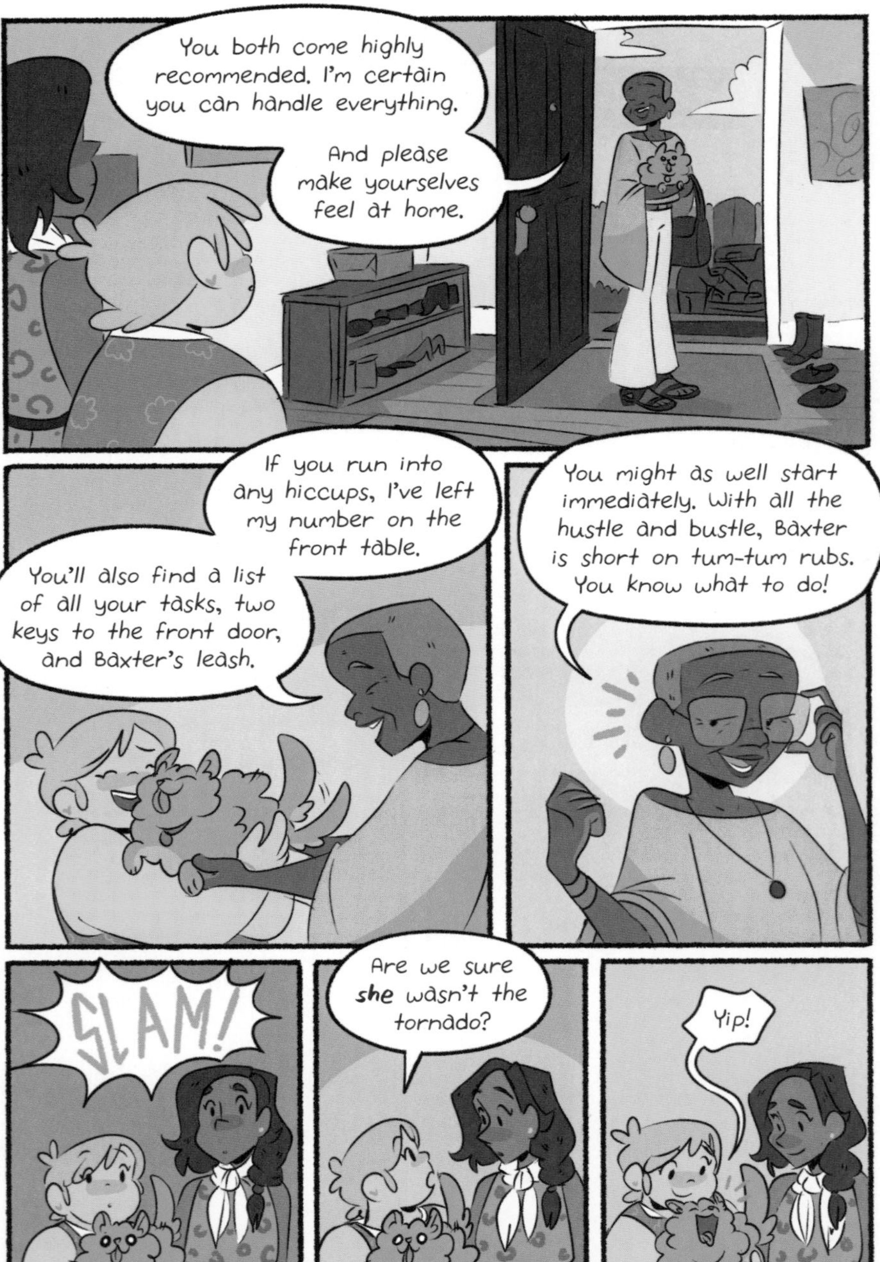
You both come highly recommended. I'm certain you can handle everything.
And please make yourselves feel at home.
If you run into any hiccups, I've left my number on the front table.
You'll also find a list of all your tasks, two keys to the front door, and Baxter's leash.
You might as well start immediately. With all the hustle and bustle, Baxter is short on tum-tum rubs. You know what to do!
SLAM!
Are we sure **she** wasn't the tornado?
Yip!

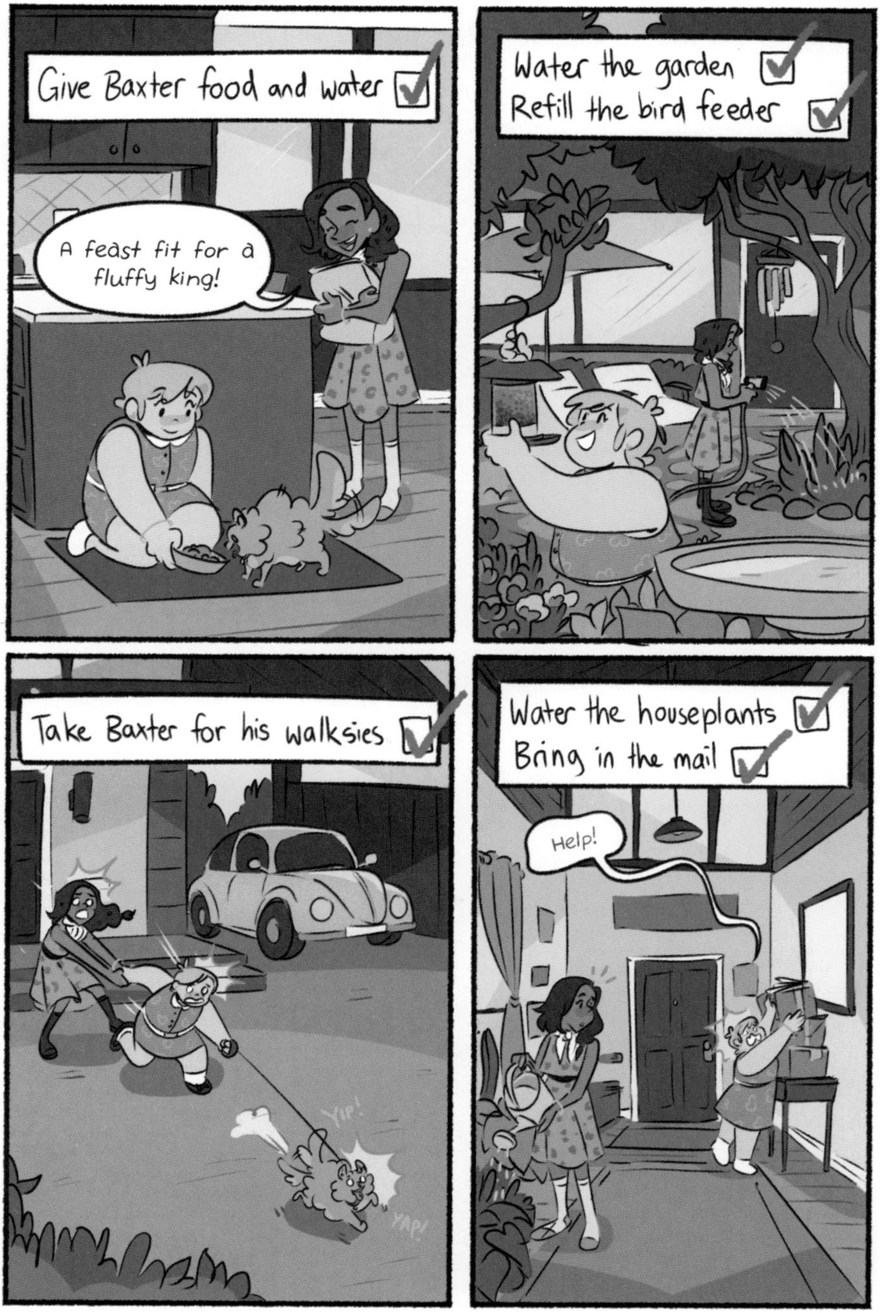
Give Baxter food and water
A feast fit for a fluffy king!
Water the garden
Refill the bird feeder
Take Baxter for his walksies
YIP!
YAP!
Water the houseplants
Bring in the mail
Help!

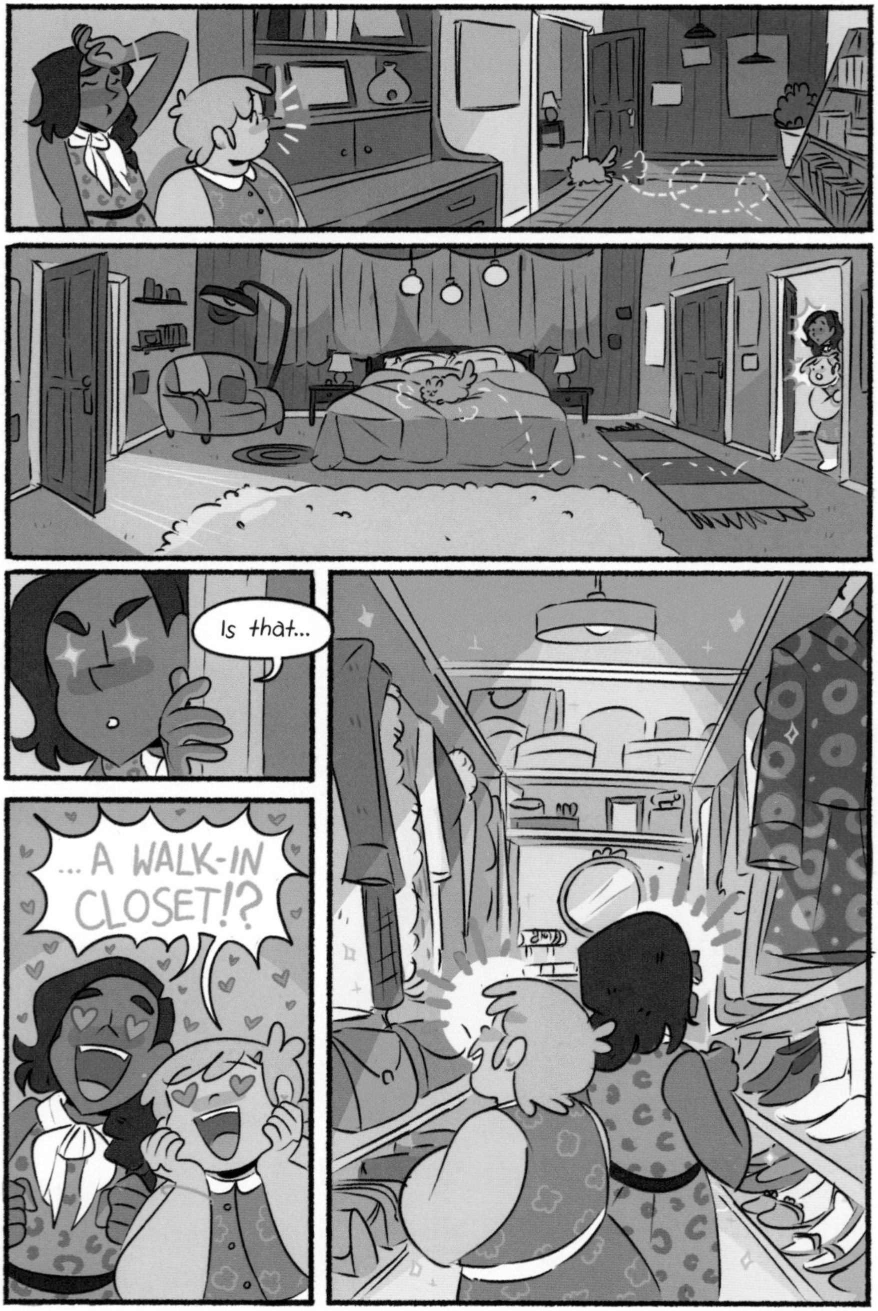
Is that...
...A WALK-IN CLOSET!?

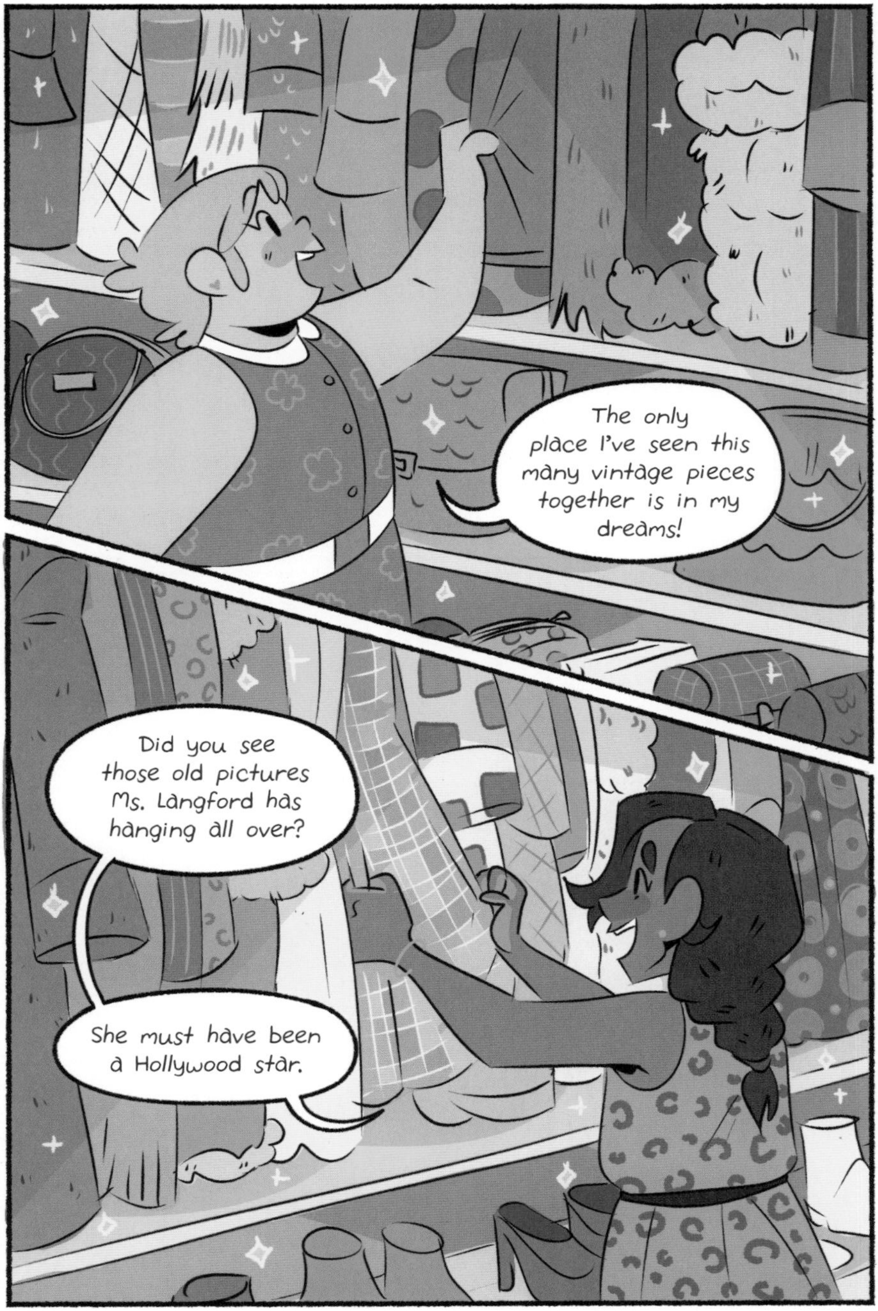
The only place I've seen this many vintage pieces together is in my dreams!
Did you see those old pictures Ms. Langford has hanging all over?
She must have been a Hollywood star.

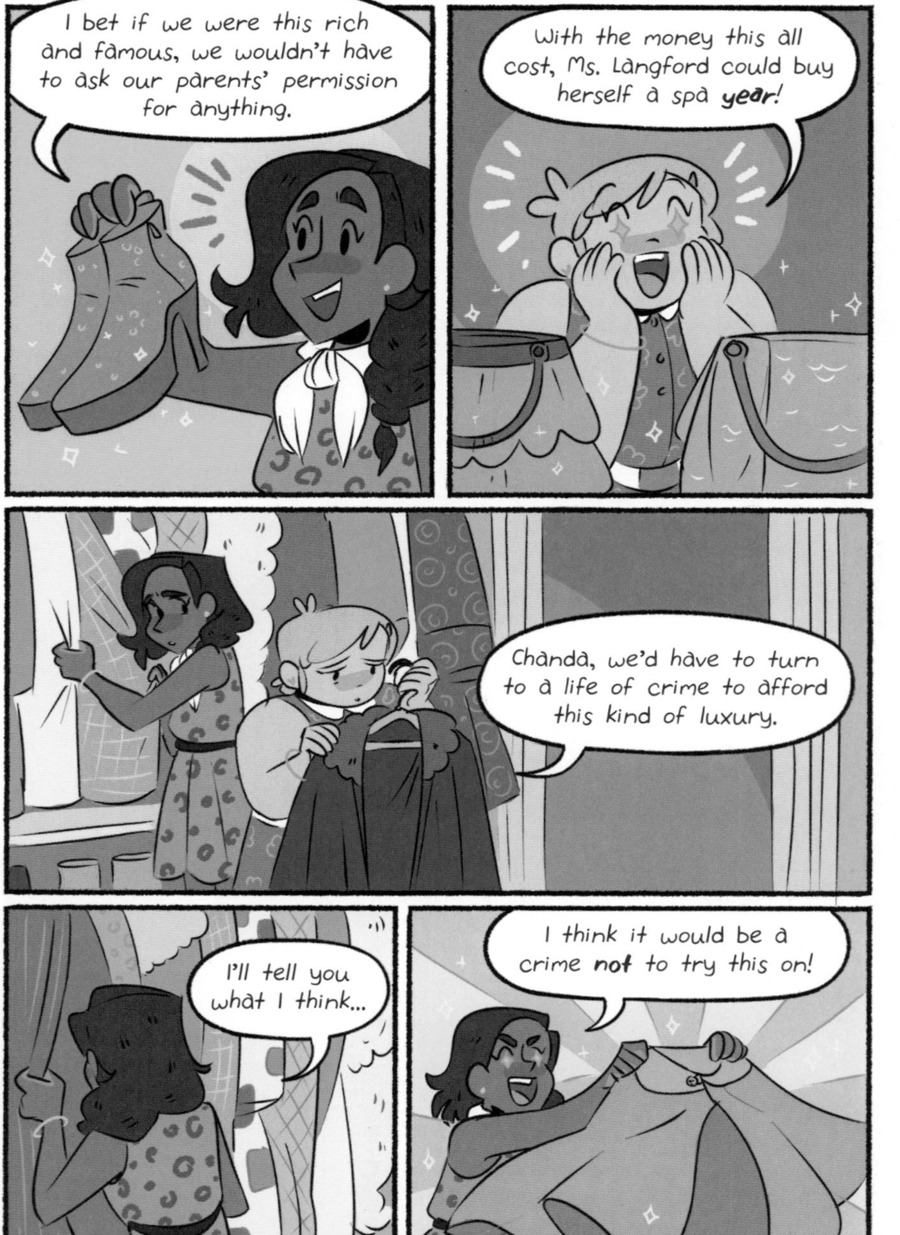
I bet if we were this rich and famous, we wouldn't have to ask our parents' permission for anything.
With the money this all cost, Ms. Langford could buy herself a spa **year**!
Chanda, we'd have to turn to a life of crime to afford this kind of luxury.
I'll tell you what I think...
I think it would be a crime **not** to try this on!

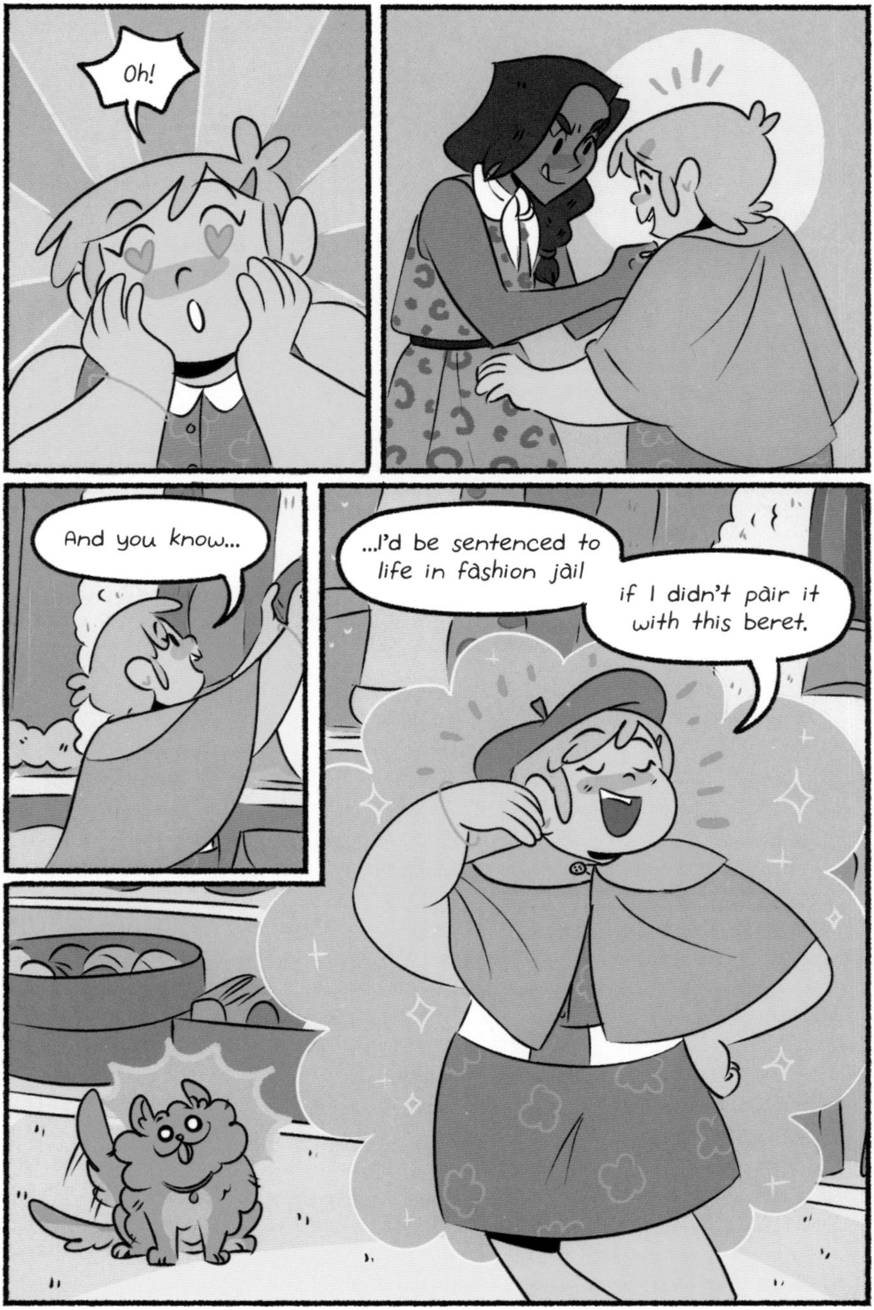
Oh!
And you know...
...I'd be sentenced to life in fashion jail
if I didn't pair it with this beret.

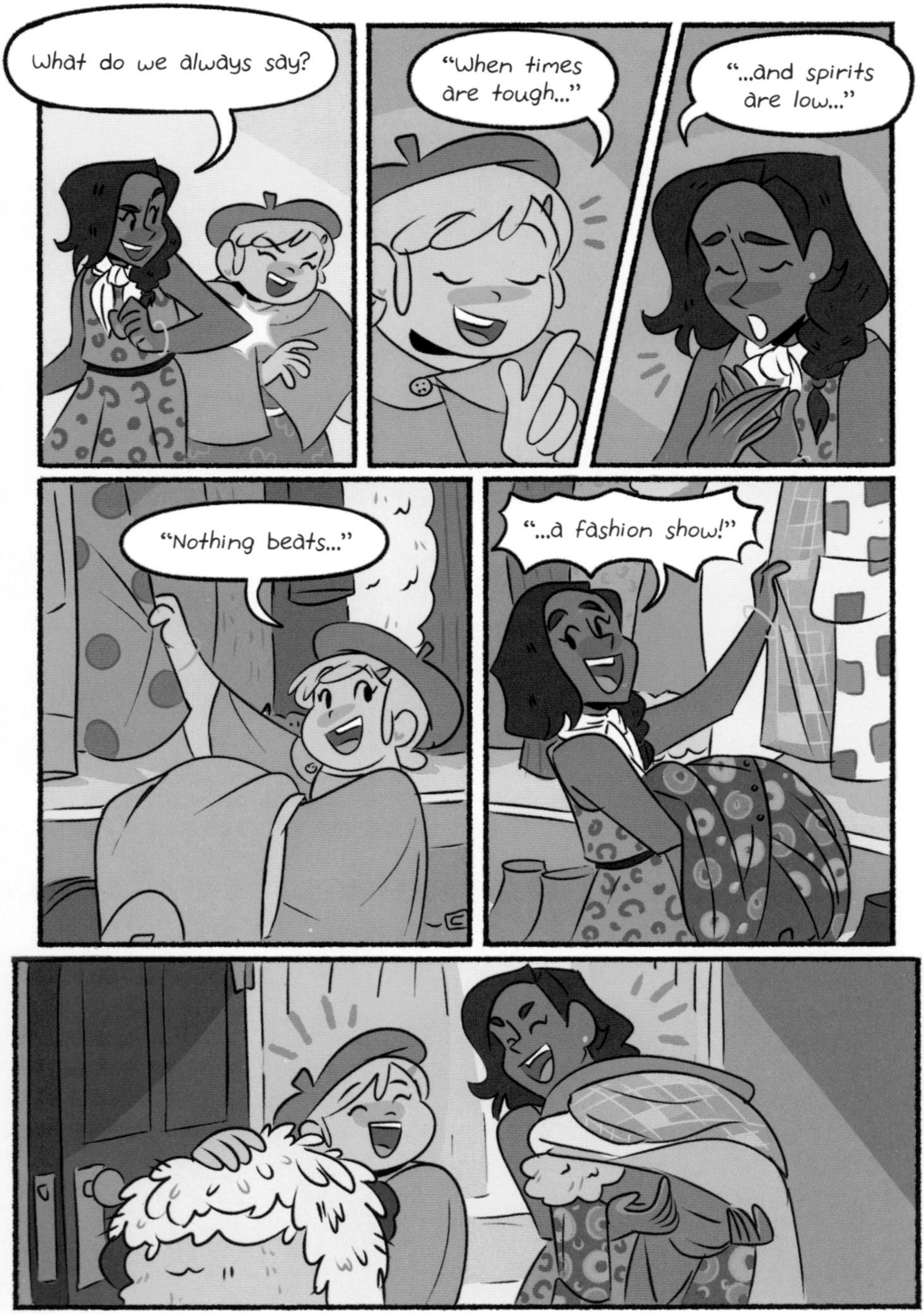
What do we always say?
"When times are tough..."
"...and spirits are low..."
"Nothing beats..."
"...a fashion show!"

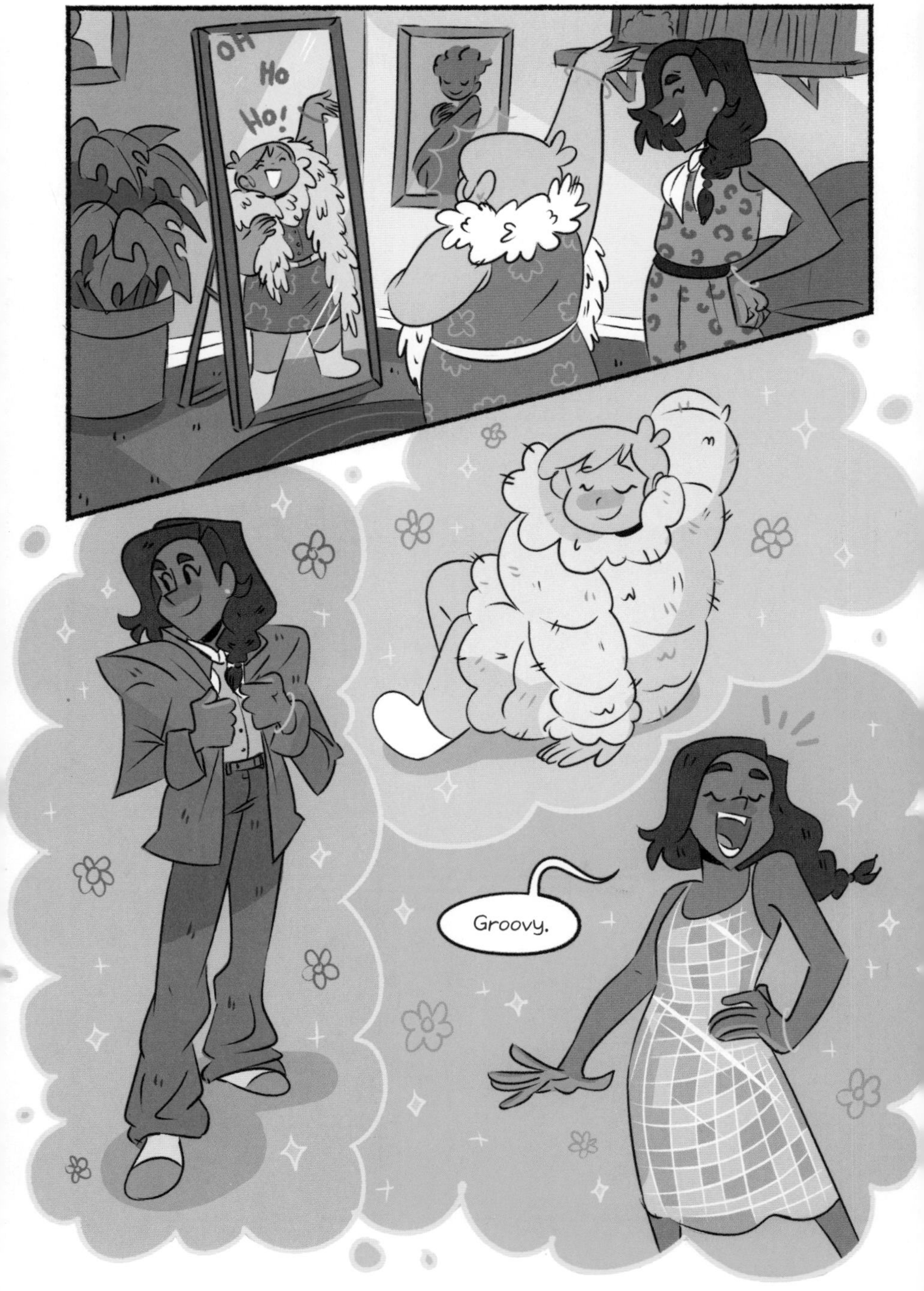
OH Ho Ho!
Groovy.

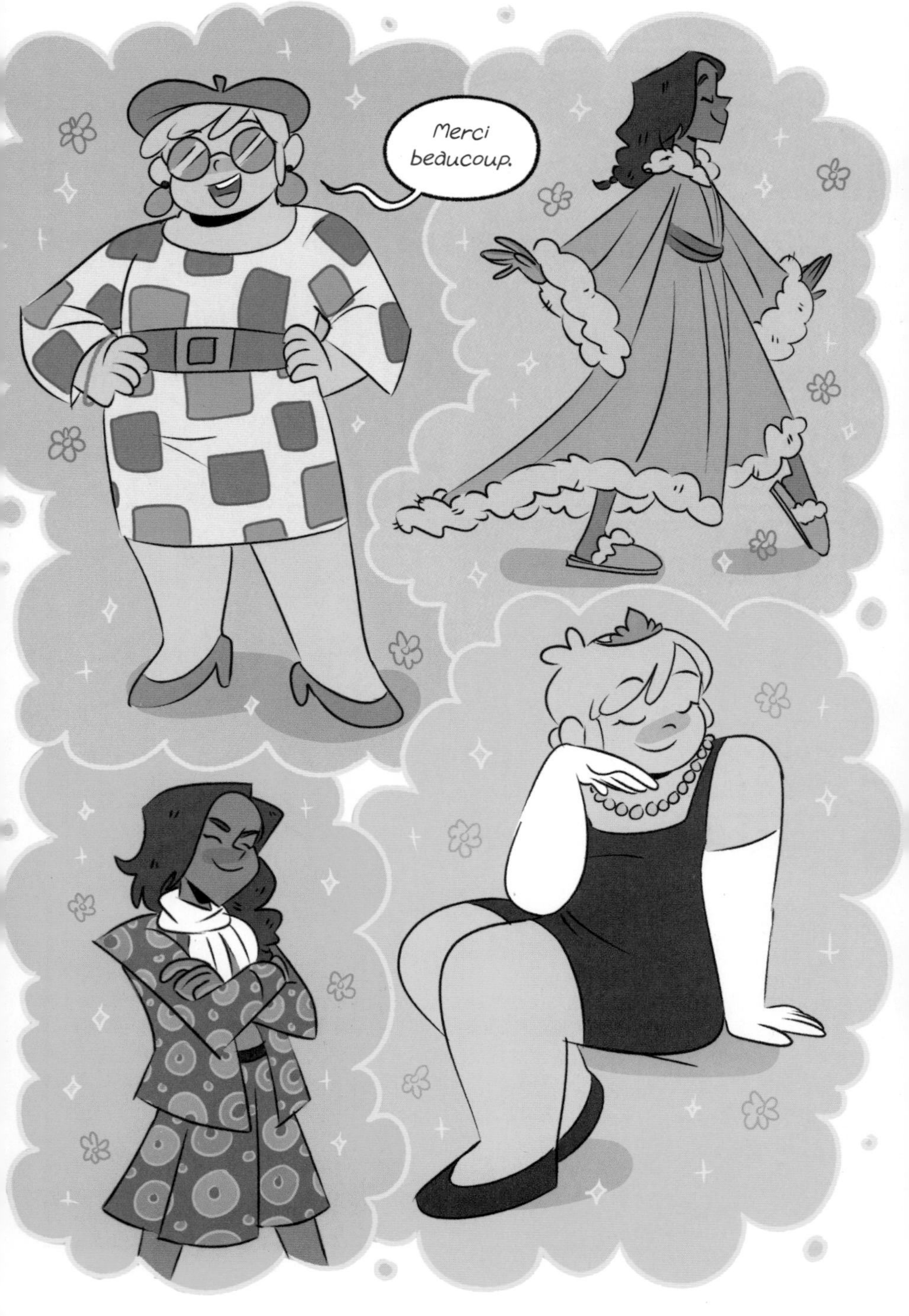
Merci beaucoup.

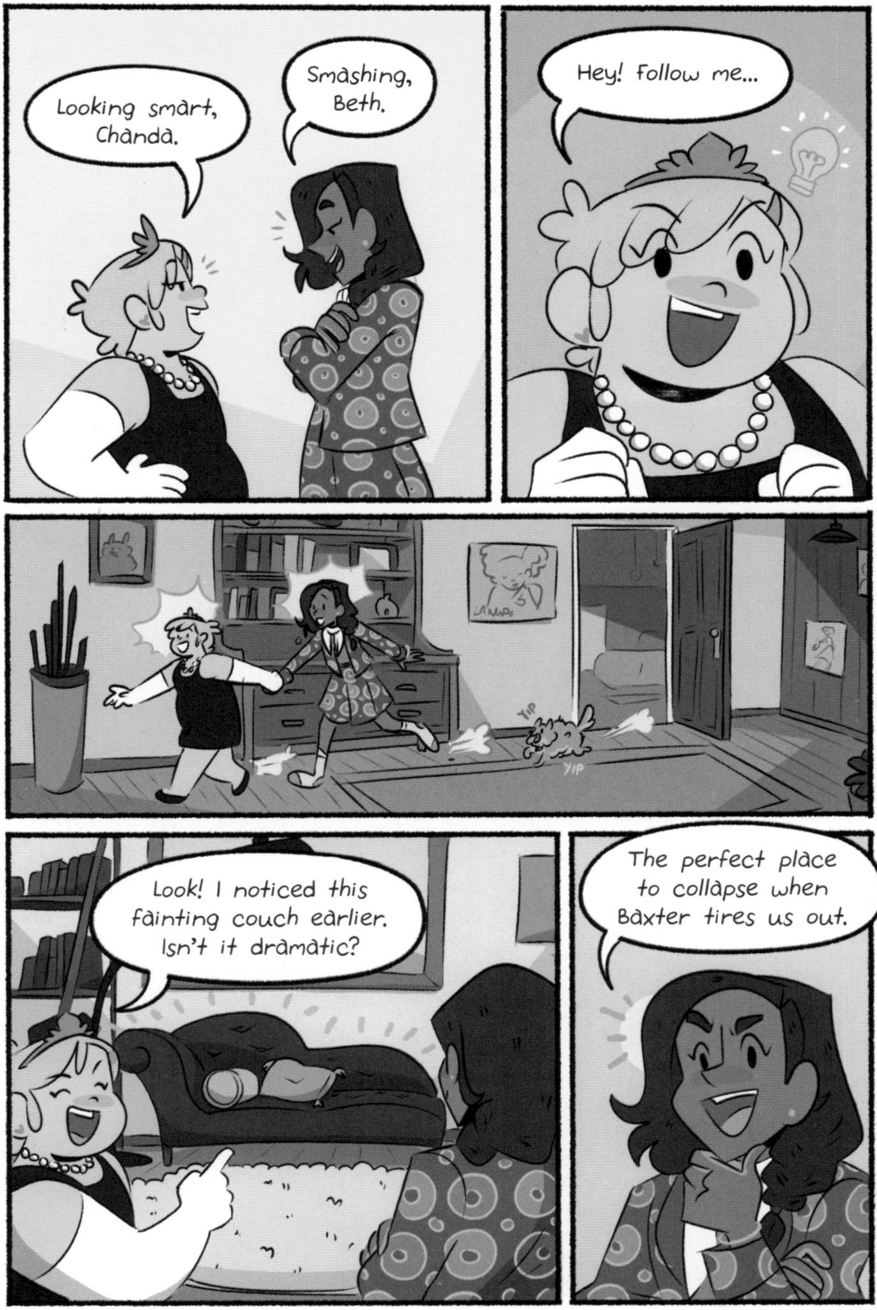
Looking smart, Chanda.
Smashing, Beth.
Hey! Follow me...
YIP
YIP
Look! I noticed this fainting couch earlier. Isn't it dramatic?
The perfect place to collapse when Baxter tires us out.

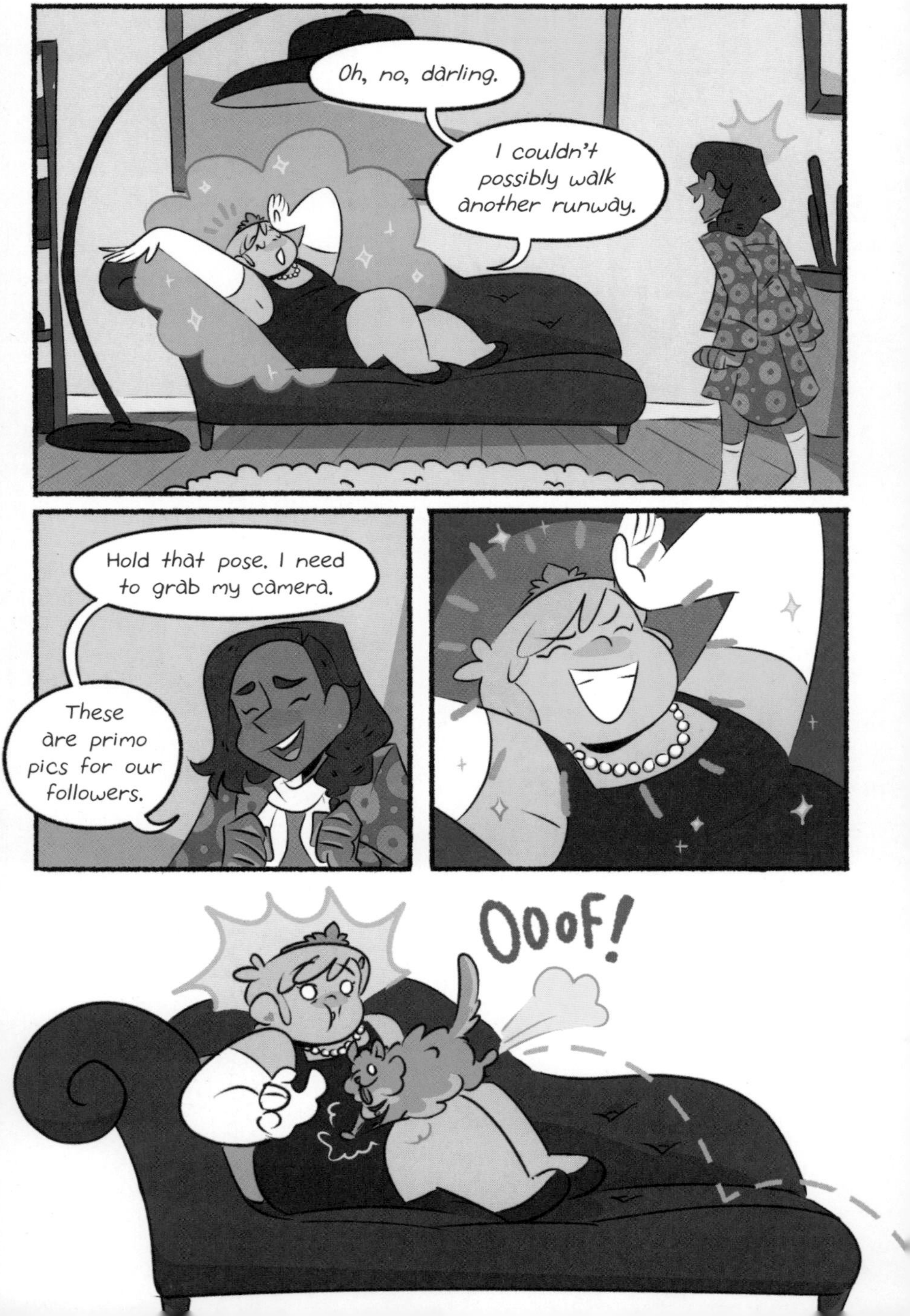

Oh, no, darling.
I couldn't possibly walk another runway.
Hold that pose. I need to grab my camera.
These are primo pics for our followers.
OOOF!

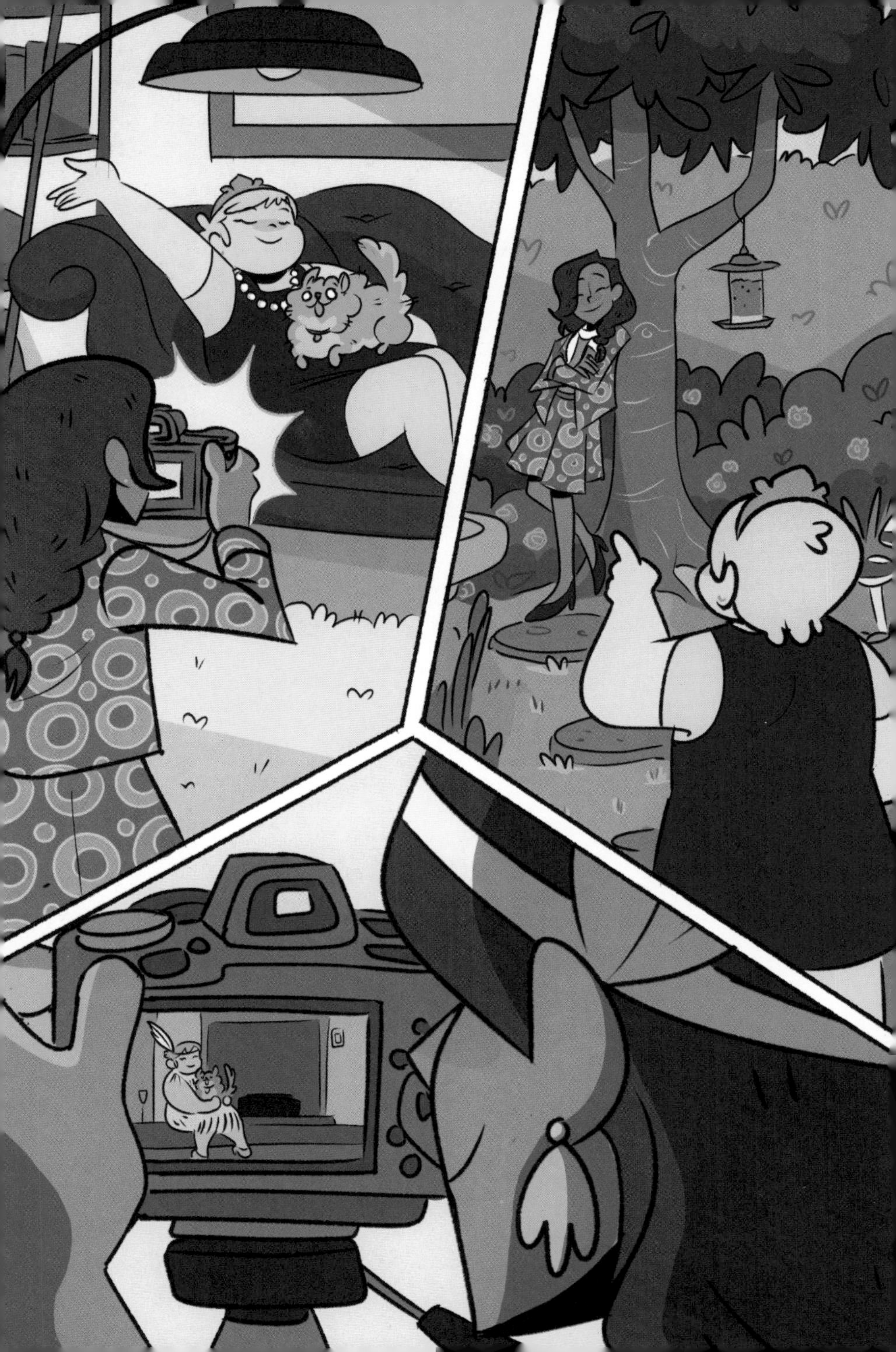

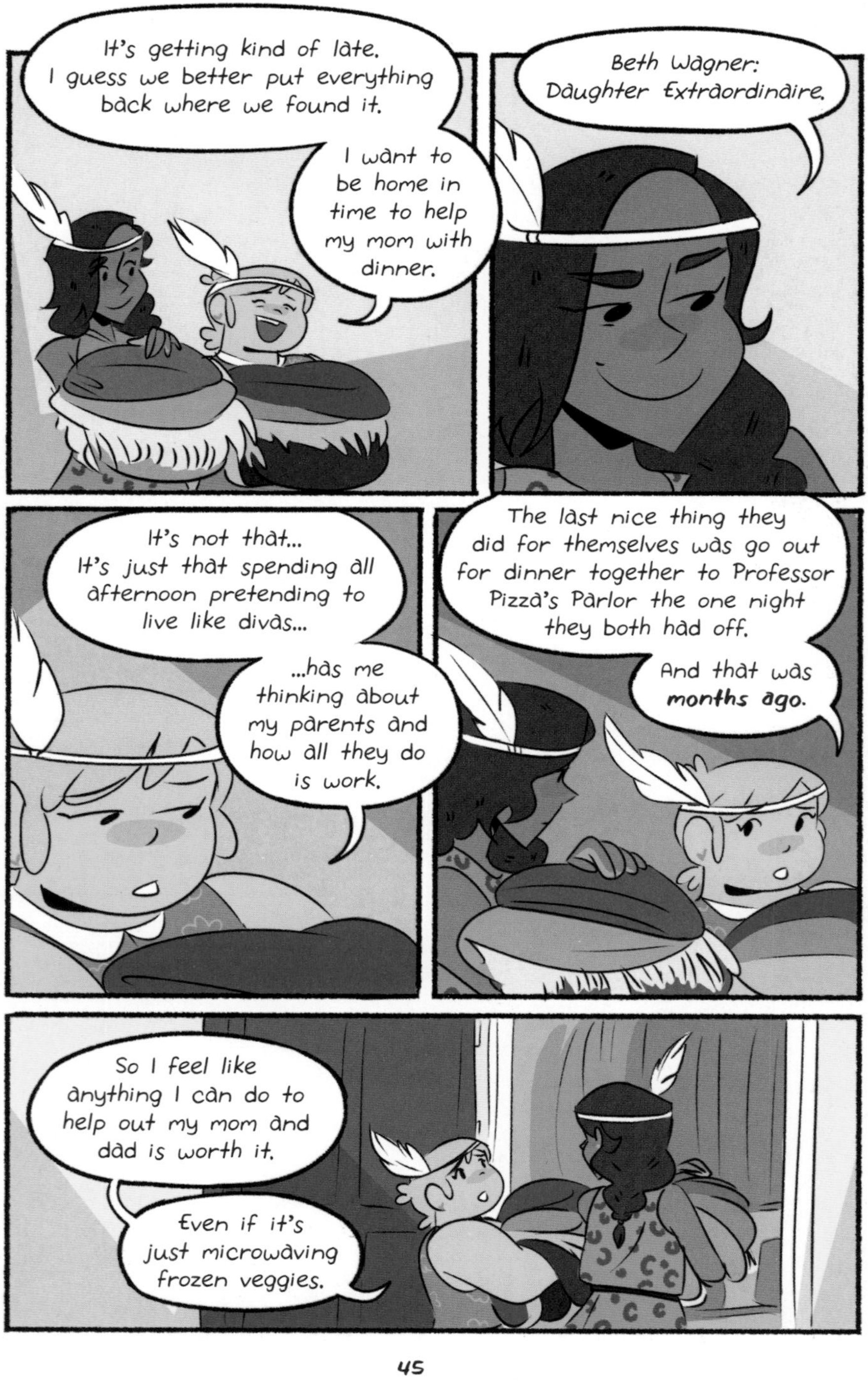
It's getting kind of late. I guess we better put everything back where we found it.
I want to be home in time to help my mom with dinner.
Beth Wagner: Daughter Extraordinaire.
It's not that... It's just that spending all afternoon pretending to live like divas...
...has me thinking about my parents and how all they do is work.
The last nice thing they did for themselves was go out for dinner together to Professor Pizza's Parlor the one night they both had off.
And that was **months ago.**
So I feel like anything I can do to help out my mom and dad is worth it.
Even if it's just microwaving frozen veggies.

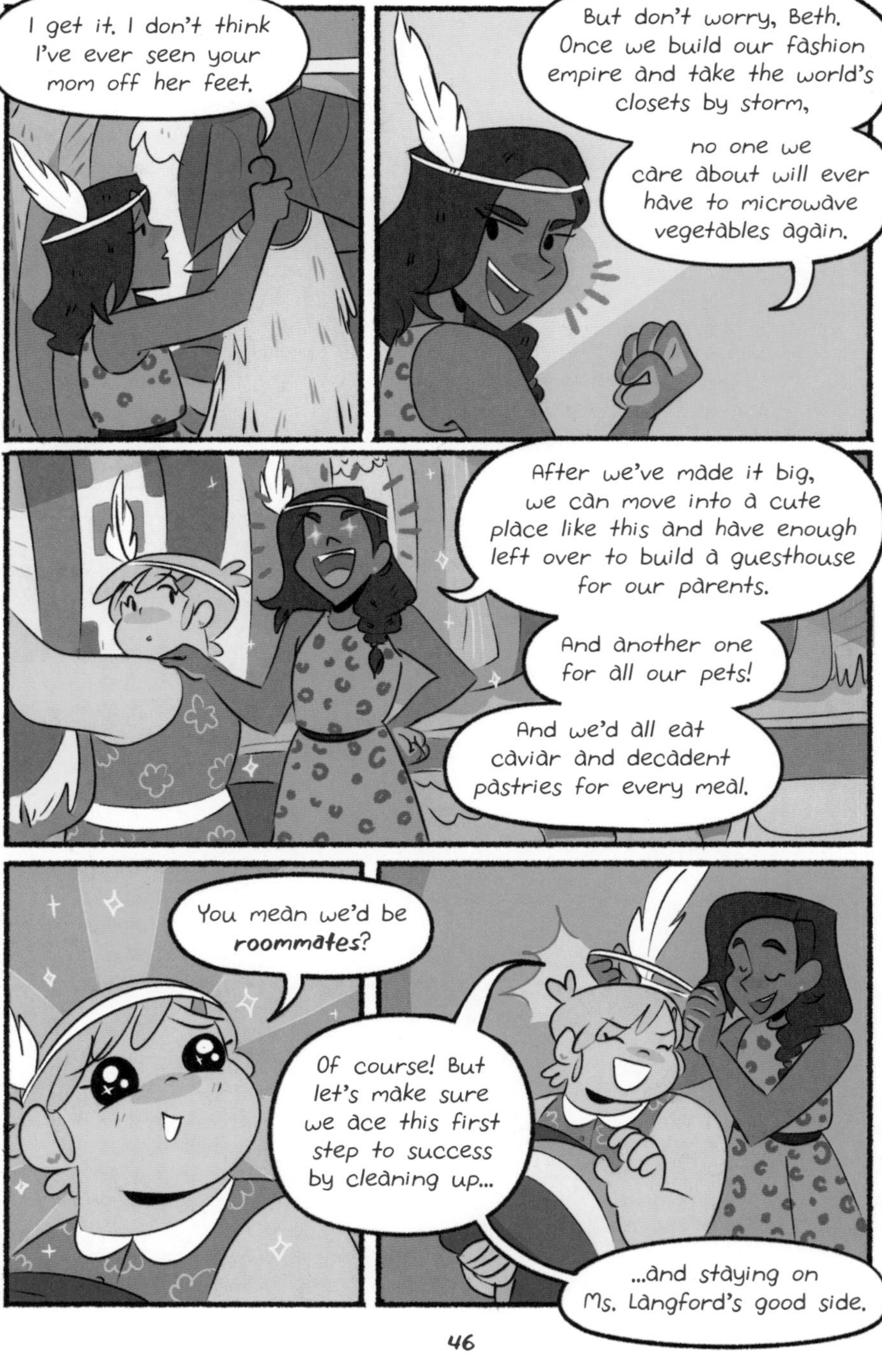
I get it. I don't think I've ever seen your mom off her feet.
But don't worry, Beth. Once we build our fashion empire and take the world's closets by storm,
no one we care about will ever have to microwave vegetables again.
After we've made it big, we can move into a cute place like this and have enough left over to build a guesthouse for our parents.
And another one for all our pets!
And we'd all eat caviar and decadent pastries for every meal.
You mean we'd be **roommates**?
Of course! But let's make sure we ace this first step to success by cleaning up...
...and staying on Ms. Langford's good side.

STYLE

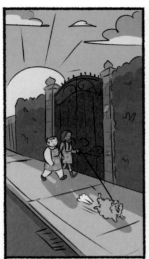

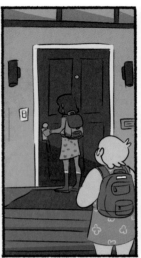

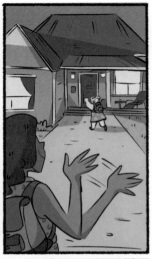

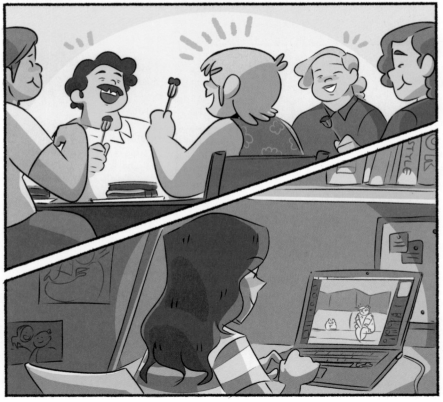

crystalchandalier:
Flowers: growing.
Beth: glowing.
#garden #vintagefashion
#adorbs
frantastic09:
ooooOOOOoooooooooo!!
willowXtheXwisp: This
is SO good <3 <3

⭐ 73   💬 6   📤

crystalchandalier:
Teatime all the time.
#scrumptious #scrump
#pinkiesup
trentsk8s808: save
some cookies for
meeeeeeee!!!!!
graaaceful: classy and
classic

⭐ 70   💬 10   📤

crystalchandalier: Which one of you has been shedding on the couch? **@b3thw** #baddog #badbaxter #badbeth
avacheers4u: I hope that's faux
crystalchandalier: @avacheers4u Beth's is acrylic, Baxter's is homegrown

⭐ 83 💬 19 ⬆️

crystalchandalier: It's not New Year's, but we're still having a ball! #besties #bestdog #clink
livitup1016: lol i always cheers with orange juice too #nopulp
naturalbornchiller: OMG where are you???

⭐ 76 💬 12 ⬆️

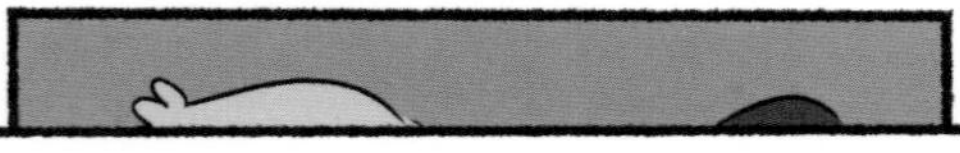

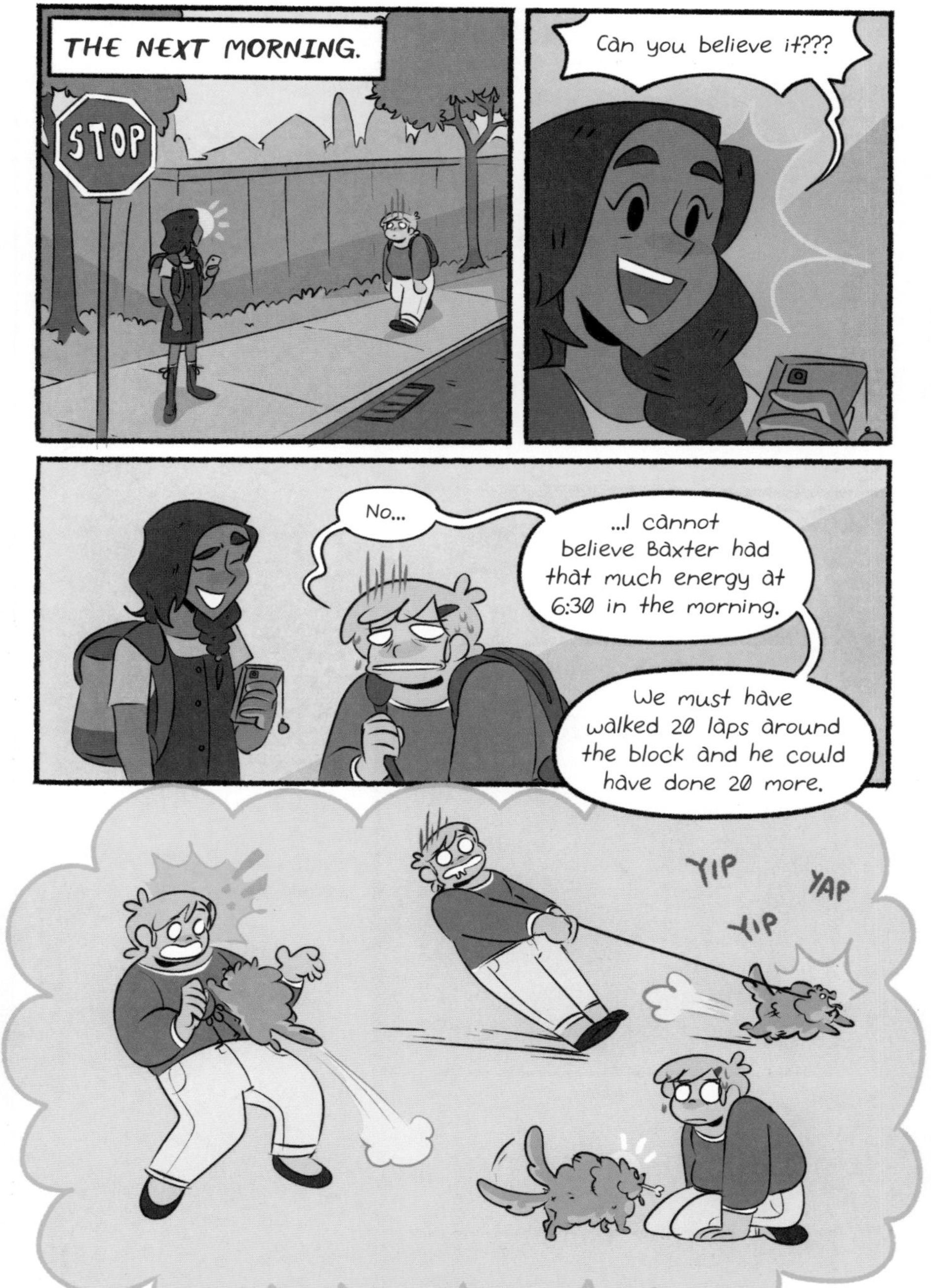
THE NEXT MORNING.
STOP
Can you believe it???
No...
...I cannot believe Baxter had that much energy at 6:30 in the morning.
We must have walked 20 laps around the block and he could have done 20 more.
YIP
YAP
YIP

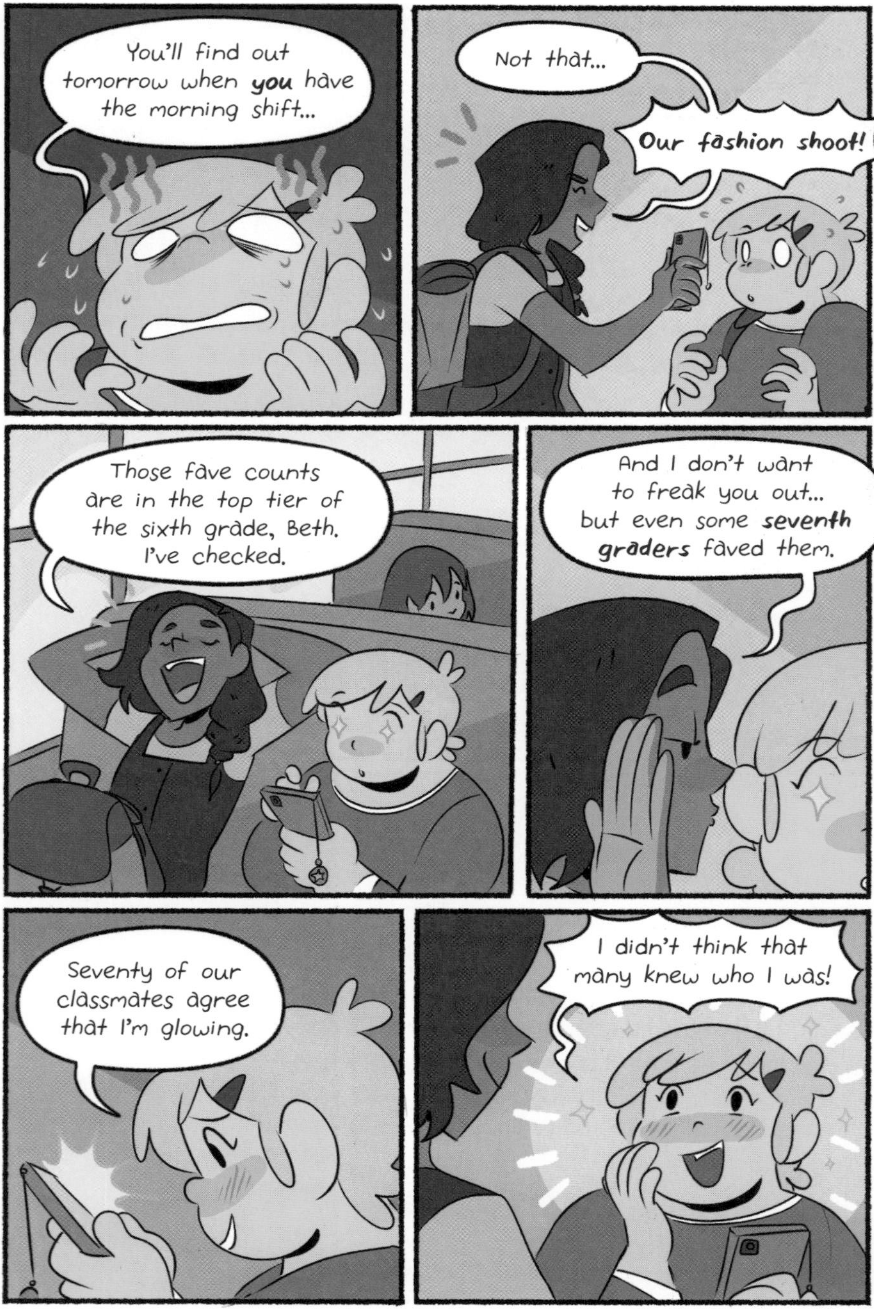
You'll find out tomorrow when **you** have the morning shift...
Not that...
Our fashion shoot!
Those fave counts are in the top tier of the sixth grade, Beth. I've checked.
And I don't want to freak you out... but even some **seventh graders** faved them.
Seventy of our classmates agree that I'm glowing.
I didn't think that many knew who I was!

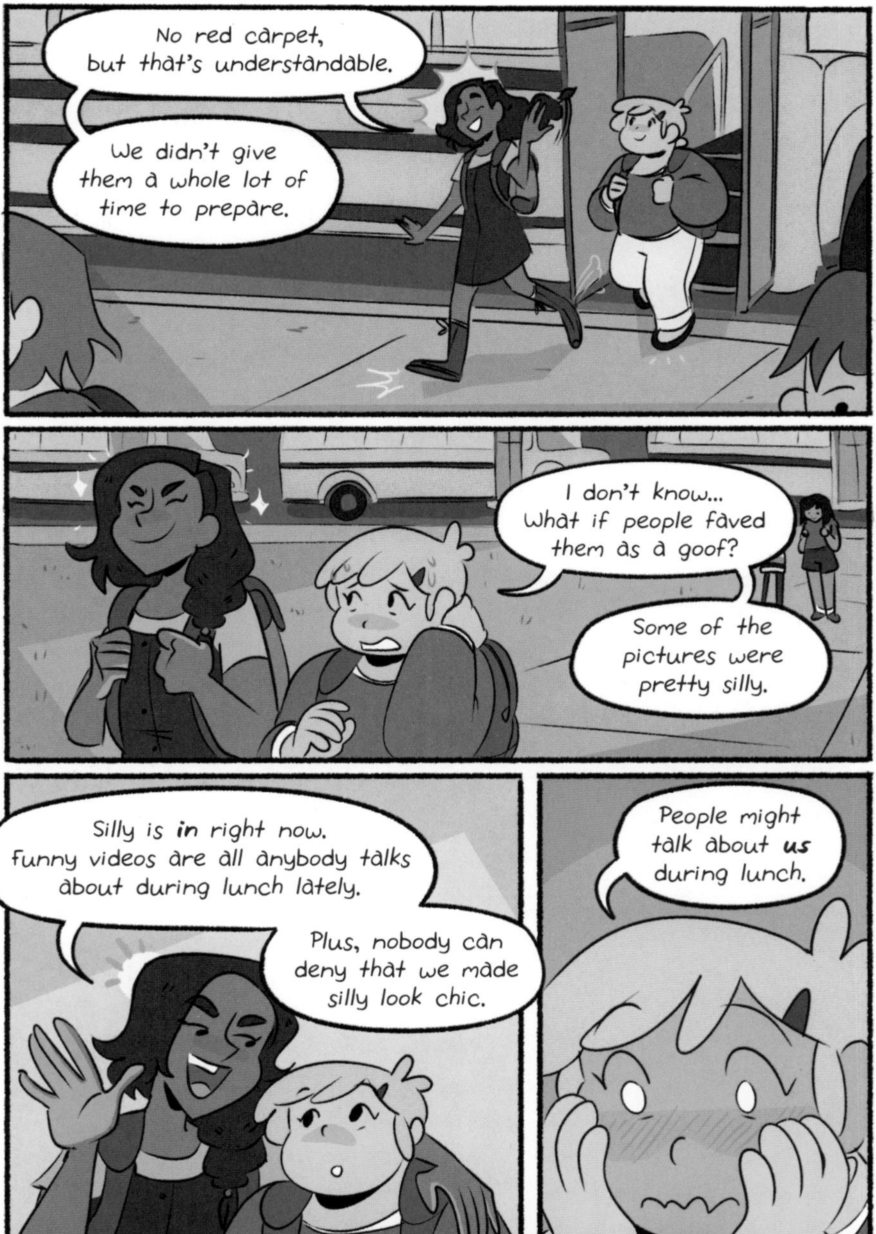
No red carpet, but that's understandable.
We didn't give them a whole lot of time to prepare.
I don't know... What if people faved them as a goof?
Some of the pictures were pretty silly.
Silly is **in** right now. Funny videos are all anybody talks about during lunch lately.
Plus, nobody can deny that we made silly look chic.
People might talk about **us** during lunch.

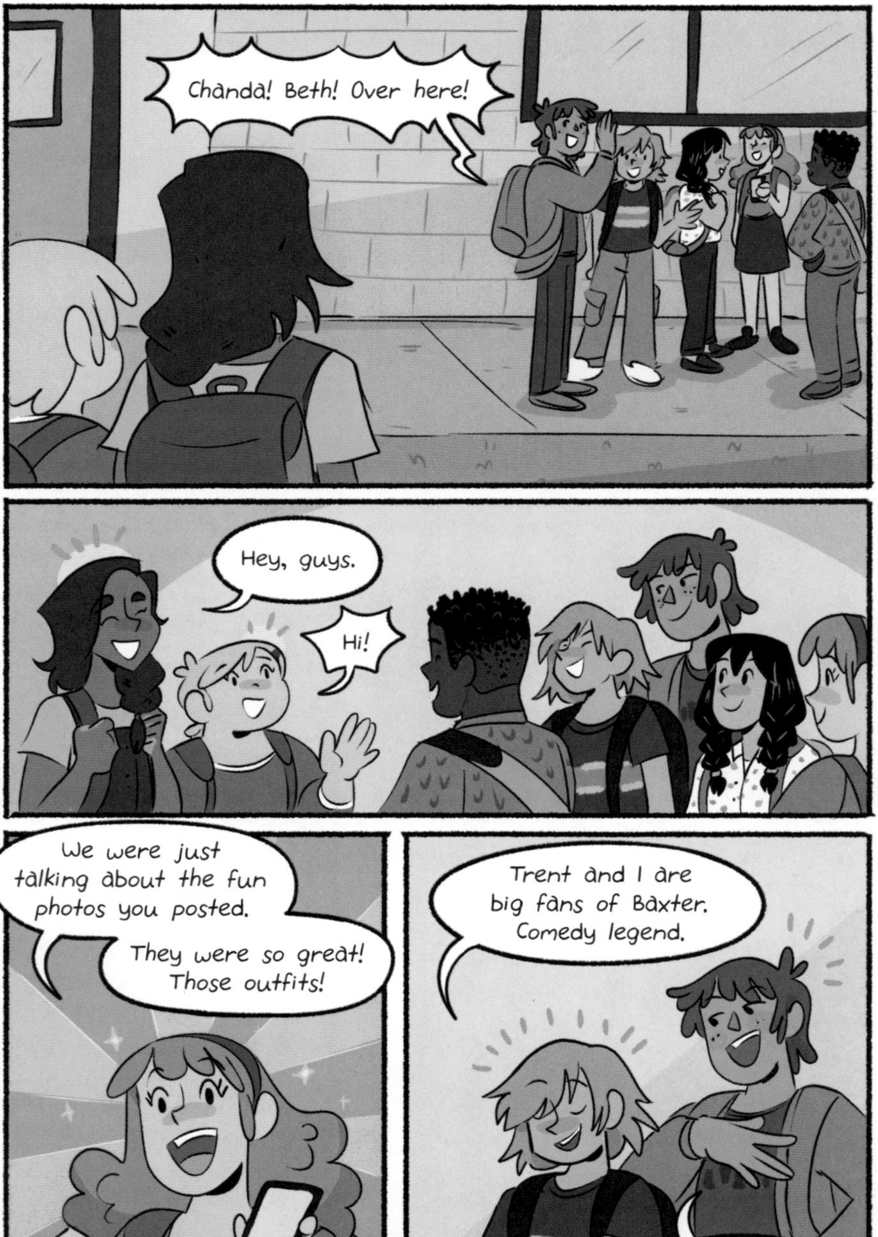
Chanda! Beth! Over here!
Hey, guys.
Hi!
We were just talking about the fun photos you posted.
They were so great! Those outfits!
Trent and I are big fans of Baxter. Comedy legend.
I'd like to shake his paw.

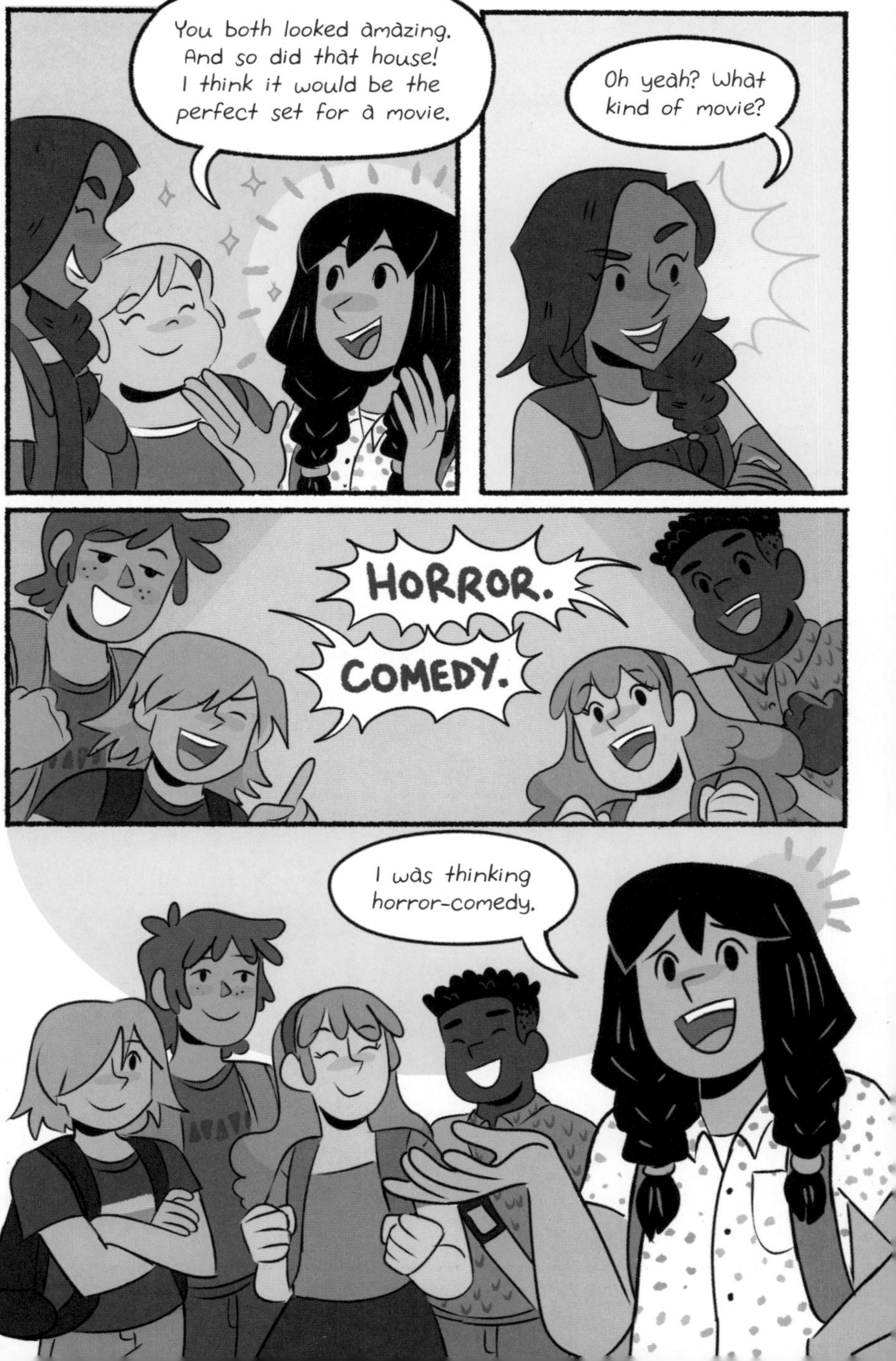
You both looked amazing. And so did that house! I think it would be the perfect set for a movie.
Oh yeah? What kind of movie?
HORROR.
COMEDY.
I was thinking horror-comedy.

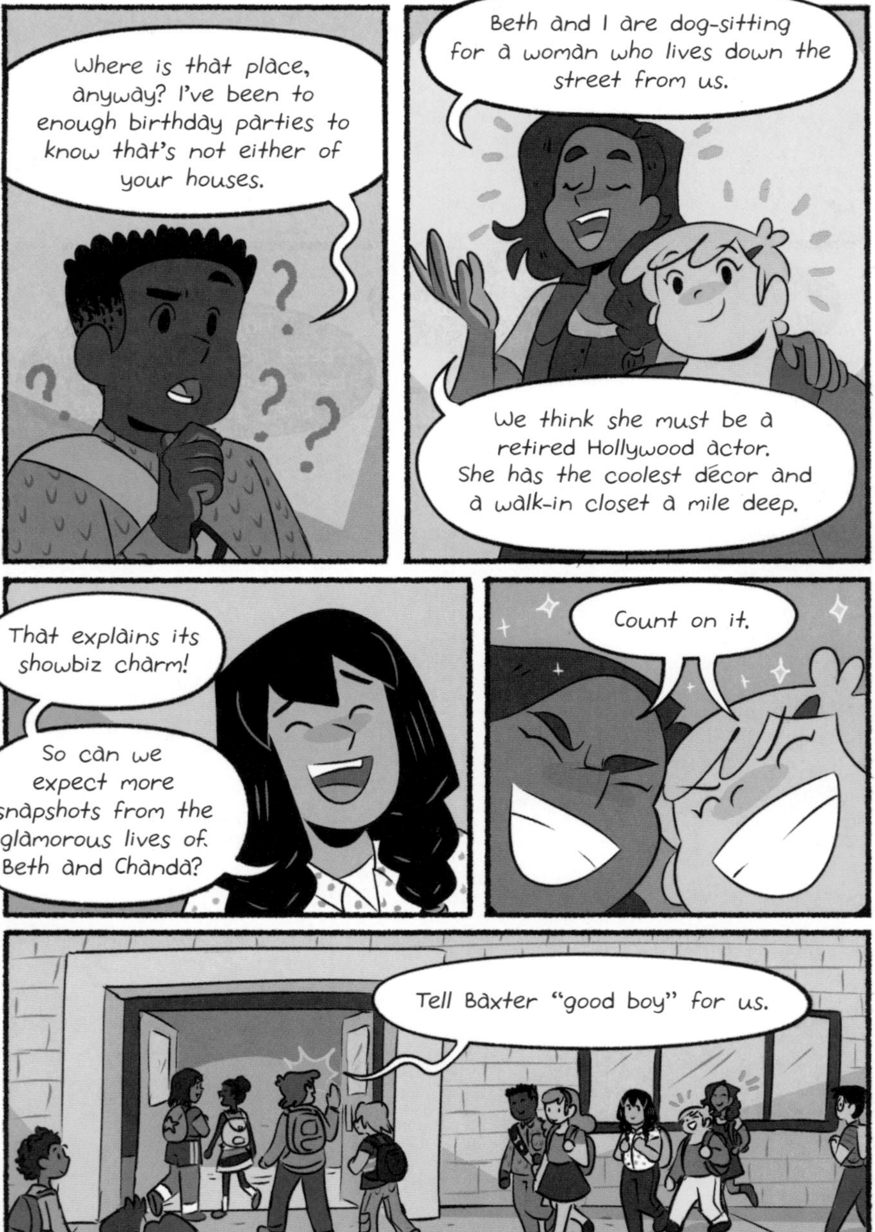
Where is that place, anyway? I've been to enough birthday parties to know that's not either of your houses.
Beth and I are dog-sitting for a woman who lives down the street from us.
We think she must be a retired Hollywood actor. She has the coolest décor and a walk-in closet a mile deep.
That explains its showbiz charm!
So can we expect more snapshots from the glamorous lives of Beth and Chanda?
Count on it.
Tell Baxter "good boy" for us.

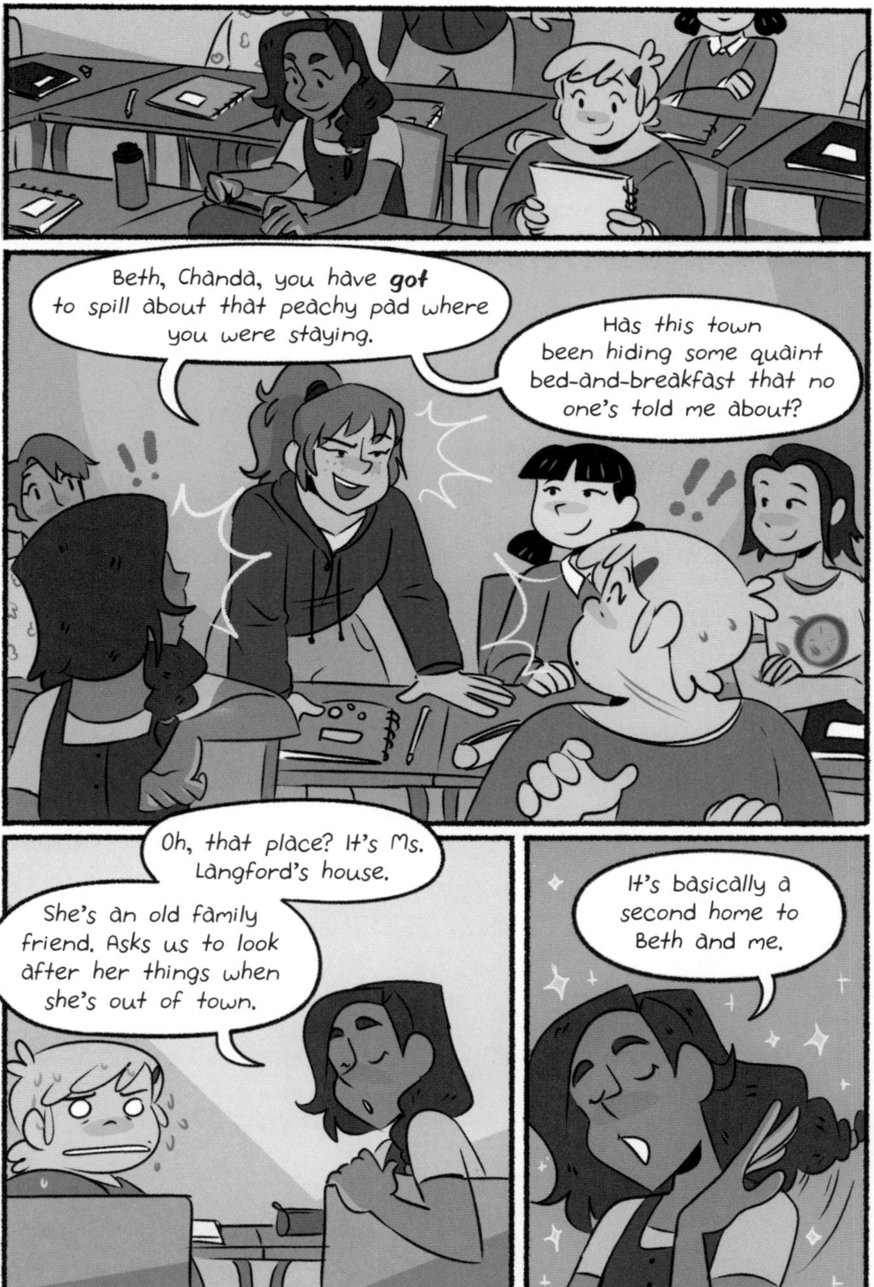
Beth, Chanda, you have **got** to spill about that peachy pad where you were staying.
Has this town been hiding some quaint bed-and-breakfast that no one's told me about?
Oh, that place? It's Ms. Langford's house.
She's an old family friend. Asks us to look after her things when she's out of town.
It's basically a second home to Beth and me.

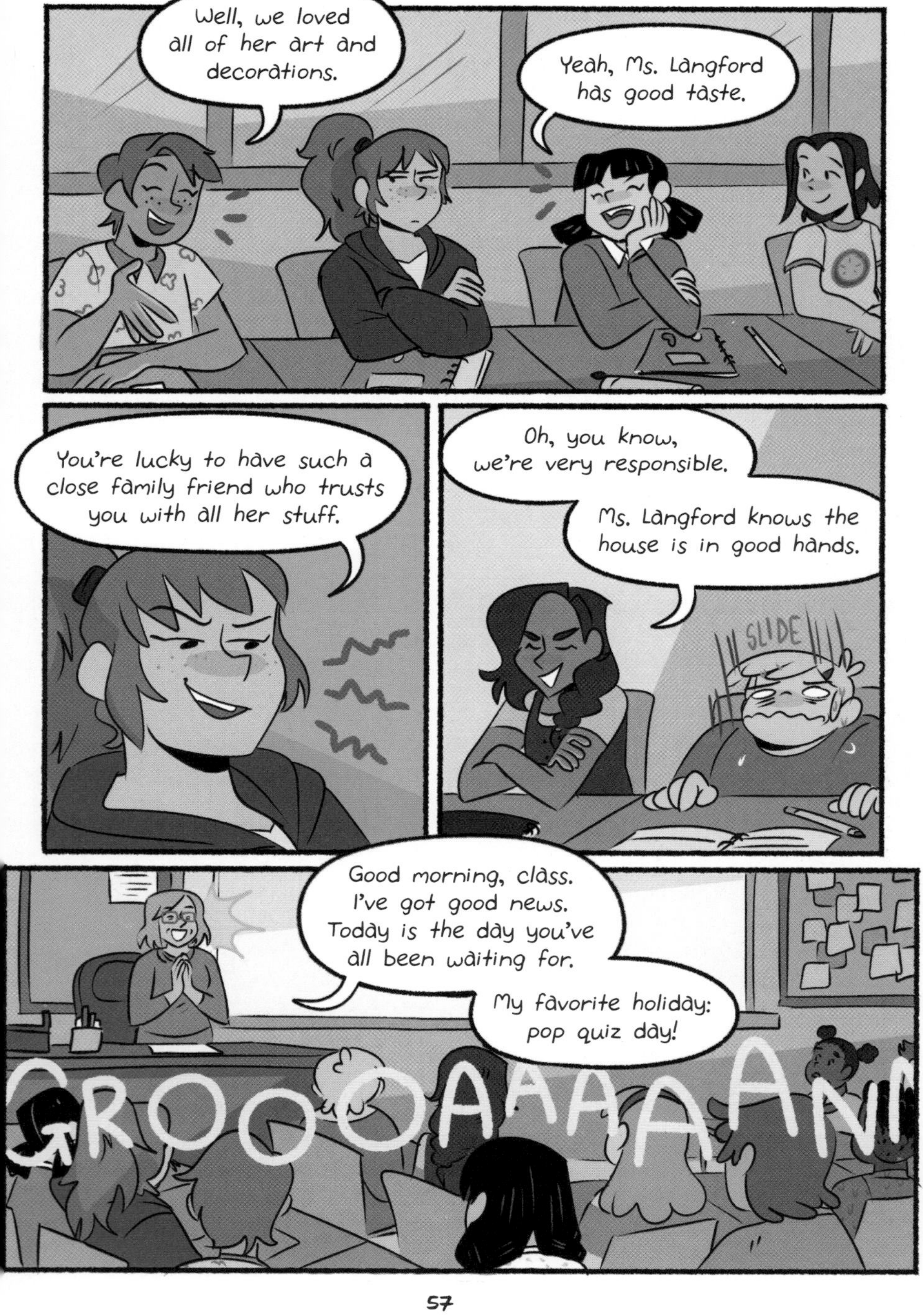
Well, we loved all of her art and decorations.
Yeah, Ms. Langford has good taste.
You're lucky to have such a close family friend who trusts you with all her stuff.
Oh, you know, we're very responsible.
Ms. Langford knows the house is in good hands.
SLIDE
Good morning, class. I've got good news. Today is the day you've all been waiting for.
My favorite holiday: pop quiz day!
GROOOAAAAAN

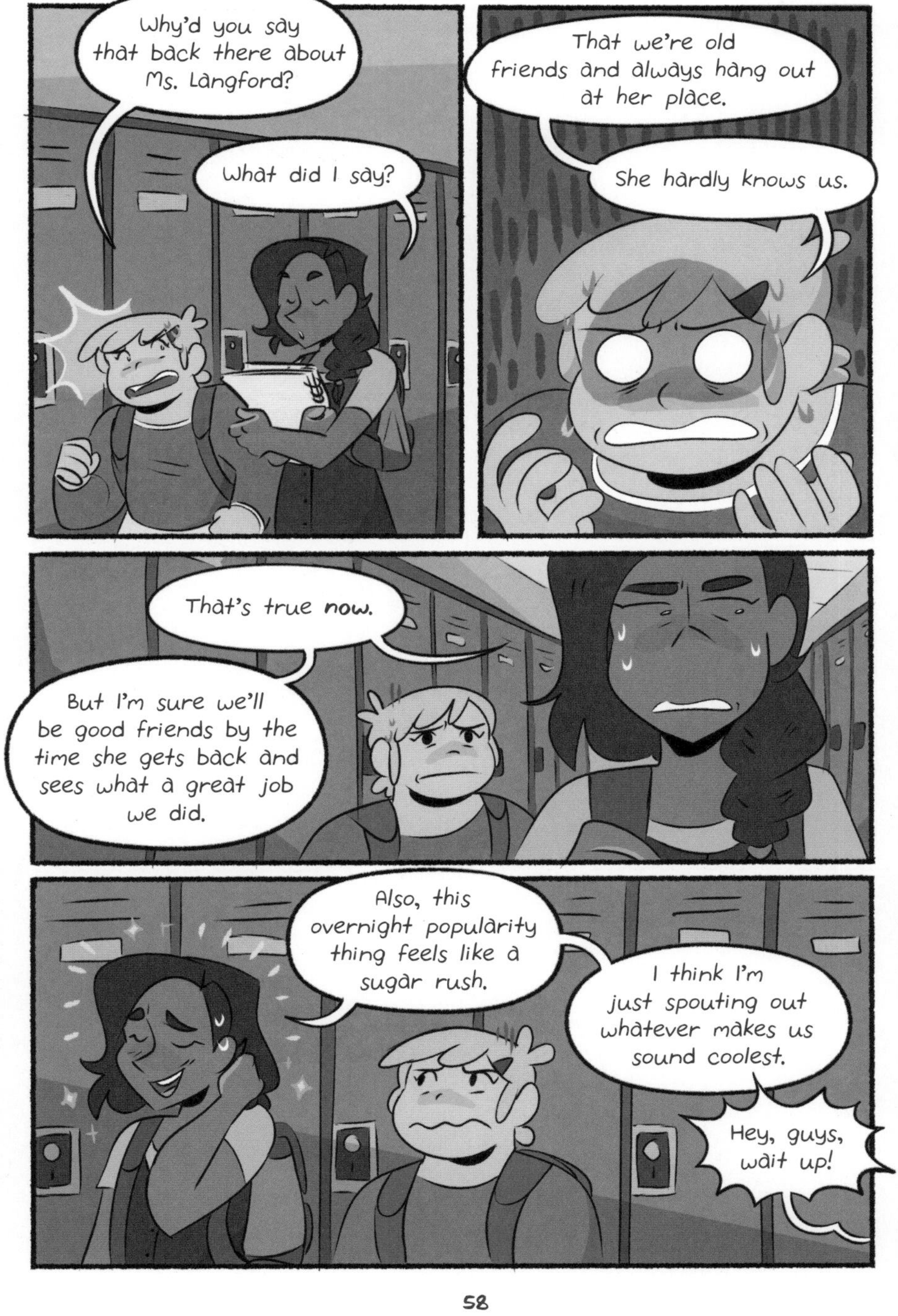
Why'd you say that back there about Ms. Langford?
What did I say?
That we're old friends and always hang out at her place.
She hardly knows us.
That's true **now.**
But I'm sure we'll be good friends by the time she gets back and sees what a great job we did.
Also, this overnight popularity thing feels like a sugar rush.
I think I'm just spouting out whatever makes us sound coolest.
Hey, guys, wait up!

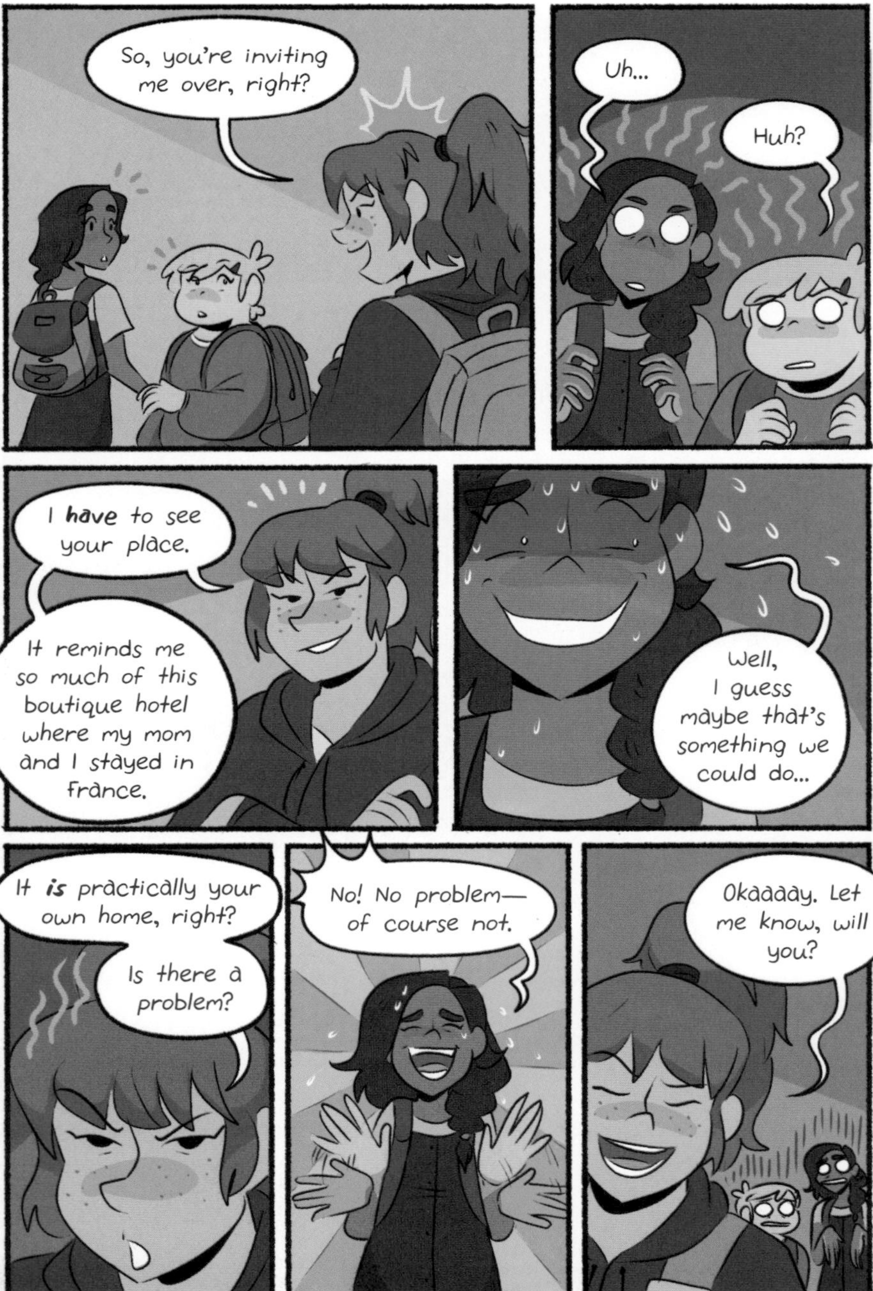
So, you're inviting me over, right?
Uh...
Huh?
I **have** to see your place.
It reminds me so much of this boutique hotel where my mom and I stayed in France.
Well, I guess maybe that's something we could do...
It ***is*** practically your own home, right?
Is there a problem?
No! No problem— of course not.
Okaaaay. Let me know, will you?

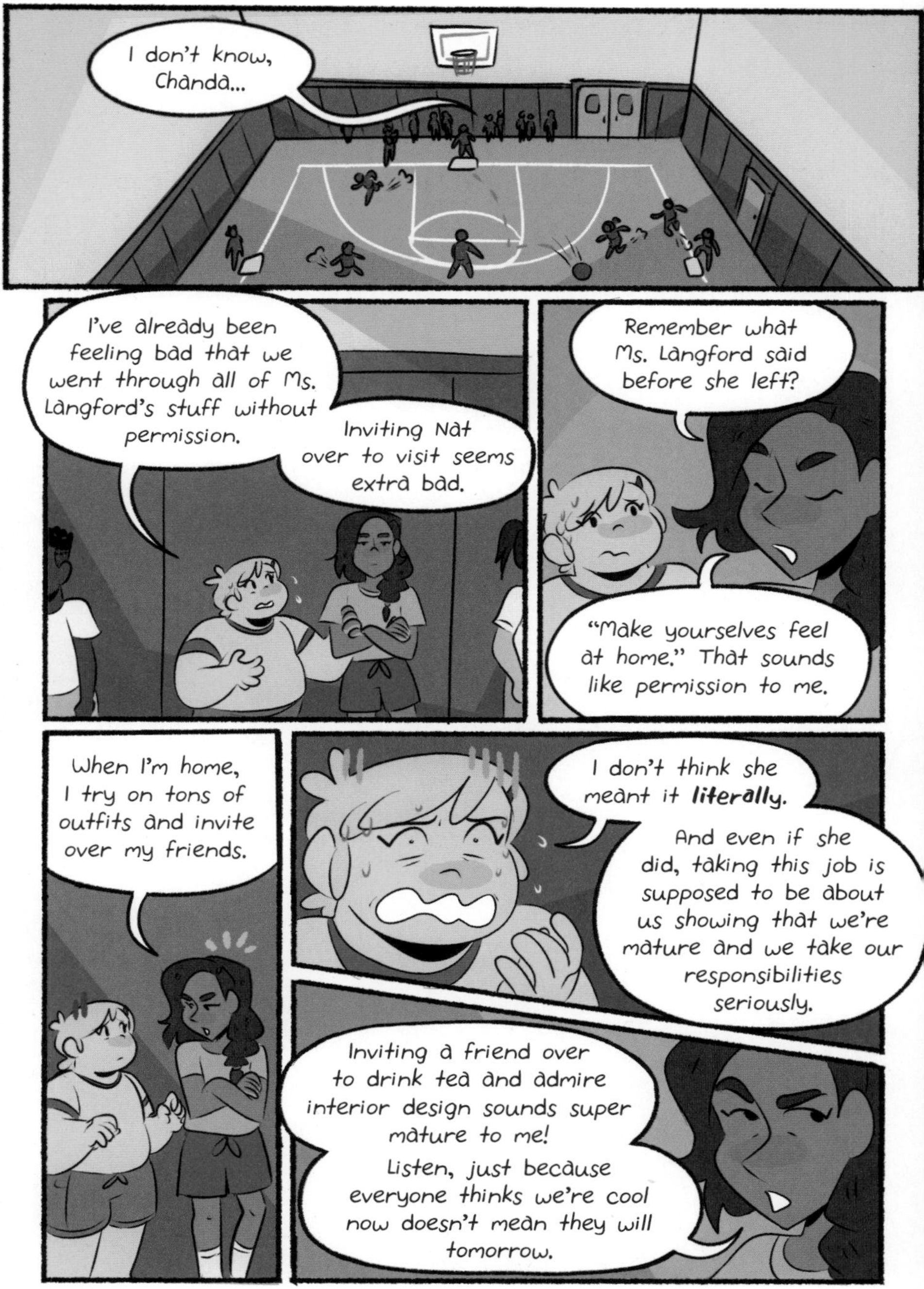
I don't know, Chanda...
I've already been feeling bad that we went through all of Ms. Langford's stuff without permission.
Inviting Nat over to visit seems extra bad.
Remember what Ms. Langford said before she left?
"Make yourselves feel at home." That sounds like permission to me.
When I'm home, I try on tons of outfits and invite over my friends.
I don't think she meant it **literally**.
And even if she did, taking this job is supposed to be about us showing that we're mature and we take our responsibilities seriously.
Inviting a friend over to drink tea and admire interior design sounds super mature to me!
Listen, just because everyone thinks we're cool now doesn't mean they will tomorrow.

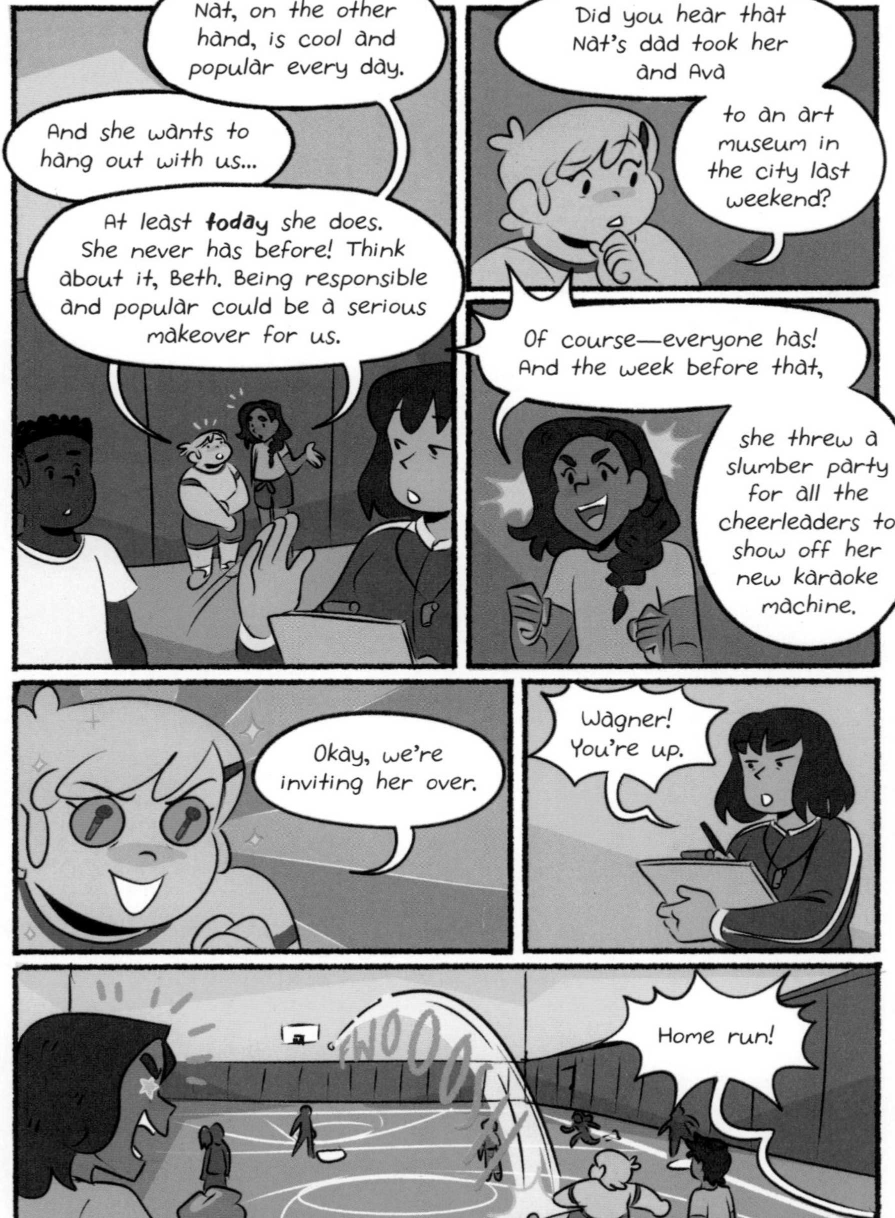

Nat, on the other hand, is cool and popular every day.
And she wants to hang out with us...
At least **today** she does. She never has before! Think about it, Beth. Being responsible and popular could be a serious makeover for us.
Did you hear that Nat's dad took her and Ava
to an art museum in the city last weekend?
Of course—everyone has! And the week before that,
she threw a slumber party for all the cheerleaders to show off her new karaoke machine.
Okay, we're inviting her over.
Wagner! You're up.
FWOOOSH
Home run!

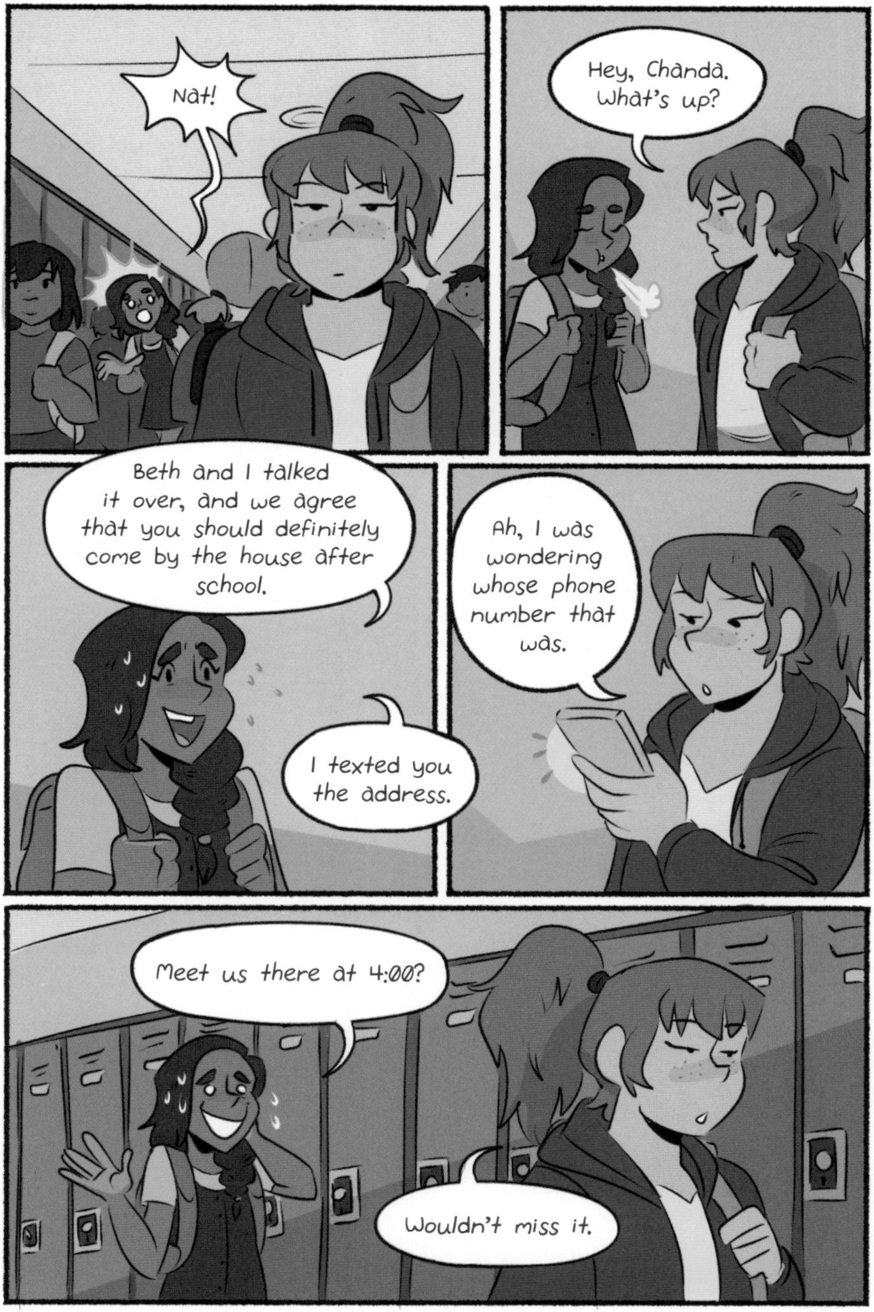

Nat!
Hey, Chanda. What's up?
Beth and I talked it over, and we agree that you should definitely come by the house after school.
I texted you the address.
Ah, I was wondering whose phone number that was.
Meet us there at 4:00?
Wouldn't miss it.

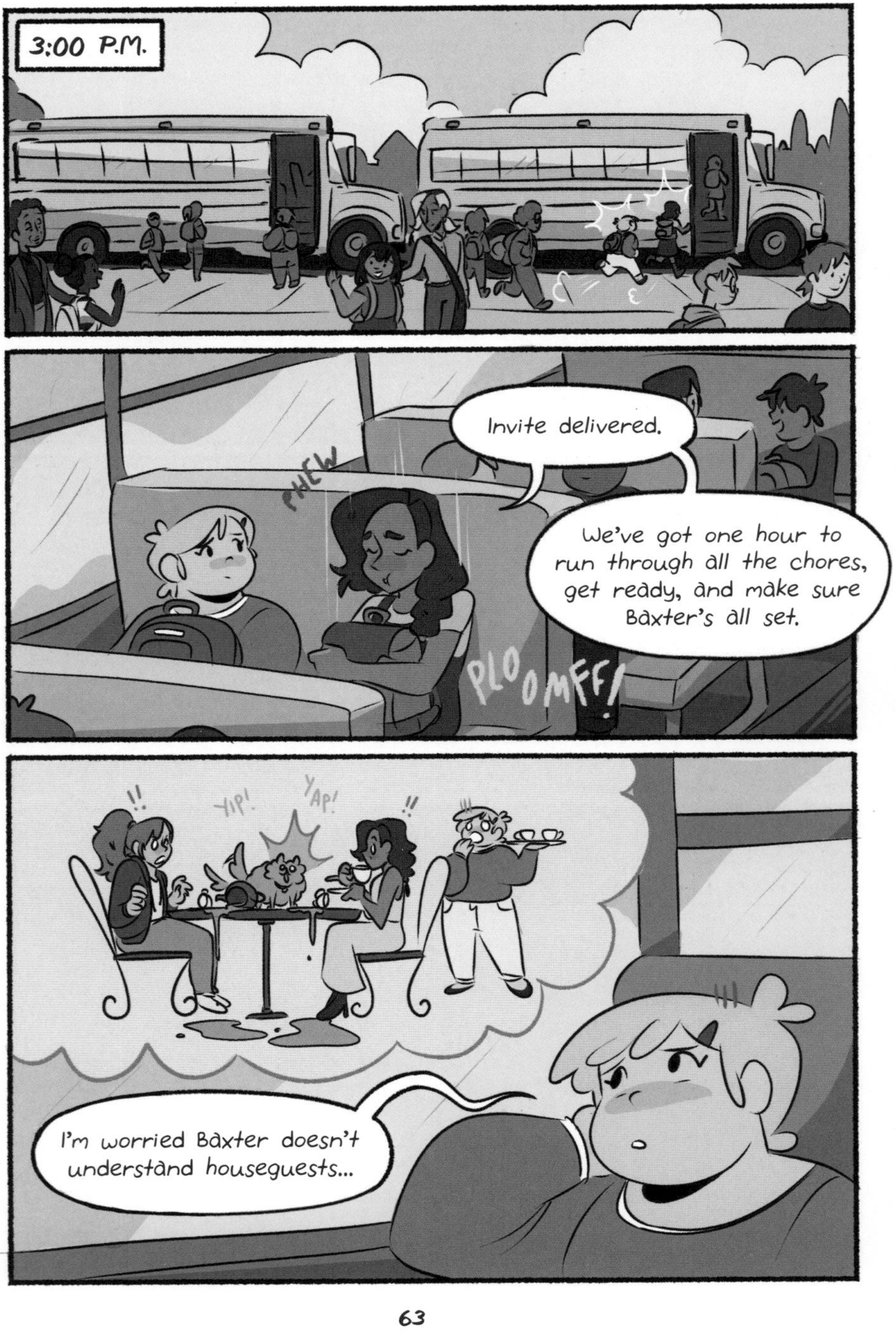
3:00 P.M.
Invite delivered.
PHEW
We've got one hour to run through all the chores, get ready, and make sure Baxter's all set.
PLOOMFF!
!!
YIP!
YAP!
!!
I'm worried Baxter doesn't understand houseguests...

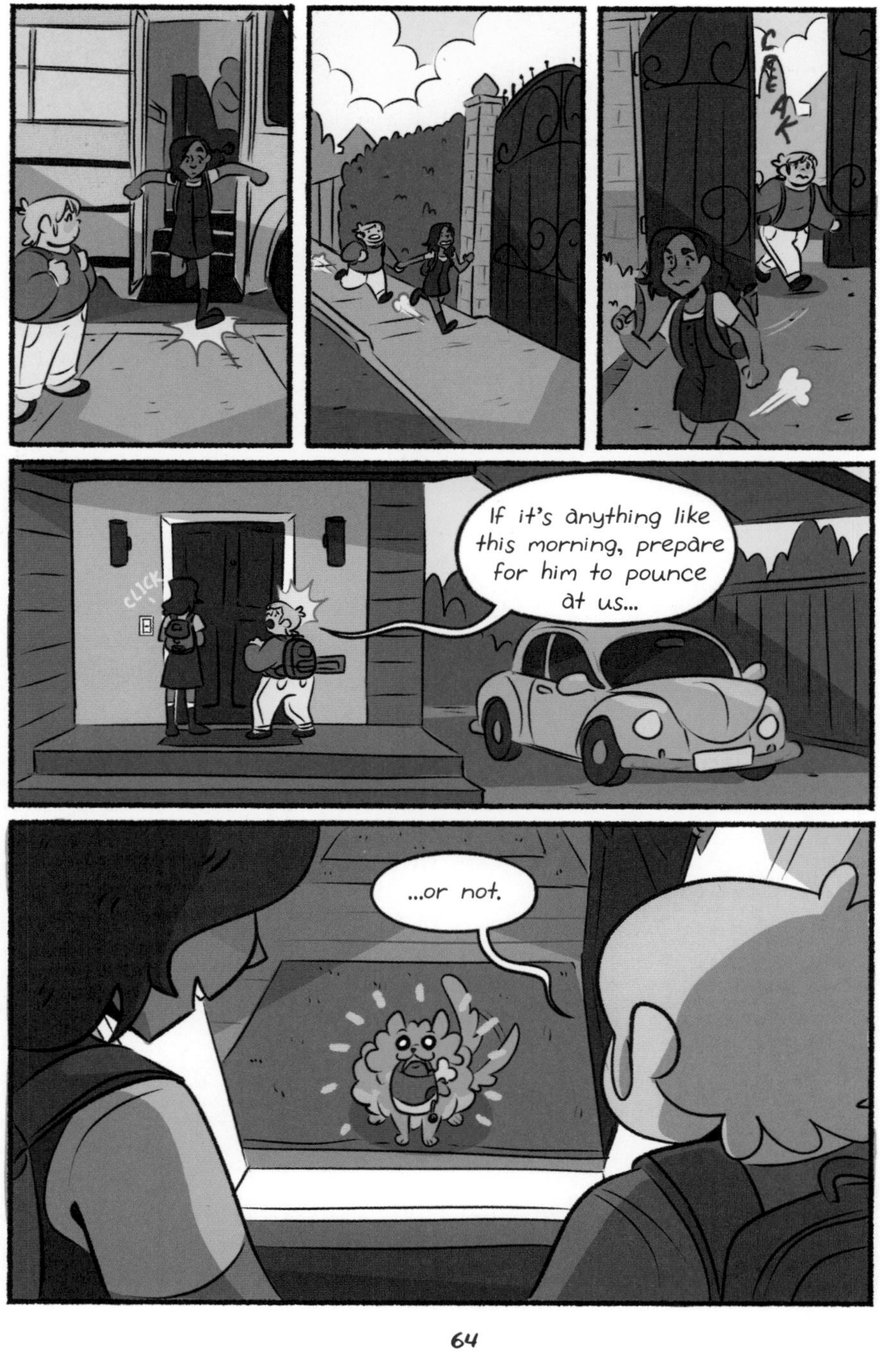
CREAK
CLICK
If it's anything like this morning, prepare for him to pounce at us...
...or not.

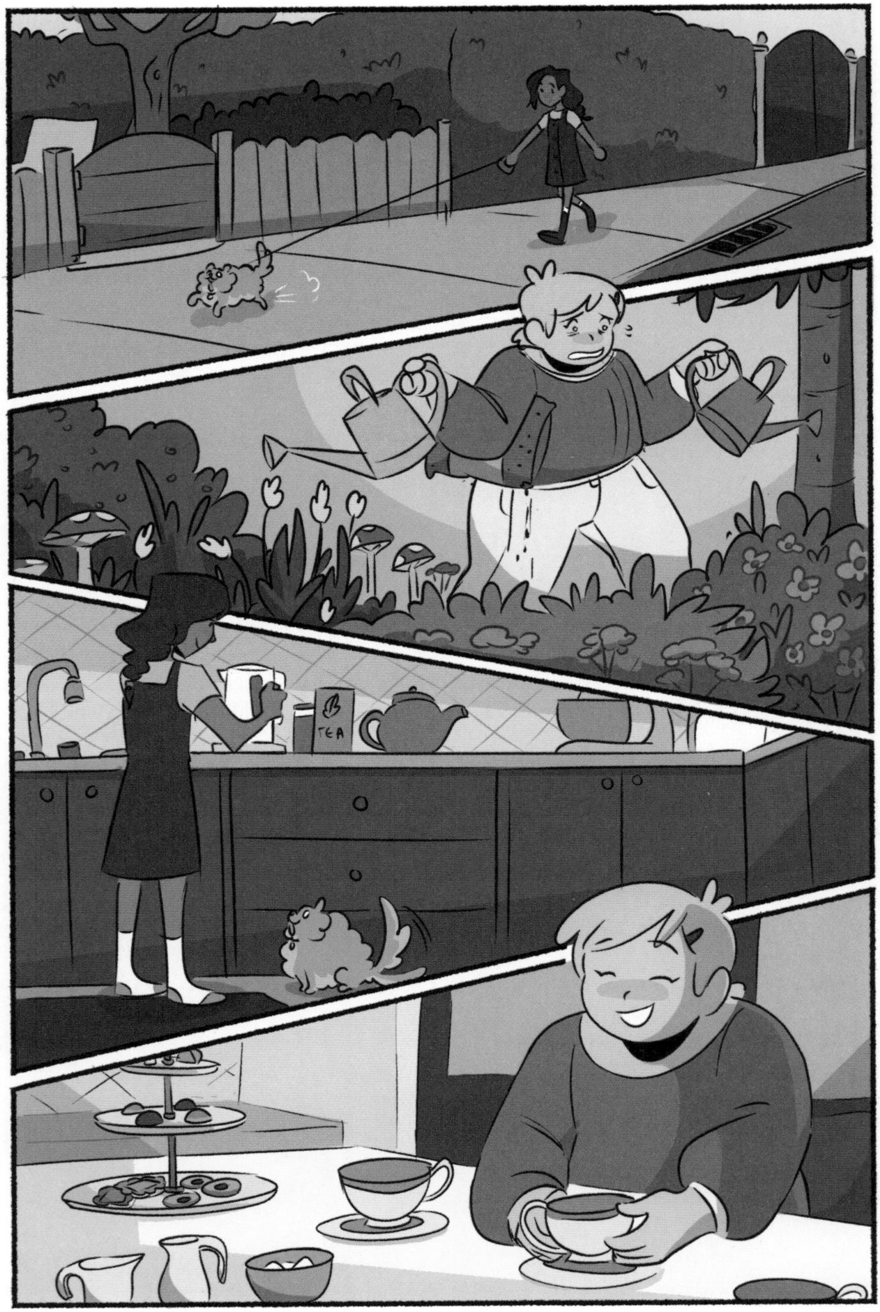
TEA

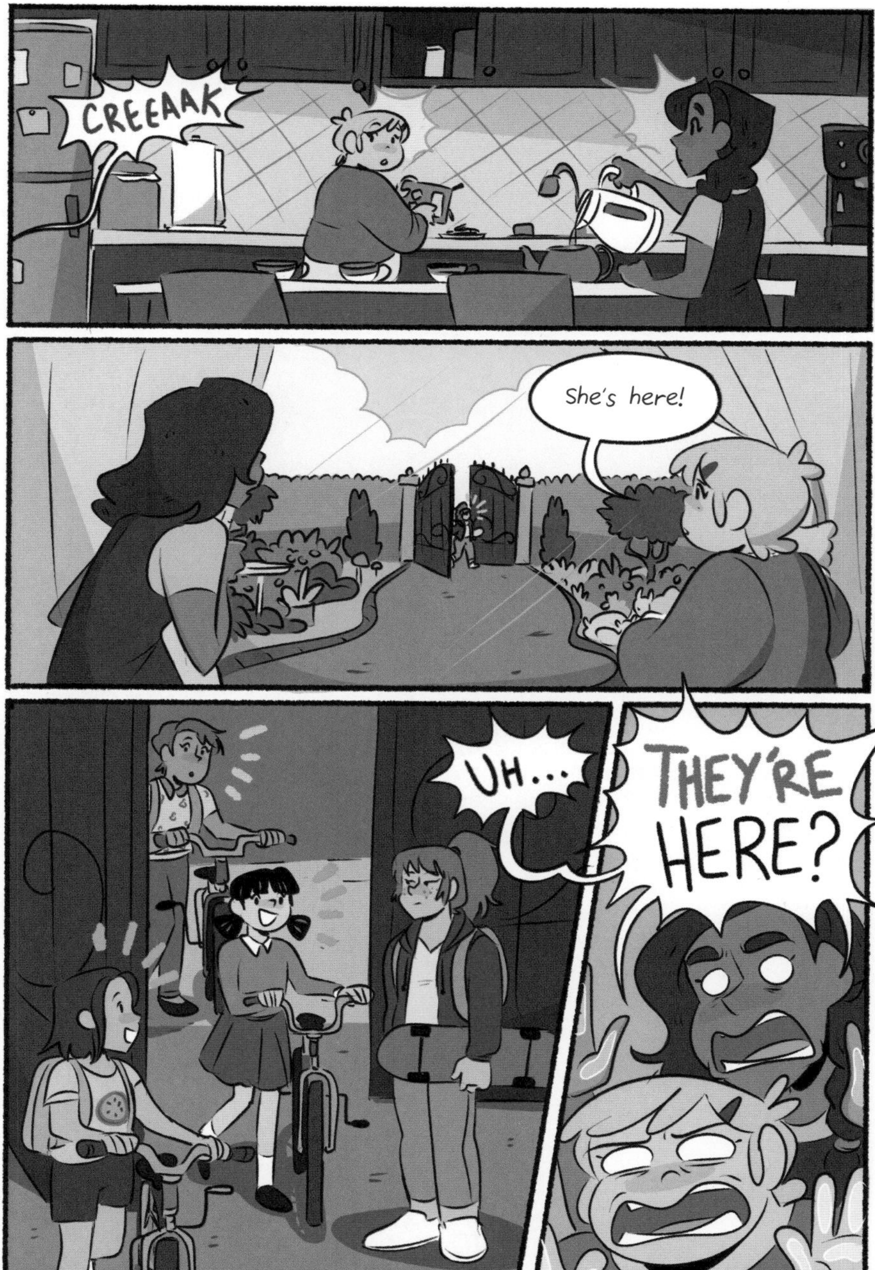
CREEAAK
She's here!
UH...
THEY'RE HERE?

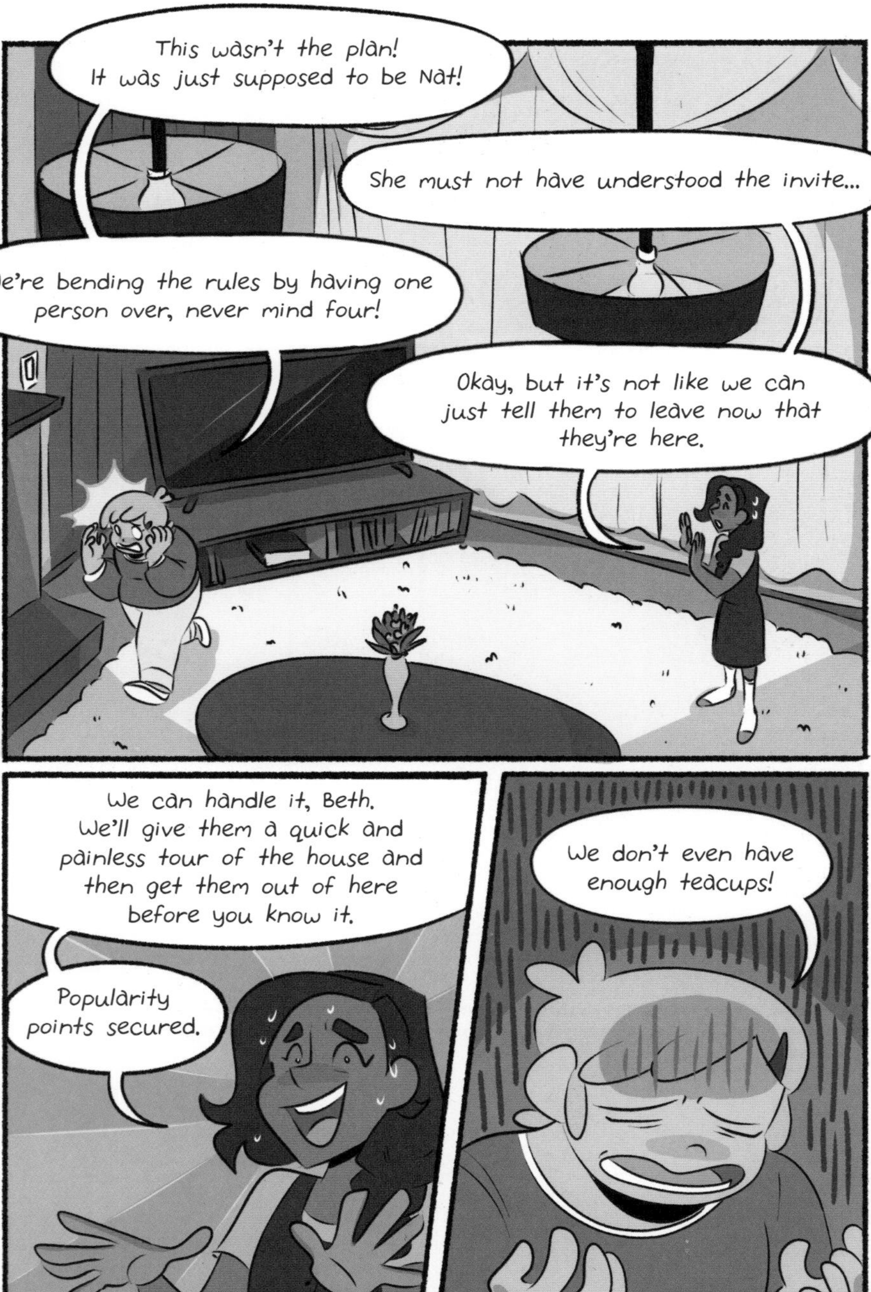
This wasn't the plan! It was just supposed to be Nat!
She must not have understood the invite...
We're bending the rules by having one person over, never mind four!
Okay, but it's not like we can just tell them to leave now that they're here.
We can handle it, Beth. We'll give them a quick and painless tour of the house and then get them out of here before you know it.
Popularity points secured.
We don't even have enough teacups!

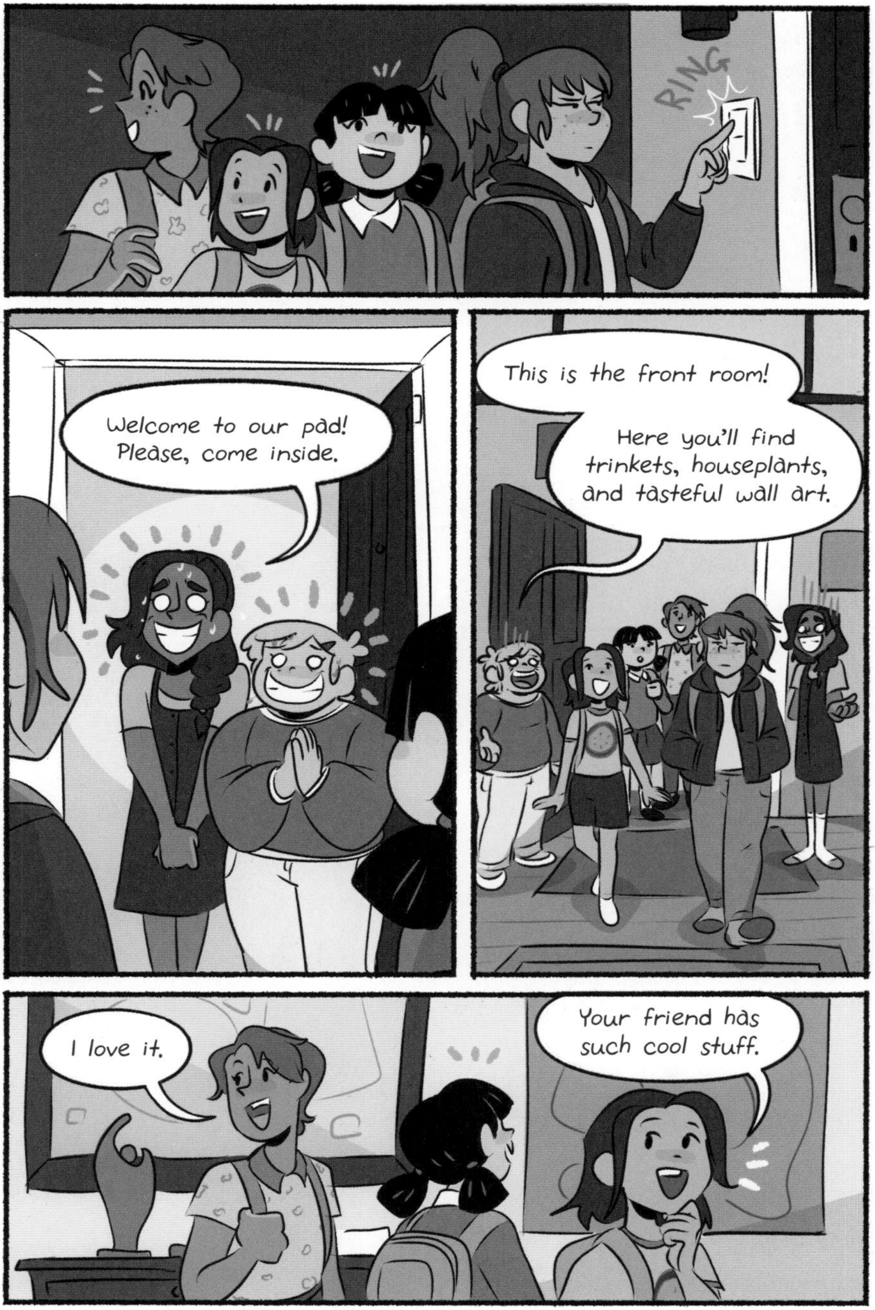
RING
Welcome to our pad! Please, come inside.
This is the front room!
Here you'll find trinkets, houseplants, and tasteful wall art.
I love it.
Your friend has such cool stuff.

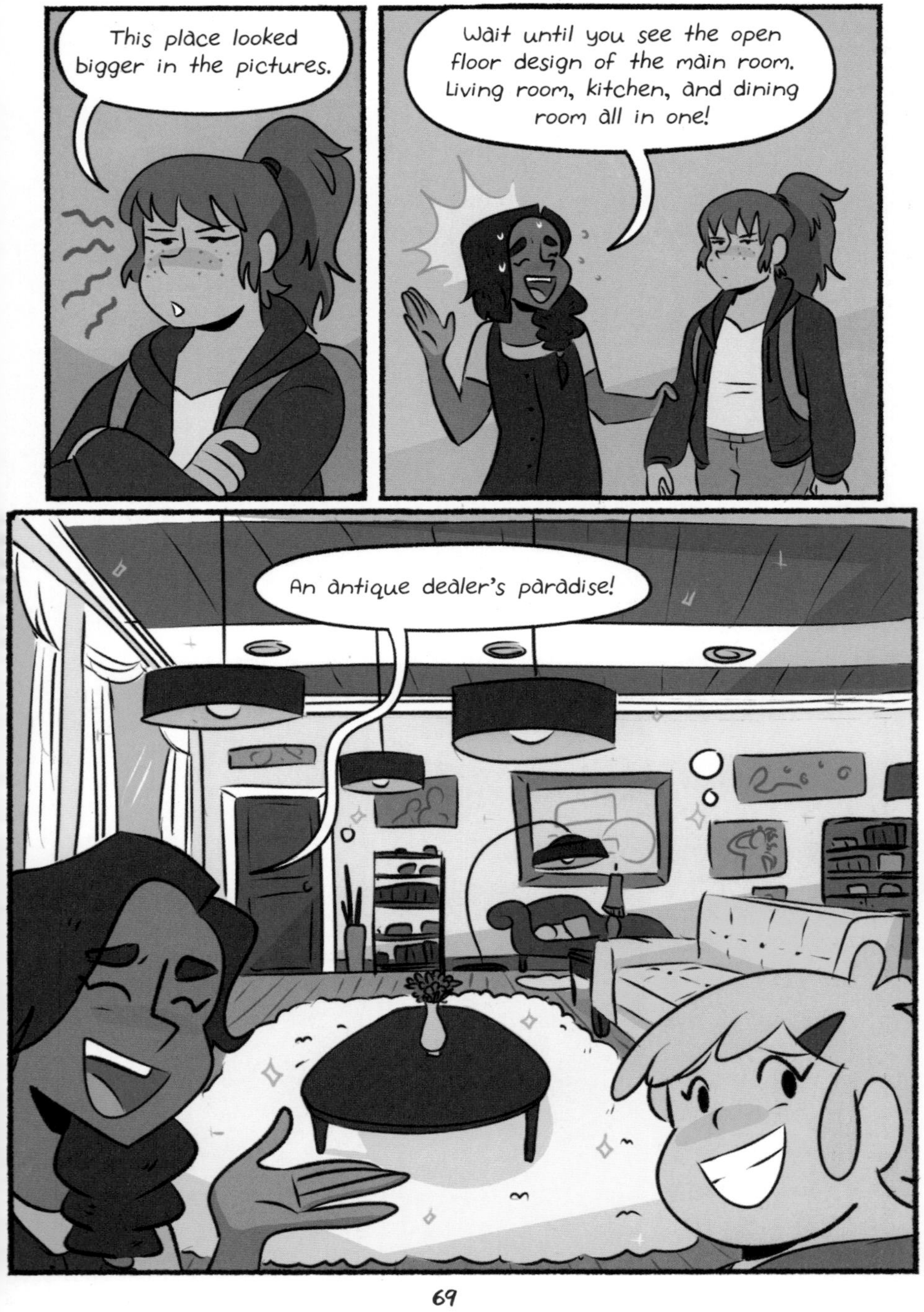
This place looked bigger in the pictures.
Wait until you see the open floor design of the main room. Living room, kitchen, and dining room all in one!
An antique dealer's paradise!

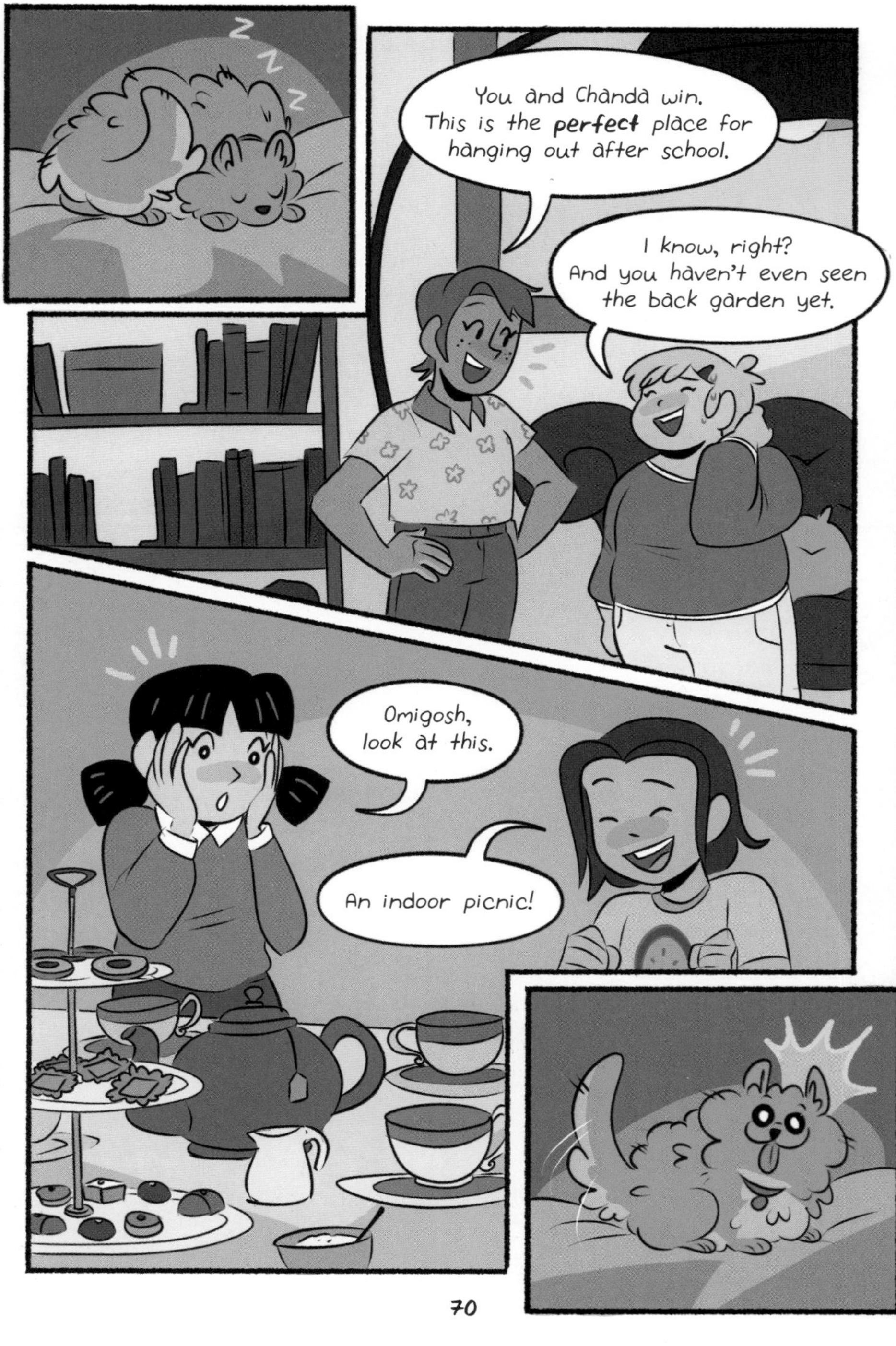
Z Z Z
You and Chanda win. This is the **perfect** place for hanging out after school.
I know, right? And you haven't even seen the back garden yet.
Omigosh, look at this.
An indoor picnic!

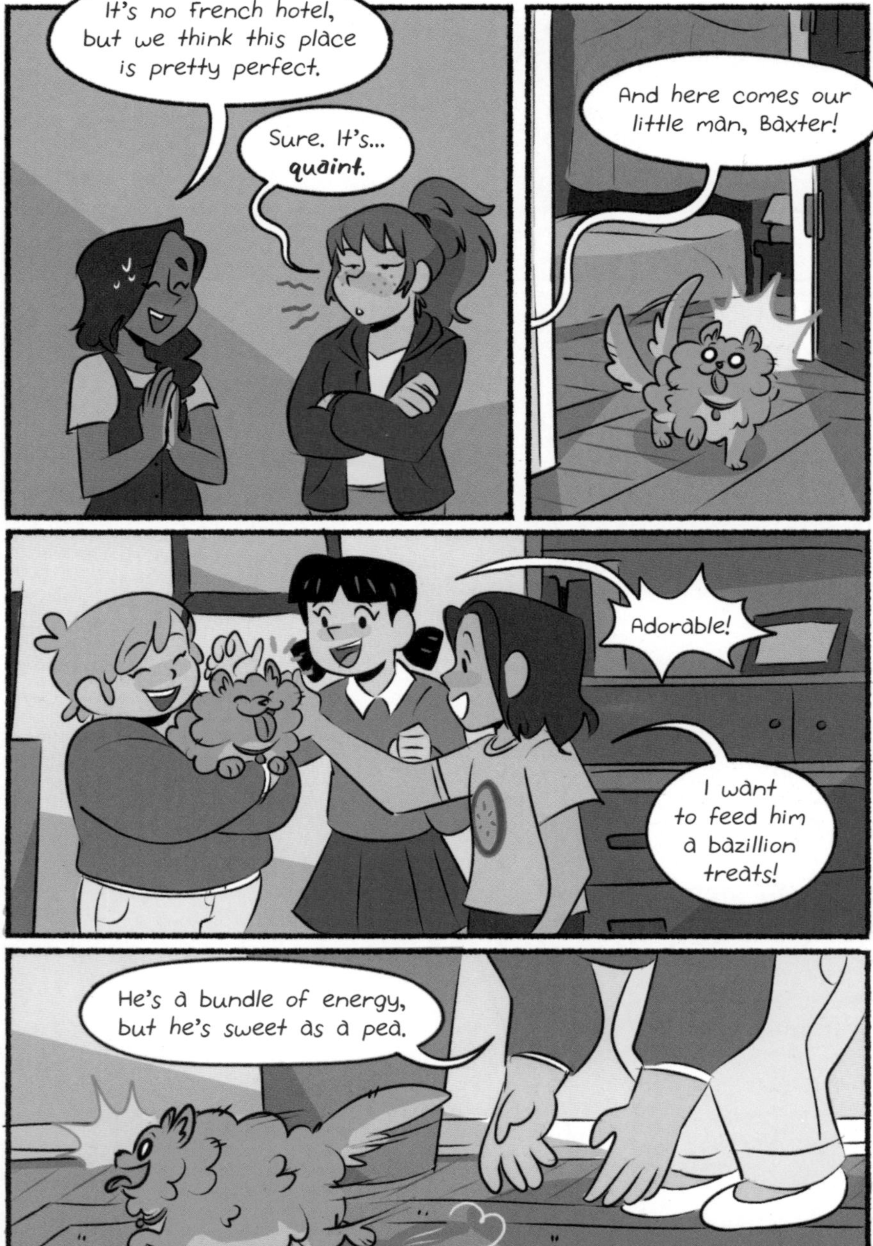
It's no French hotel, but we think this place is pretty perfect.
Sure. It's... **quaint.**
And here comes our little man, Baxter!
Adorable!
I want to feed him a bazillion treats!
He's a bundle of energy, but he's sweet as a pea.

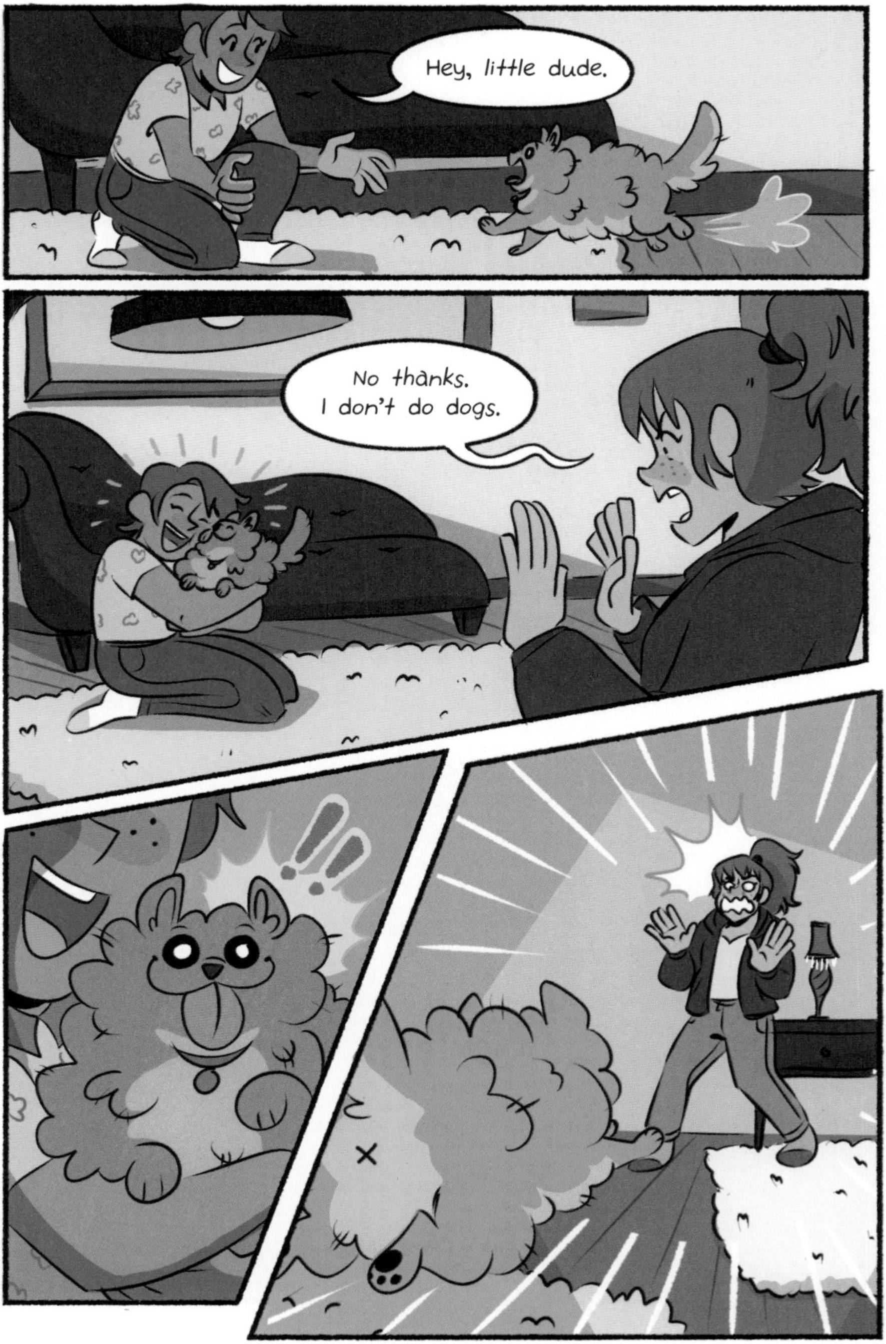
Hey, little dude.
No thanks.
I don't do dogs.

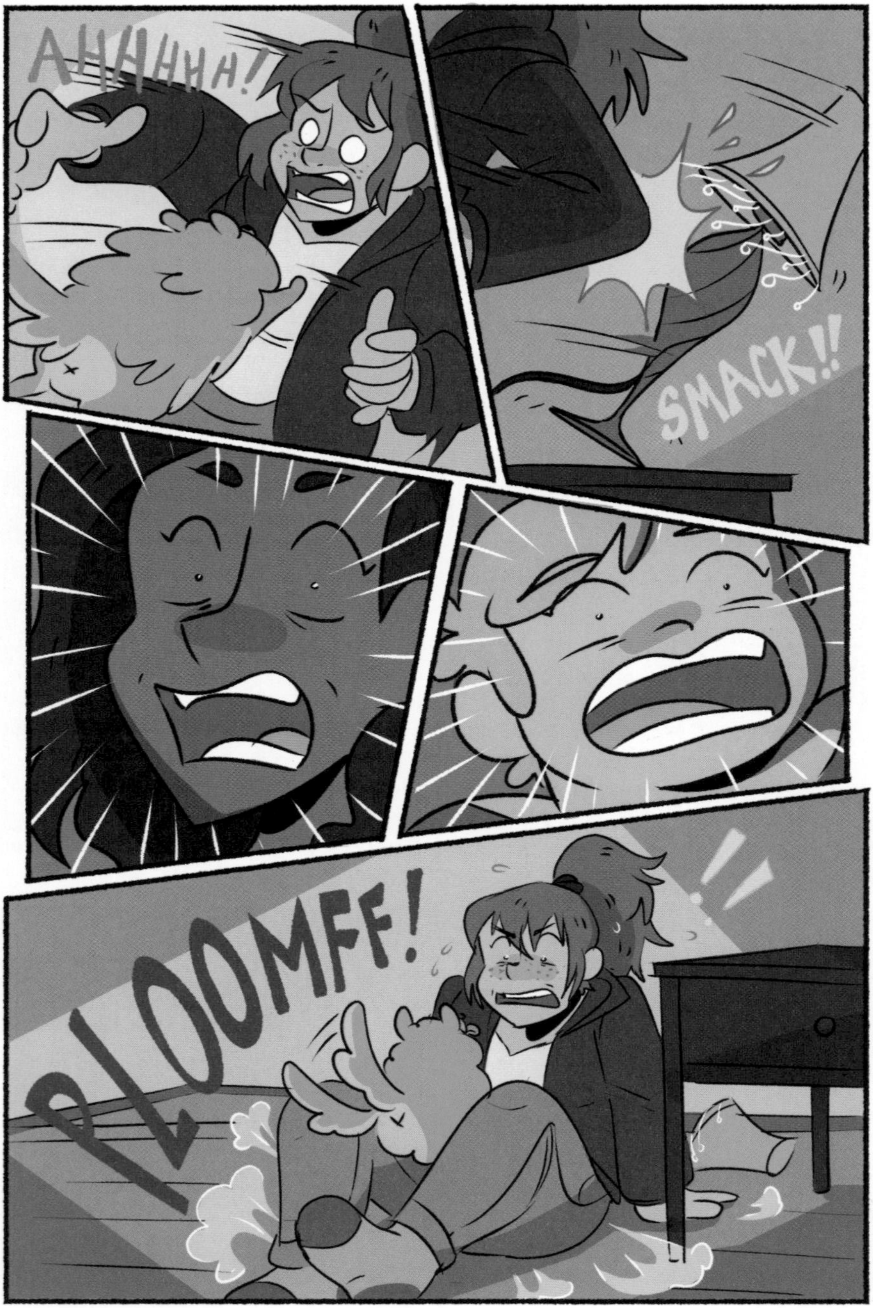

AHHHHHA!
SMACK!!
PLOOMFF!
!!

Are you okay, Nat?
That dog **attacked** me.
A bit of an overstatement. Baxter's slobber will dry, I think.
But the lamp...

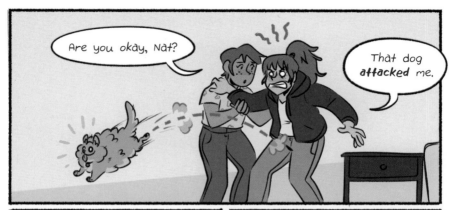

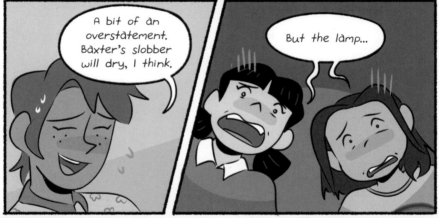

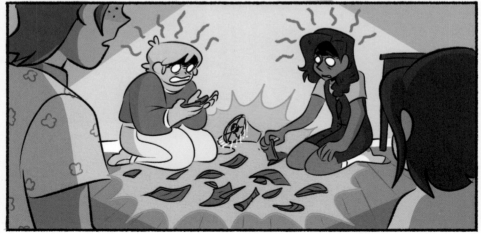

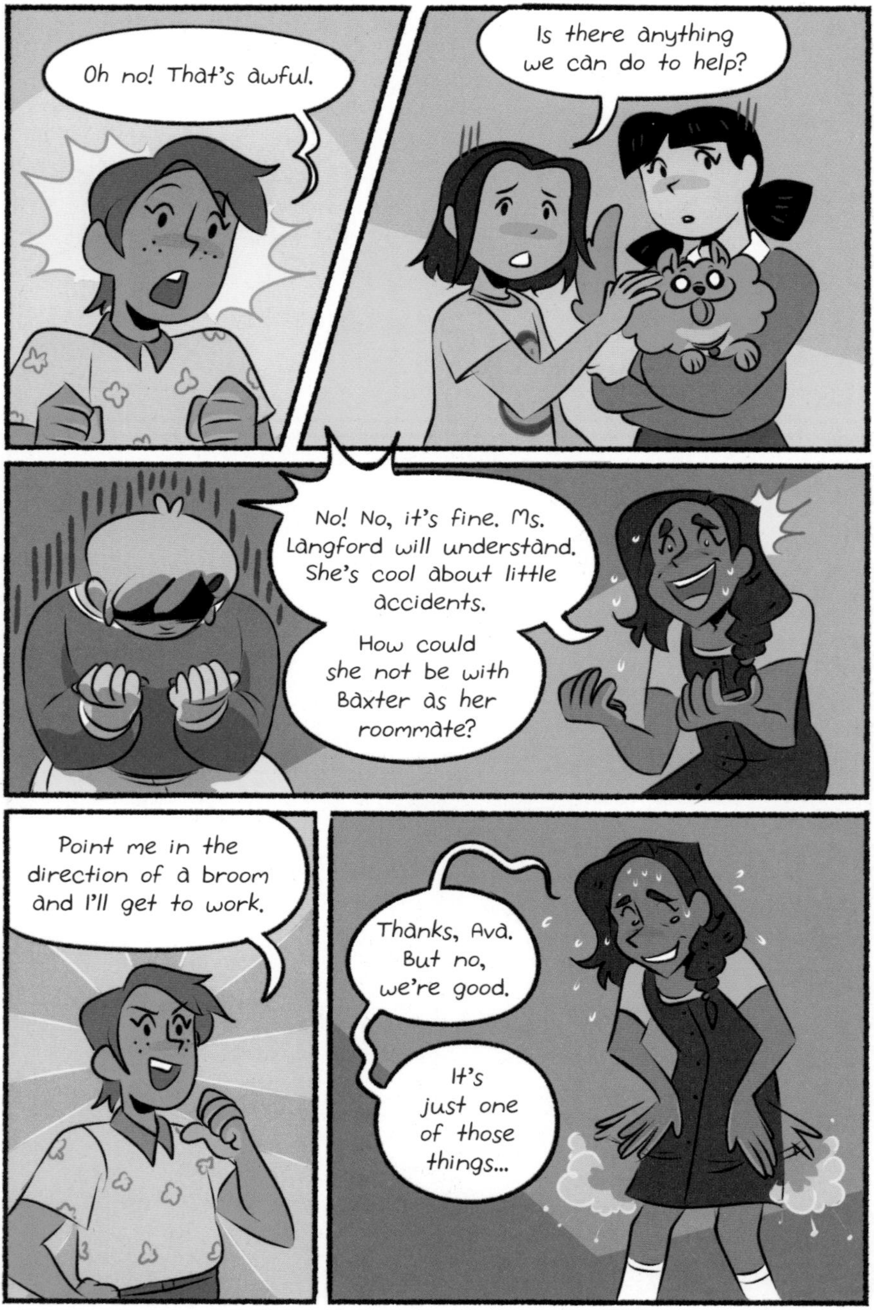
Oh no! That's awful.
Is there anything we can do to help?
No! No, it's fine. Ms. Langford will understand. She's cool about little accidents.
How could she not be with Baxter as her roommate?
Point me in the direction of a broom and I'll get to work.
Thanks, Ava. But no, we're good.
It's just one of those things...

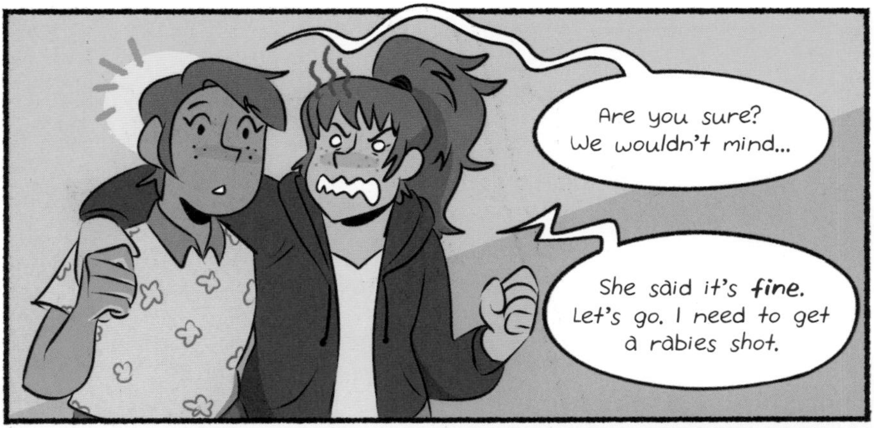
Are you sure? We wouldn't mind...
She said it's **fine.** Let's go. I need to get a rabies shot.

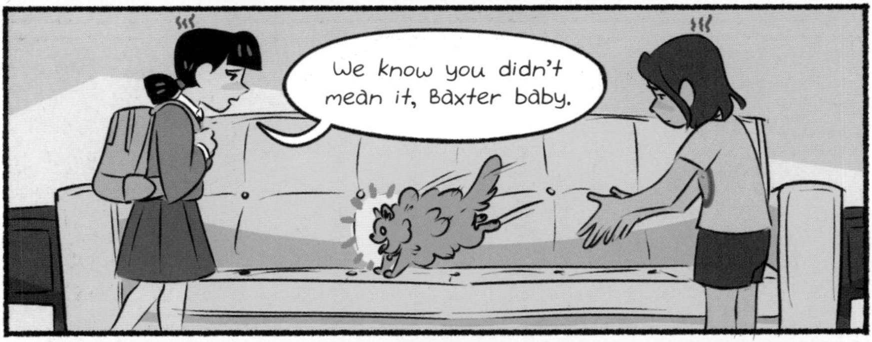
We know you didn't mean it, Baxter baby.

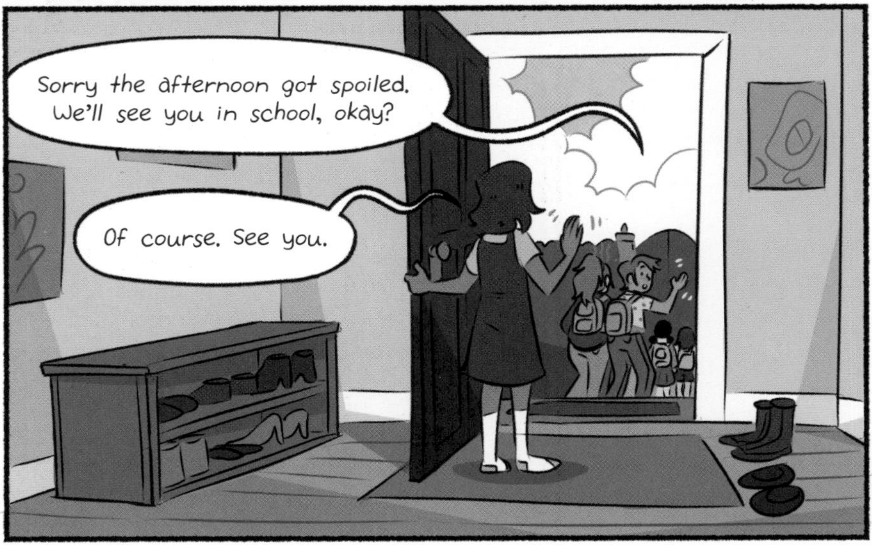
Sorry the afternoon got spoiled. We'll see you in school, okay?
Of course. See you.

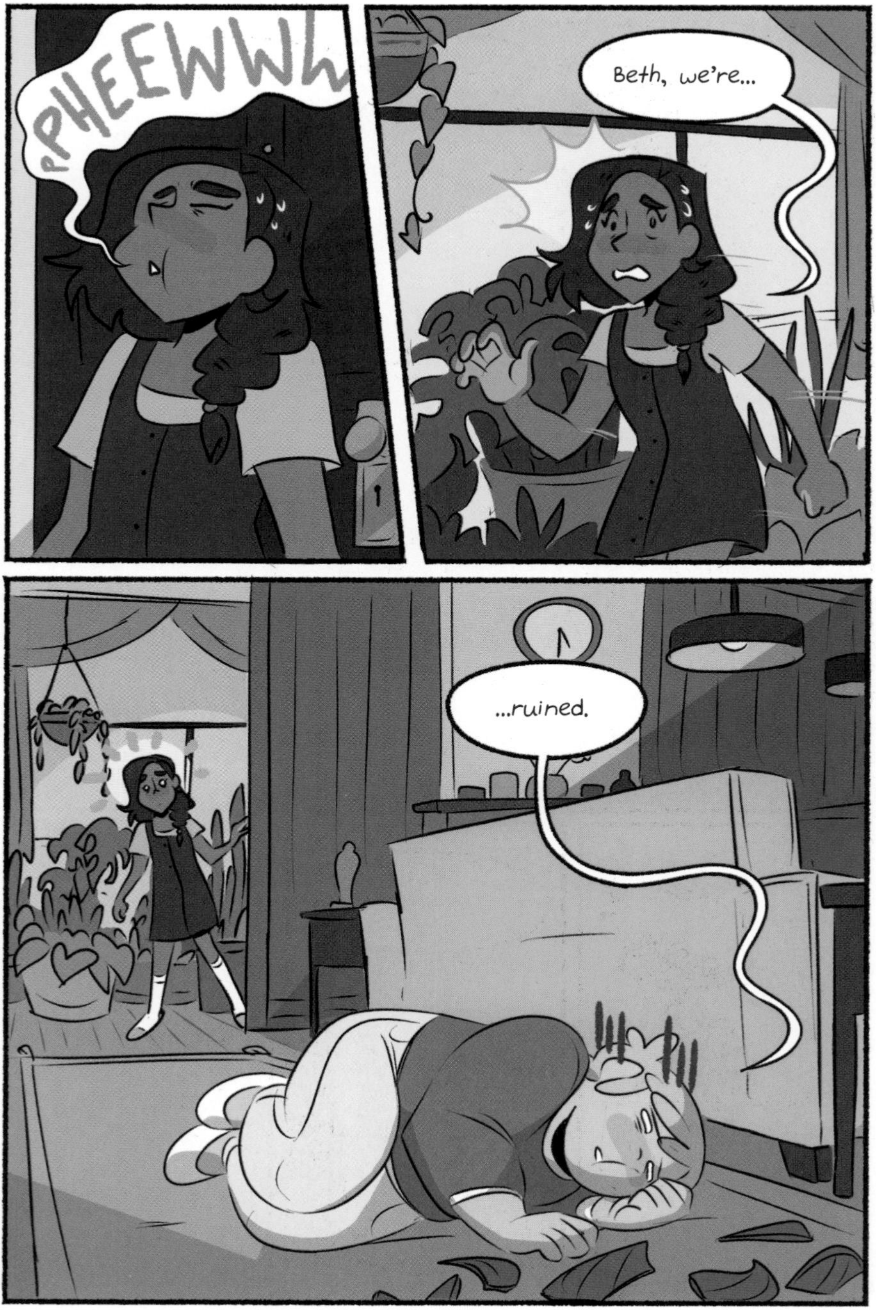
PHEEWWW
Beth, we're...
...ruined.

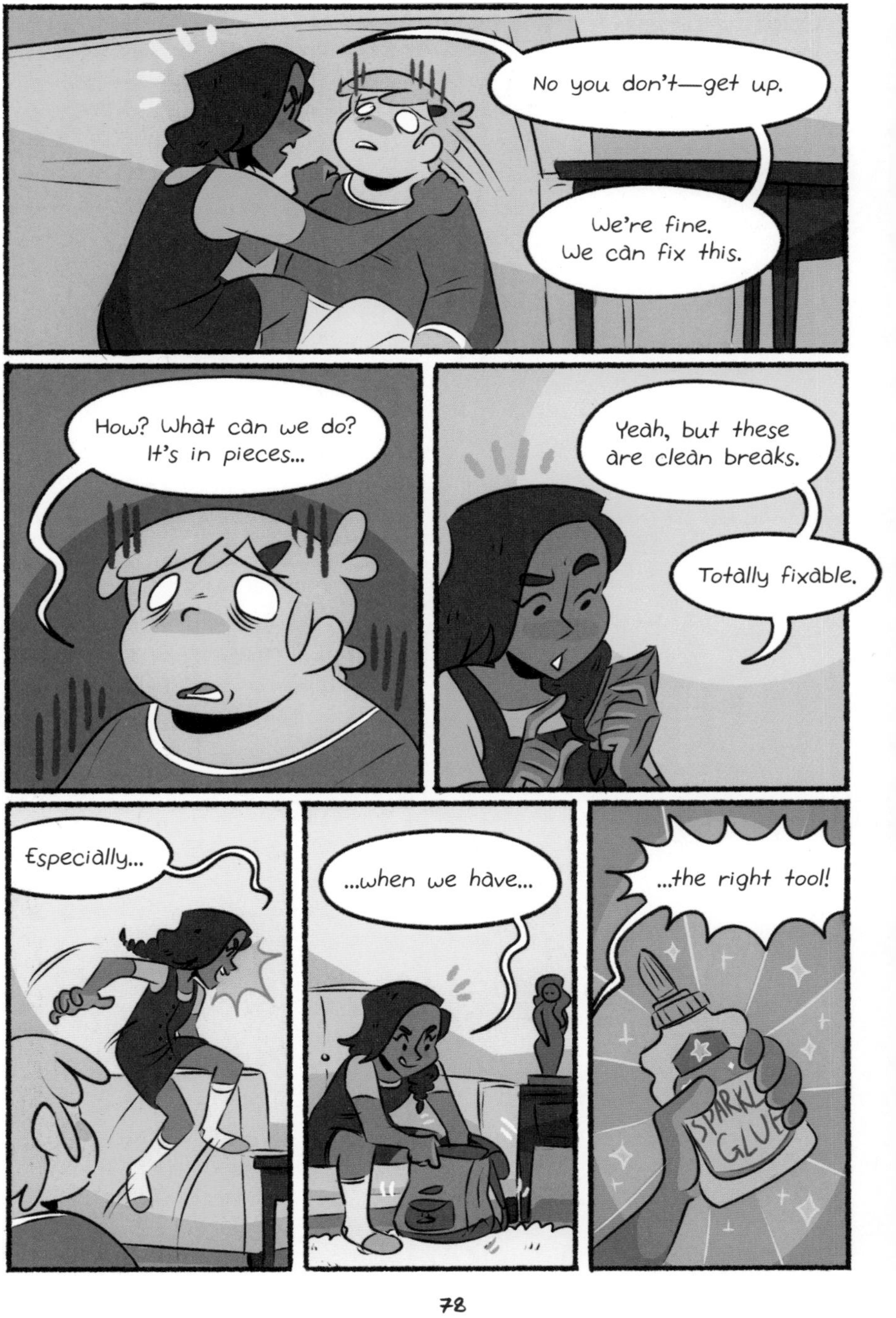
No you don't—get up.
We're fine. We can fix this.
How? What can we do? It's in pieces...
Yeah, but these are clean breaks.
Totally fixable.
Especially...
...when we have...
...the right tool!
SPARKL GLUE

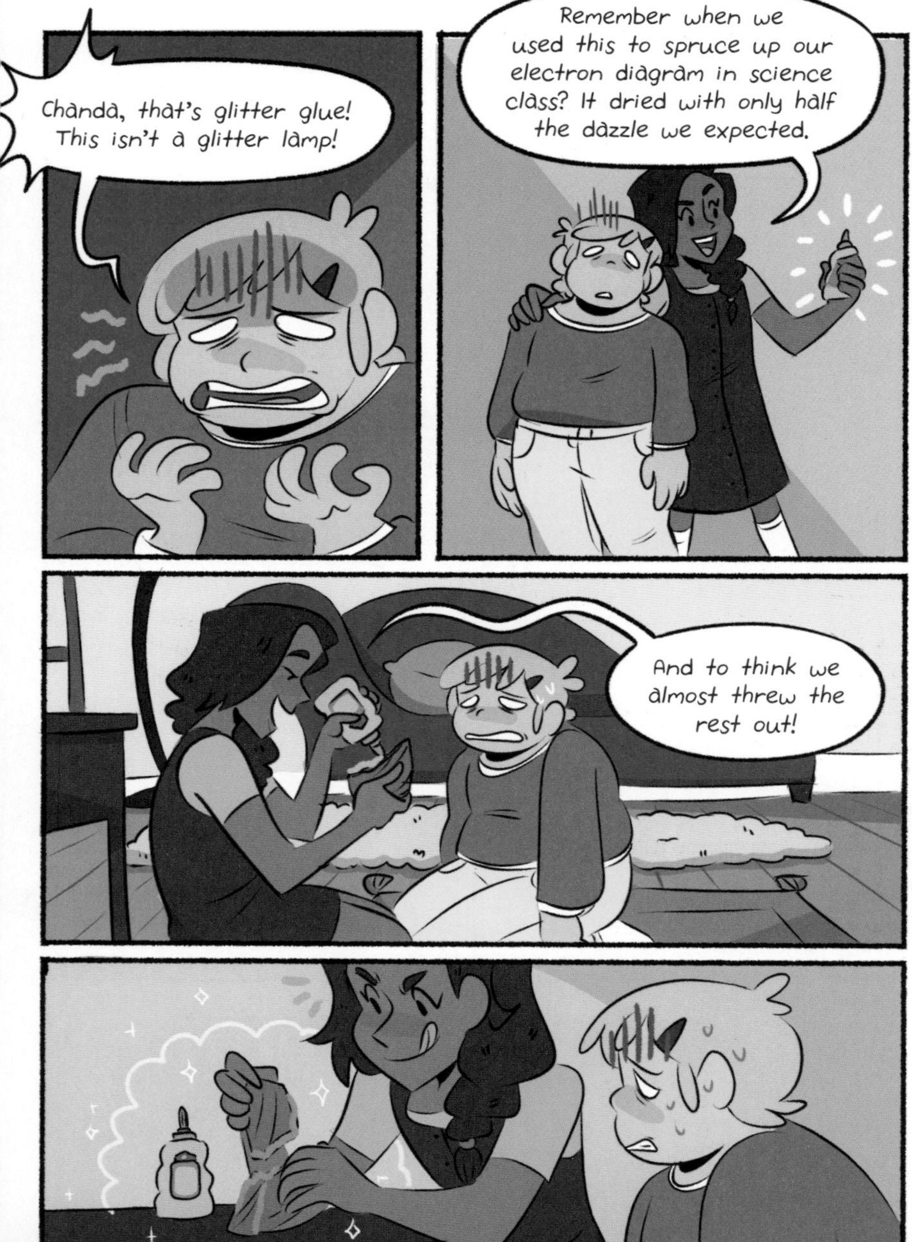
Chanda, that's glitter glue! This isn't a glitter lamp!
Remember when we used this to spruce up our electron diagram in science class? It dried with only half the dazzle we expected.
And to think we almost threw the rest out!

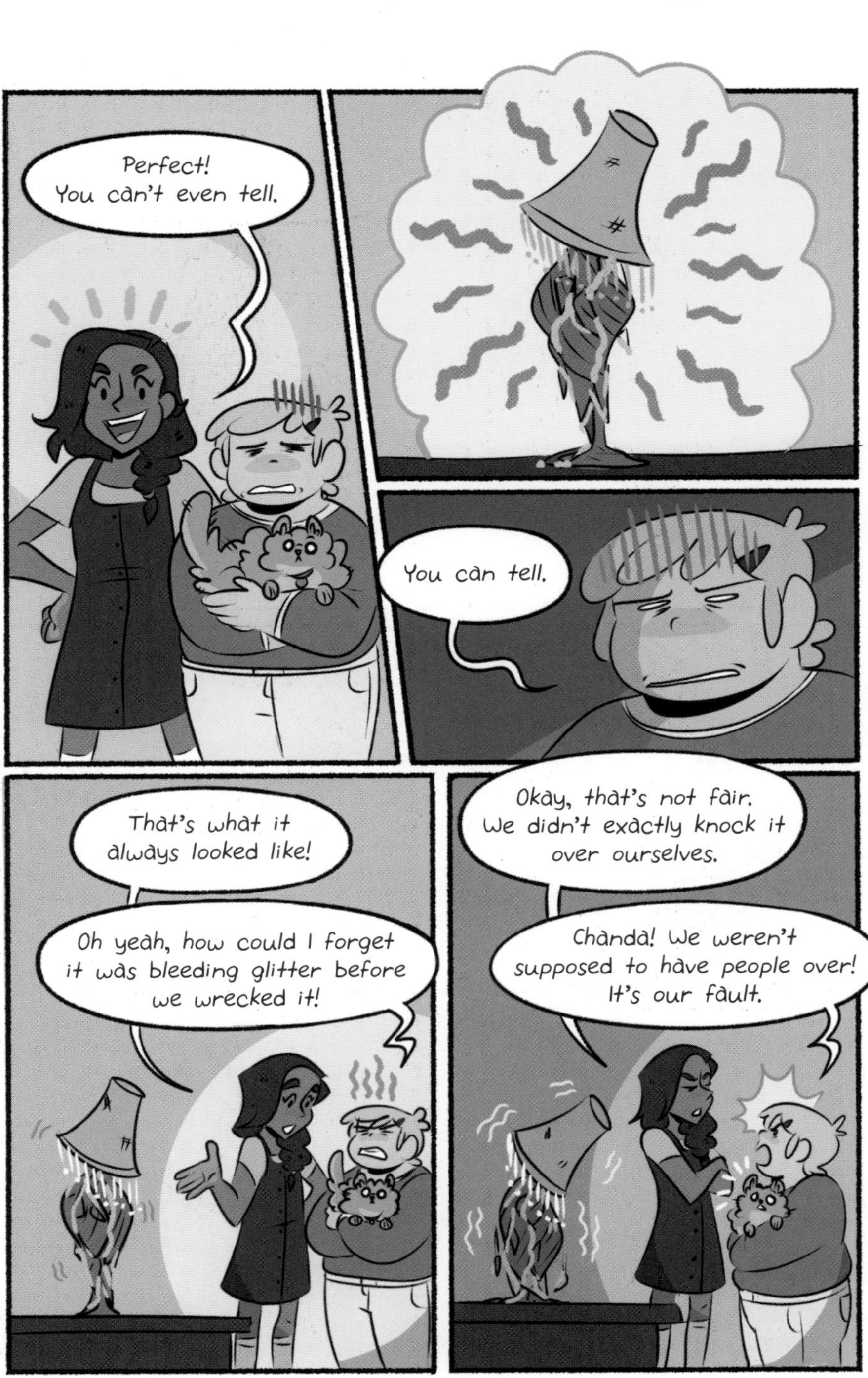
Perfect!
You can't even tell.
You can tell.
That's what it always looked like!
Oh yeah, how could I forget it was bleeding glitter before we wrecked it!
Okay, that's not fair. We didn't exactly knock it over ourselves.
Chanda! We weren't supposed to have people over! It's our fault.

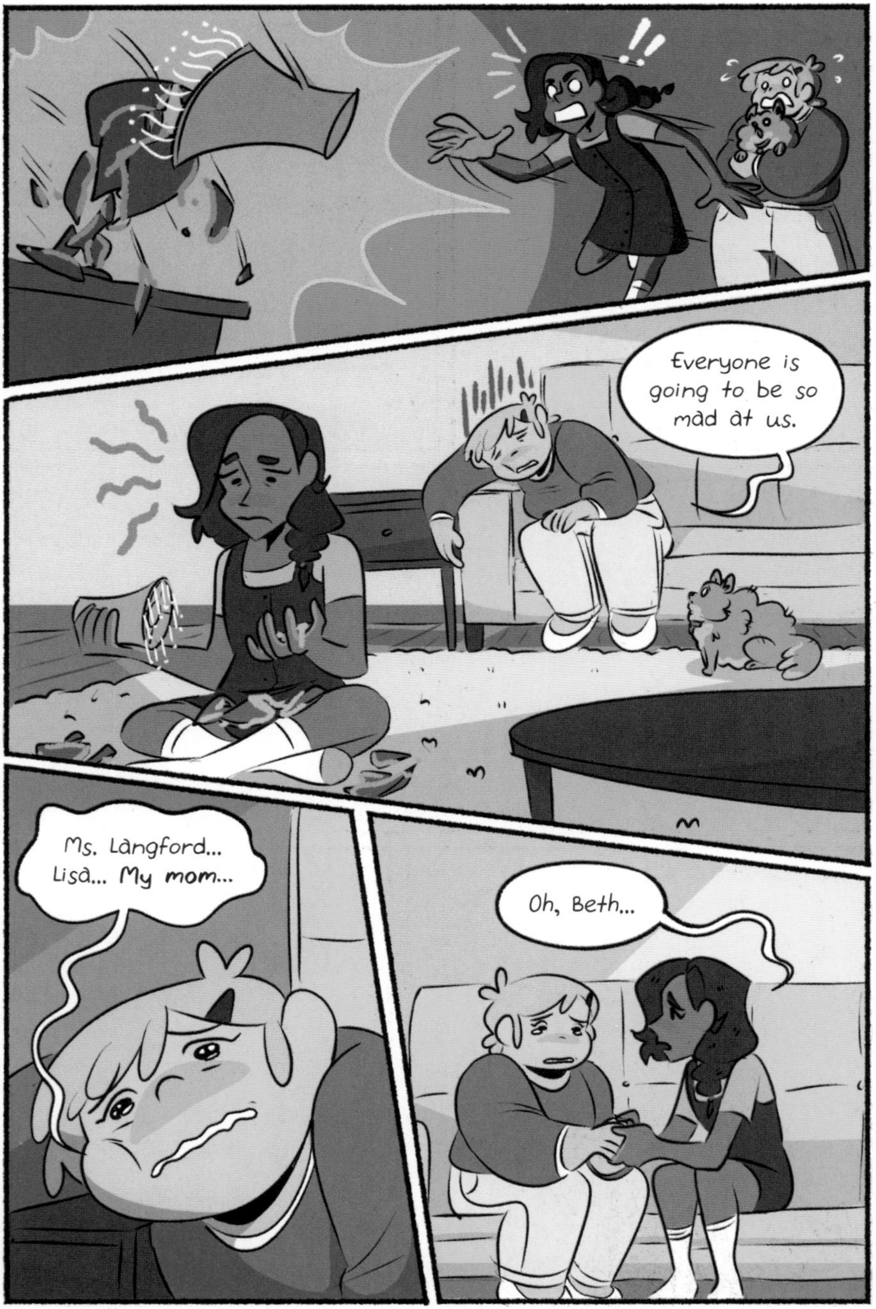
!!
Everyone is going to be so mad at us.
Ms. Langford... Lisa... My mom...
Oh, Beth...

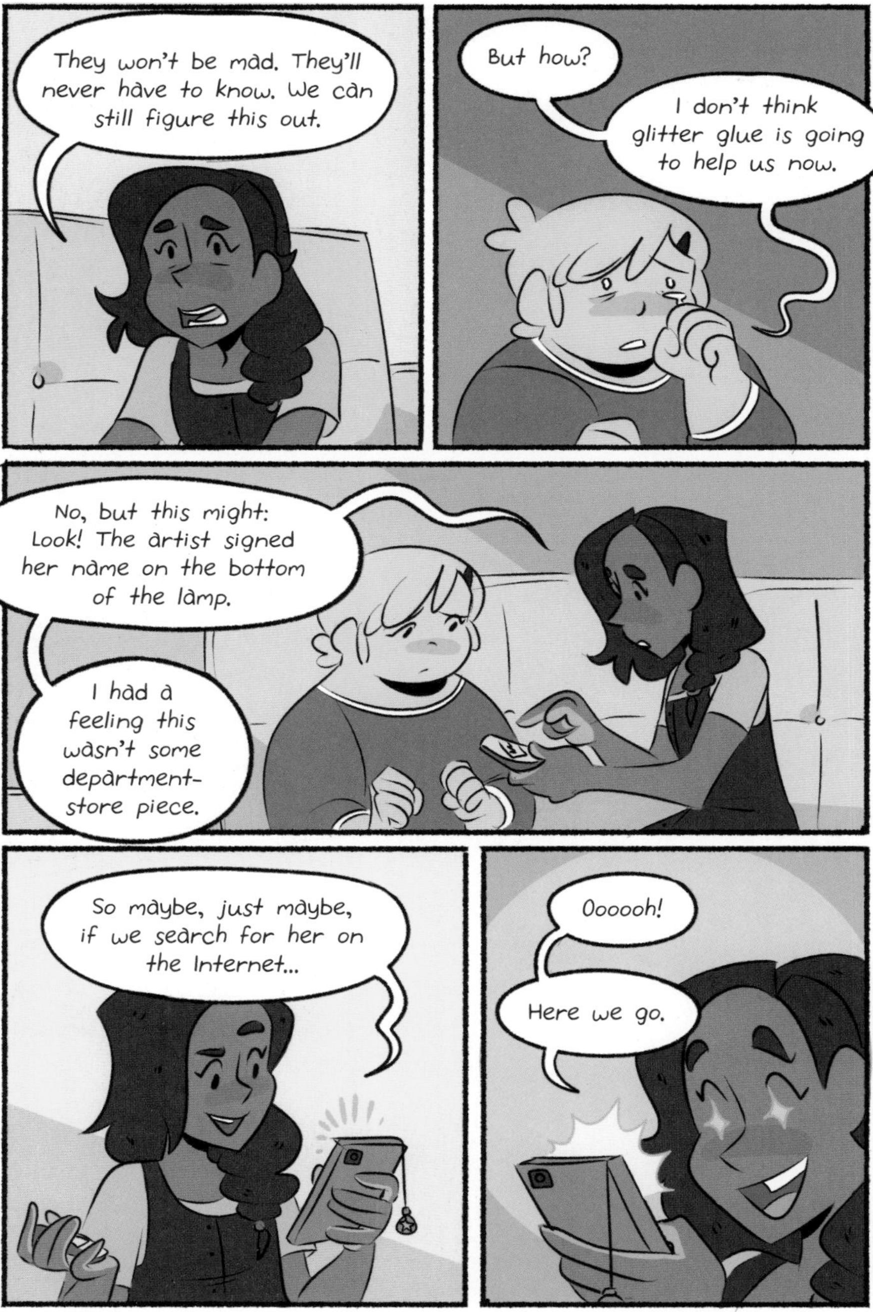
They won't be mad. They'll never have to know. We can still figure this out.
But how?
I don't think glitter glue is going to help us now.
No, but this might: Look! The artist signed her name on the bottom of the lamp.
I had a feeling this wasn't some department-store piece.
So maybe, just maybe, if we search for her on the Internet...
Oooooh!
Here we go.

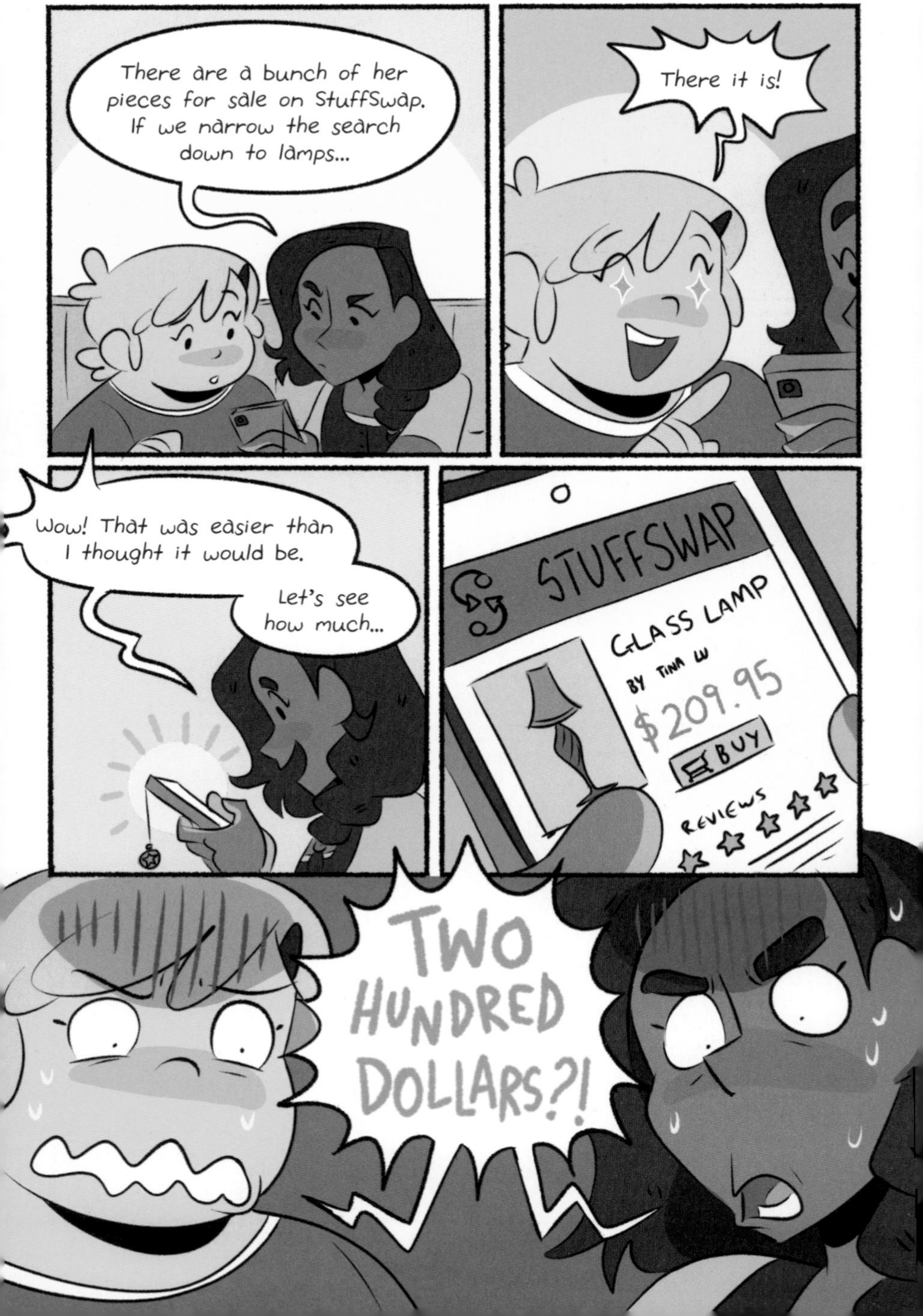
There are a bunch of her pieces for sale on StuffSwap. If we narrow the search down to lamps...
There it is!
Wow! That was easier than I thought it would be.
Let's see how much...
STUFFSWAP
GLASS LAMP
BY TINA W
$209.95
BUY
REVIEWS
TWO HUNDRED DOLLARS?!

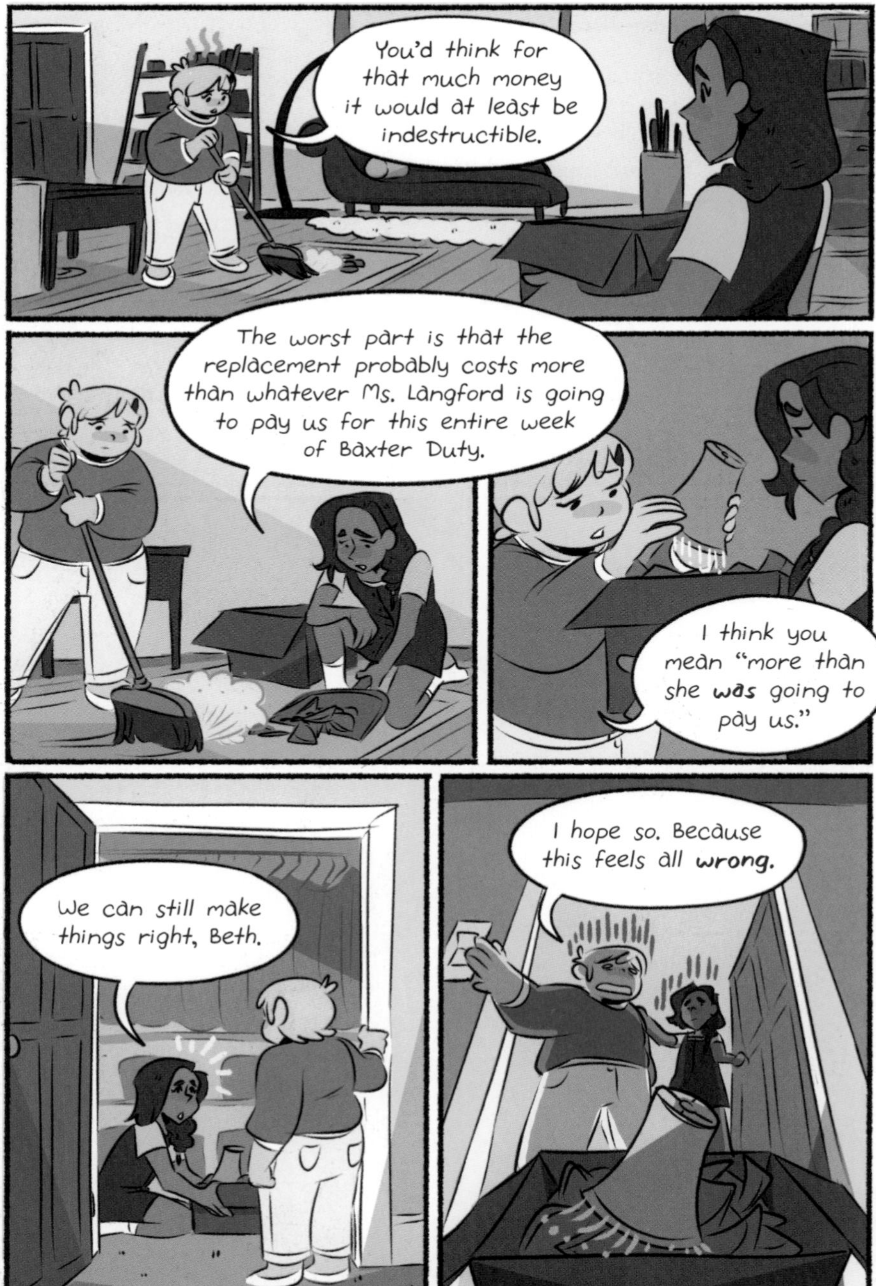
You'd think for that much money it would at least be indestructible.
The worst part is that the replacement probably costs more than whatever Ms. Langford is going to pay us for this entire week of Baxter Duty.
I think you mean "more than she **was** going to pay us."
We can still make things right, Beth.
I hope so. Because this feels all **wrong.**

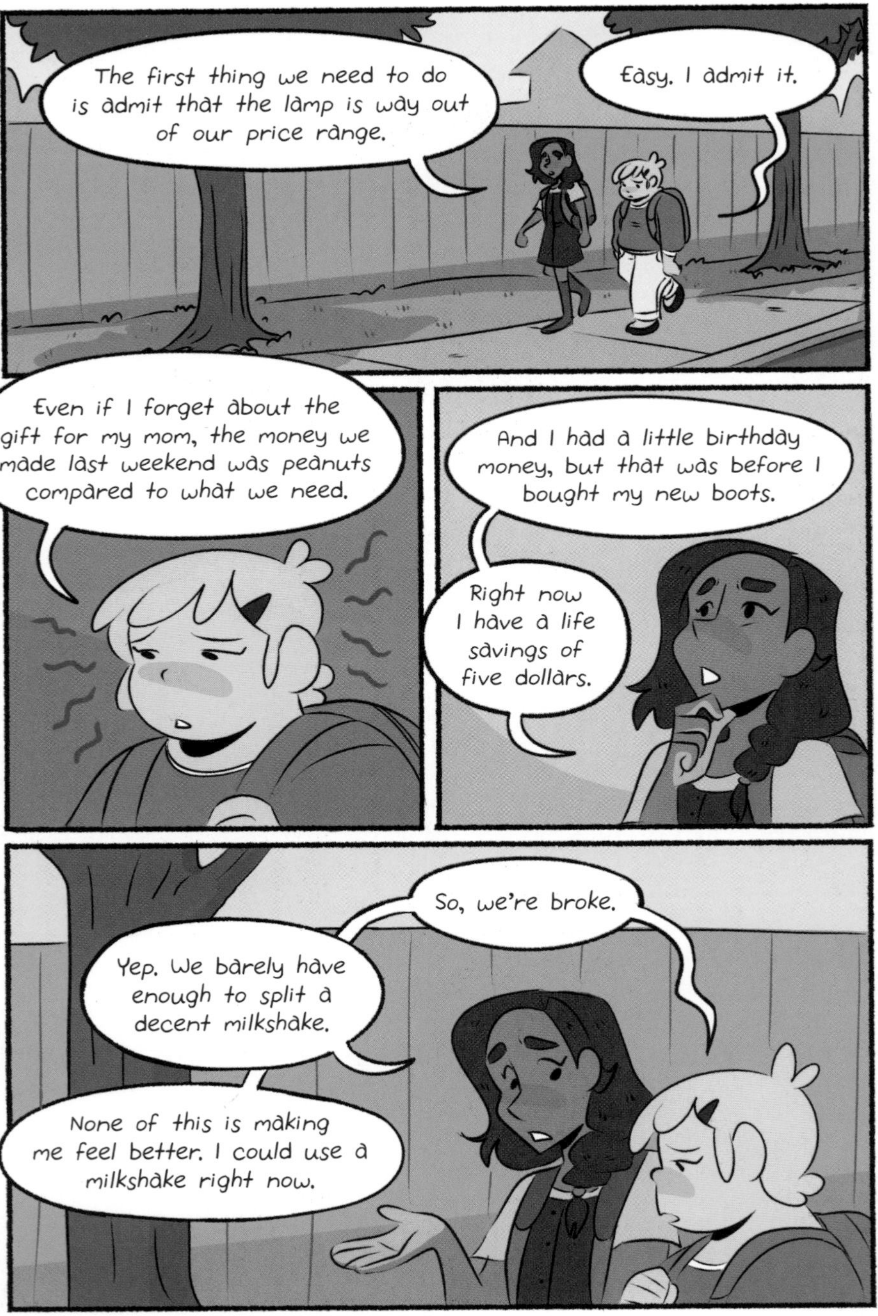
The first thing we need to do is admit that the lamp is way out of our price range.
Easy. I admit it.
Even if I forget about the gift for my mom, the money we made last weekend was peanuts compared to what we need.
And I had a little birthday money, but that was before I bought my new boots.
Right now I have a life savings of five dollars.
So, we're broke.
Yep. We barely have enough to split a decent milkshake.
None of this is making me feel better. I could use a milkshake right now.

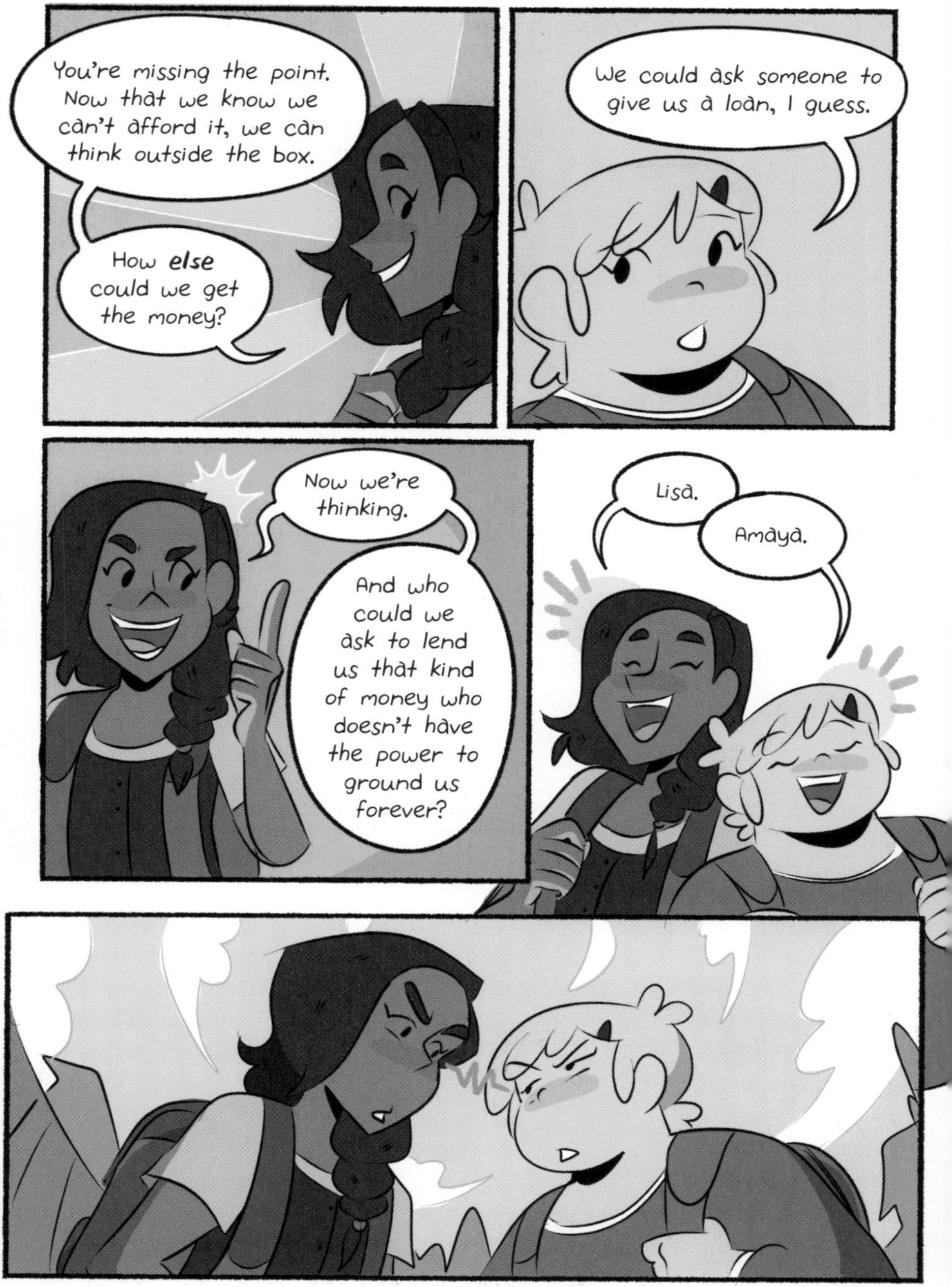
You're missing the point. Now that we know we can't afford it, we can think outside the box.
How **else** could we get the money?
We could ask someone to give us a loan, I guess.
Now we're thinking.
And who could we ask to lend us that kind of money who doesn't have the power to ground us forever?
Lisa.
Amaya.

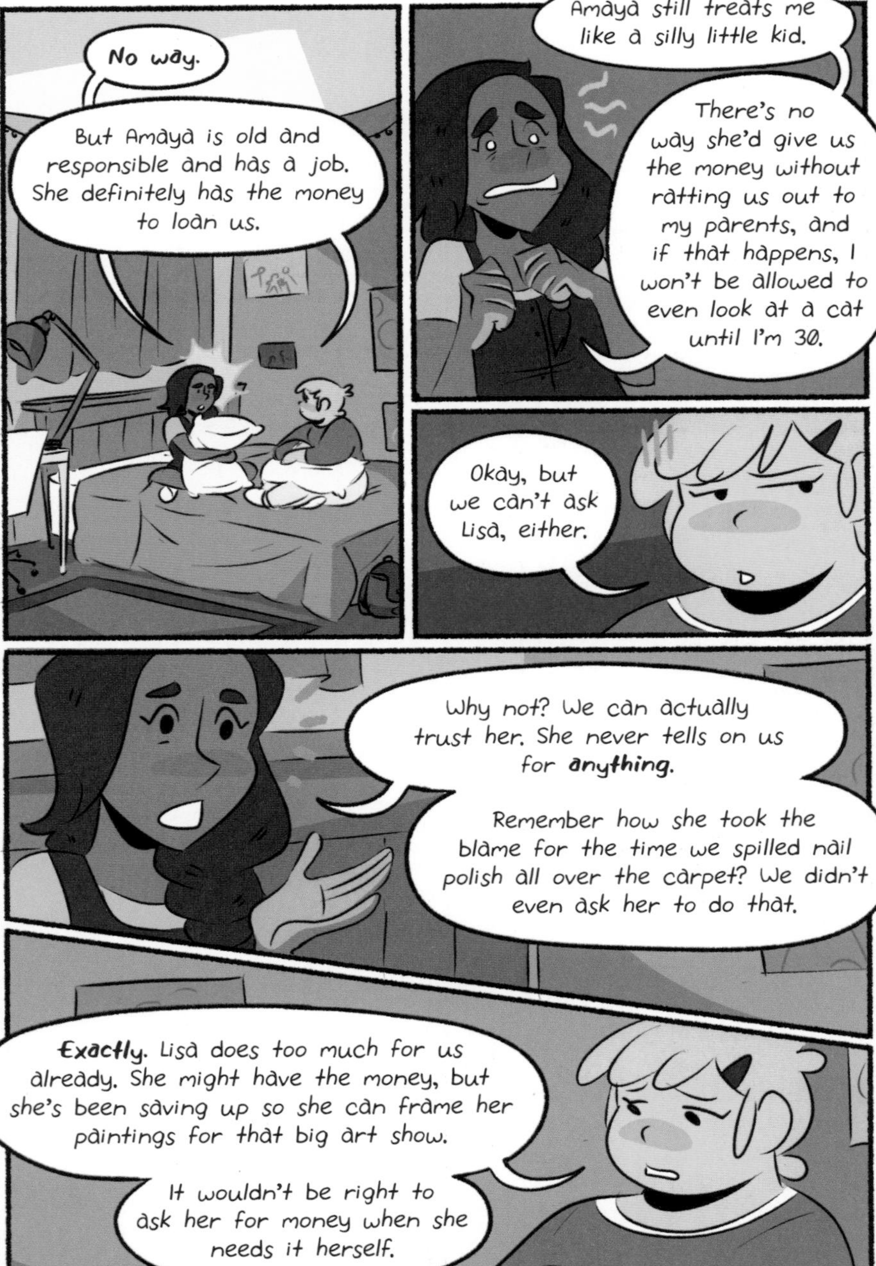
No way.
But Amaya is old and responsible and has a job. She definitely has the money to loan us.
Amaya still treats me like a silly little kid.
There's no way she'd give us the money without ratting us out to my parents, and if that happens, I won't be allowed to even look at a cat until I'm 30.
Okay, but we can't ask Lisa, either.
Why not? We can actually trust her. She never tells on us for **anything**.
Remember how she took the blame for the time we spilled nail polish all over the carpet? We didn't even ask her to do that.
Exactly. Lisa does too much for us already. She might have the money, but she's been saving up so she can frame her paintings for that big art show.
It wouldn't be right to ask her for money when she needs it herself.

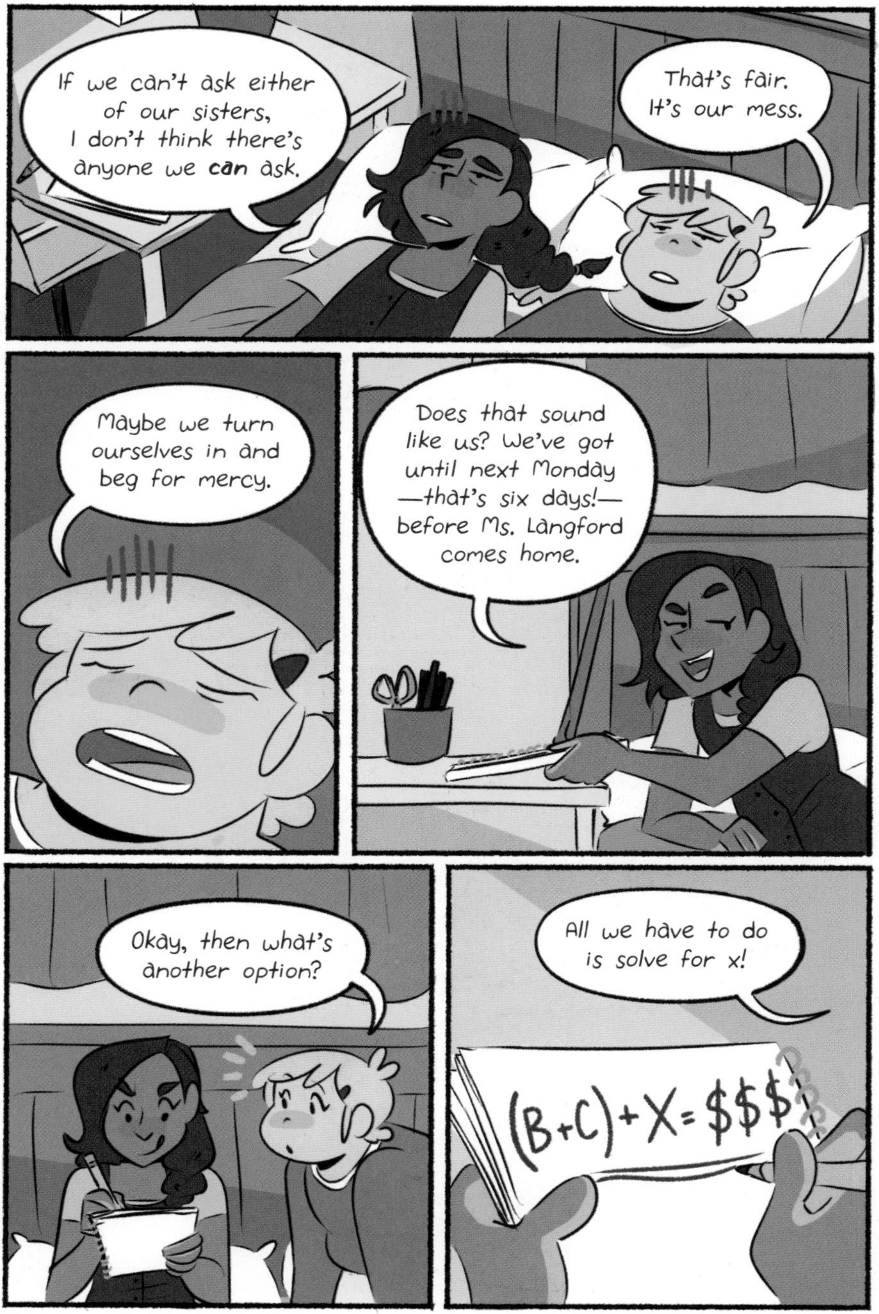
If we can't ask either of our sisters, I don't think there's anyone we **can** ask.
That's fair. It's our mess.
Maybe we turn ourselves in and beg for mercy.
Does that sound like us? We've got until next Monday —that's six days!— before Ms. Langford comes home.
Okay, then what's another option?
All we have to do is solve for x!
(B+C)+X=$$$

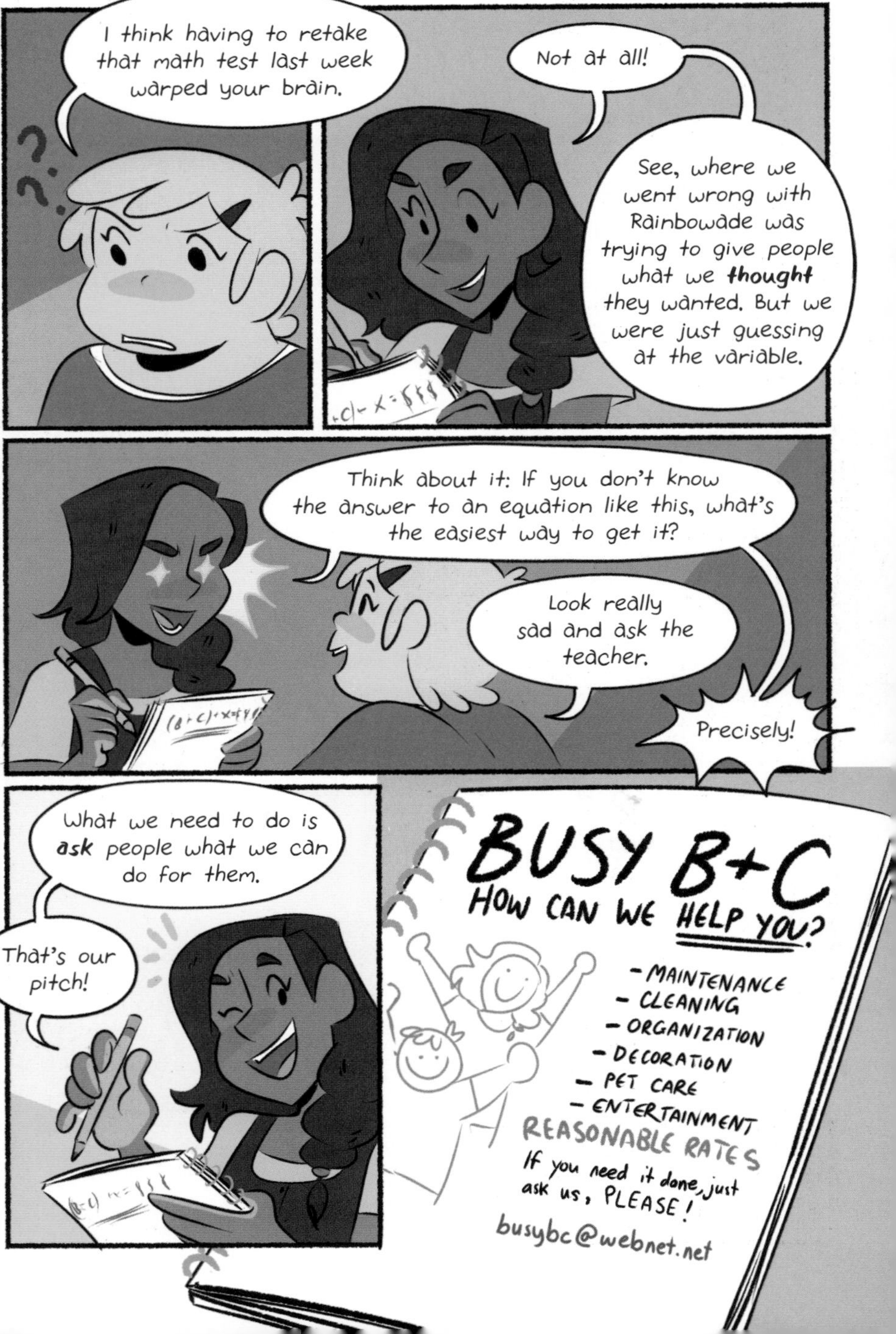

I think having to retake that math test last week warped your brain.
Not at all!
See, where we went wrong with Rainbowade was trying to give people what we **thought** they wanted. But we were just guessing at the variable.
Think about it: If you don't know the answer to an equation like this, what's the easiest way to get it?
Look really sad and ask the teacher.
Precisely!
What we need to do is **ask** people what we can do for them.
That's our pitch!
BUSY B+C
HOW CAN WE HELP YOU?
- MAINTENANCE
- CLEANING
- ORGANIZATION
- DECORATION
- PET CARE
- ENTERTAINMENT
REASONABLE RATES
If you need it done, just ask us, PLEASE!
busybc@webnet.net

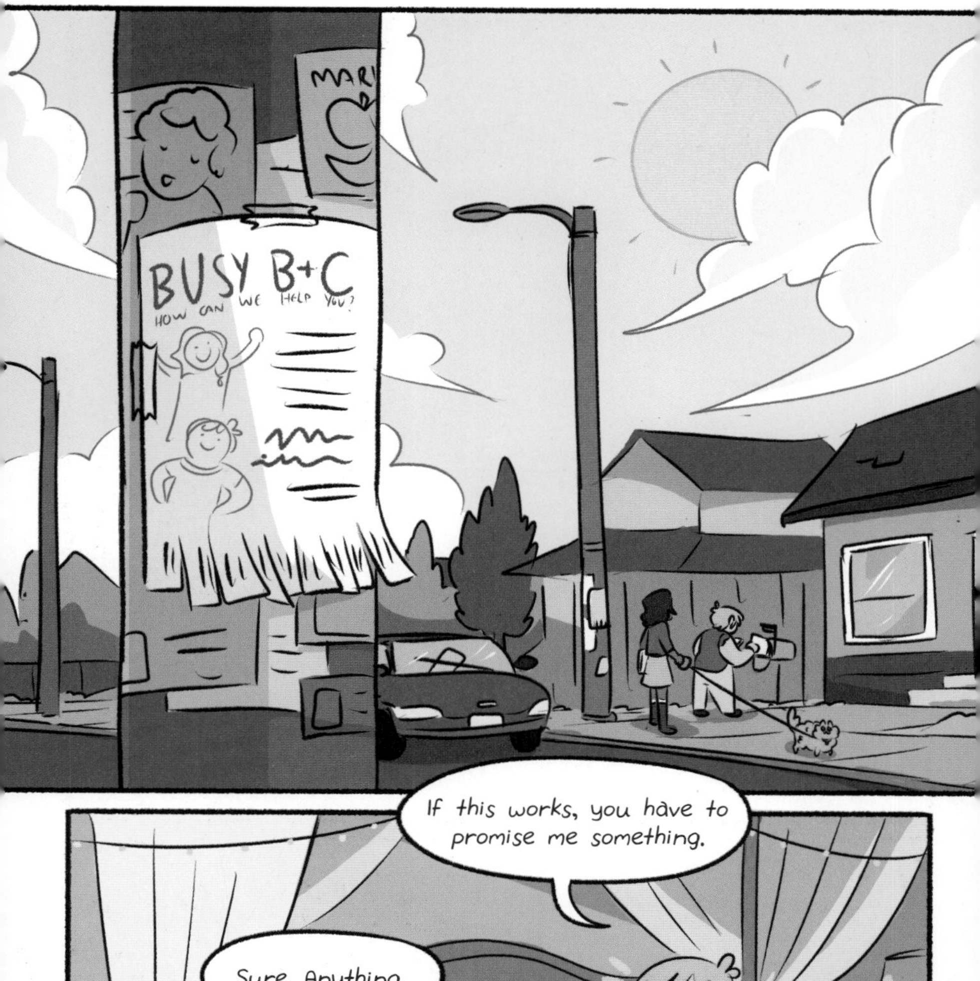
BUSY B+C
HOW CAN WE HELP YOU?

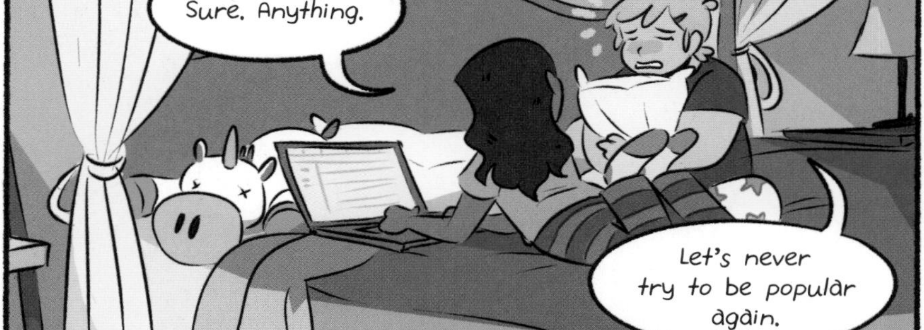
If this works, you have to promise me something.
Sure. Anything.
Let's never try to be popular again.

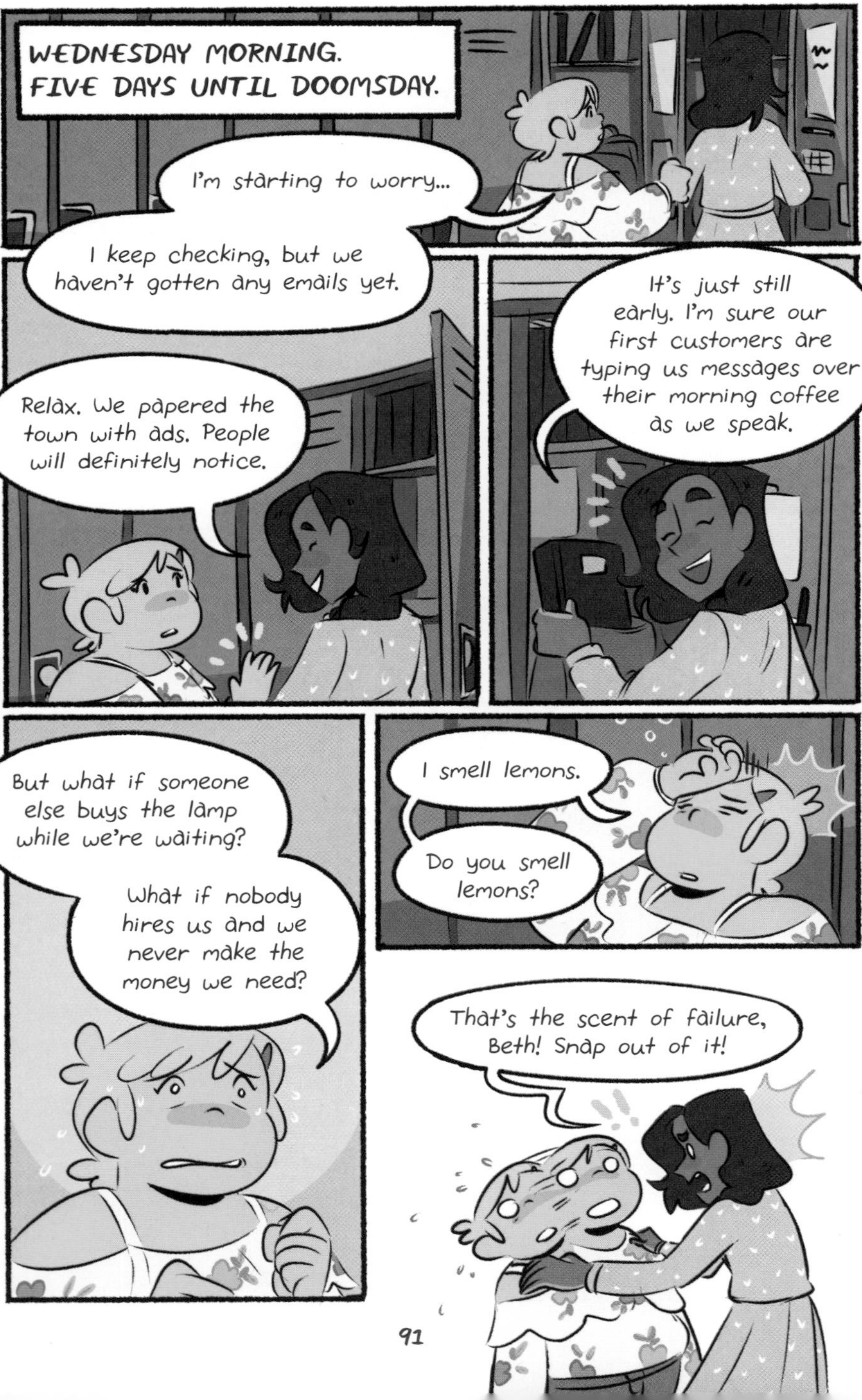
WEDNESDAY MORNING. FIVE DAYS UNTIL DOOMSDAY.
I'm starting to worry...
I keep checking, but we haven't gotten any emails yet.
Relax. We papered the town with ads. People will definitely notice.
It's just still early. I'm sure our first customers are typing us messages over their morning coffee as we speak.
But what if someone else buys the lamp while we're waiting?
What if nobody hires us and we never make the money we need?
I smell lemons.
Do you smell lemons?
That's the scent of failure, Beth! Snap out of it!

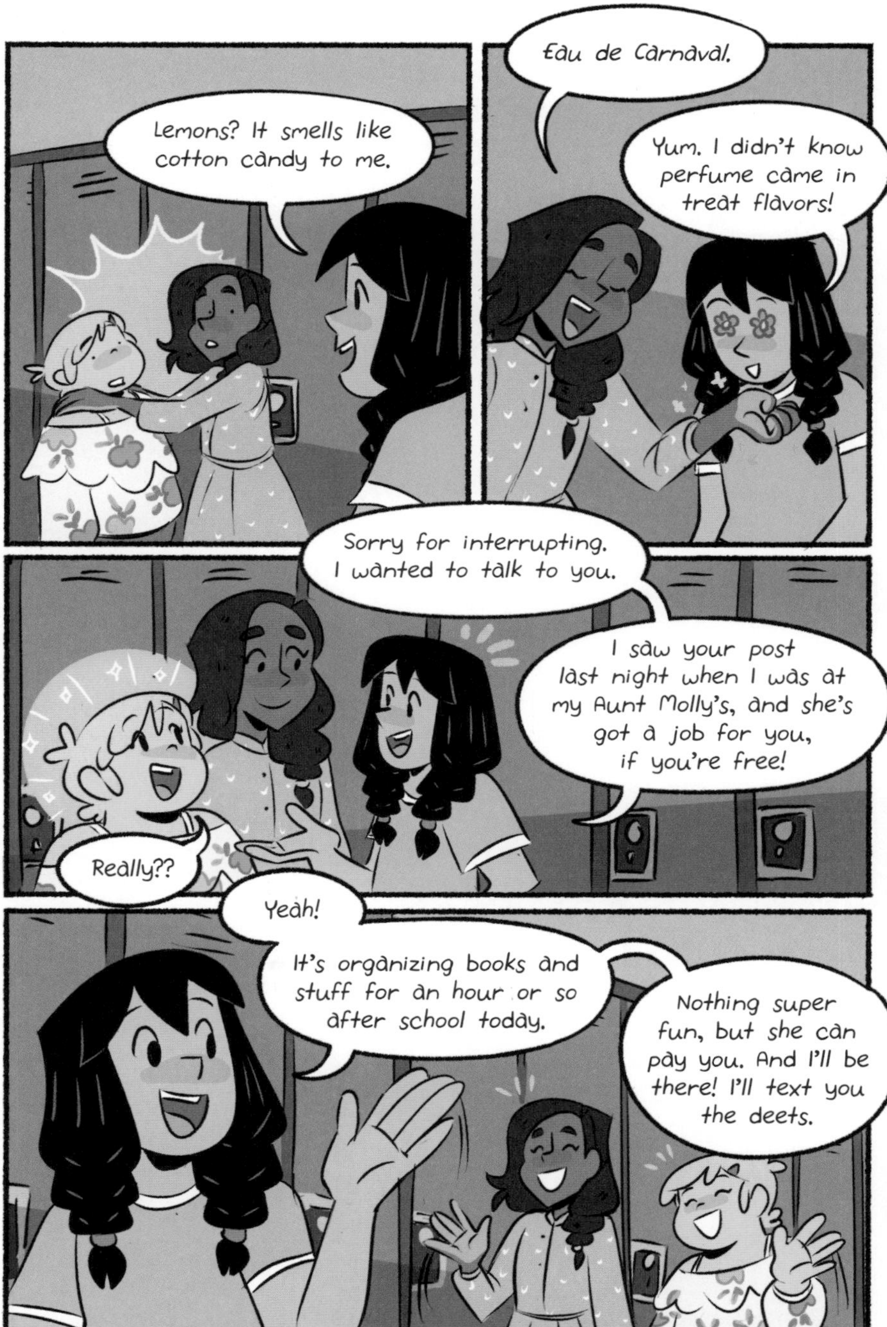
Lemons? It smells like cotton candy to me.
Eau de Carnaval.
Yum. I didn't know perfume came in treat flavors!
Sorry for interrupting. I wanted to talk to you.
I saw your post last night when I was at my Aunt Molly's, and she's got a job for you, if you're free!
Really??
Yeah!
It's organizing books and stuff for an hour or so after school today.
Nothing super fun, but she can pay you. And I'll be there! I'll text you the deets.

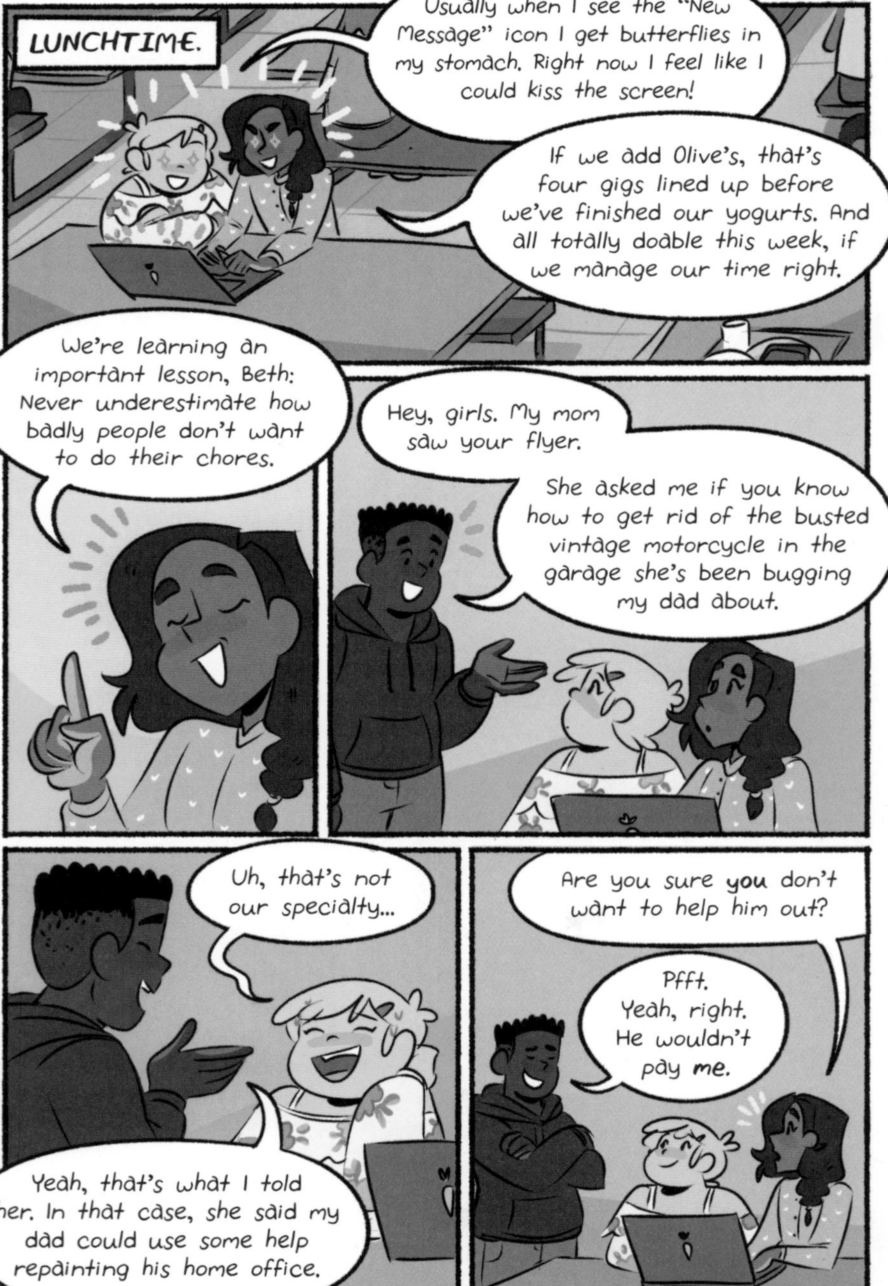
LUNCHTIME.
Usually when I see the "New Message" icon I get butterflies in my stomach. Right now I feel like I could kiss the screen!
If we add Olive's, that's four gigs lined up before we've finished our yogurts. And all totally doable this week, if we manage our time right.
We're learning an important lesson, Beth: Never underestimate how badly people don't want to do their chores.
Hey, girls. My mom saw your flyer.
She asked me if you know how to get rid of the busted vintage motorcycle in the garage she's been bugging my dad about.
Uh, that's not our specialty...
Yeah, that's what I told her. In that case, she said my dad could use some help repainting his home office.
Are you sure **you** don't want to help him out?
Pfft.
Yeah, right.
He wouldn't pay **me**.

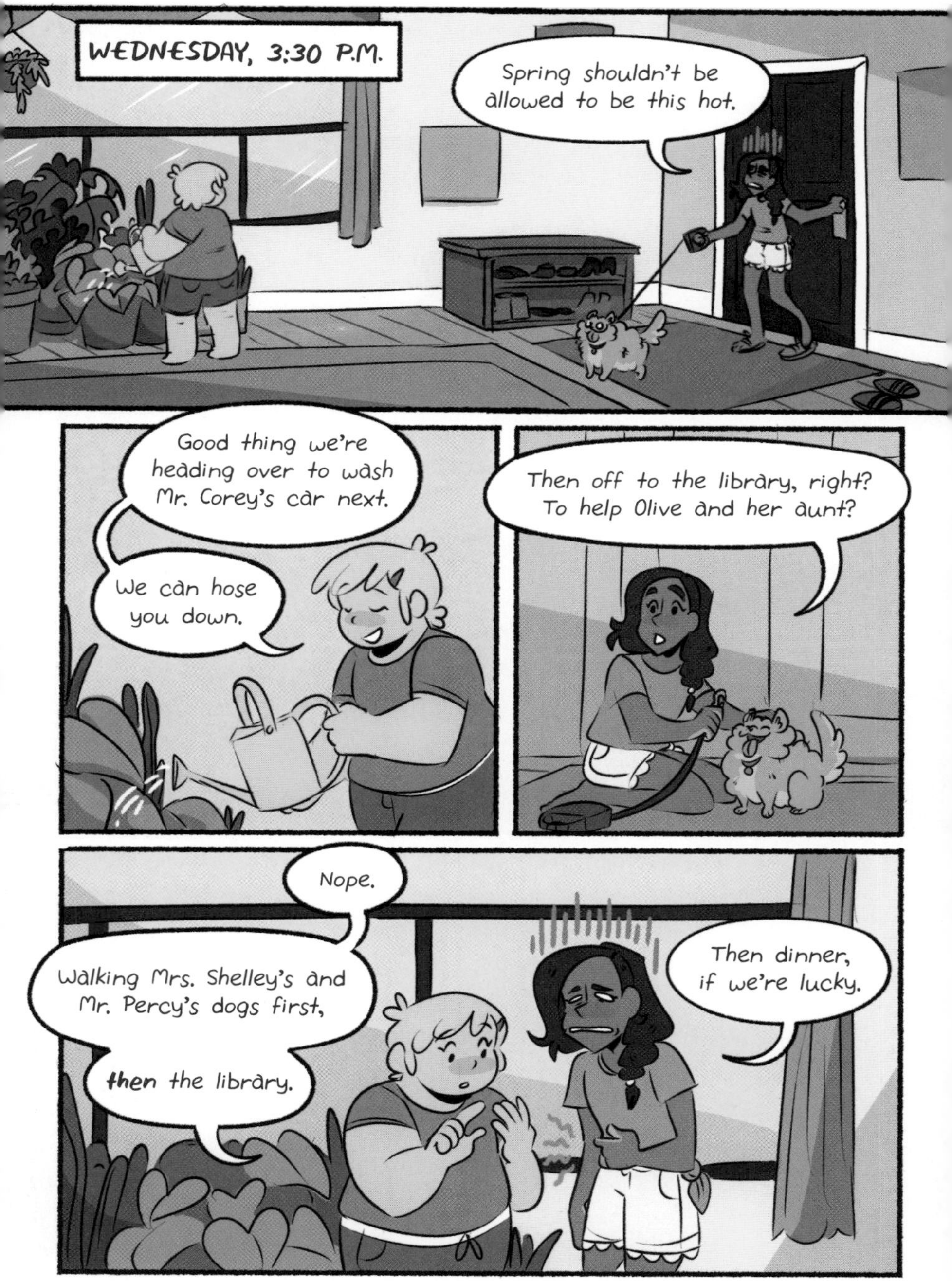
WEDNESDAY, 3:30 P.M.
Spring shouldn't be allowed to be this hot.
Good thing we're heading over to wash Mr. Corey's car next.
We can hose you down.
Then off to the library, right? To help Olive and her aunt?
Nope.
Walking Mrs. Shelley's and Mr. Percy's dogs first,
then the library.
Then dinner, if we're lucky.

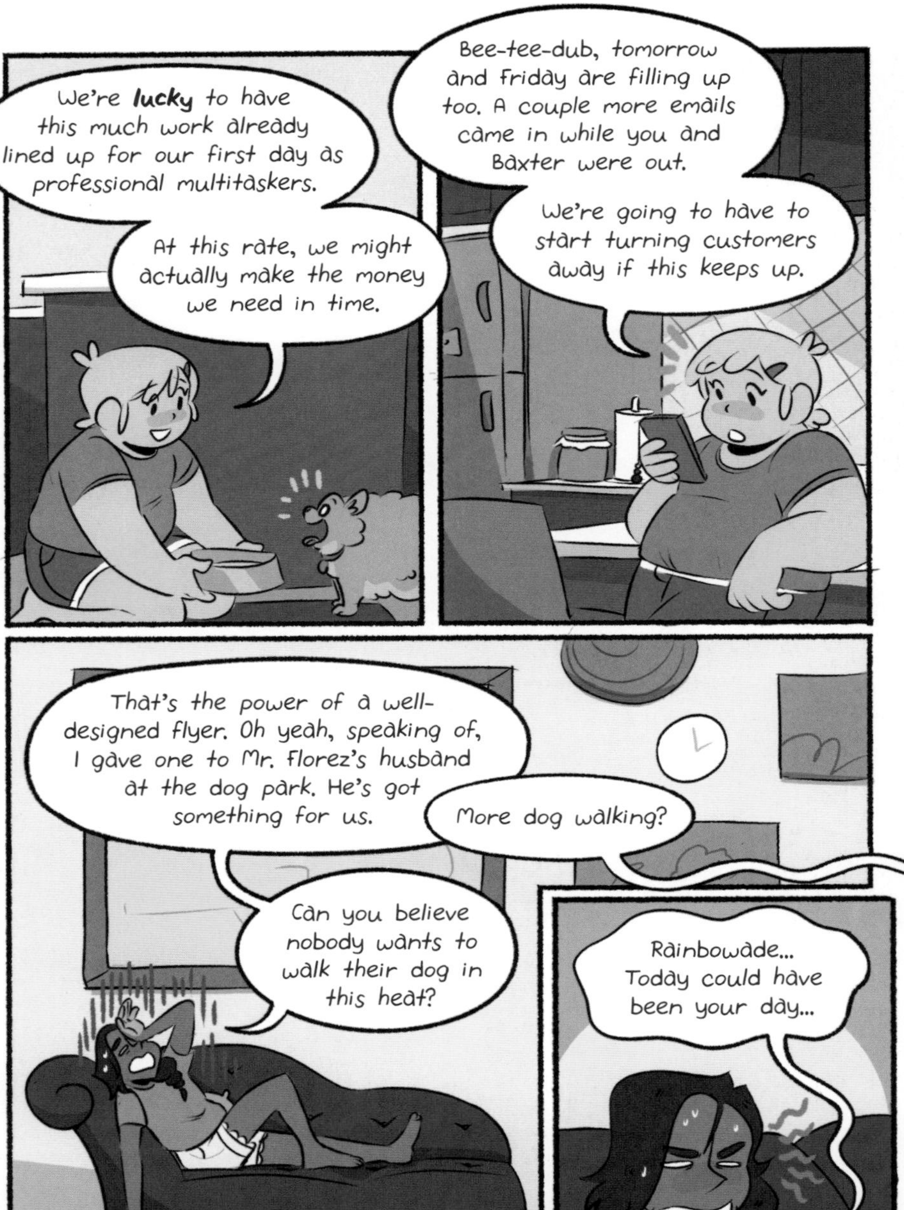
We're **lucky** to have this much work already lined up for our first day as professional multitaskers.
At this rate, we might actually make the money we need in time.
Bee-tee-dub, tomorrow and Friday are filling up too. A couple more emails came in while you and Baxter were out.
We're going to have to start turning customers away if this keeps up.
That's the power of a well-designed flyer. Oh yeah, speaking of, I gave one to Mr. Florez's husband at the dog park. He's got something for us.
More dog walking?
Can you believe nobody wants to walk their dog in this heat?
Rainbowade... Today could have been your day...

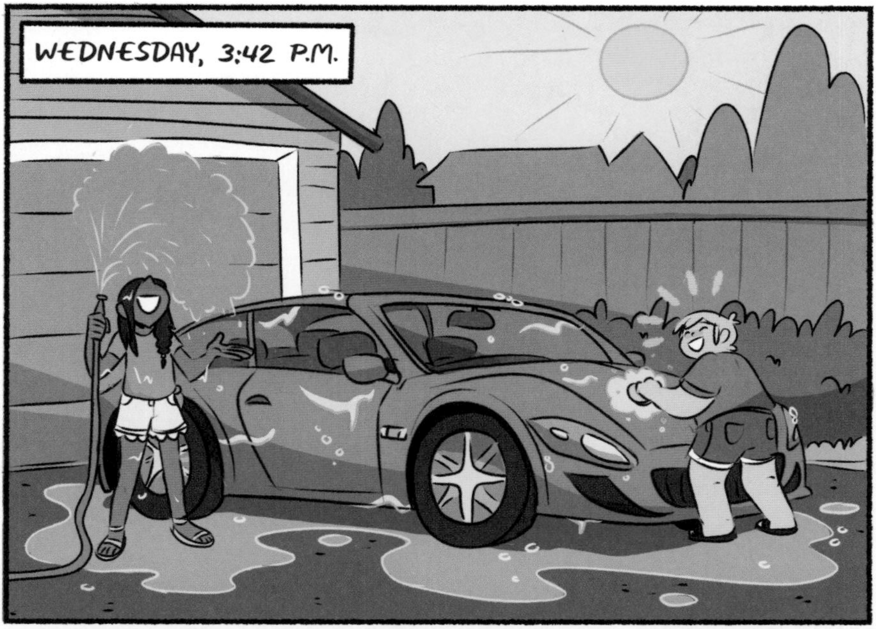
WEDNESDAY, 3:42 P.M.

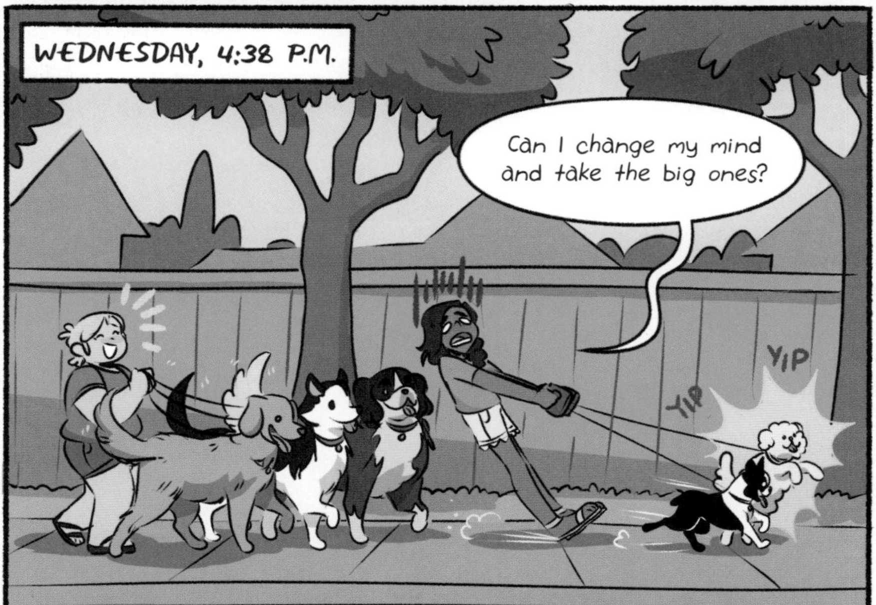
WEDNESDAY, 4:38 P.M.
Can I change my mind and take the big ones?
YIP
YIP

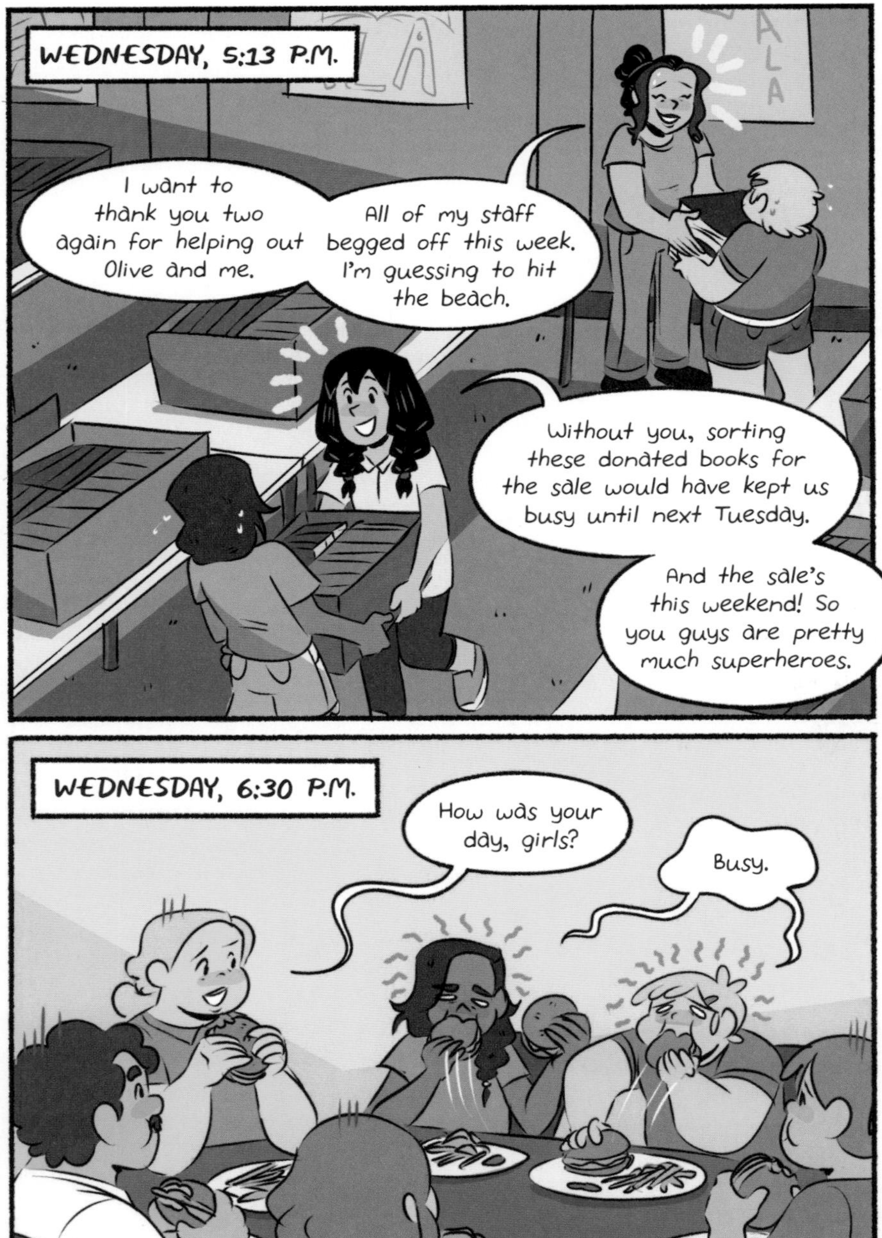
WEDNESDAY, 5:13 P.M.
I want to thank you two again for helping out Olive and me.
All of my staff begged off this week. I'm guessing to hit the beach.
Without you, sorting these donated books for the sale would have kept us busy until next Tuesday.
And the sale's this weekend! So you guys are pretty much superheroes.
WEDNESDAY, 6:30 P.M.
How was your day, girls?
Busy.

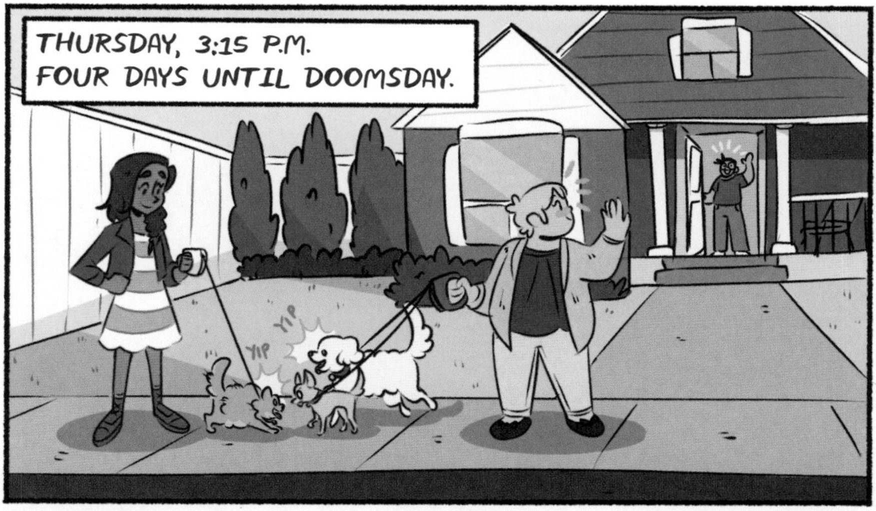
THURSDAY, 3:15 P.M.
FOUR DAYS UNTIL DOOMSDAY.
YIP
YIP

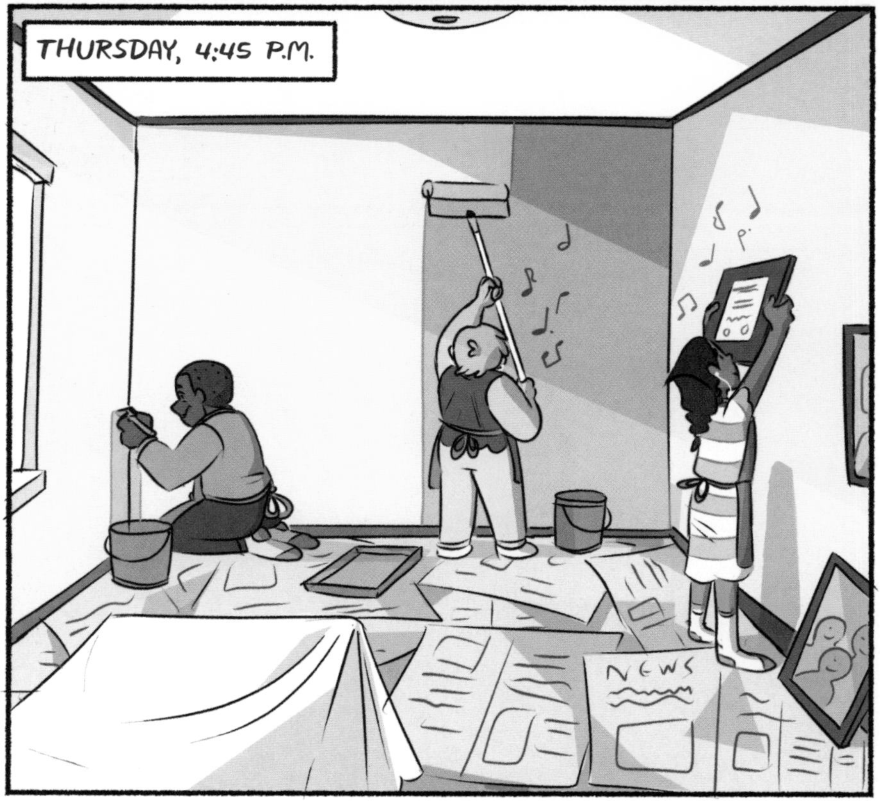
THURSDAY, 4:45 P.M.
NEWS

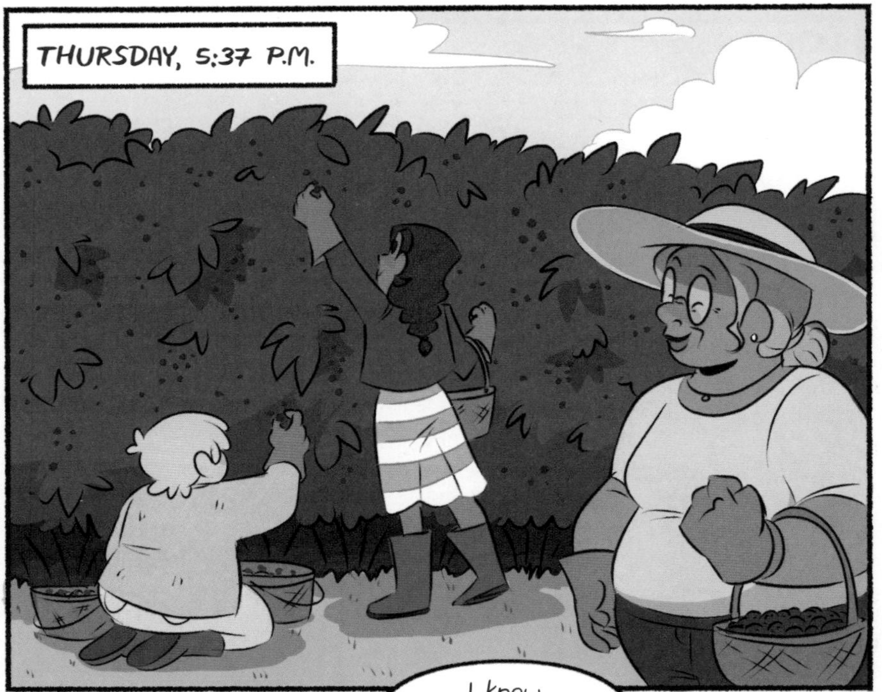
THURSDAY, 5:37 P.M.

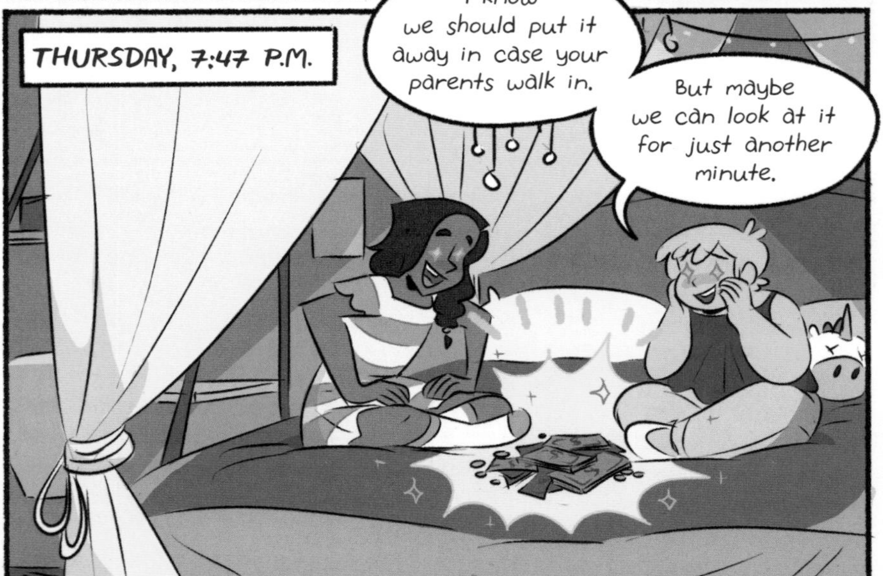
THURSDAY, 7:47 P.M.
I know we should put it away in case your parents walk in.
But maybe we can look at it for just another minute.

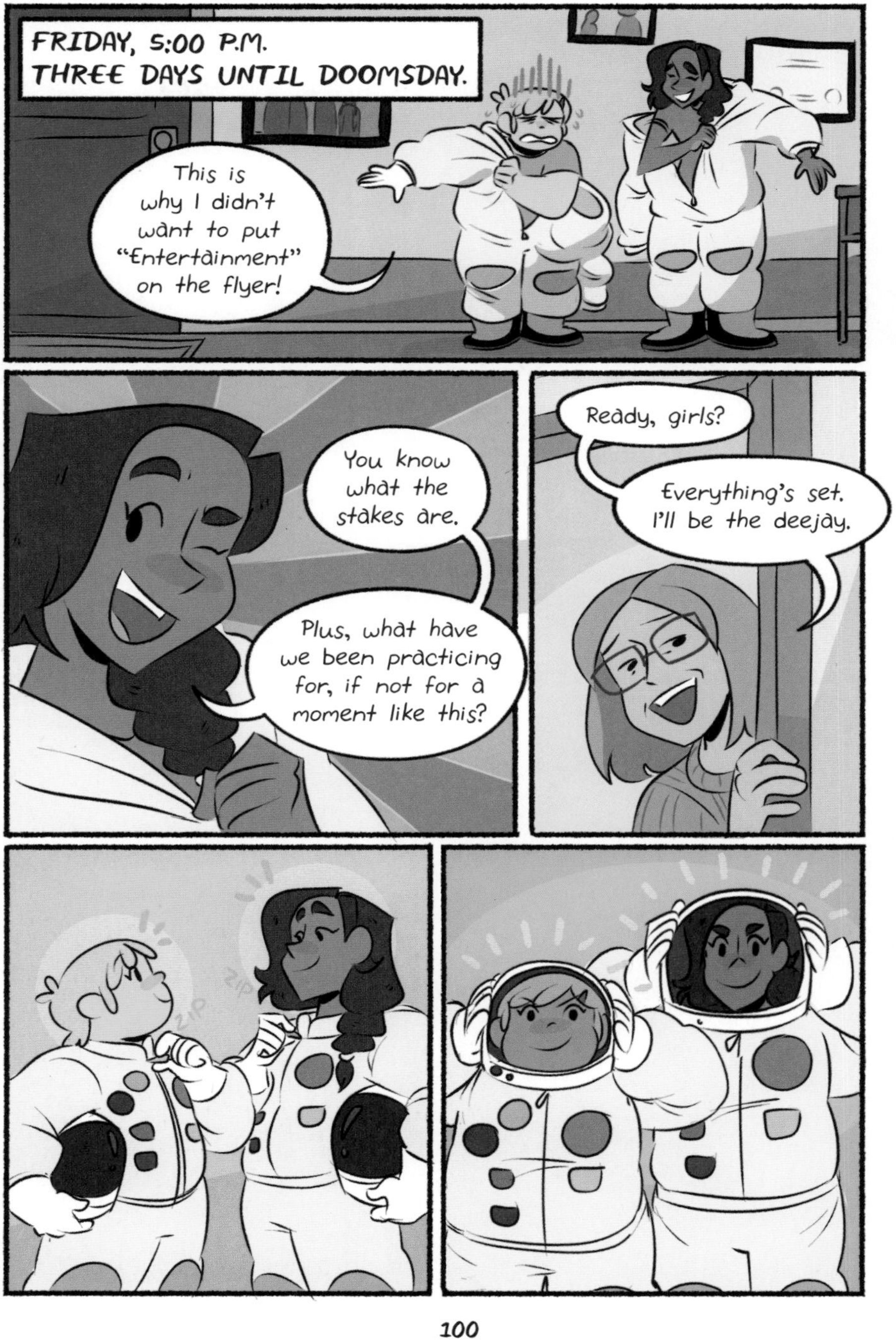
FRIDAY, 5:00 P.M.
THREE DAYS UNTIL DOOMSDAY.
This is why I didn't want to put "Entertainment" on the flyer!
You know what the stakes are.
Plus, what have we been practicing for, if not for a moment like this?
Ready, girls?
Everything's set. I'll be the deejay.
ZIP ZIP

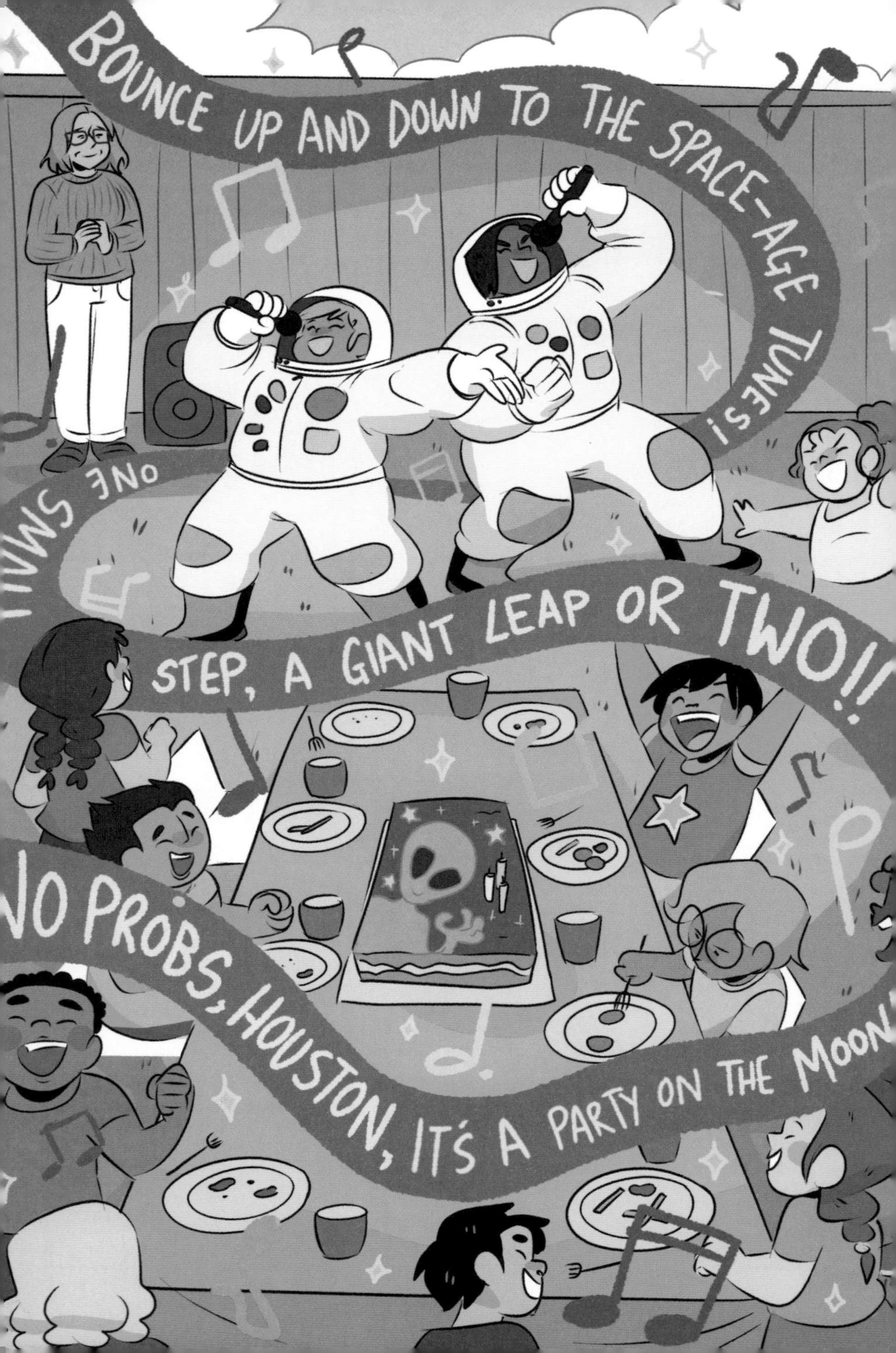
BOUNCE UP AND DOWN TO THE SPACE-AGE TUNES!
ONE SMALL STEP, A GIANT LEAP OR TWO!!
NO PROBS, HOUSTON, IT'S A PARTY ON THE MOON

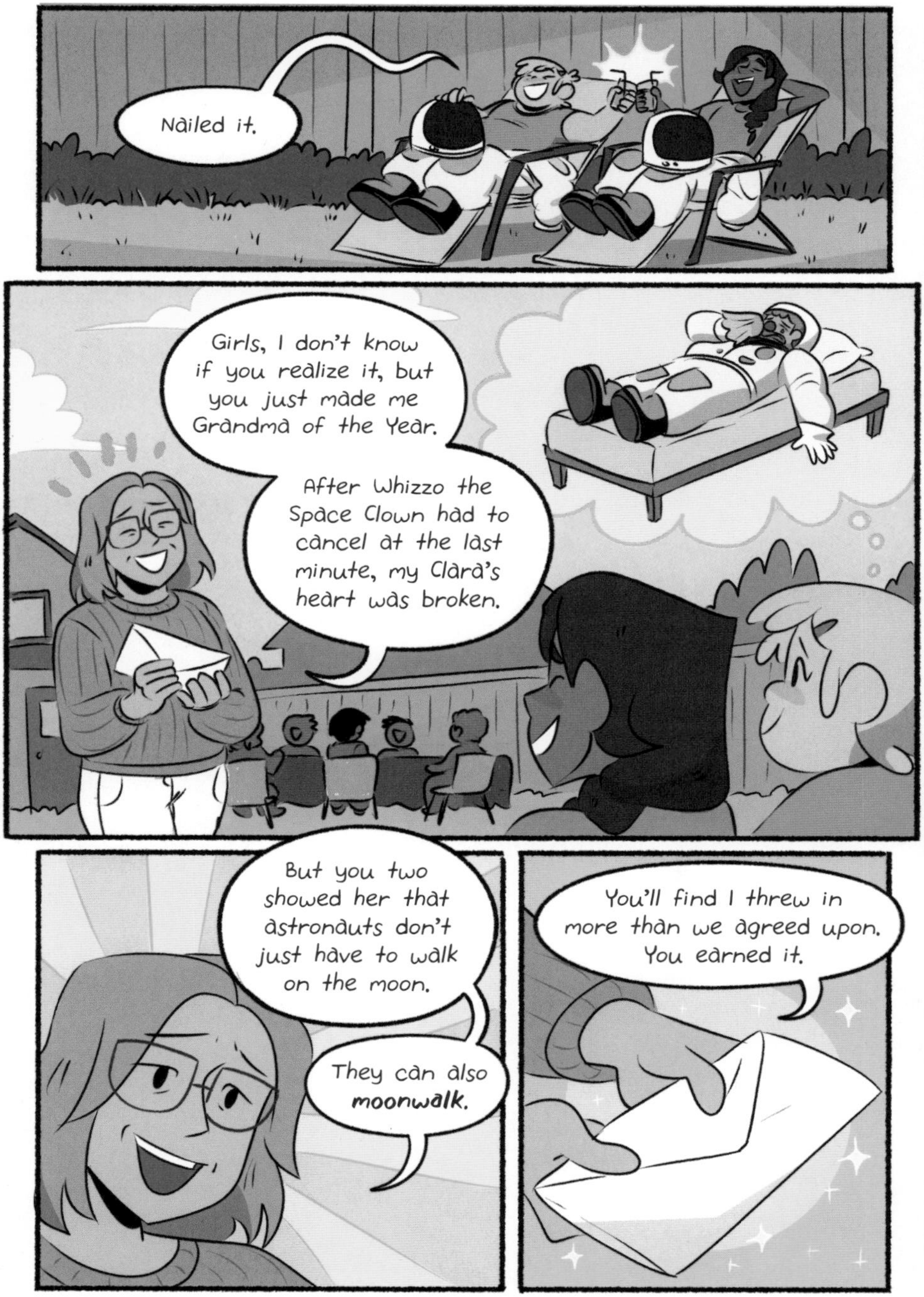
Nailed it.
Girls, I don't know if you realize it, but you just made me Grandma of the Year.
After Whizzo the Space Clown had to cancel at the last minute, my Clara's heart was broken.
But you two showed her that astronauts don't just have to walk on the moon.
They can also **moonwalk.**
You'll find I threw in more than we agreed upon. You earned it.

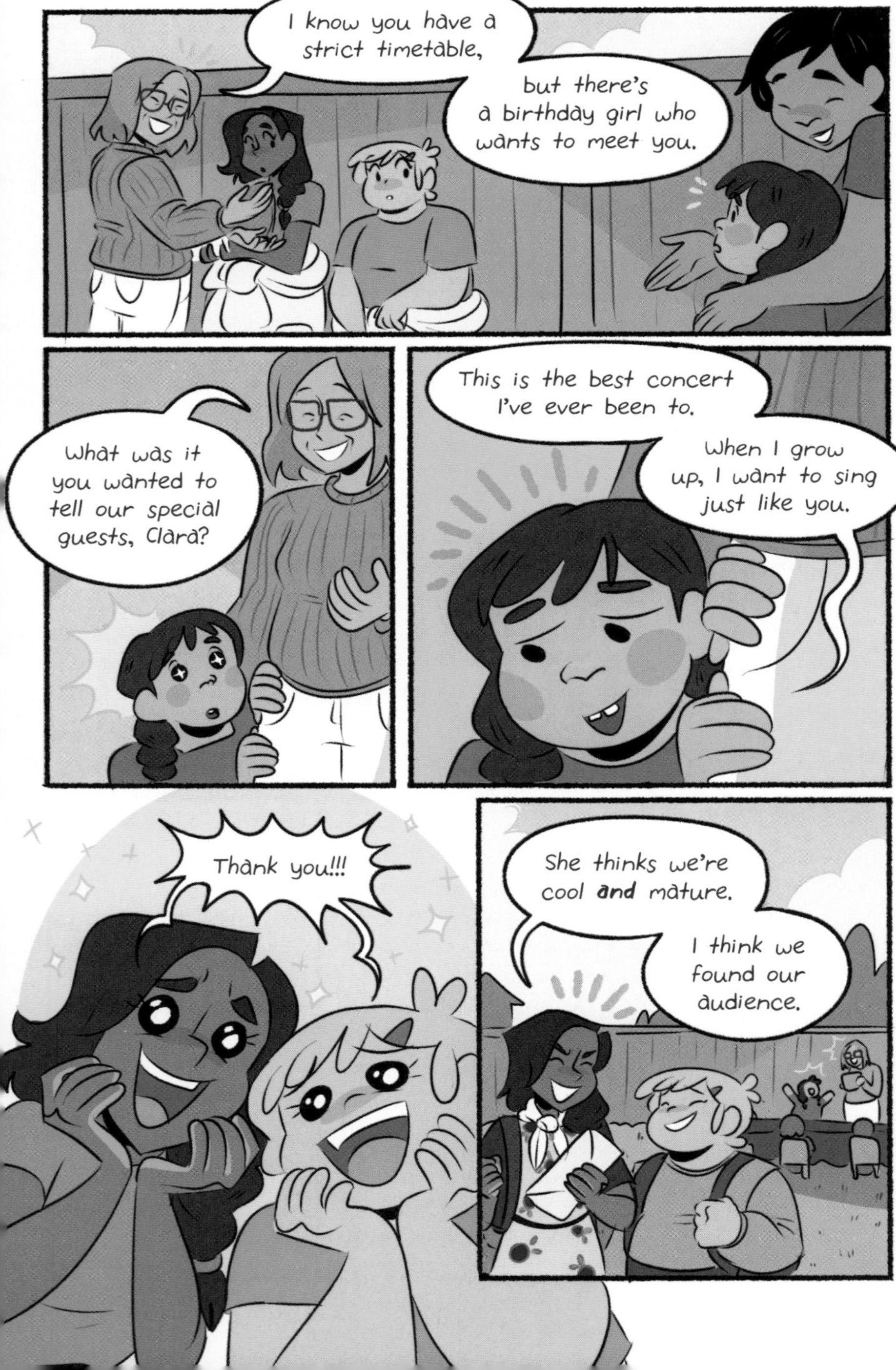
I know you have a strict timetable,
but there's a birthday girl who wants to meet you.
What was it you wanted to tell our special guests, Clara?
This is the best concert I've ever been to.
When I grow up, I want to sing just like you.
Thank you!!!
She thinks we're cool **and** mature.
I think we found our audience.

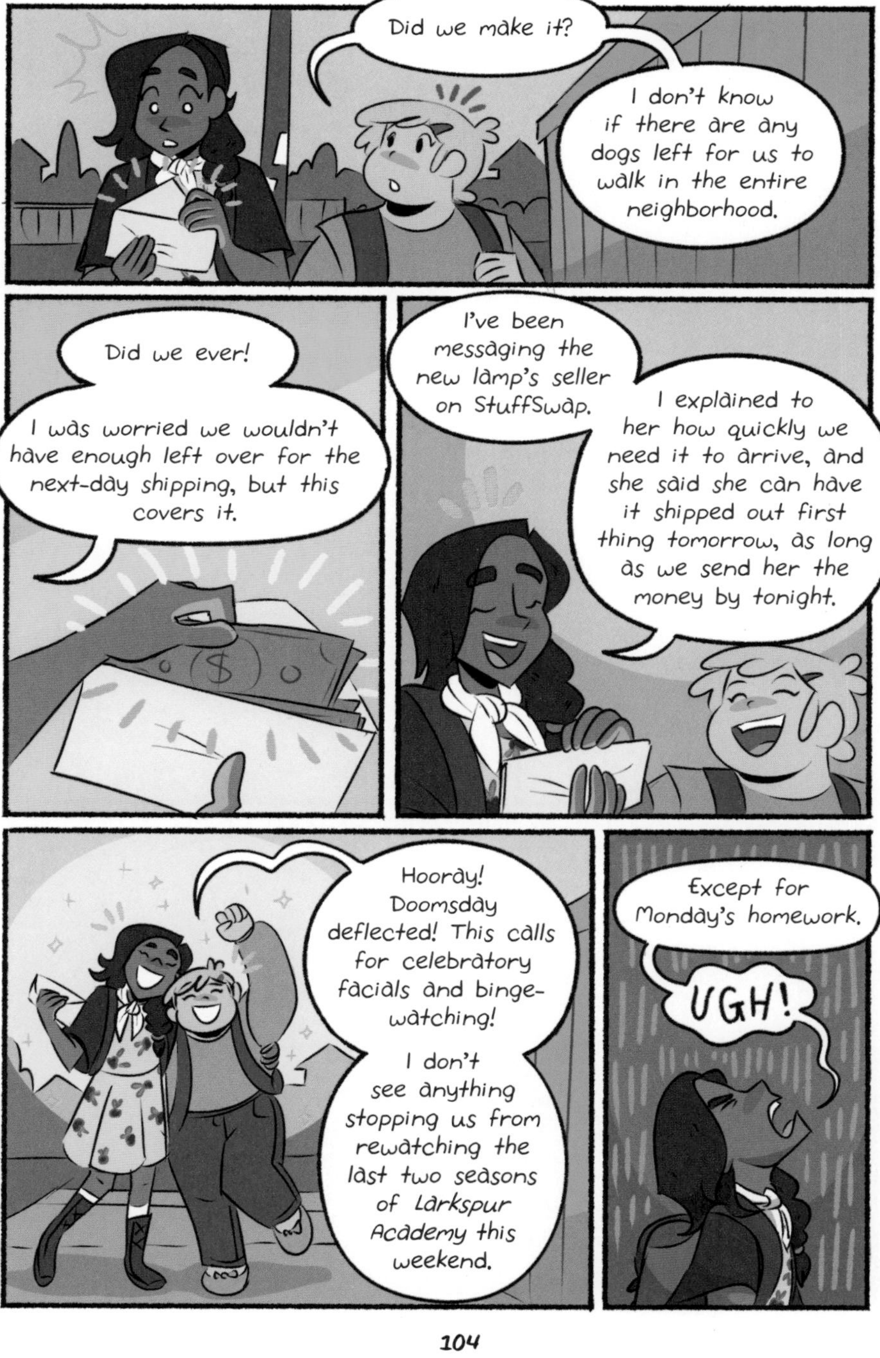
Did we make it?
I don't know if there are any dogs left for us to walk in the entire neighborhood.
Did we ever!
I was worried we wouldn't have enough left over for the next-day shipping, but this covers it.
I've been messaging the new lamp's seller on StuffSwap.
I explained to her how quickly we need it to arrive, and she said she can have it shipped out first thing tomorrow, as long as we send her the money by tonight.
Hooray! Doomsday deflected! This calls for celebratory facials and binge-watching!
I don't see anything stopping us from rewatching the last two seasons of *Larkspur Academy* this weekend.
Except for Monday's homework.
UGH!

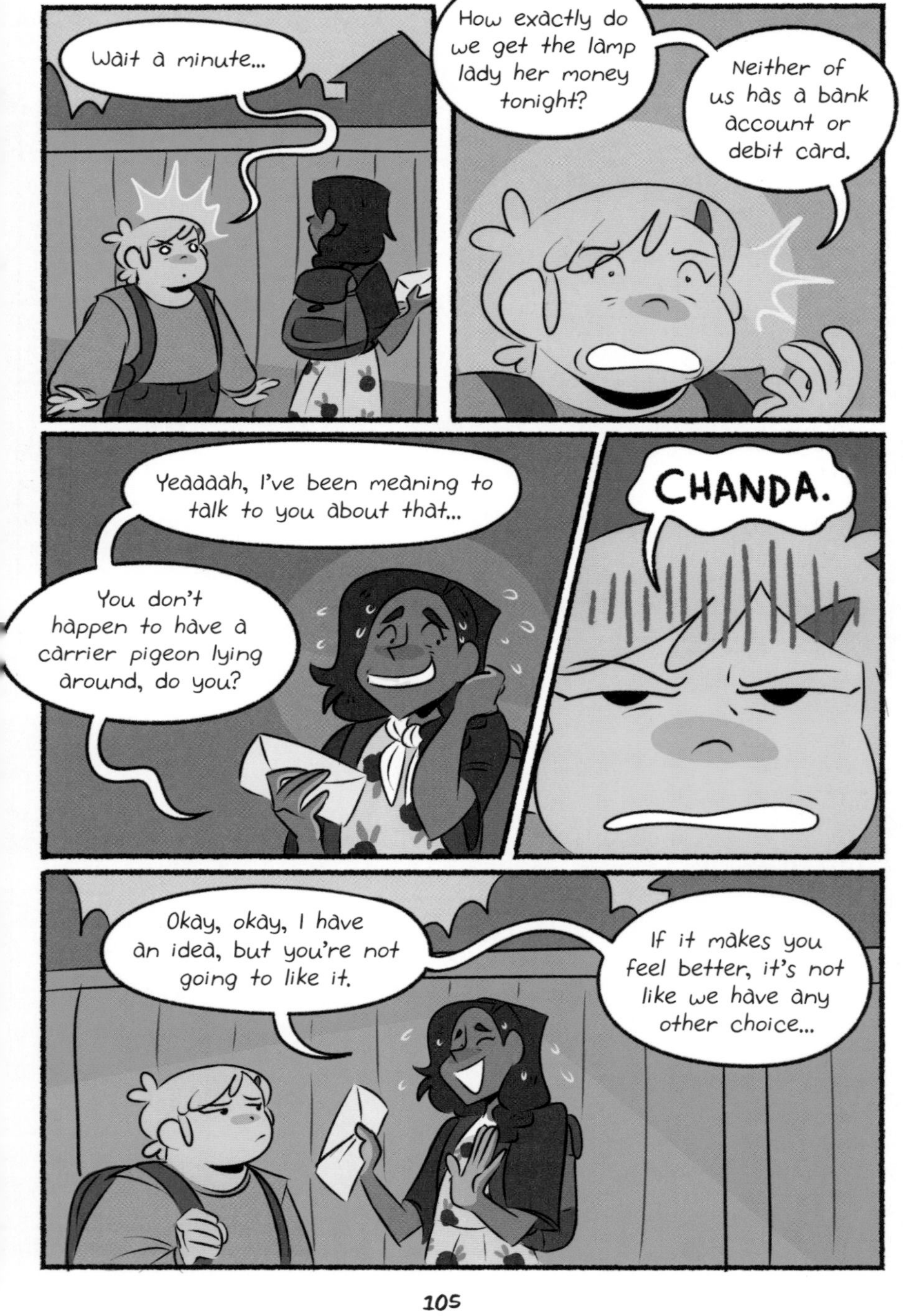

Wait a minute...
How exactly do we get the lamp lady her money tonight?
Neither of us has a bank account or debit card.
Yeaaaah, I've been meaning to talk to you about that...
You don't happen to have a carrier pigeon lying around, do you?
CHANDA.
Okay, okay, I have an idea, but you're not going to like it.
If it makes you feel better, it's not like we have any other choice...

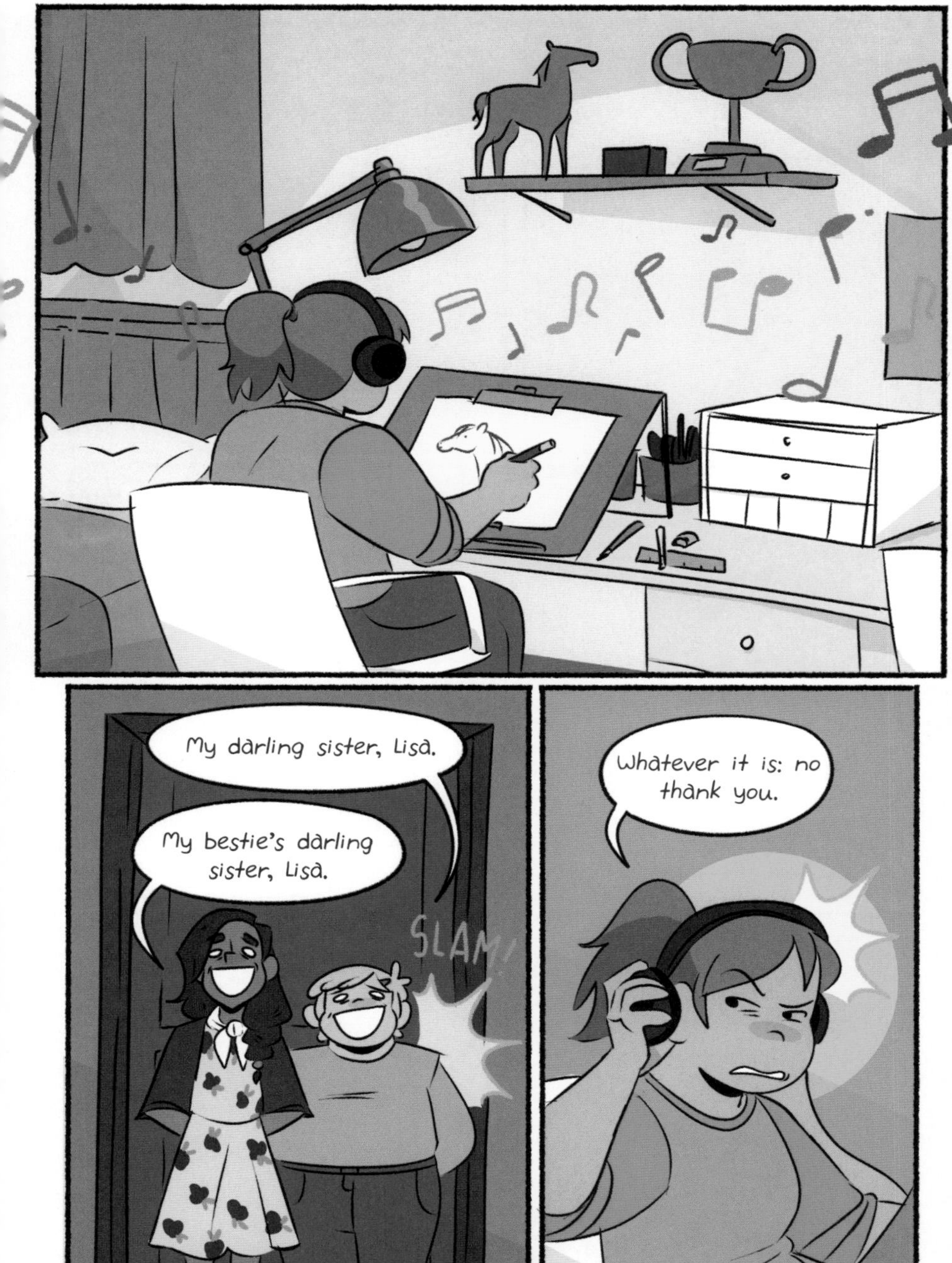
My darling sister, Lisa.
My bestie's darling sister, Lisa.
SLAM!
Whatever it is: no thank you.

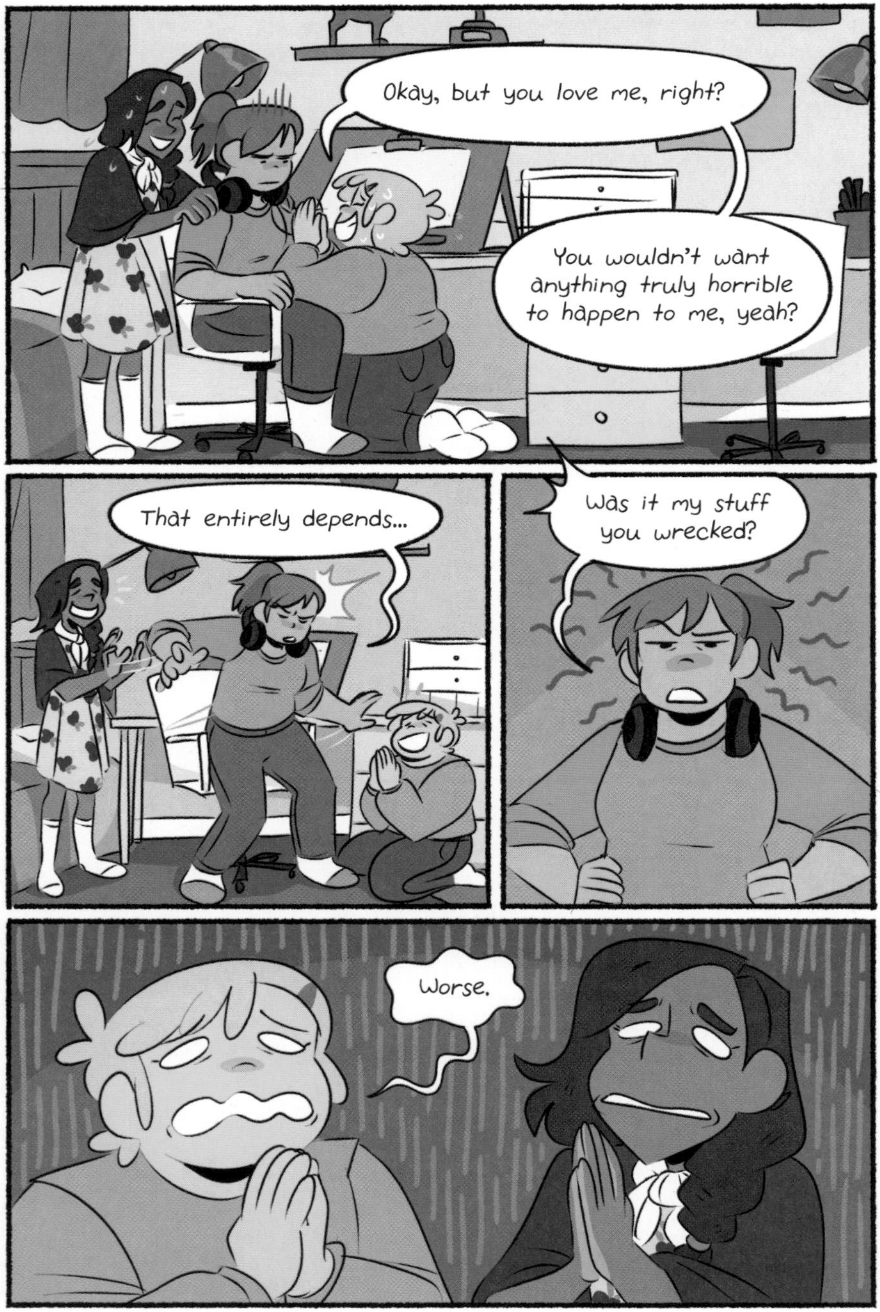
Okay, but you love me, right?
You wouldn't want anything truly horrible to happen to me, yeah?
That entirely depends...
Was it my stuff you wrecked?
Worse.

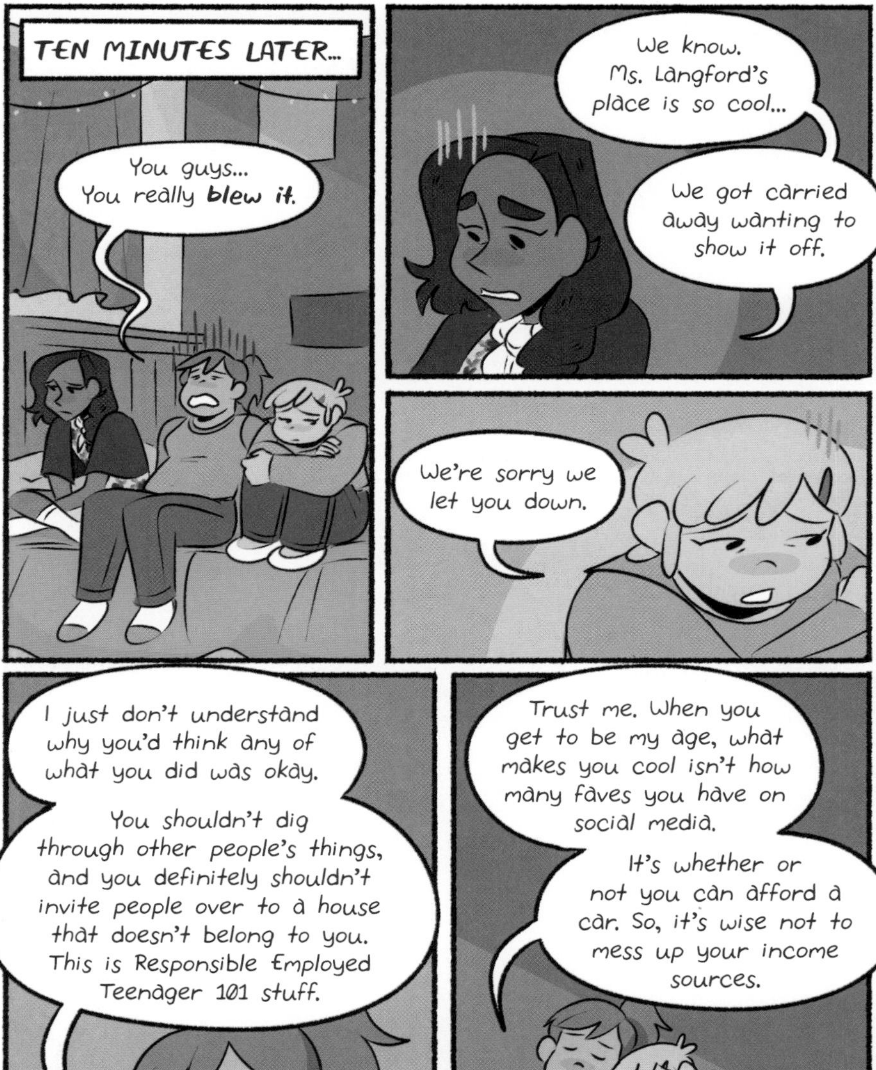
TEN MINUTES LATER...
You guys... You really **blew it**.
We know. Ms. Langford's place is so cool...
We got carried away wanting to show it off.
We're sorry we let you down.
I just don't understand why you'd think any of what you did was okay.
You shouldn't dig through other people's things, and you definitely shouldn't invite people over to a house that doesn't belong to you. This is Responsible Employed Teenager 101 stuff.
Trust me. When you get to be my age, what makes you cool isn't how many faves you have on social media.
It's whether or not you can afford a car. So, it's wise not to mess up your income sources.

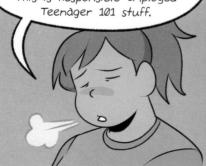

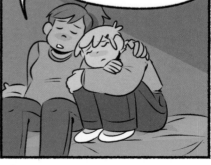

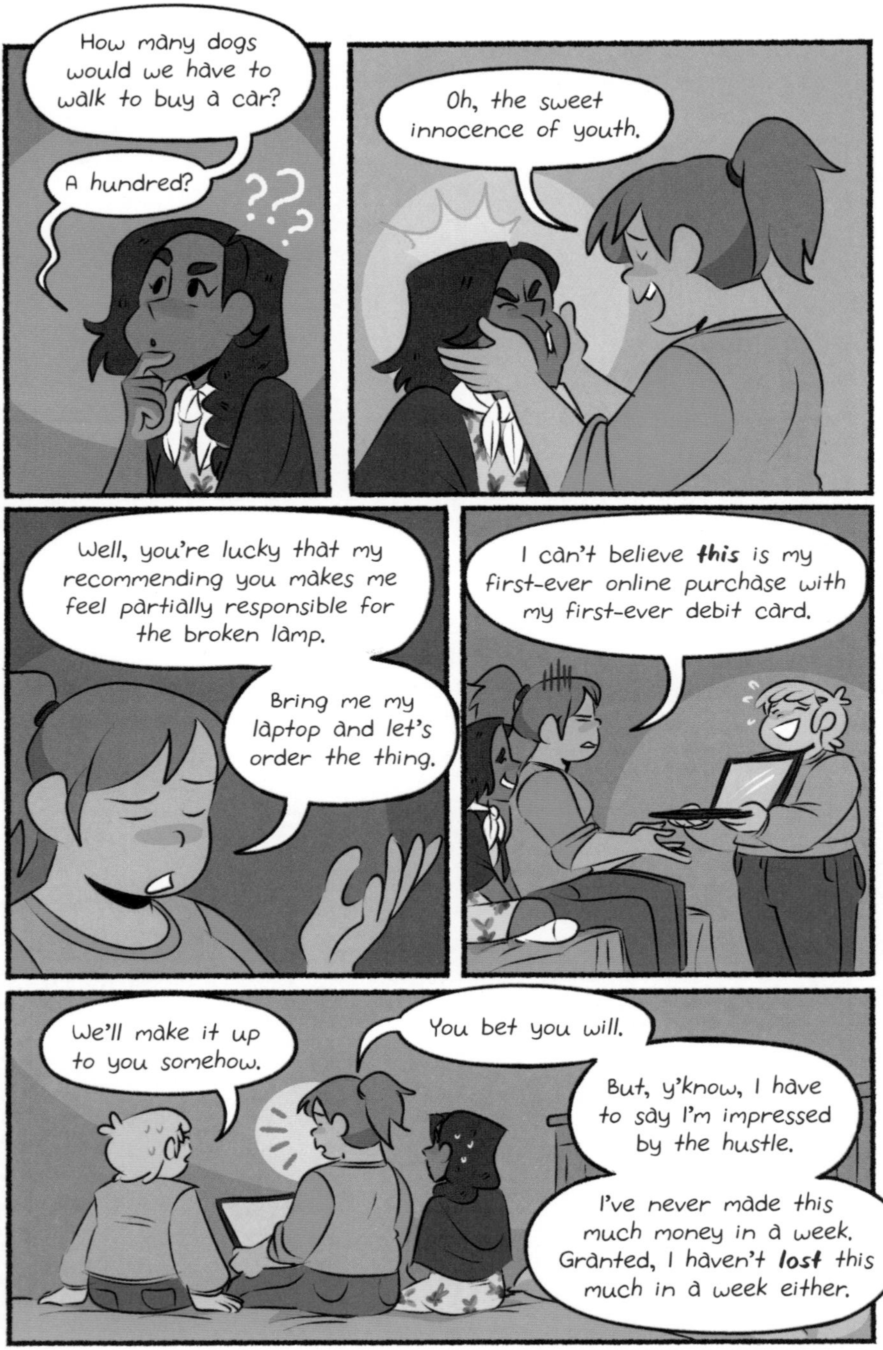
How many dogs would we have to walk to buy a car?
A hundred?
Oh, the sweet innocence of youth.
Well, you're lucky that my recommending you makes me feel partially responsible for the broken lamp.
Bring me my laptop and let's order the thing.
I can't believe **this** is my first-ever online purchase with my first-ever debit card.
We'll make it up to you somehow.
You bet you will.
But, y'know, I have to say I'm impressed by the hustle.
I've never made this much money in a week. Granted, I haven't **lost** this much in a week either.

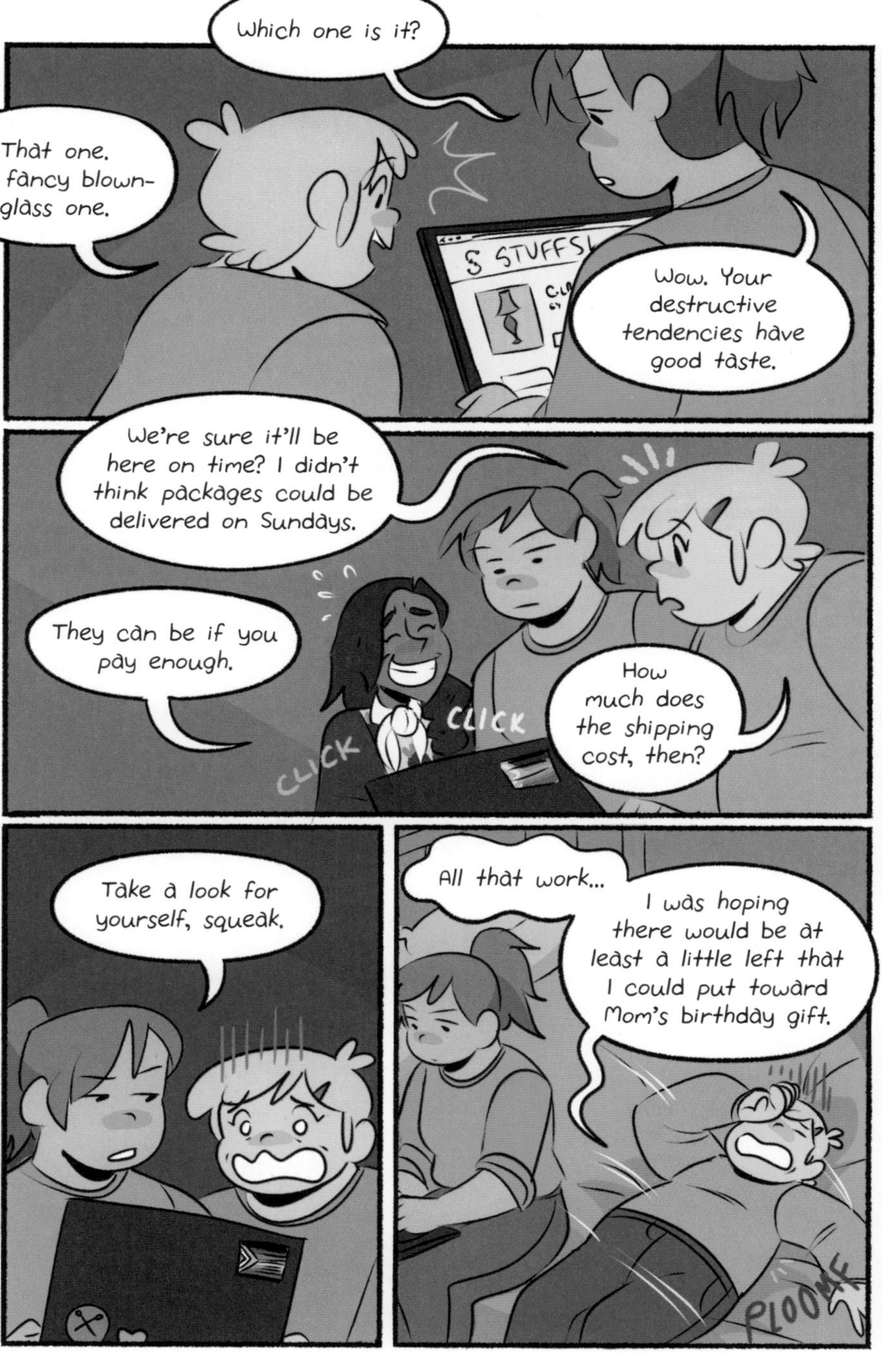
Which one is it?
That one. The fancy blown-glass one.
STUFFS
Wow. Your destructive tendencies have good taste.
We're sure it'll be here on time? I didn't think packages could be delivered on Sundays.
They can be if you pay enough.
CLICK
CLICK
How much does the shipping cost, then?
Take a look for yourself, squeak.
All that work...
I was hoping there would be at least a little left that I could put toward Mom's birthday gift.
PLOOMF

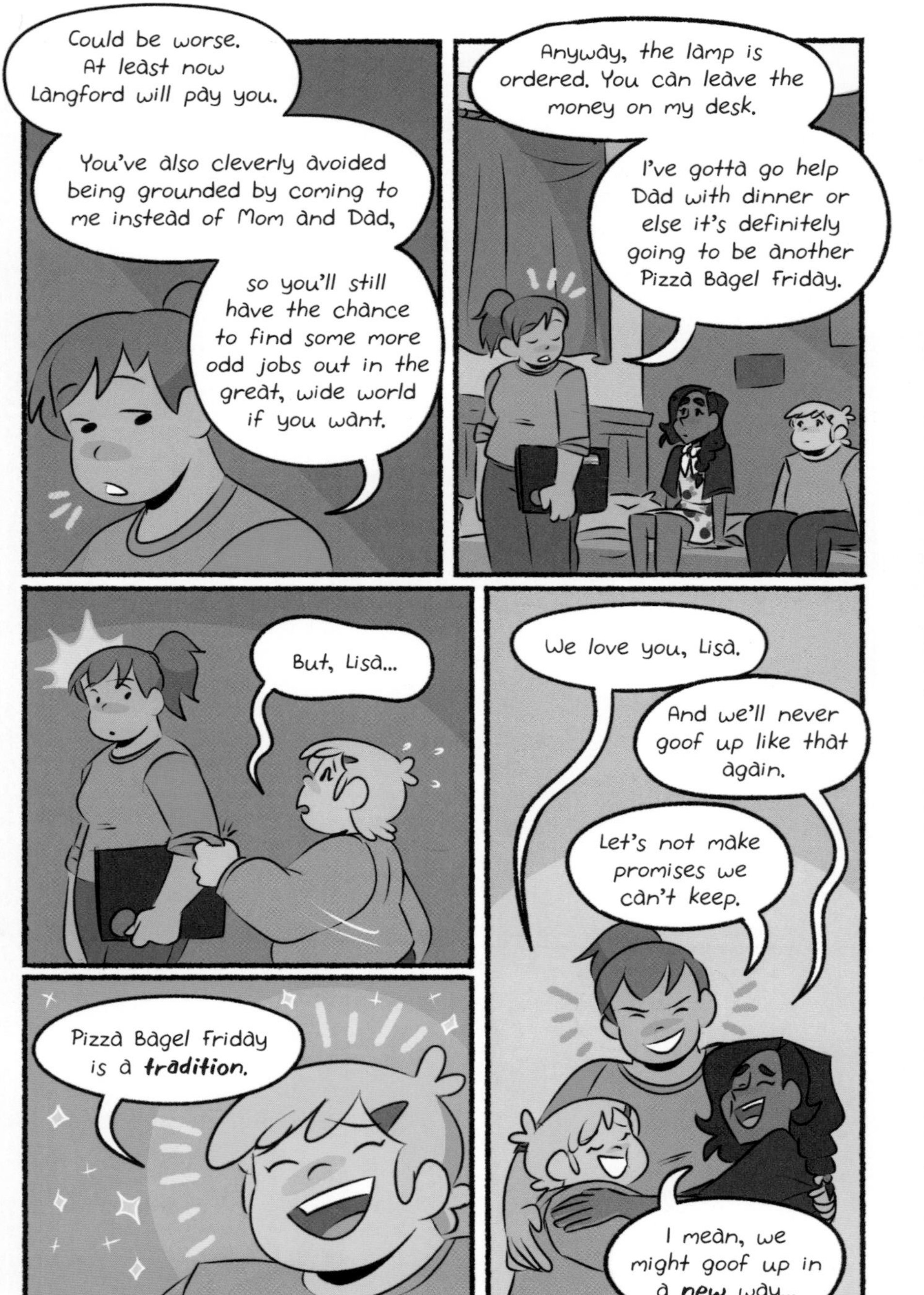
Could be worse. At least now Langford will pay you.
You've also cleverly avoided being grounded by coming to me instead of Mom and Dad,
so you'll still have the chance to find some more odd jobs out in the great, wide world if you want.
Anyway, the lamp is ordered. You can leave the money on my desk.
I've gotta go help Dad with dinner or else it's definitely going to be another Pizza Bagel Friday.
But, Lisa...
Pizza Bagel Friday is a **tradition.**
We love you, Lisa.
And we'll never goof up like that again.
Let's not make promises we can't keep.
I mean, we might goof up in a **new** way...

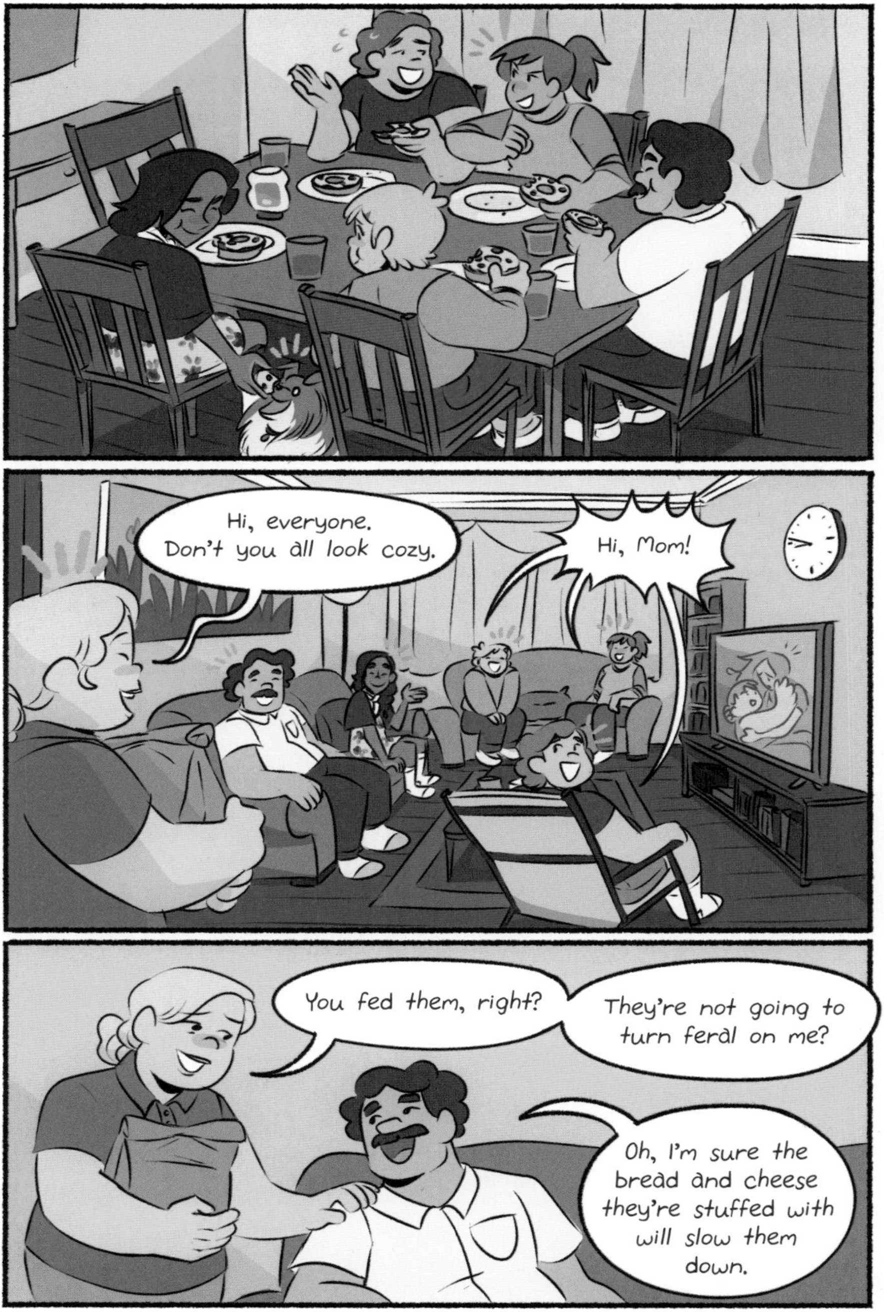
Hi, everyone.
Don't you all look cozy.
Hi, Mom!
You fed them, right?
They're not going to turn feral on me?
Oh, I'm sure the bread and cheese they're stuffed with will slow them down.

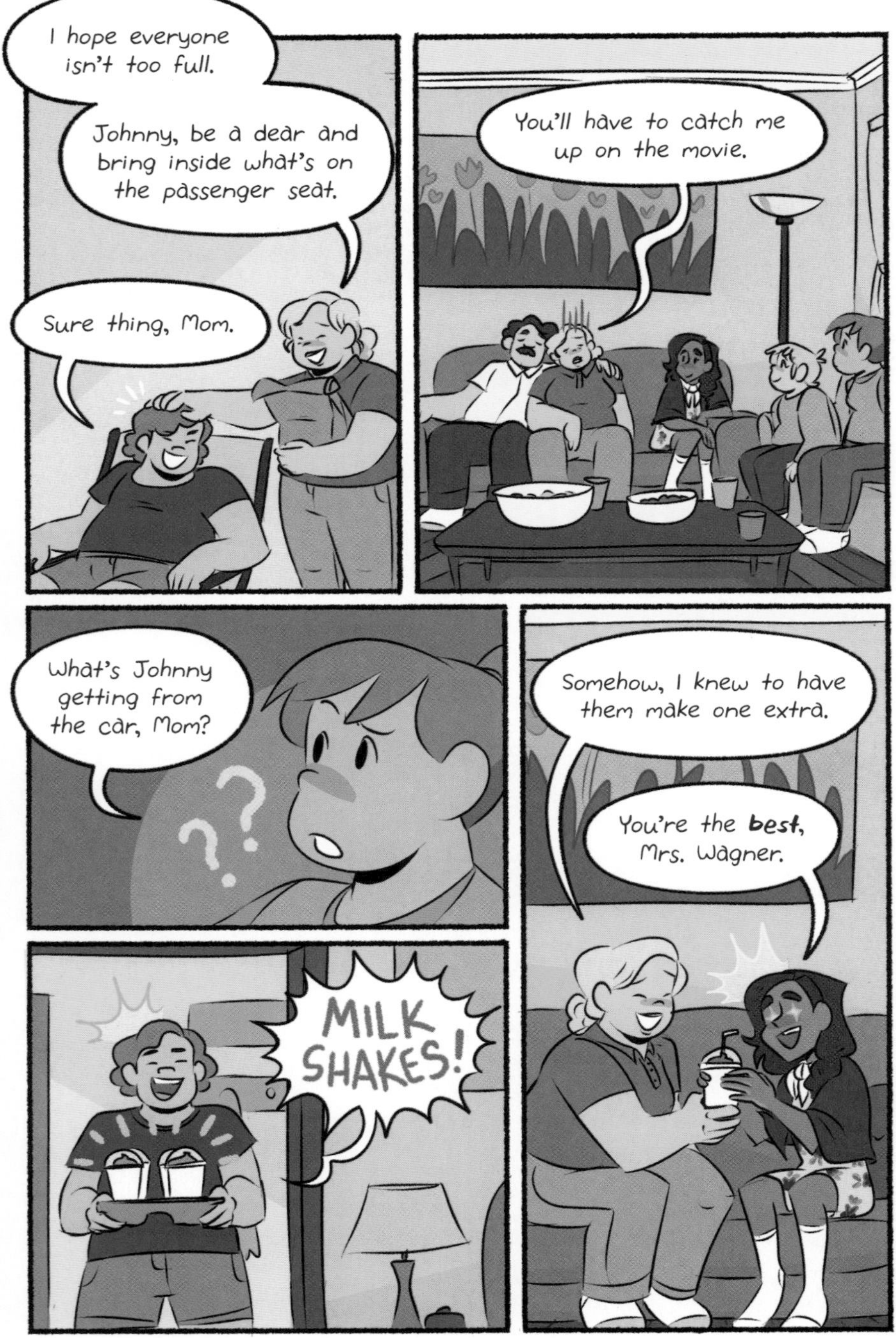
I hope everyone isn't too full.
Johnny, be a dear and bring inside what's on the passenger seat.
Sure thing, Mom.
You'll have to catch me up on the movie.
What's Johnny getting from the car, Mom?
Somehow, I knew to have them make one extra.
You're the **best**, Mrs. Wagner.
MILK SHAKES!

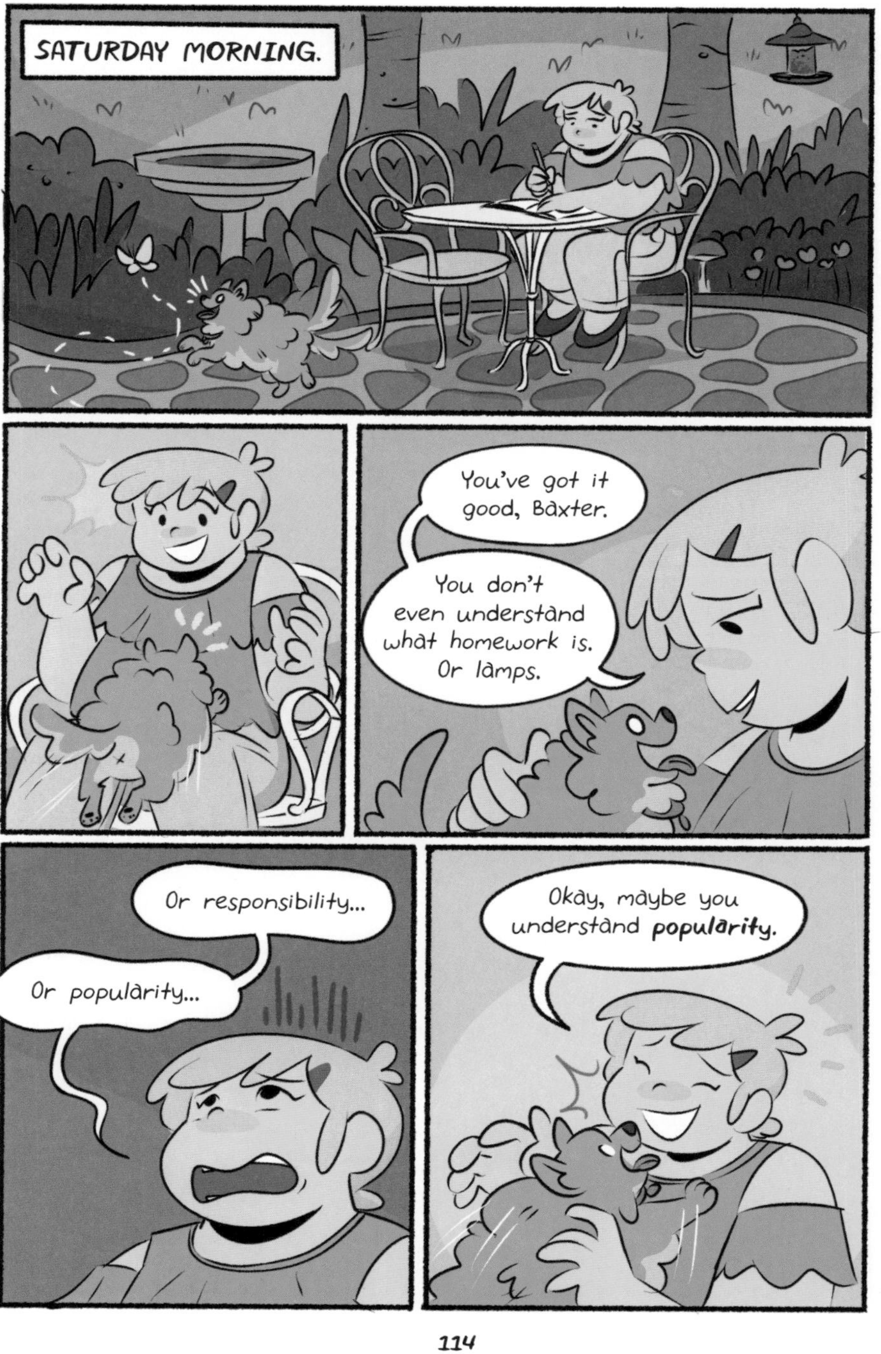
SATURDAY MORNING.
You've got it good, Baxter.
You don't even understand what homework is. Or lamps.
Or responsibility...
Or popularity...
Okay, maybe you understand **popularity**.

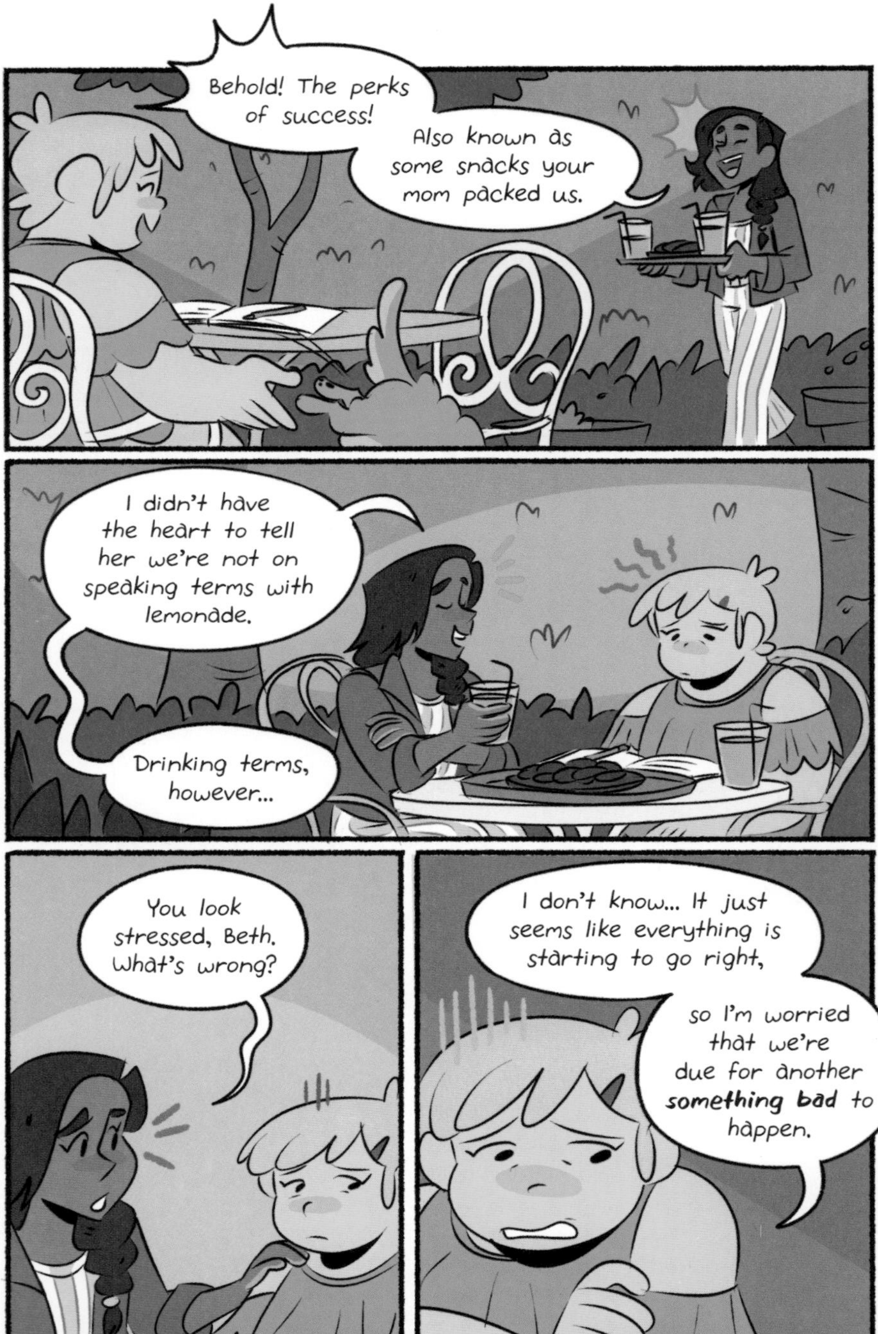
Behold! The perks of success!
Also known as some snacks your mom packed us.
I didn't have the heart to tell her we're not on speaking terms with lemonade.
Drinking terms, however...
You look stressed, Beth. What's wrong?
I don't know... It just seems like everything is starting to go right,
so I'm worried that we're due for another **something bad** to happen.

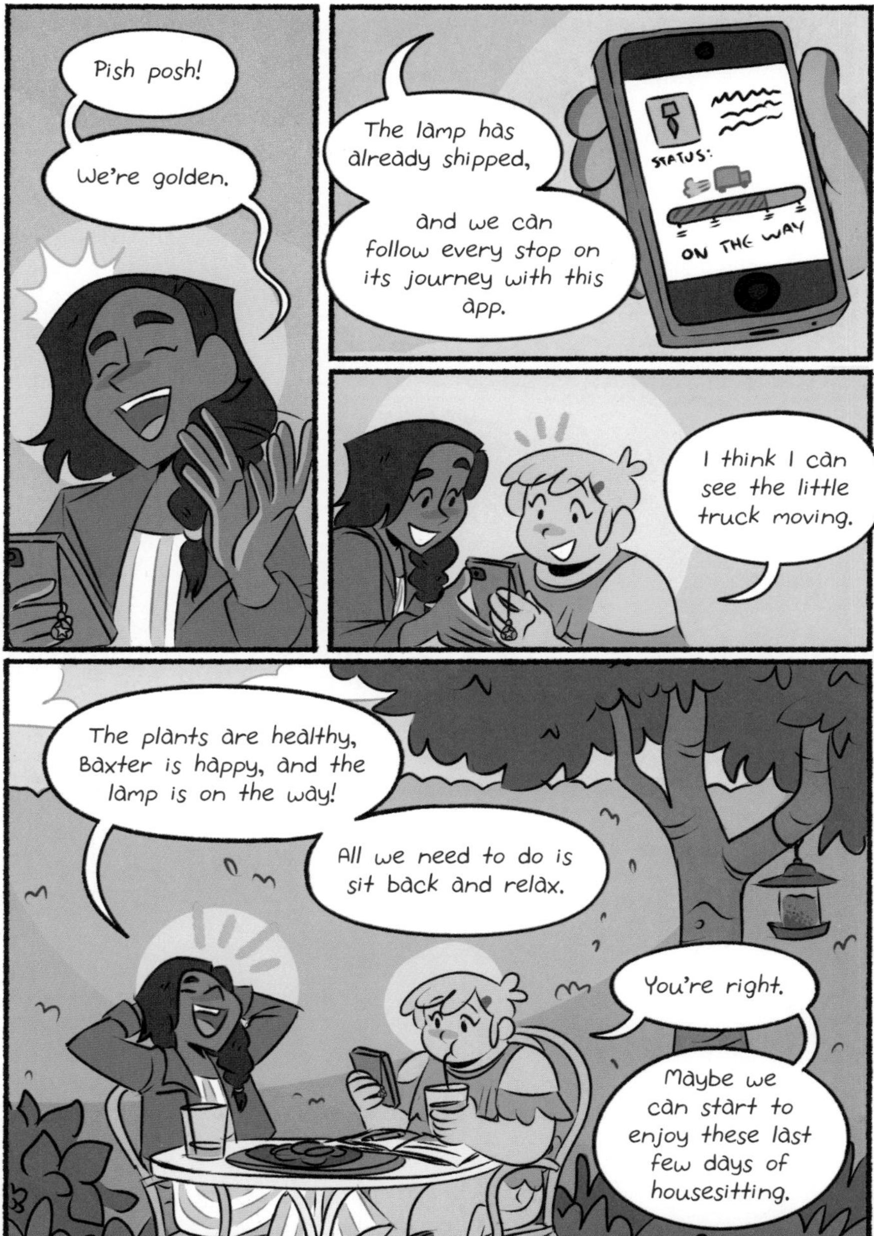
Pish posh!
We're golden.
The lamp has already shipped,
and we can follow every stop on its journey with this app.
STATUS:
ON THE WAY
I think I can see the little truck moving.
The plants are healthy, Baxter is happy, and the lamp is on the way!
All we need to do is sit back and relax.
You're right.
Maybe we can start to enjoy these last few days of housesitting.

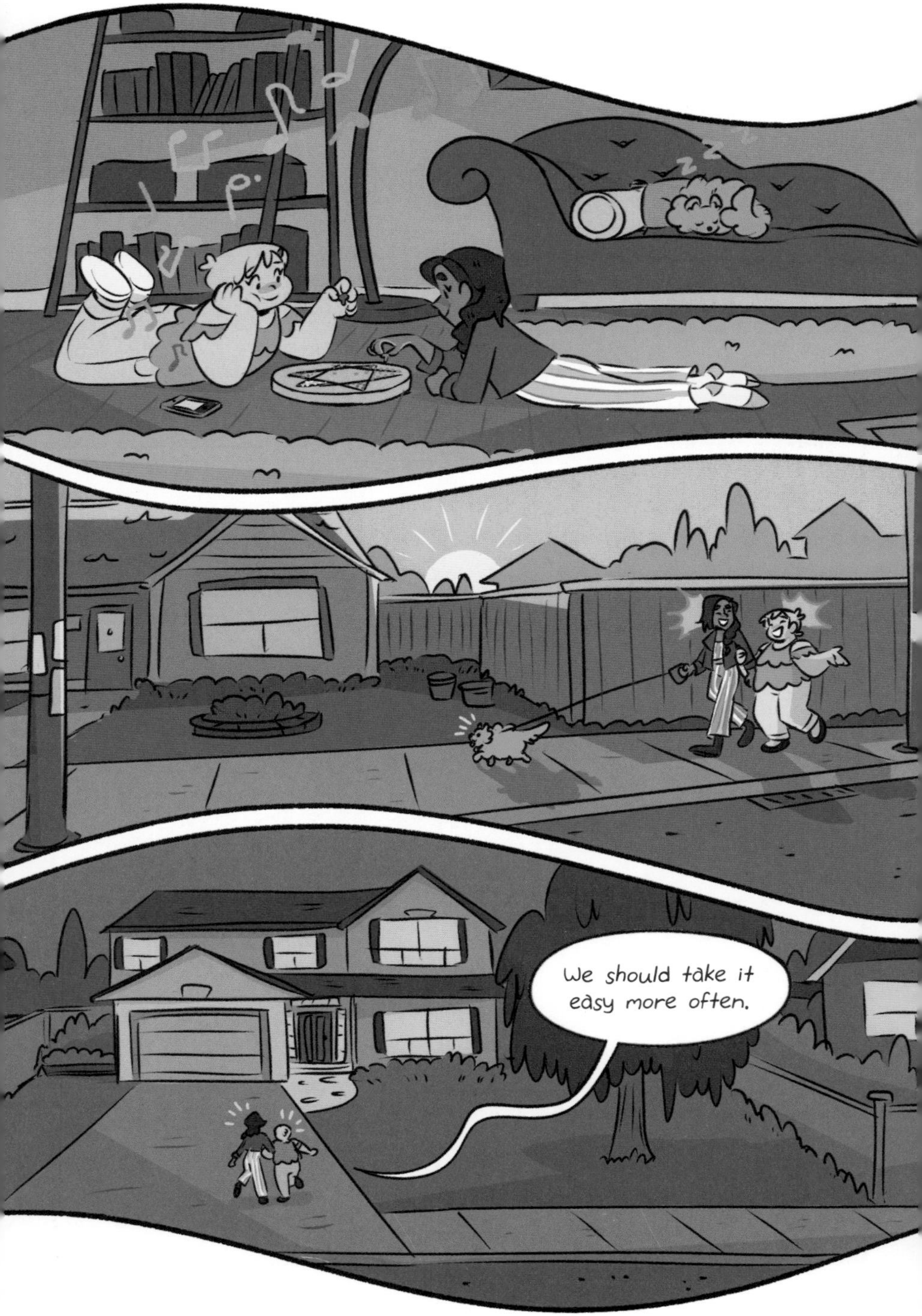
We should take it easy more often.

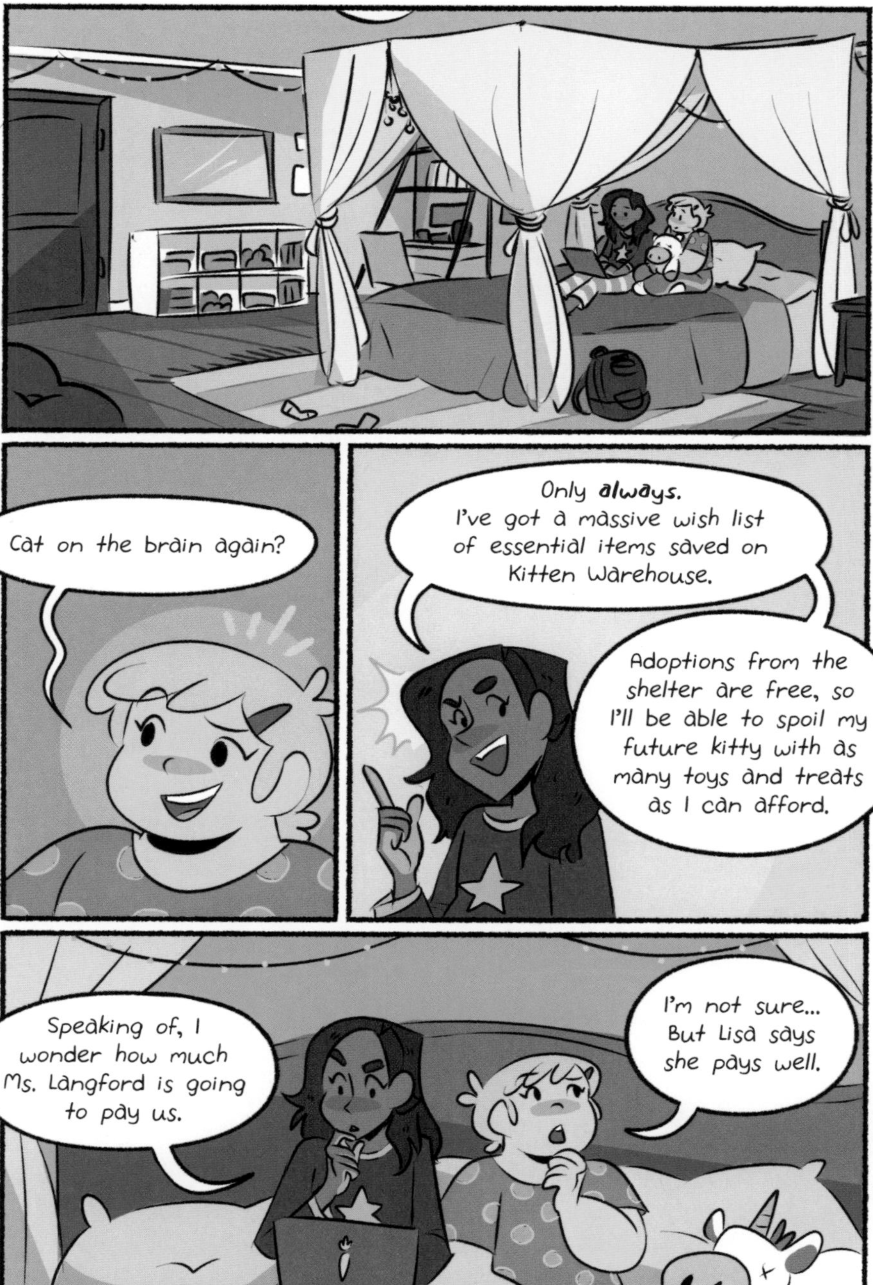
Cat on the brain again?
Only **always.** I've got a massive wish list of essential items saved on Kitten Warehouse.
Adoptions from the shelter are free, so I'll be able to spoil my future kitty with as many toys and treats as I can afford.
Speaking of, I wonder how much Ms. Langford is going to pay us.
I'm not sure... But Lisa says she pays well.

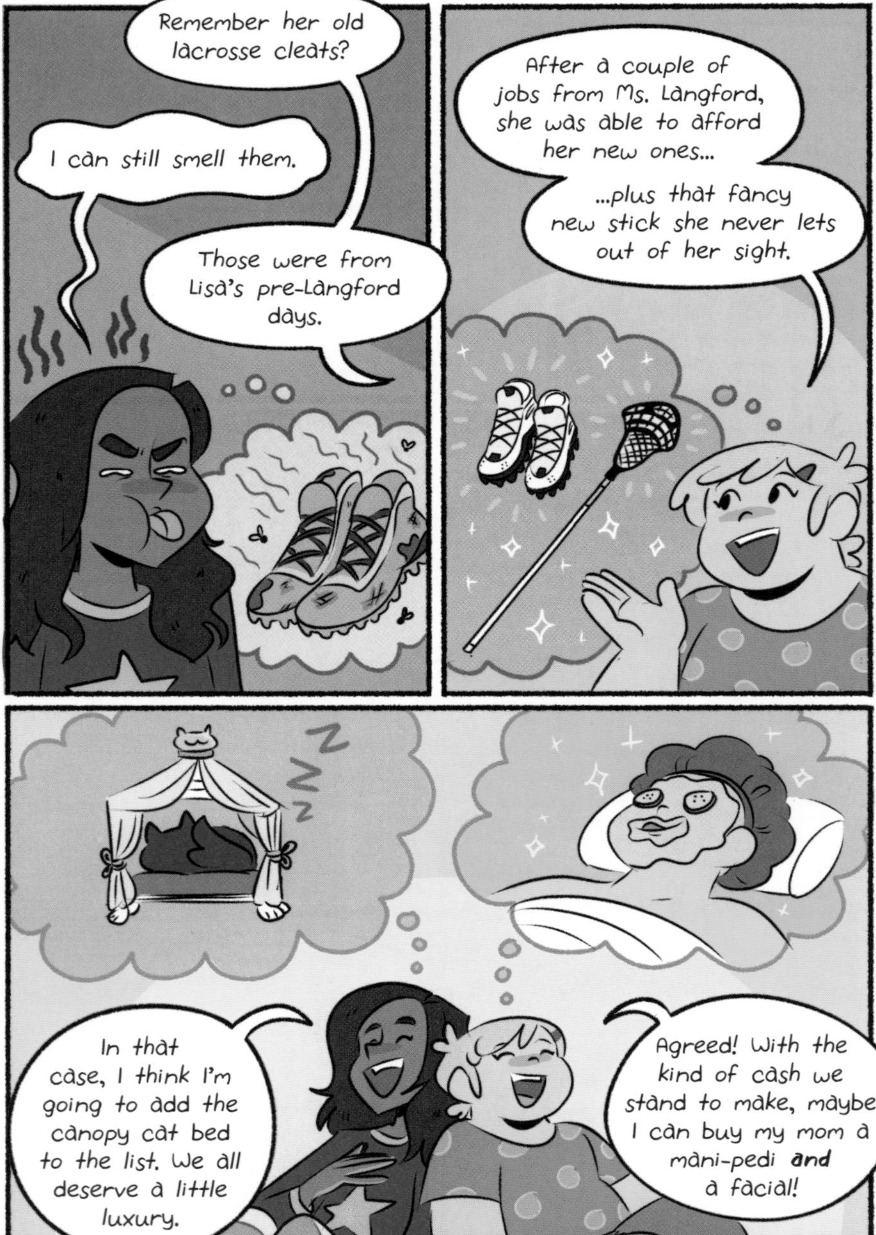
Remember her old lacrosse cleats?
I can still smell them.
Those were from Lisa's pre-Langford days.
After a couple of jobs from Ms. Langford, she was able to afford her new ones...
...plus that fancy new stick she never lets out of her sight.
In that case, I think I'm going to add the canopy cat bed to the list. We all deserve a little luxury.
Agreed! With the kind of cash we stand to make, maybe I can buy my mom a mani-pedi **and** a facial!

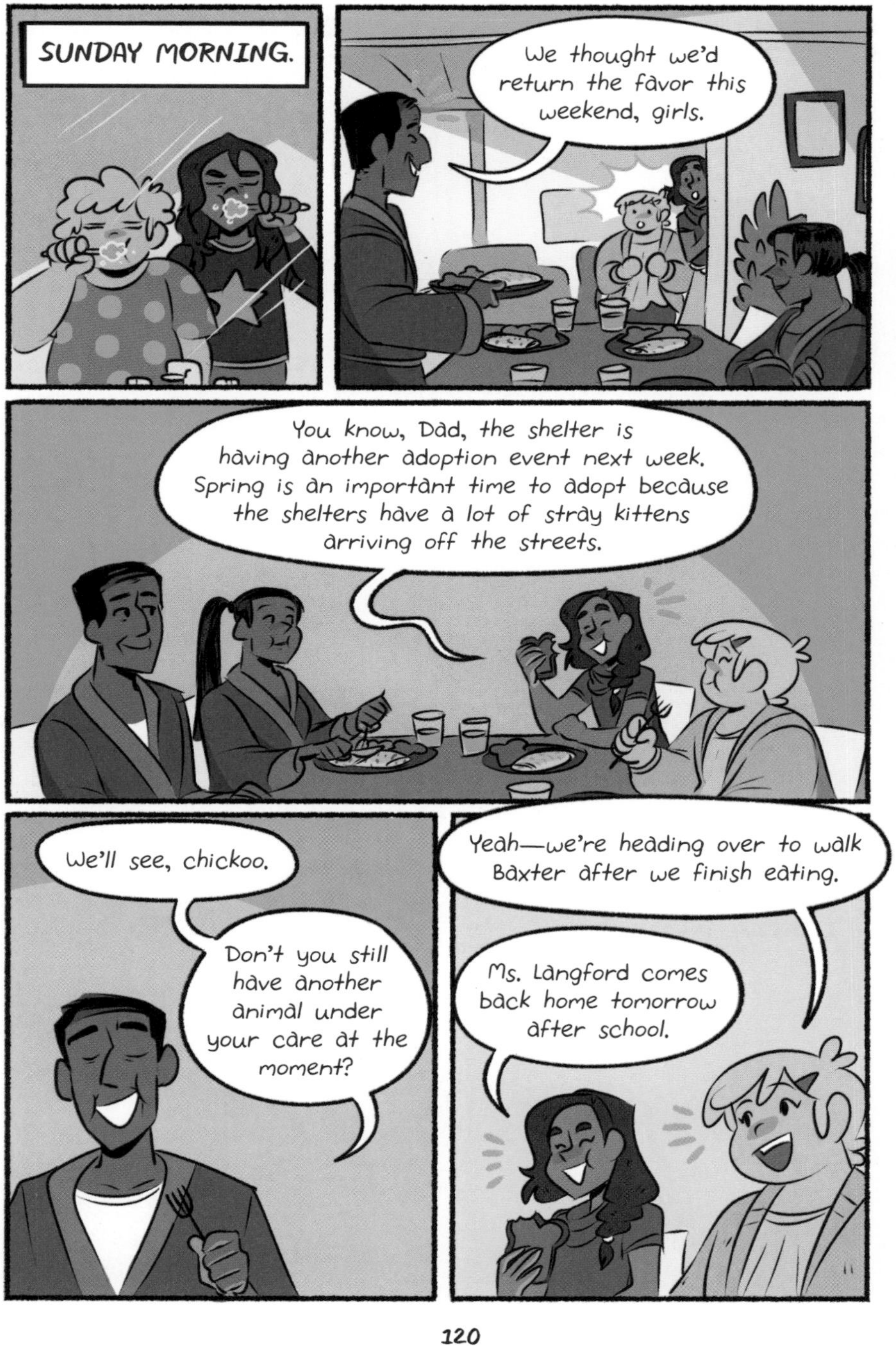
SUNDAY MORNING.
We thought we'd return the favor this weekend, girls.
You know, Dad, the shelter is having another adoption event next week. Spring is an important time to adopt because the shelters have a lot of stray kittens arriving off the streets.
We'll see, chickoo.
Don't you still have another animal under your care at the moment?
Yeah—we're heading over to walk Baxter after we finish eating.
Ms. Langford comes back home tomorrow after school.

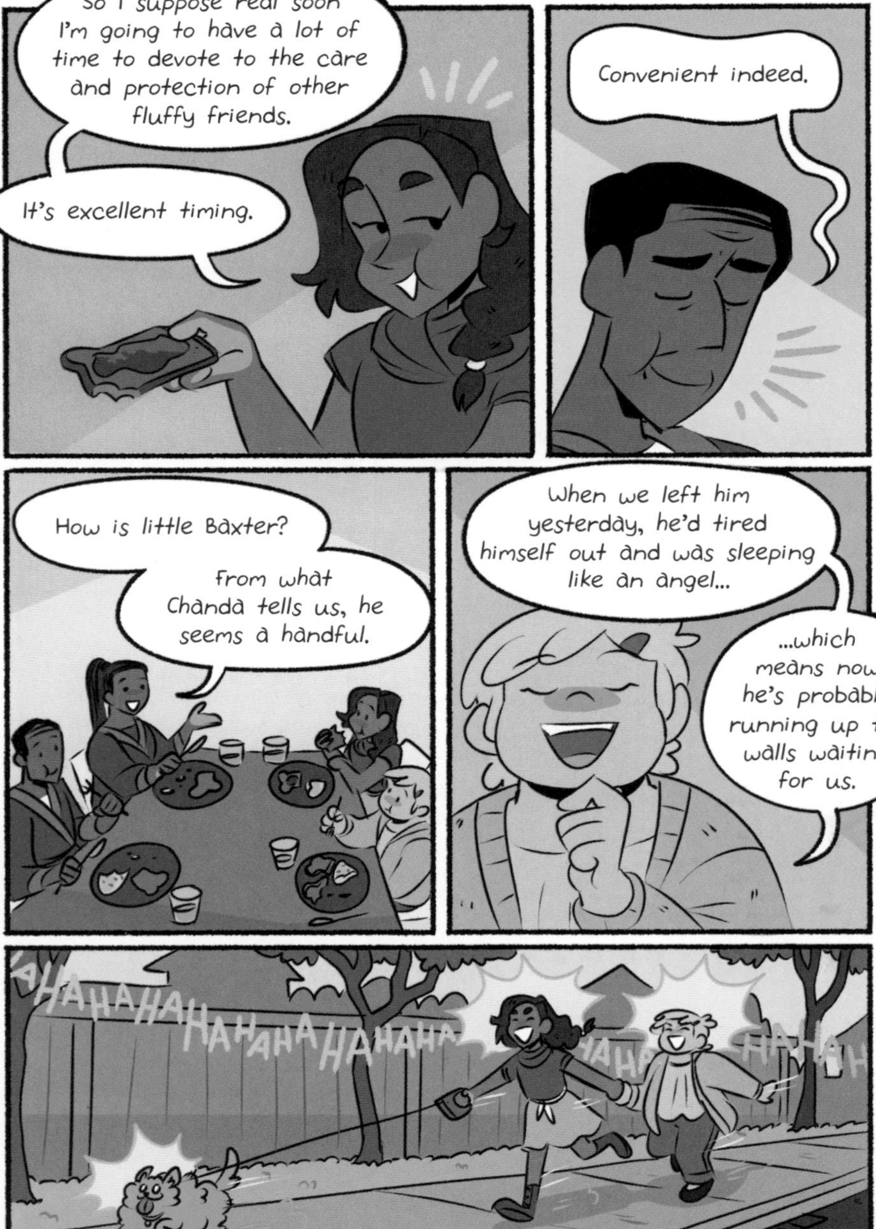
So I suppose real soon I'm going to have a lot of time to devote to the care and protection of other fluffy friends.
It's excellent timing.
Convenient indeed.
How is little Baxter?
From what Chanda tells us, he seems a handful.
When we left him yesterday, he'd tired himself out and was sleeping like an angel...
...which means now he's probably running up the walls waiting for us.
HAHAHAHAHAHAHAHAHAHAHA
HAHA
HAHAH

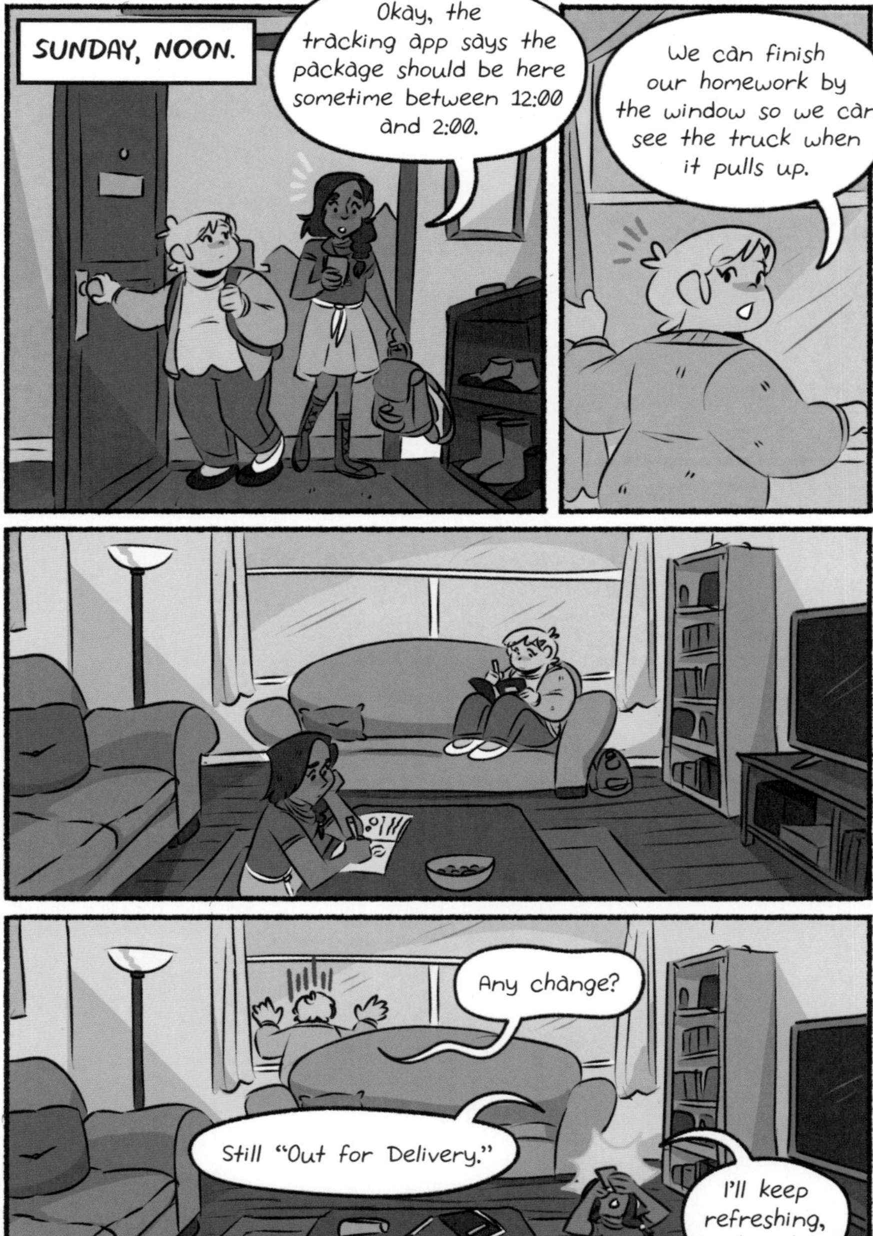
SUNDAY, NOON.
Okay, the tracking app says the package should be here sometime between 12:00 and 2:00.
We can finish our homework by the window so we can see the truck when it pulls up.
Any change?
Still "Out for Delivery."
I'll keep refreshing, though.

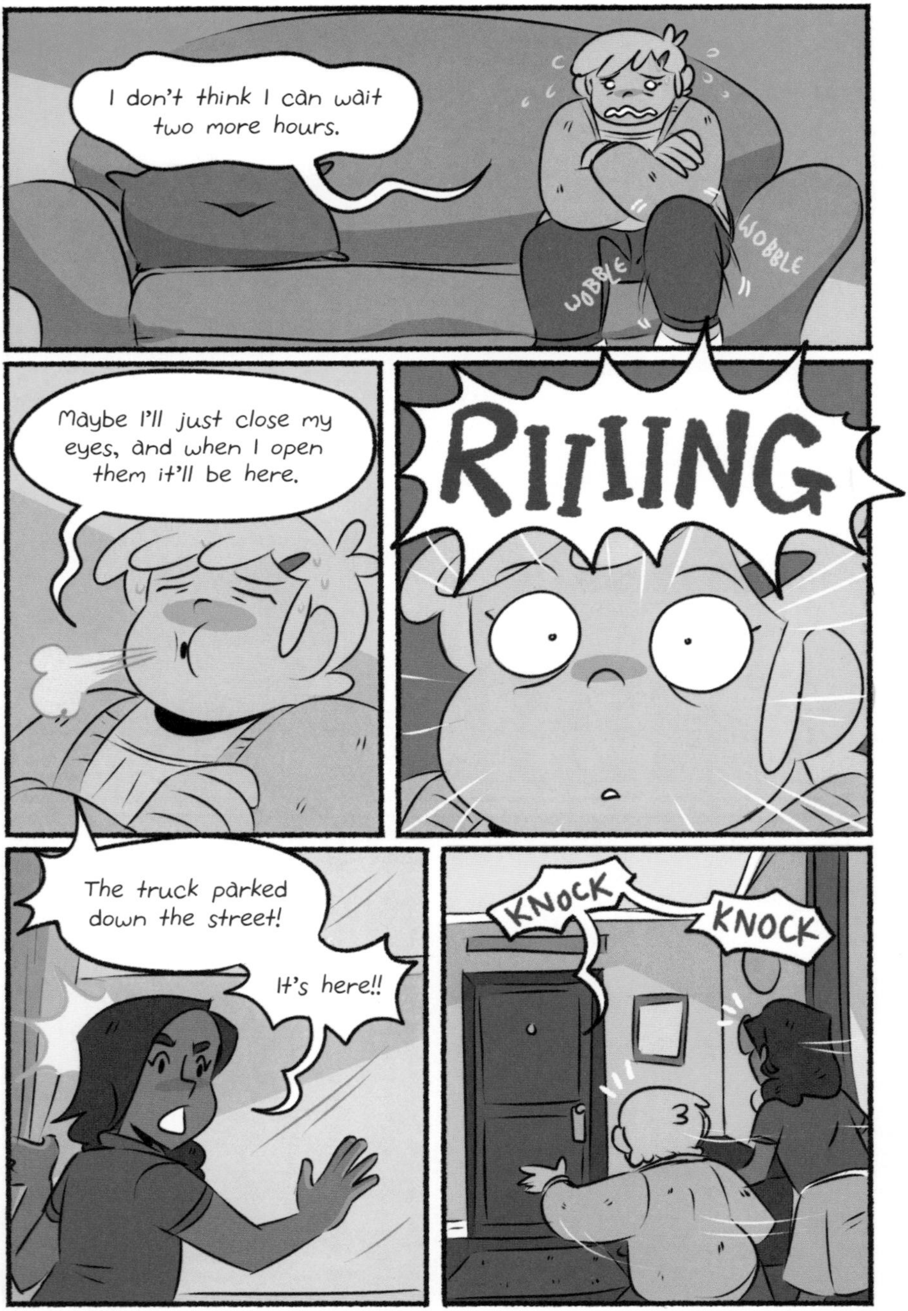

I don't think I can wait two more hours.
WOBBLE
WOBBLE
Maybe I'll just close my eyes, and when I open them it'll be here.
RIIIING
The truck parked down the street!
It's here!!
KNOCK
KNOCK

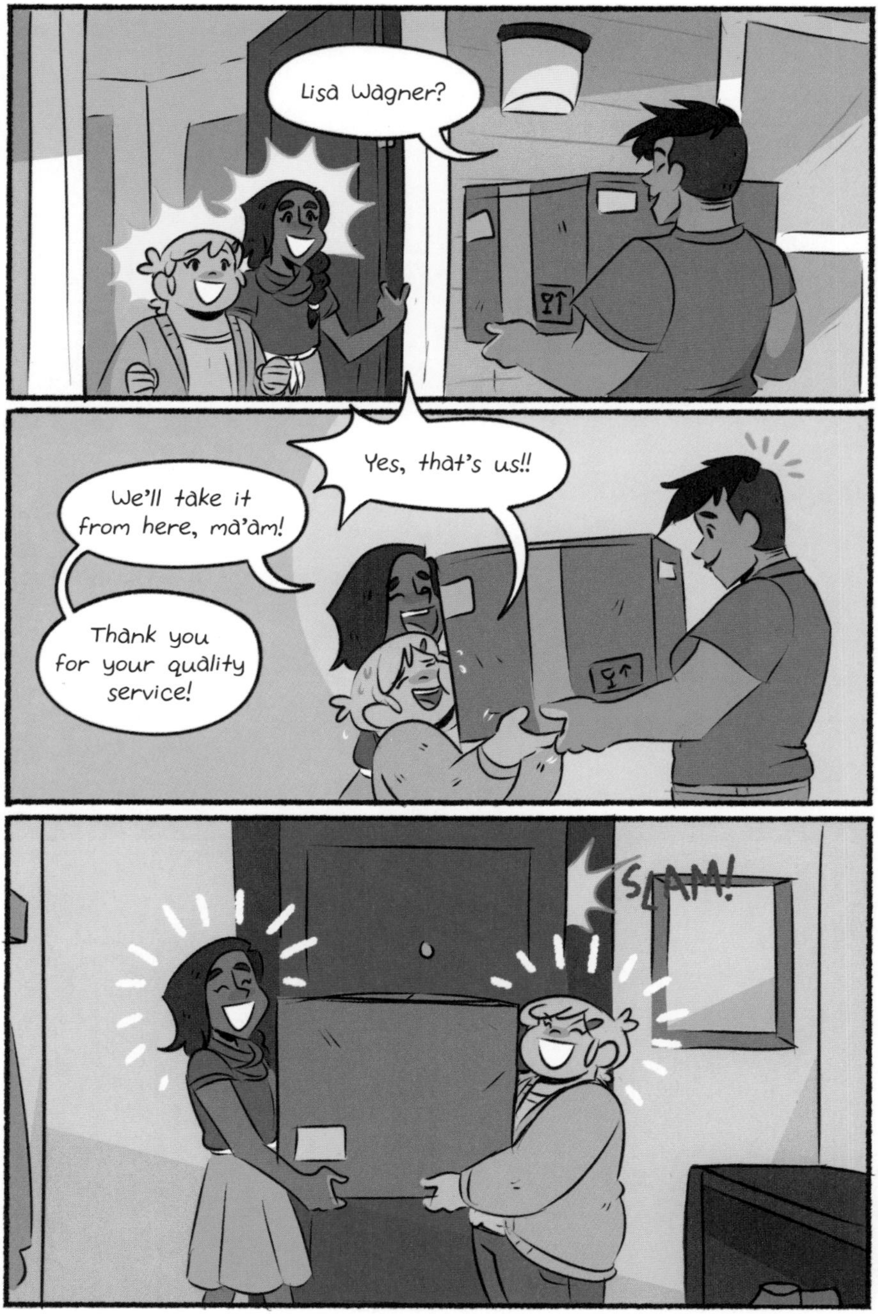
Lisa Wagner?
Yes, that's us!!
We'll take it from here, ma'am!
Thank you for your quality service!
SLAM!

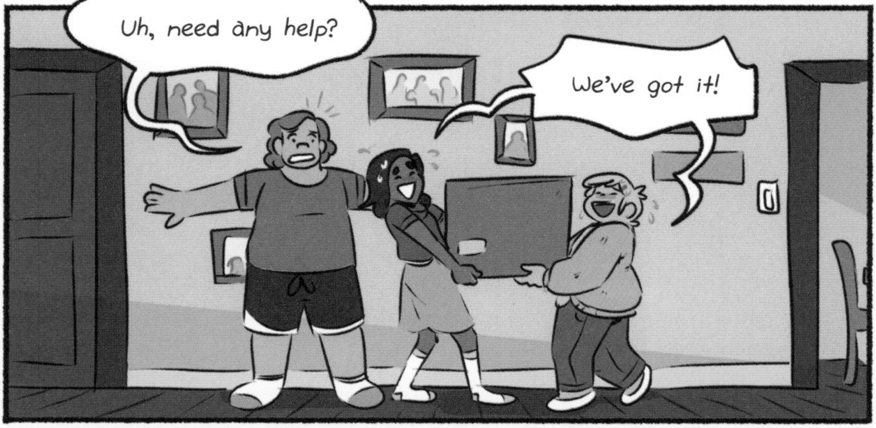
Uh, need any help?
We've got it!

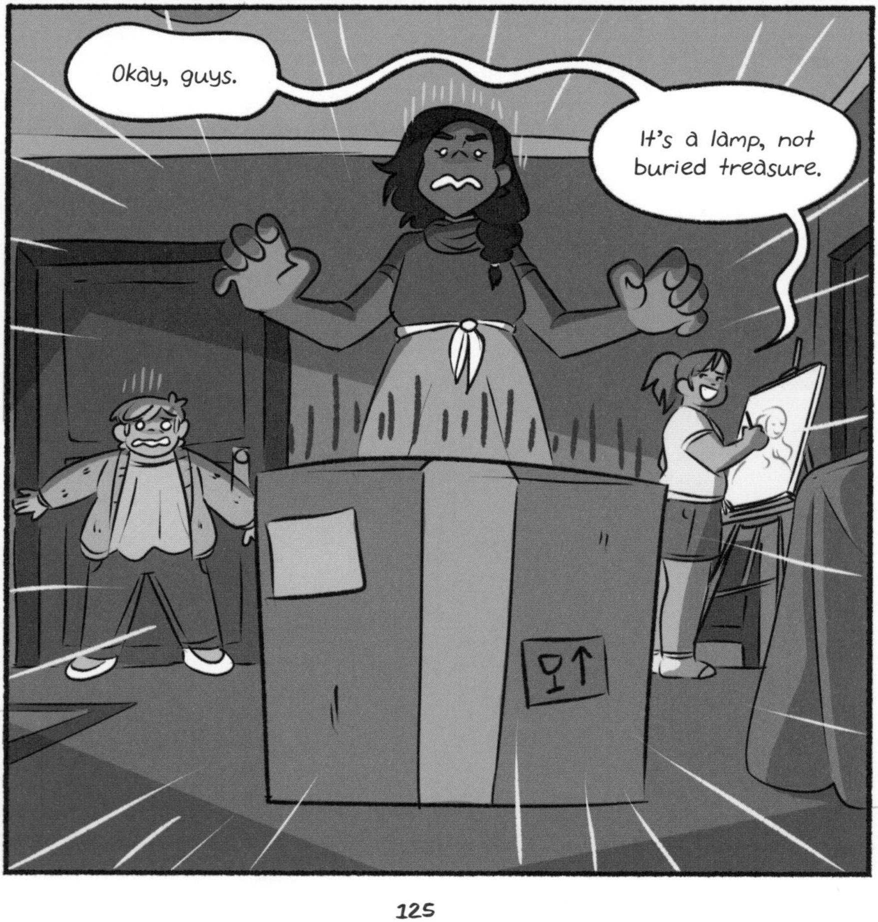
Okay, guys.
It's a lamp, not buried treasure.

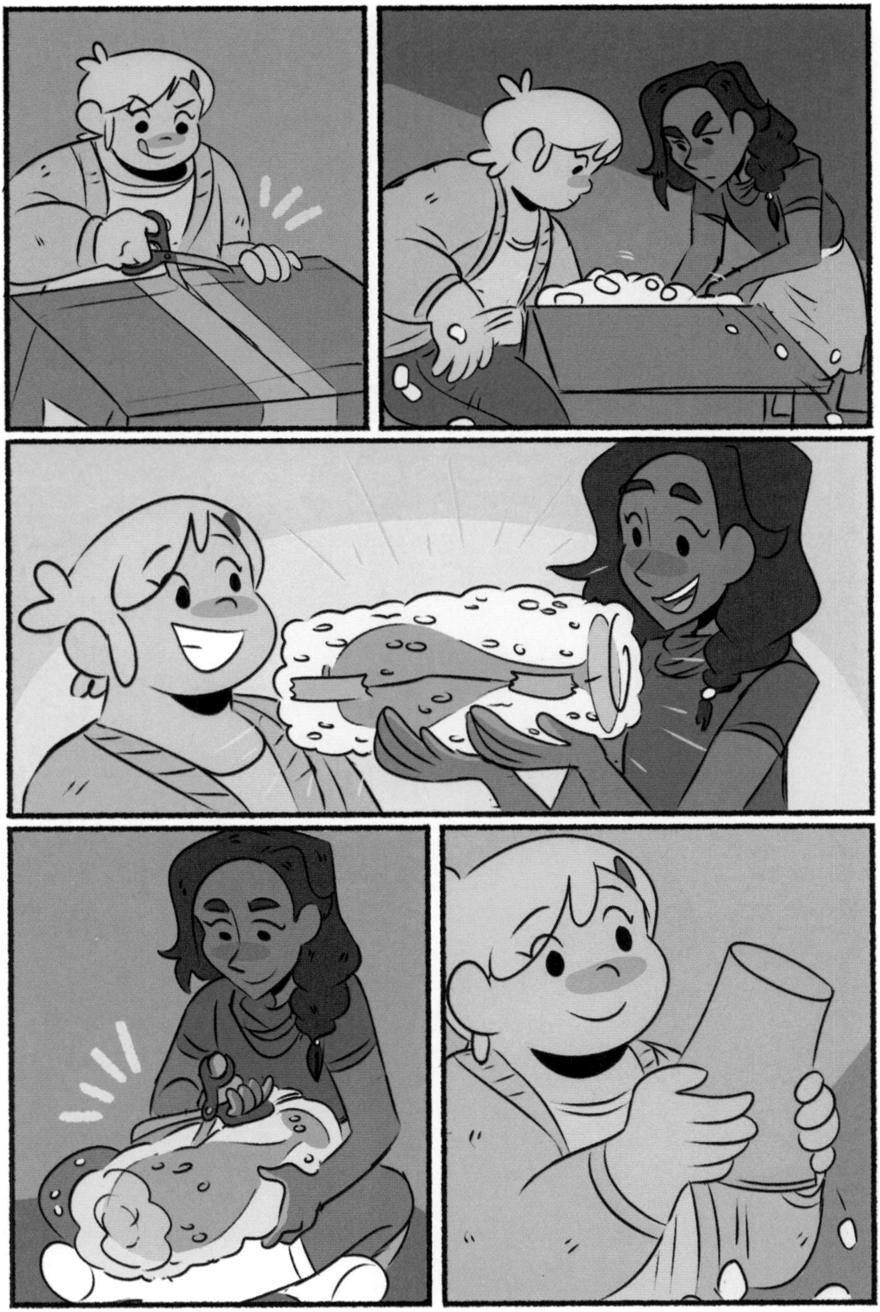

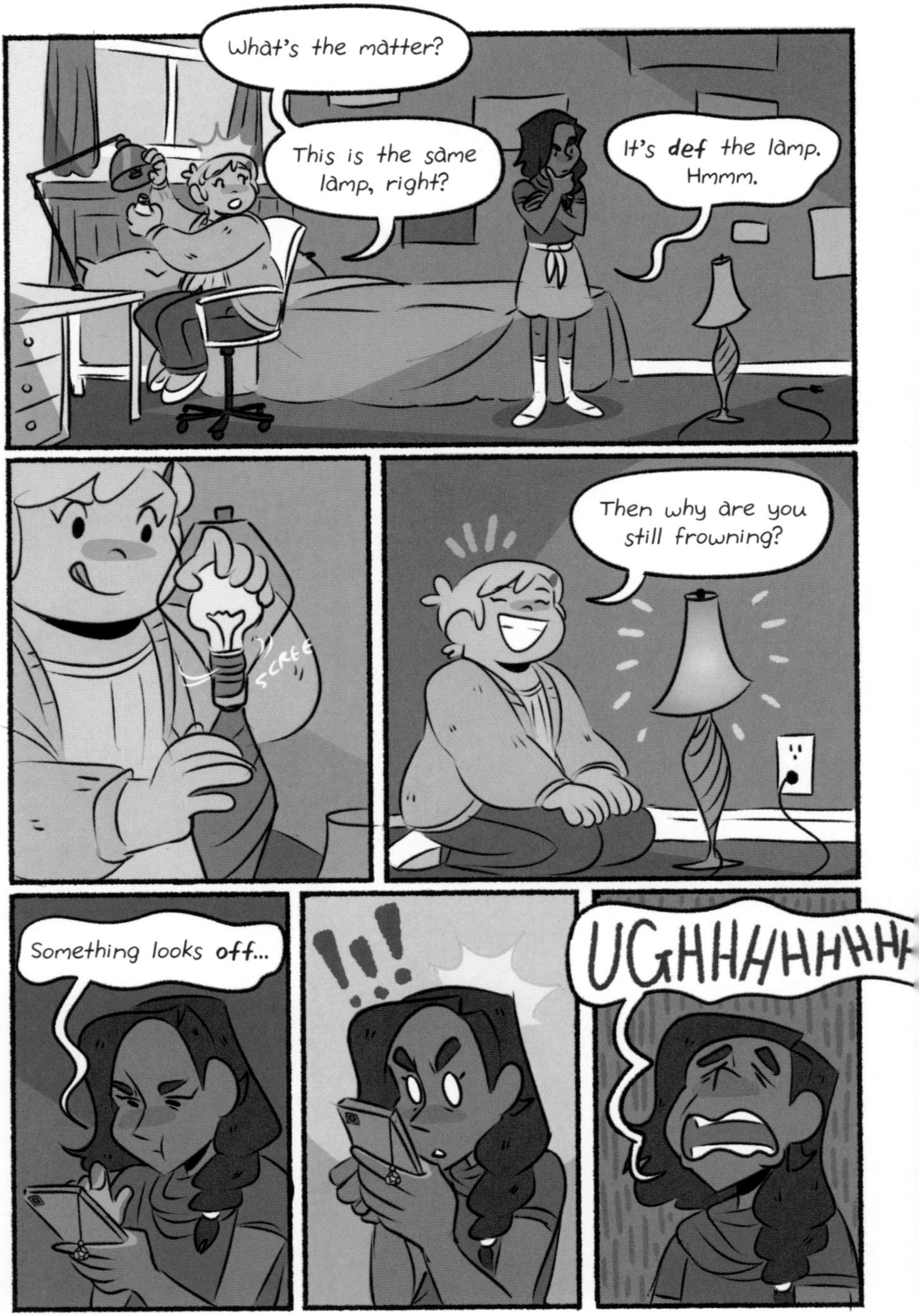
What's the matter?
This is the same lamp, right?
It's **def** the lamp. Hmmm.
SCREE
Then why are you still frowning?
Something looks **off**...
!!!
UGHHHHHHH

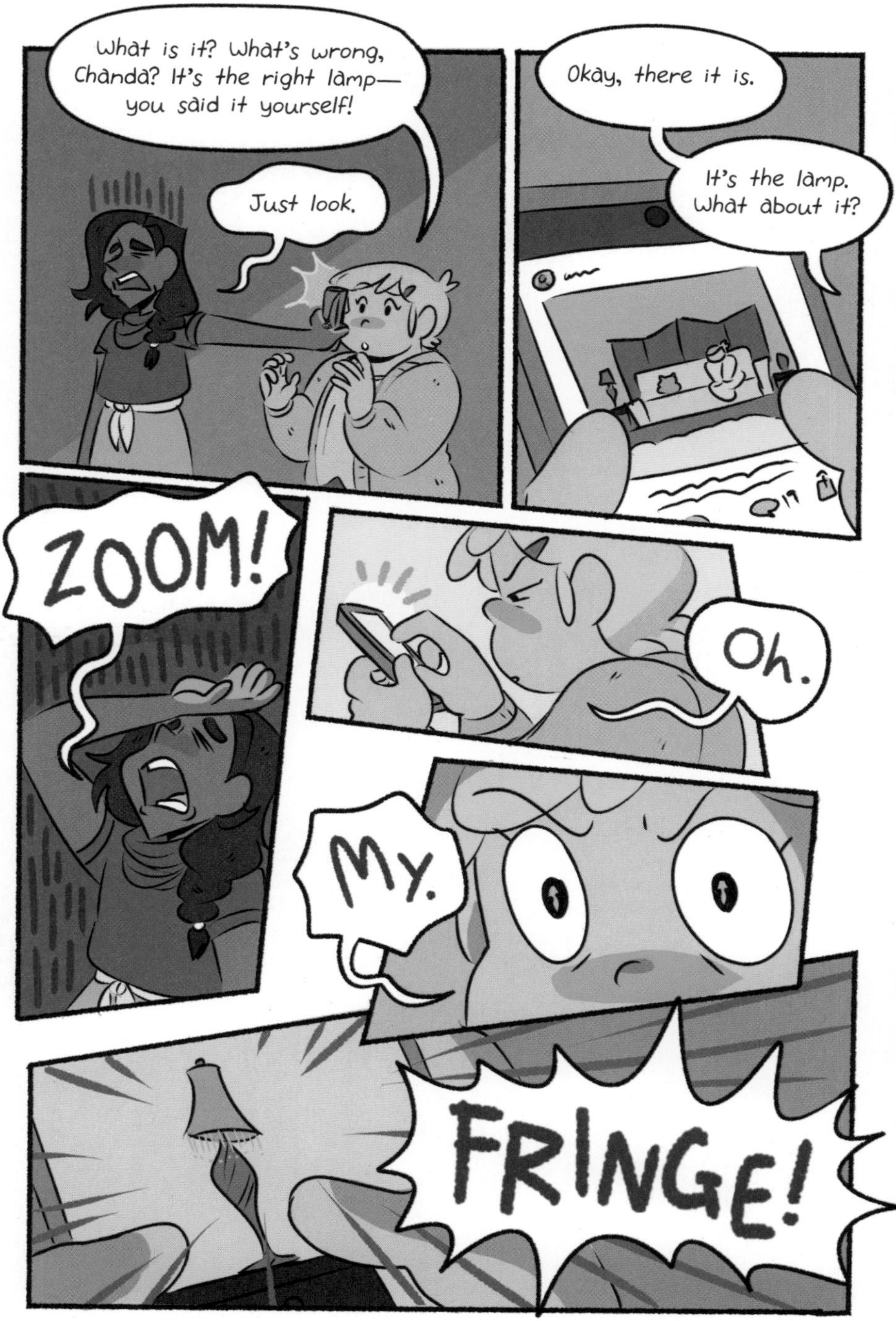
What is it? What's wrong, Chanda? It's the right lamp—you said it yourself!
Just look.
Okay, there it is.
It's the lamp. What about it?
ZOOM!
Oh.
My.
FRINGE!

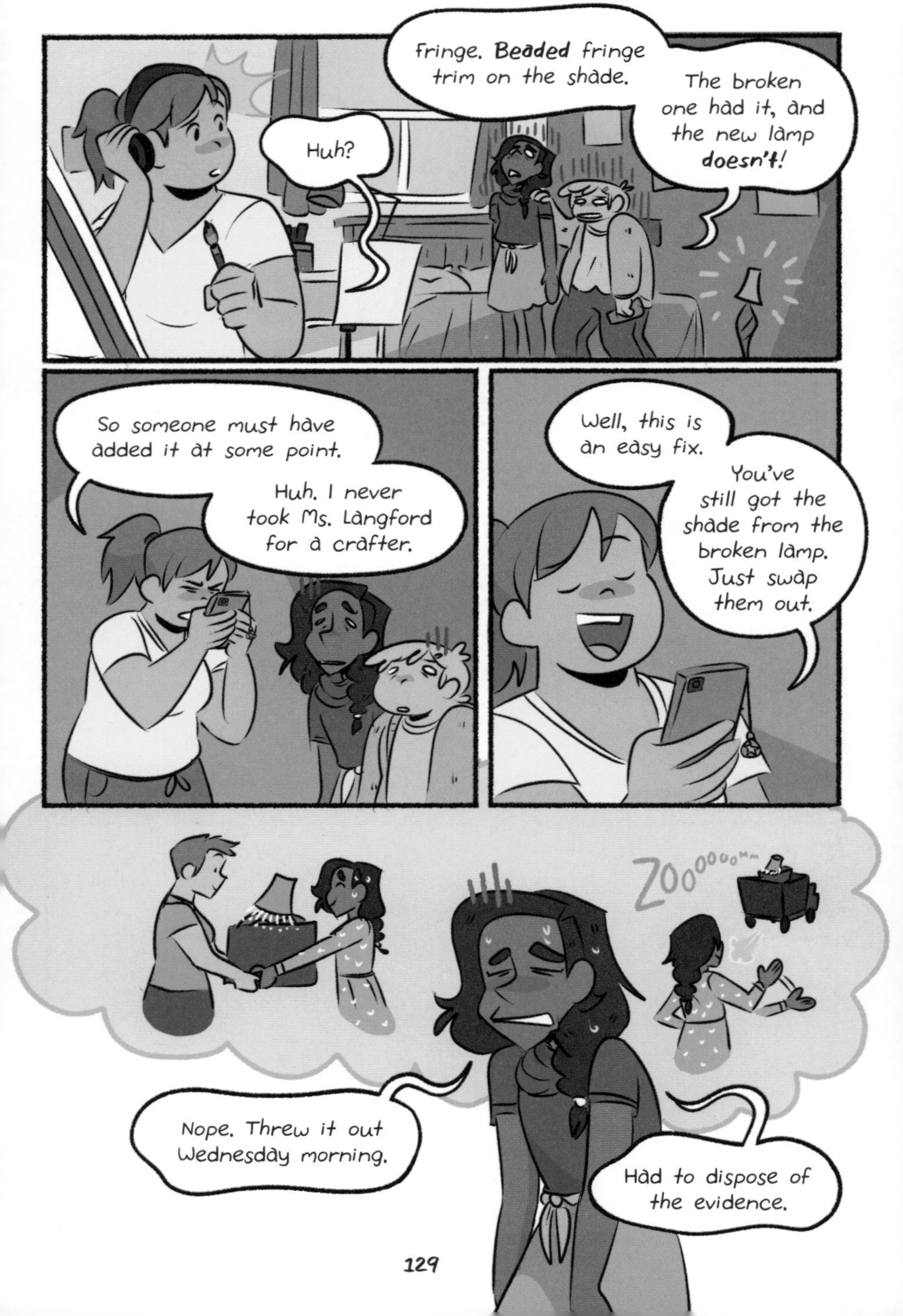
Huh?
Fringe. **Beaded** fringe trim on the shade.
The broken one had it, and the new lamp **doesn't**!
So someone must have added it at some point.
Huh. I never took Ms. Langford for a crafter.
Well, this is an easy fix.
You've still got the shade from the broken lamp. Just swap them out.
ZOOOOOOMM
Nope. Threw it out Wednesday morning.
Had to dispose of the evidence.

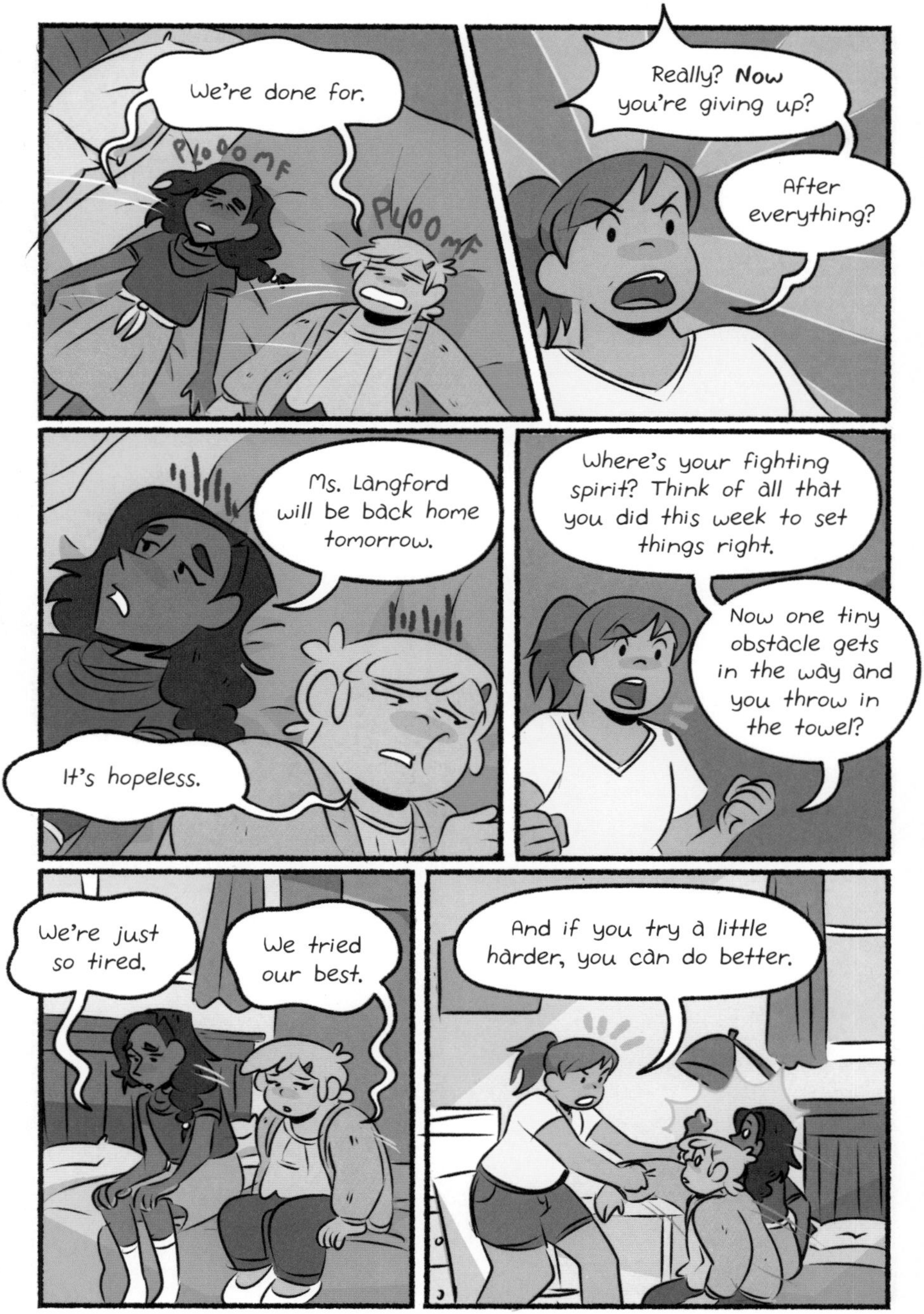
We're done for.
PLOOOMF
PLOOOMF
Really? **Now** you're giving up?
After everything?
Ms. Langford will be back home tomorrow.
It's hopeless.
Where's your fighting spirit? Think of all that you did this week to set things right.
Now one tiny obstacle gets in the way and you throw in the towel?
We're just so tired.
We tried our best.
And if you try a little harder, you can do better.

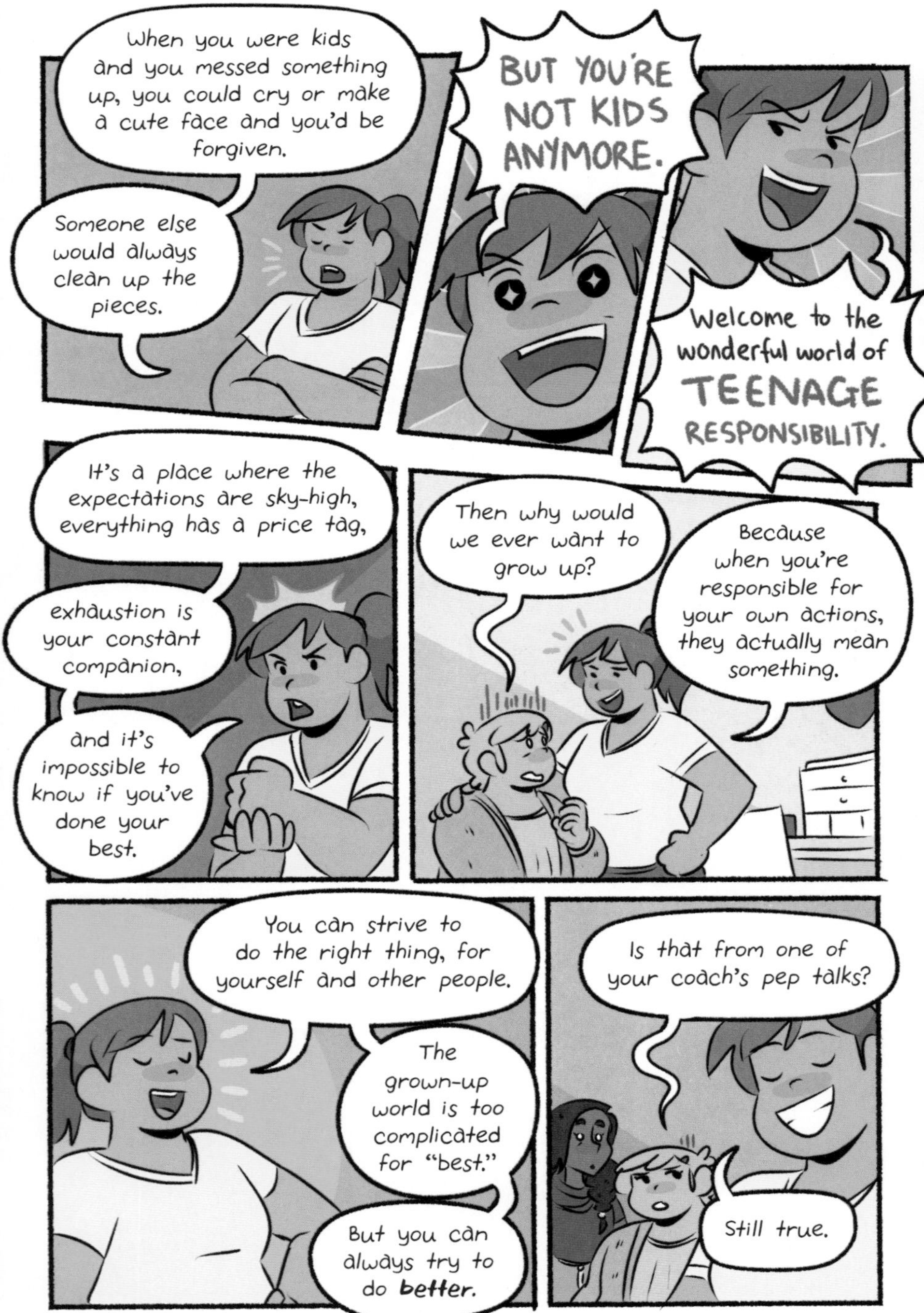

When you were kids and you messed something up, you could cry or make a cute face and you'd be forgiven.
Someone else would always clean up the pieces.
BUT YOU'RE NOT KIDS ANYMORE.
Welcome to the wonderful world of TEENAGE RESPONSIBILITY.
It's a place where the expectations are sky-high, everything has a price tag,
exhaustion is your constant companion,
and it's impossible to know if you've done your best.
Then why would we ever want to grow up?
Because when you're responsible for your own actions, they actually mean something.
You can strive to do the right thing, for yourself and other people.
The grown-up world is too complicated for "best."
But you can always try to do **better**.
Is that from one of your coach's pep talks?
Still true.

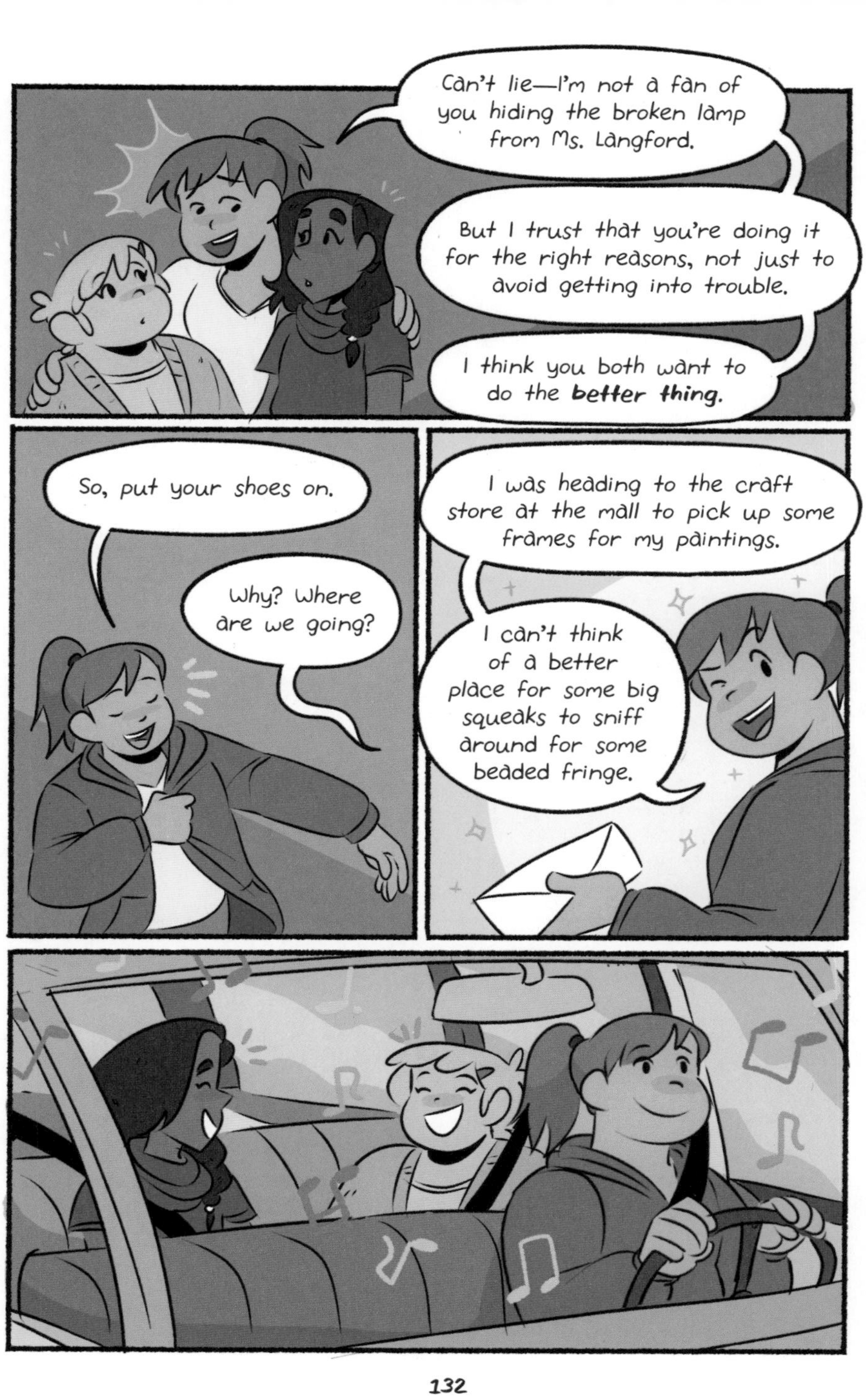
Can't lie—I'm not a fan of you hiding the broken lamp from Ms. Langford.
But I trust that you're doing it for the right reasons, not just to avoid getting into trouble.
I think you both want to do the **better thing**.
So, put your shoes on.
Why? Where are we going?
I was heading to the craft store at the mall to pick up some frames for my paintings.
I can't think of a better place for some big squeaks to sniff around for some beaded fringe.

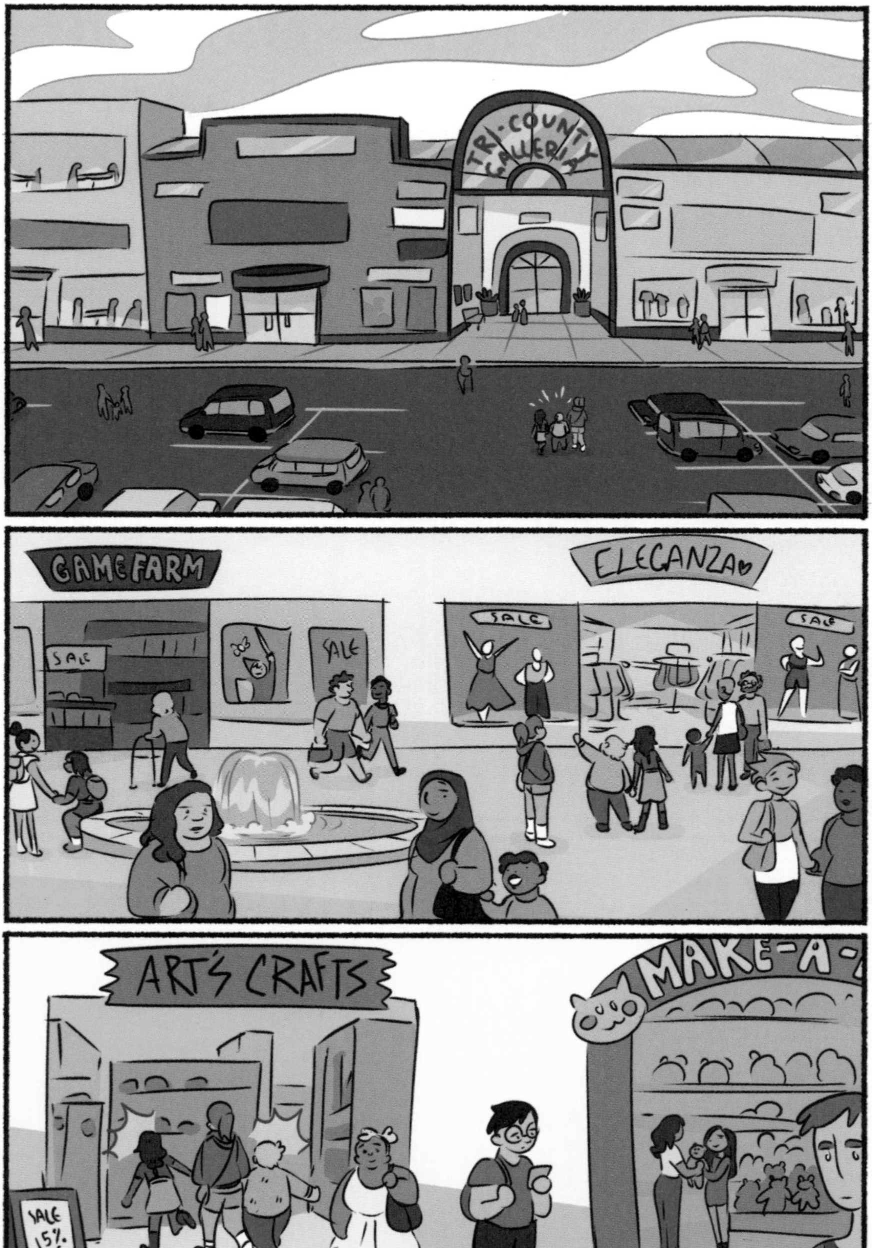

TRI-COUNTY GALLERIA
GAME FARM
SALE
SALE
ELEGANZA
SALE
SALE
ART'S CRAFTS
MAKE-A-
SALE 15% off

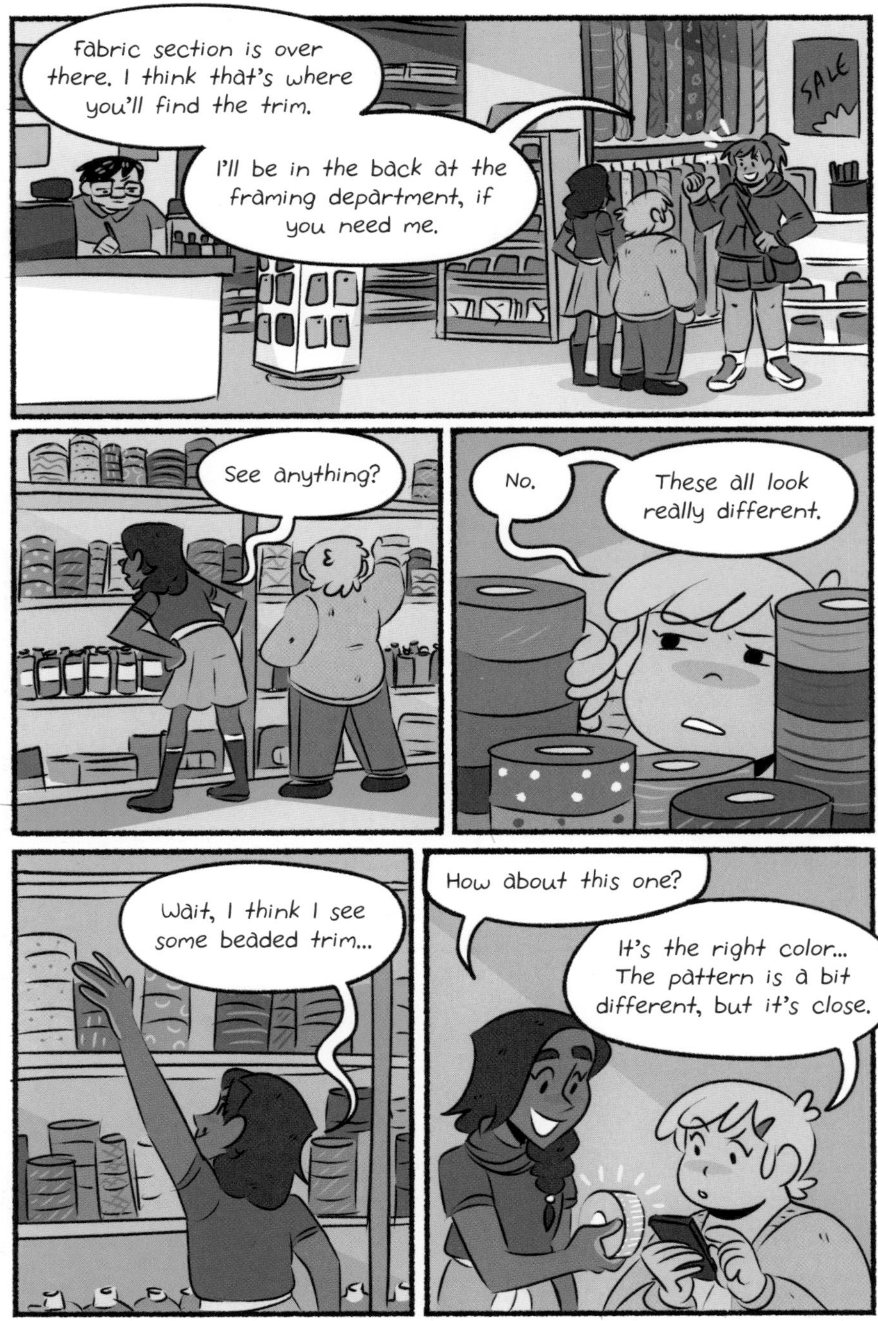
Fabric section is over there. I think that's where you'll find the trim.
I'll be in the back at the framing department, if you need me.
SALE
See anything?
No.
These all look really different.
Wait, I think I see some beaded trim...
How about this one?
It's the right color... The pattern is a bit different, but it's close.

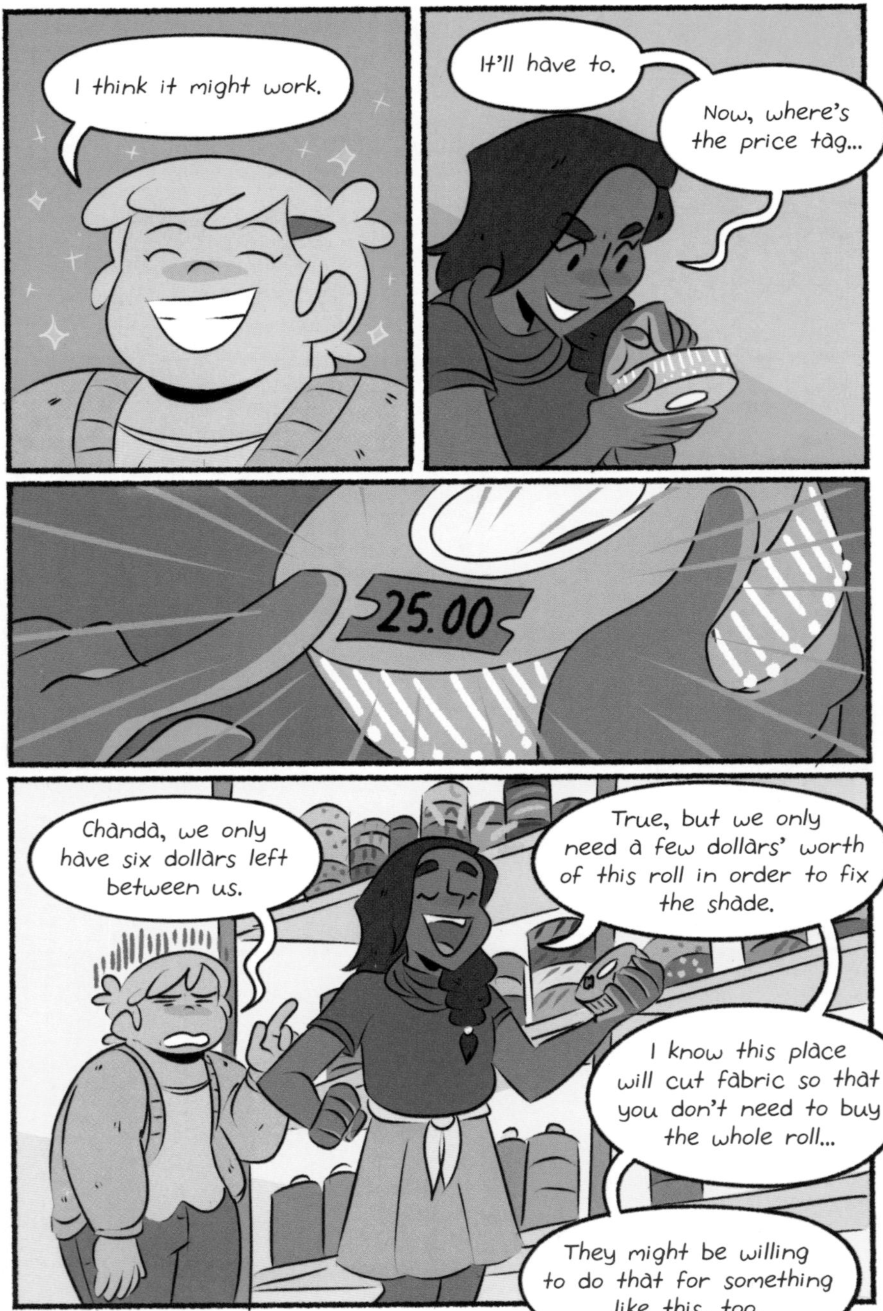
I think it might work.
It'll have to.
Now, where's the price tag...
25.00
Chanda, we only have six dollars left between us.
True, but we only need a few dollars' worth of this roll in order to fix the shade.
I know this place will cut fabric so that you don't need to buy the whole roll...
They might be willing to do that for something like this, too.

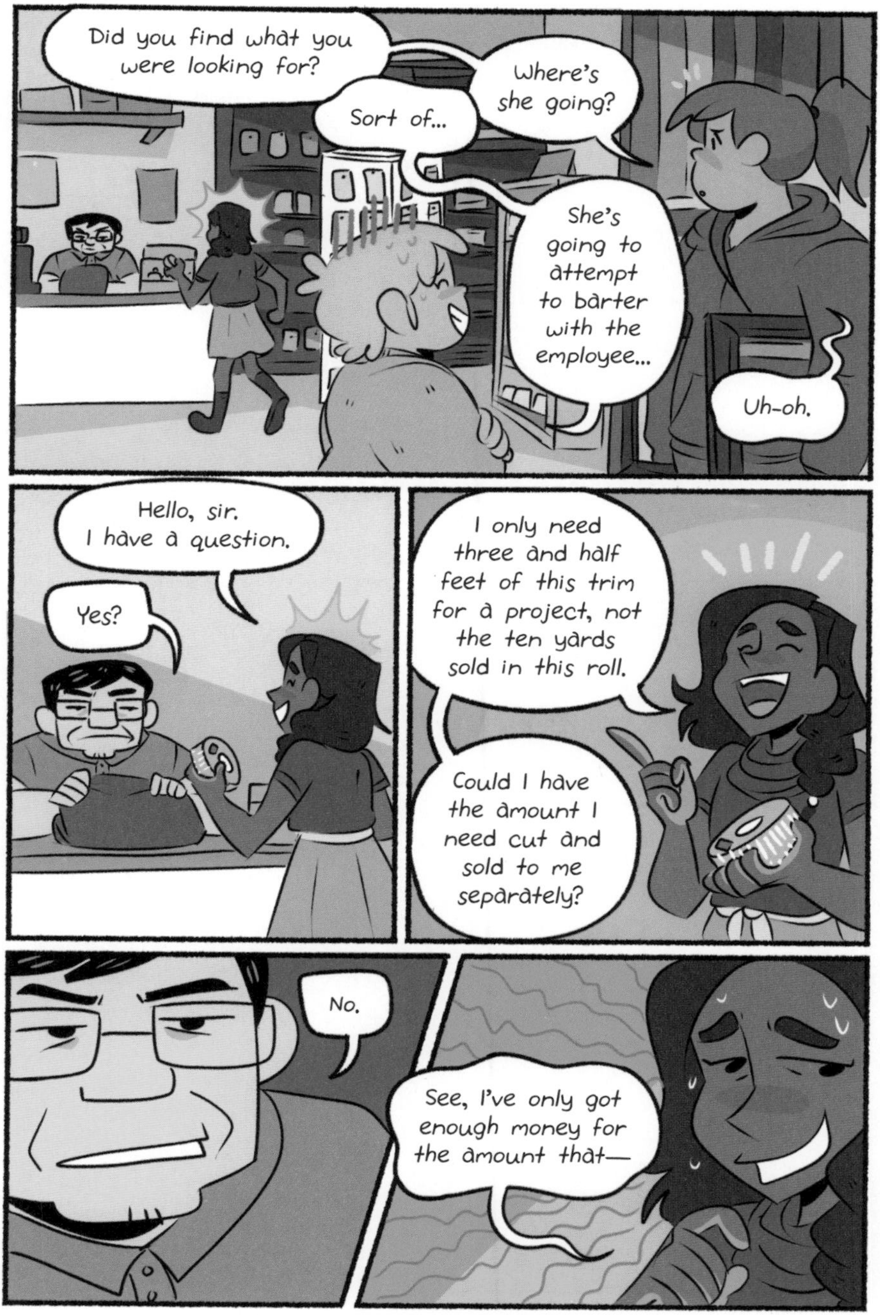
Did you find what you were looking for?
Sort of...
Where's she going?
She's going to attempt to barter with the employee...
Uh-oh.
Hello, sir. I have a question.
Yes?
I only need three and half feet of this trim for a project, not the ten yards sold in this roll.
Could I have the amount I need cut and sold to me separately?
No.
See, I've only got enough money for the amount that—

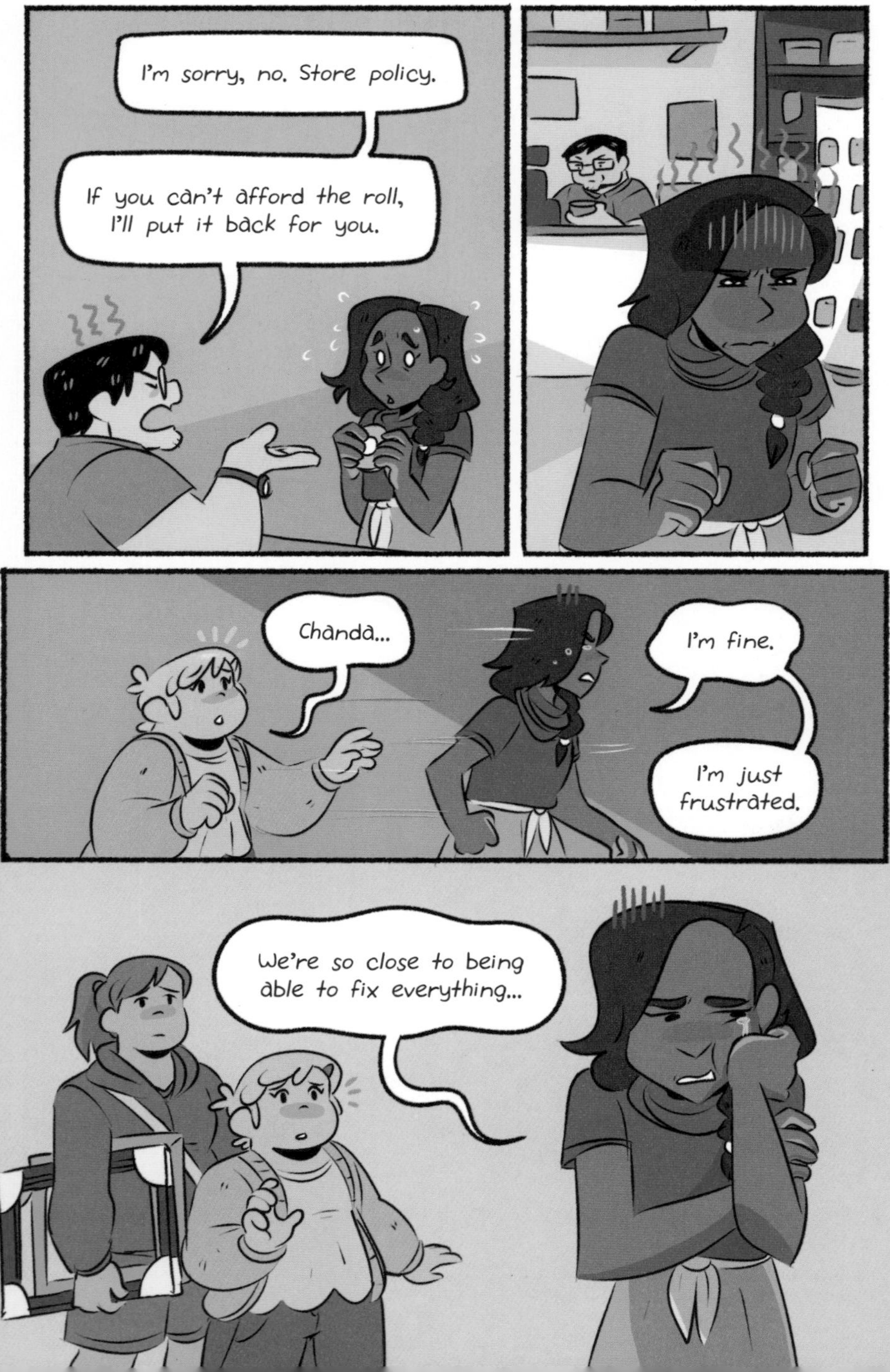
I'm sorry, no. Store policy.
If you can't afford the roll, I'll put it back for you.
Chanda...
I'm fine.
I'm just frustrated.
We're so close to being able to fix everything...

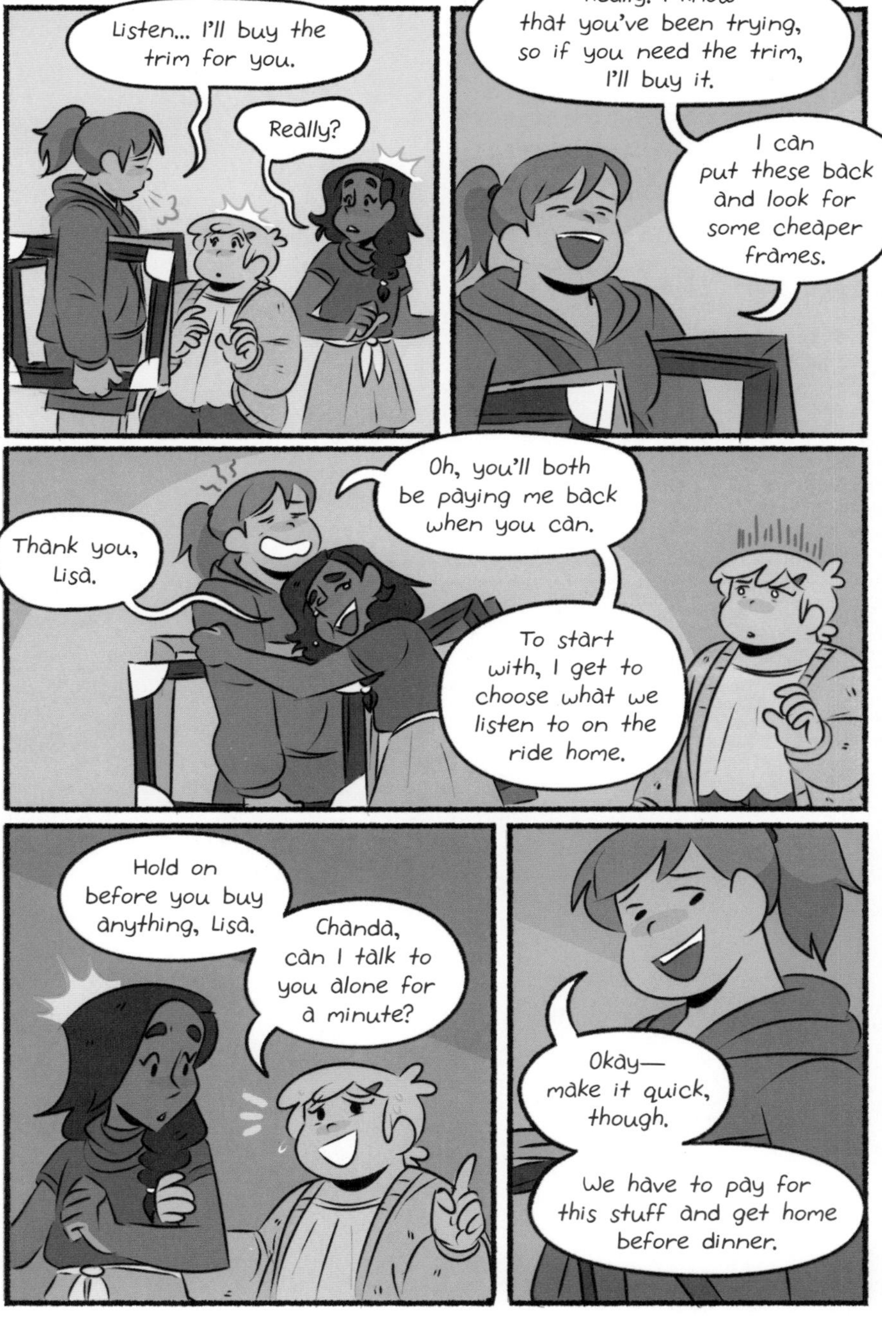
Listen... I'll buy the trim for you.
Really?
Really. I know that you've been trying, so if you need the trim, I'll buy it.
I can put these back and look for some cheaper frames.
Thank you, Lisa.
Oh, you'll both be paying me back when you can.
To start with, I get to choose what we listen to on the ride home.
Hold on before you buy anything, Lisa.
Chanda, can I talk to you alone for a minute?
Okay— make it quick, though.
We have to pay for this stuff and get home before dinner.

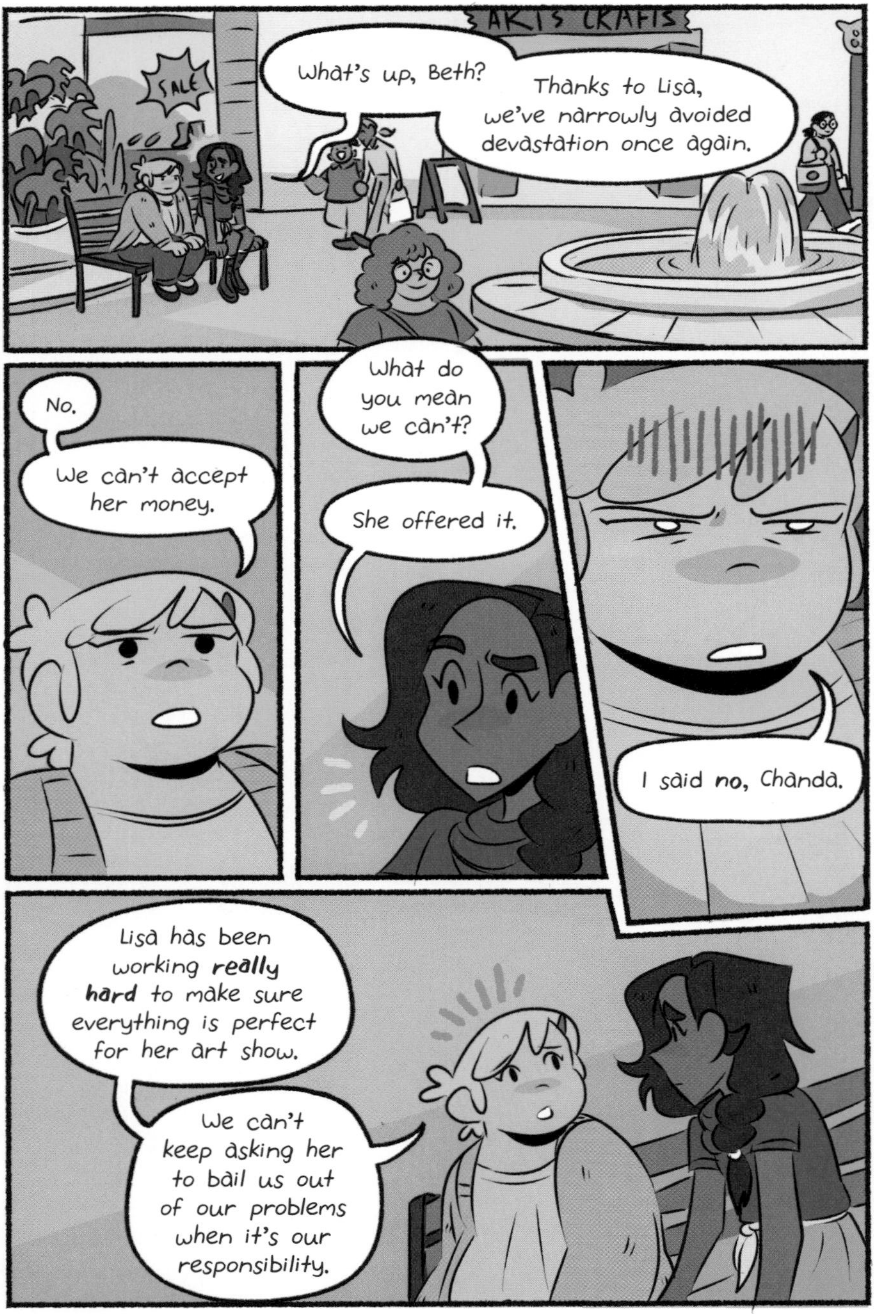
ART'S CRAFTS
SALE
What's up, Beth?
Thanks to Lisa, we've narrowly avoided devastation once again.
No.
We can't accept her money.
What do you mean we can't?
She offered it.
I said **no**, Chanda.
Lisa has been working **really hard** to make sure everything is perfect for her art show.
We can't keep asking her to bail us out of our problems when it's our responsibility.

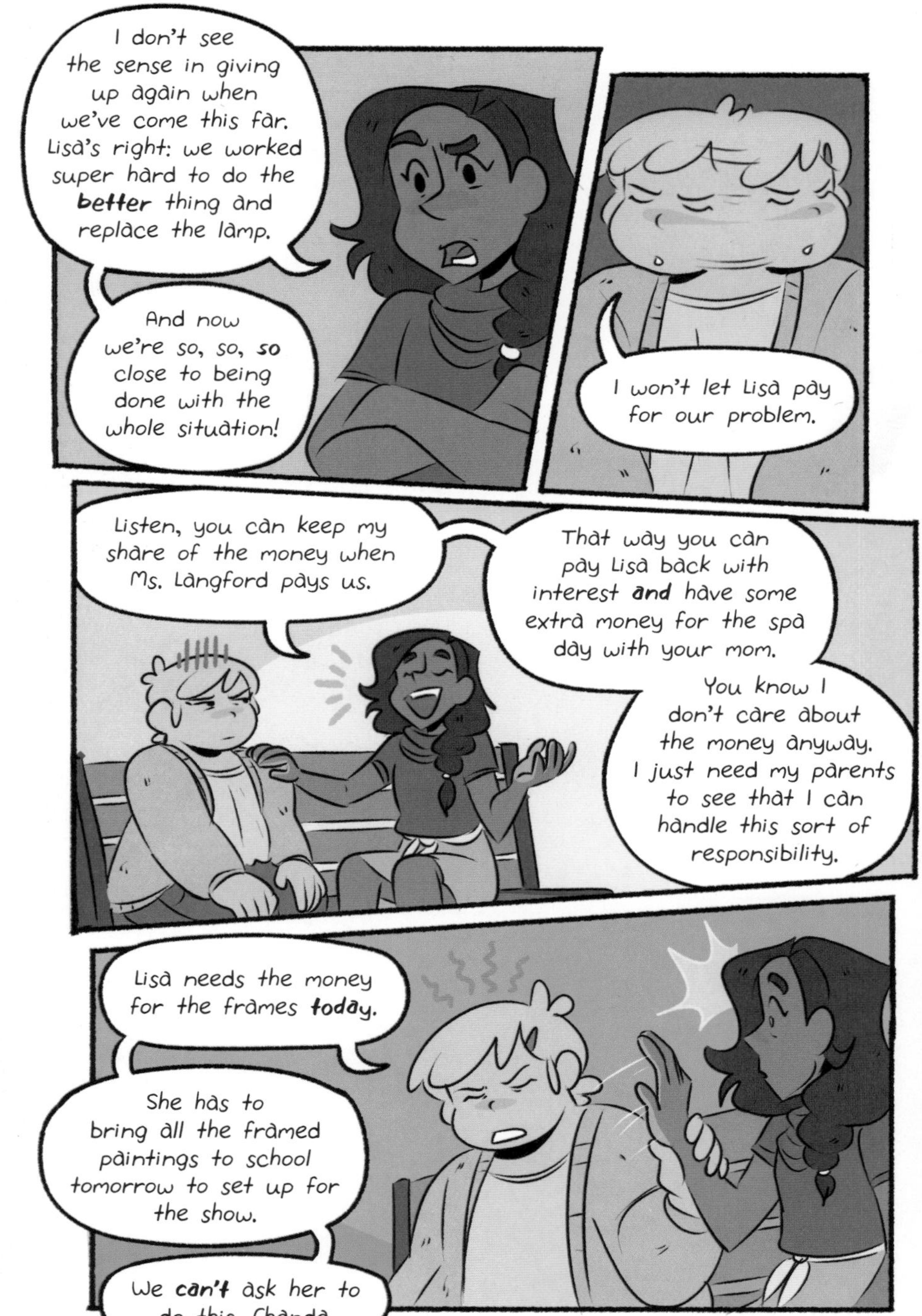
I don't see the sense in giving up again when we've come this far. Lisa's right: we worked super hard to do the **better** thing and replace the lamp.
And now we're so, so, **so** close to being done with the whole situation!
I won't let Lisa pay for our problem.
Listen, you can keep my share of the money when Ms. Langford pays us.
That way you can pay Lisa back with interest **and** have some extra money for the spa day with your mom.
You know I don't care about the money anyway. I just need my parents to see that I can handle this sort of responsibility.
Lisa needs the money for the frames **today**.
She has to bring all the framed paintings to school tomorrow to set up for the show.
We **can't** ask her to do this, Chanda.

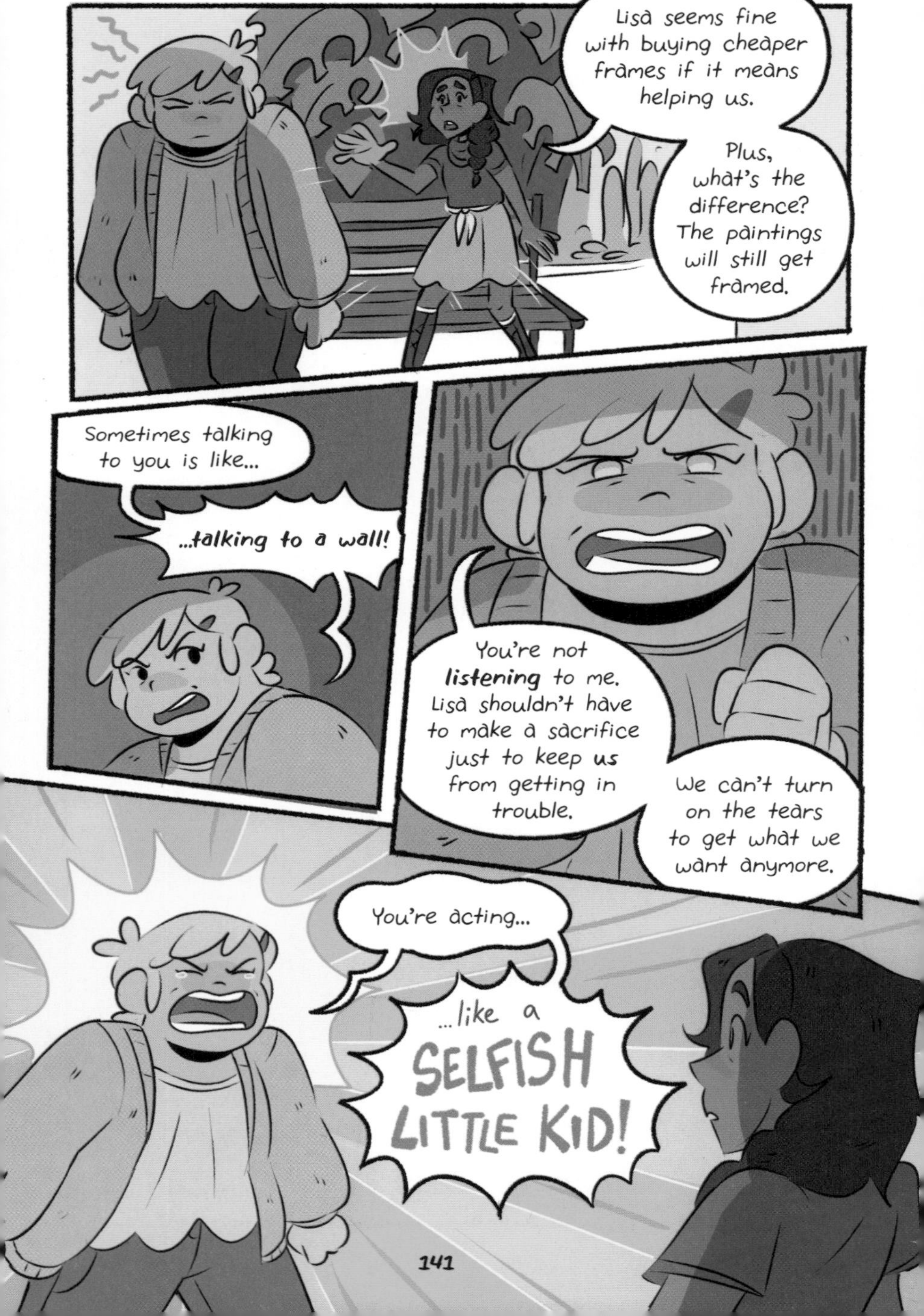

Lisa seems fine with buying cheaper frames if it means helping us.
Plus, what's the difference? The paintings will still get framed.
Sometimes talking to you is like...
...**talking to a wall!**
You're not **listening** to me. Lisa shouldn't have to make a sacrifice just to keep **us** from getting in trouble.
We can't turn on the tears to get what we want anymore.
You're acting...
...like a SELFISH LITTLE KID!

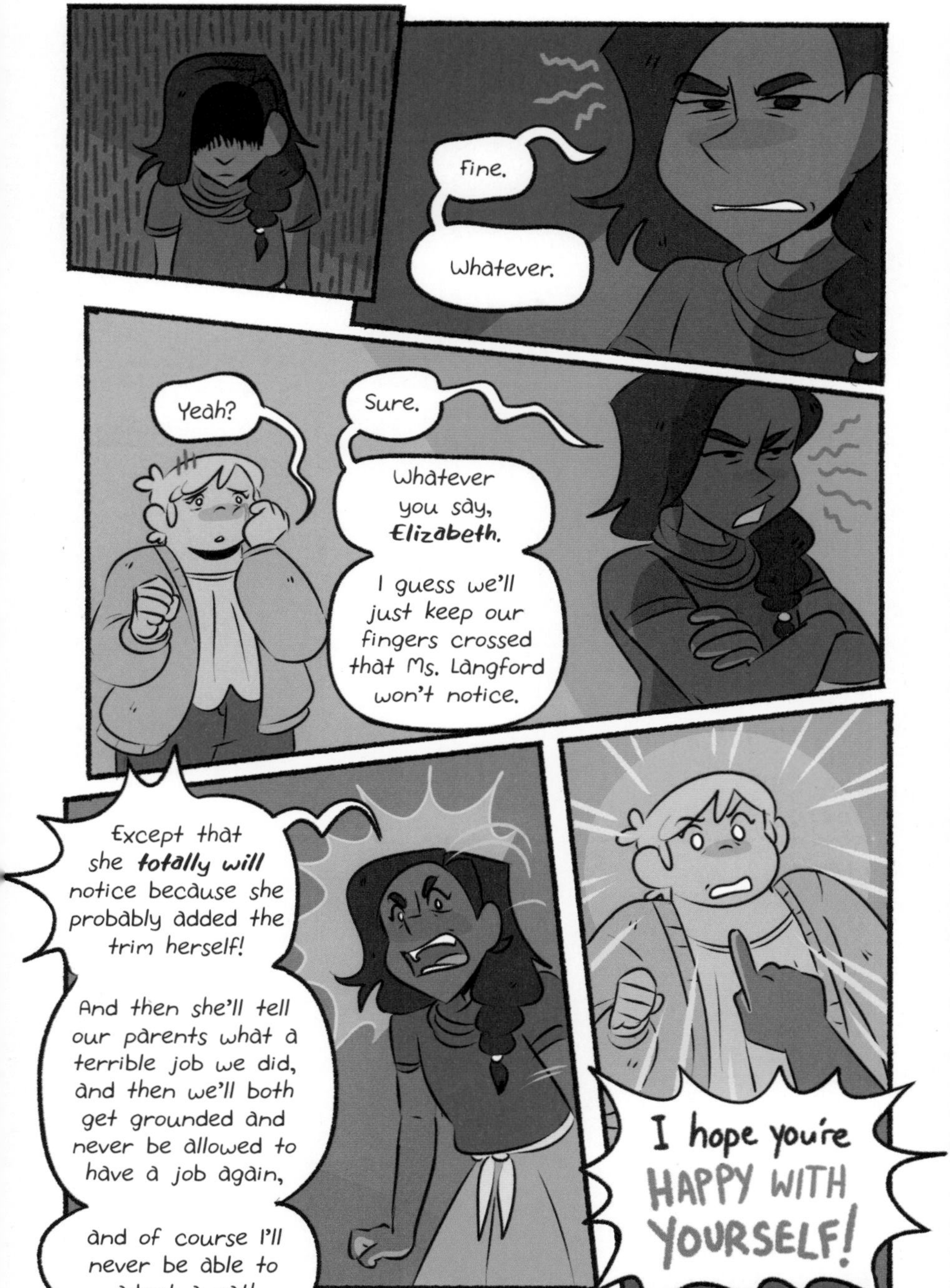
Fine.
Whatever.
Yeah?
Sure.
Whatever you say, **Elizabeth.**
I guess we'll just keep our fingers crossed that Ms. Langford won't notice.
Except that she **totally will** notice because she probably added the trim herself!
And then she'll tell our parents what a terrible job we did, and then we'll both get grounded and never be allowed to have a job again,
and of course I'll never be able to adopt a cat!
I hope you're HAPPY WITH YOURSELF!

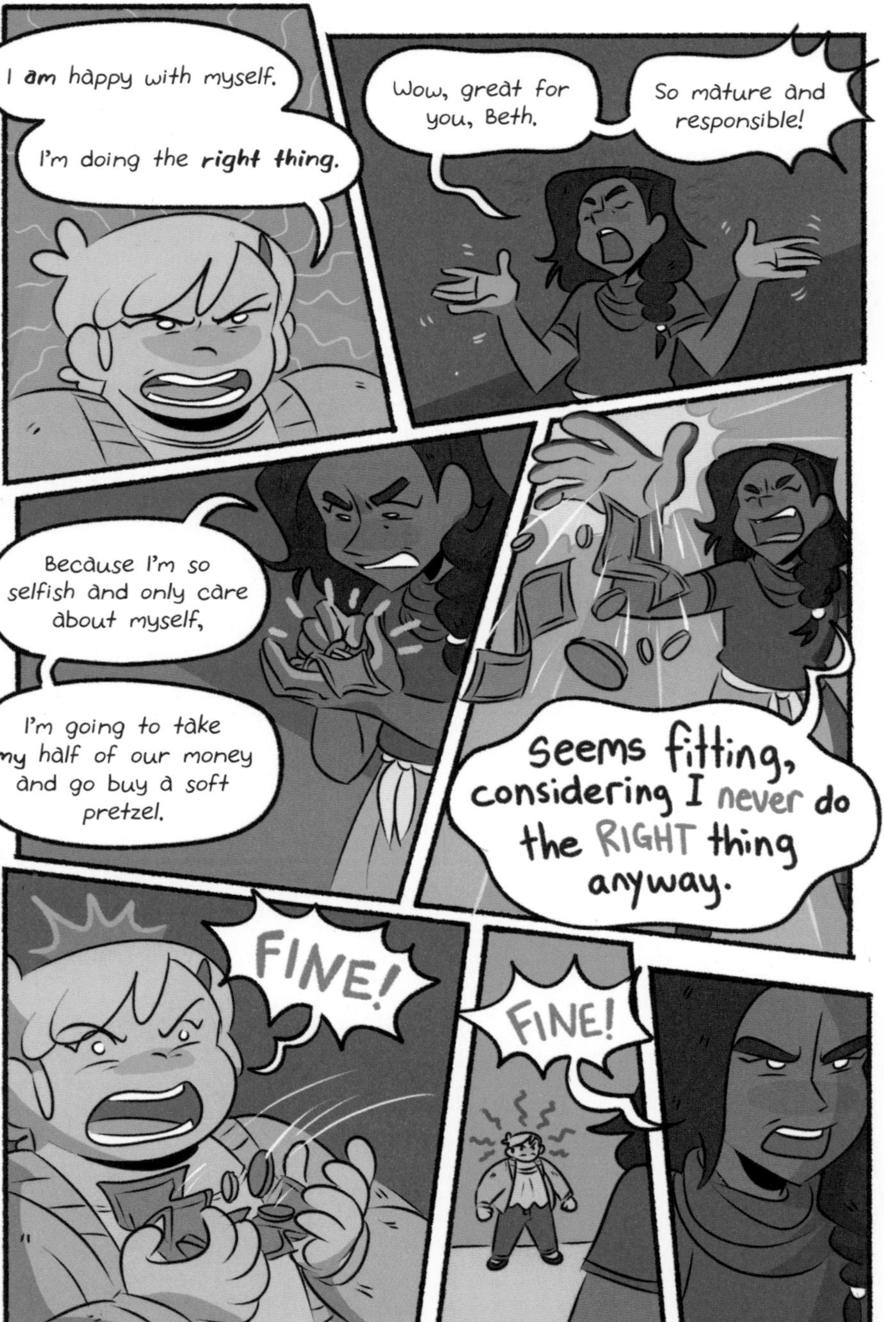
I **am** happy with myself.
I'm doing the **right thing.**
Wow, great for you, Beth.
So mature and responsible!
Because I'm so selfish and only care about myself,
I'm going to take my half of our money and go buy a soft pretzel.
Seems fitting, considering I never do the RIGHT thing anyway.
FINE!
FINE!

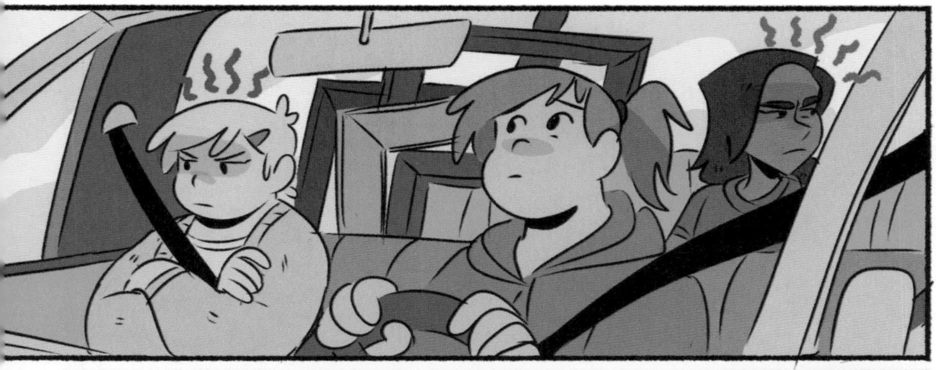
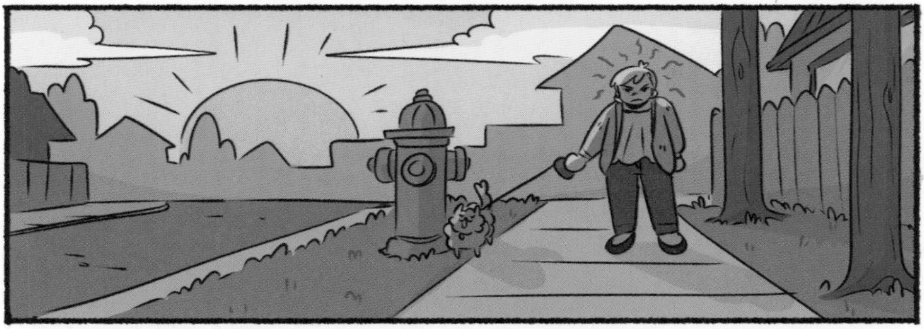
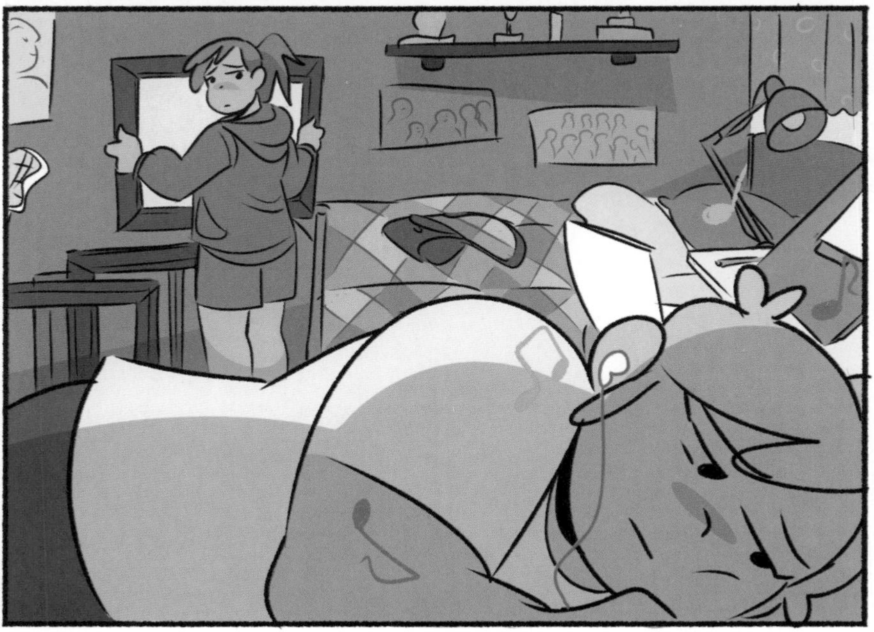

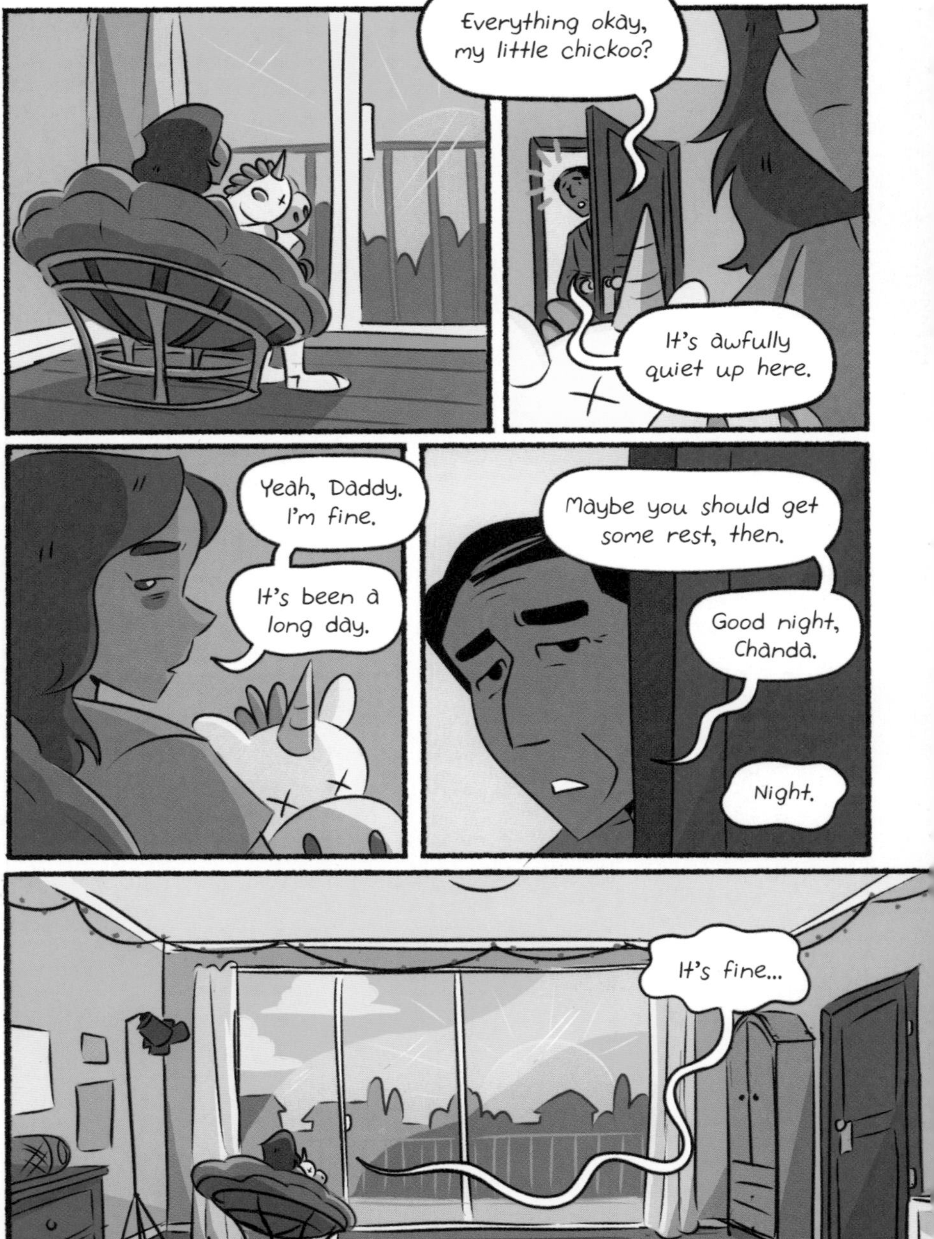
Everything okay, my little chickoo?
It's awfully quiet up here.
Yeah, Daddy. I'm fine.
It's been a long day.
Maybe you should get some rest, then.
Good night, Chanda.
Night.
It's fine...

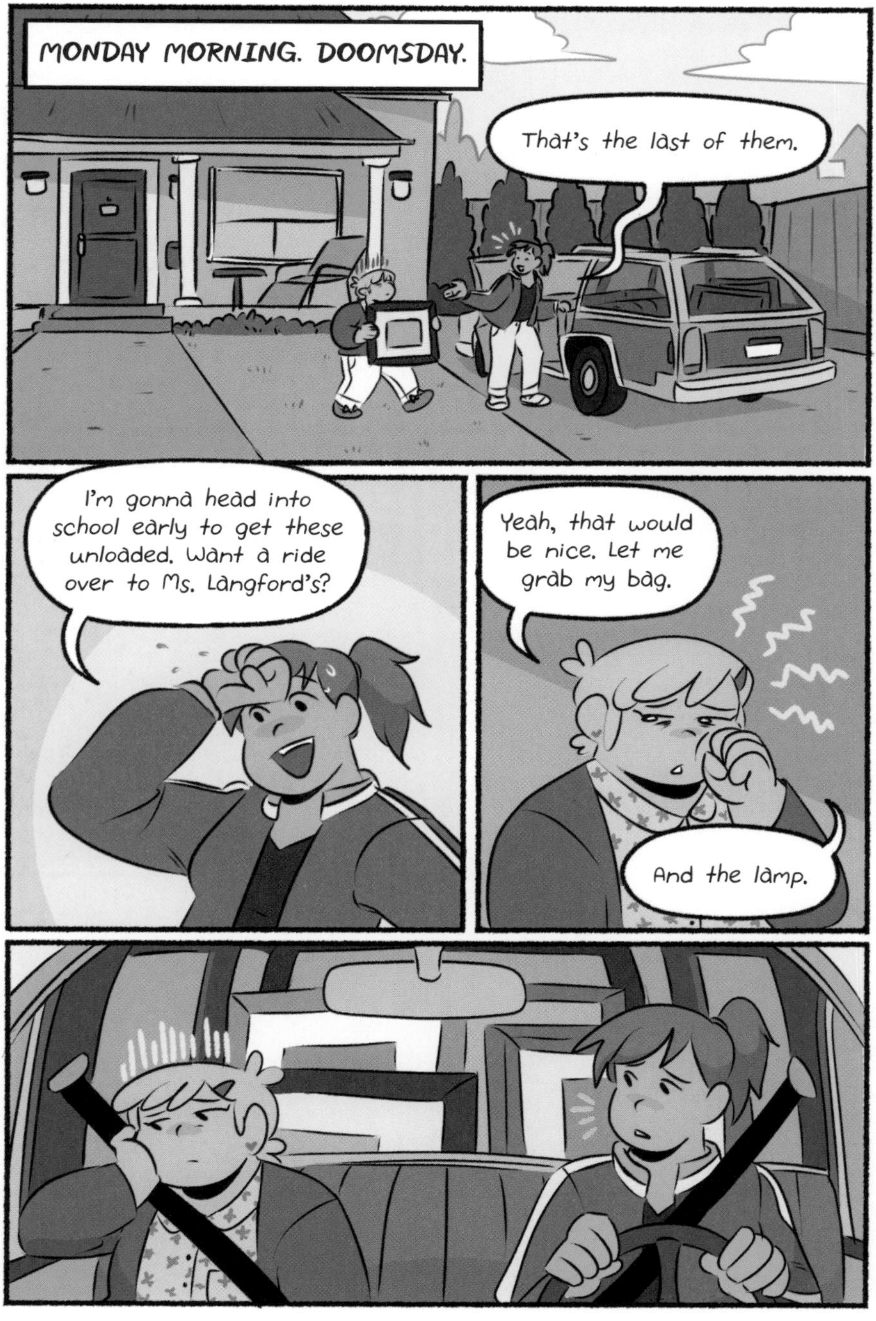
MONDAY MORNING. DOOMSDAY.
That's the last of them.
I'm gonna head into school early to get these unloaded. Want a ride over to Ms. Langford's?
Yeah, that would be nice. Let me grab my bag.
And the lamp.

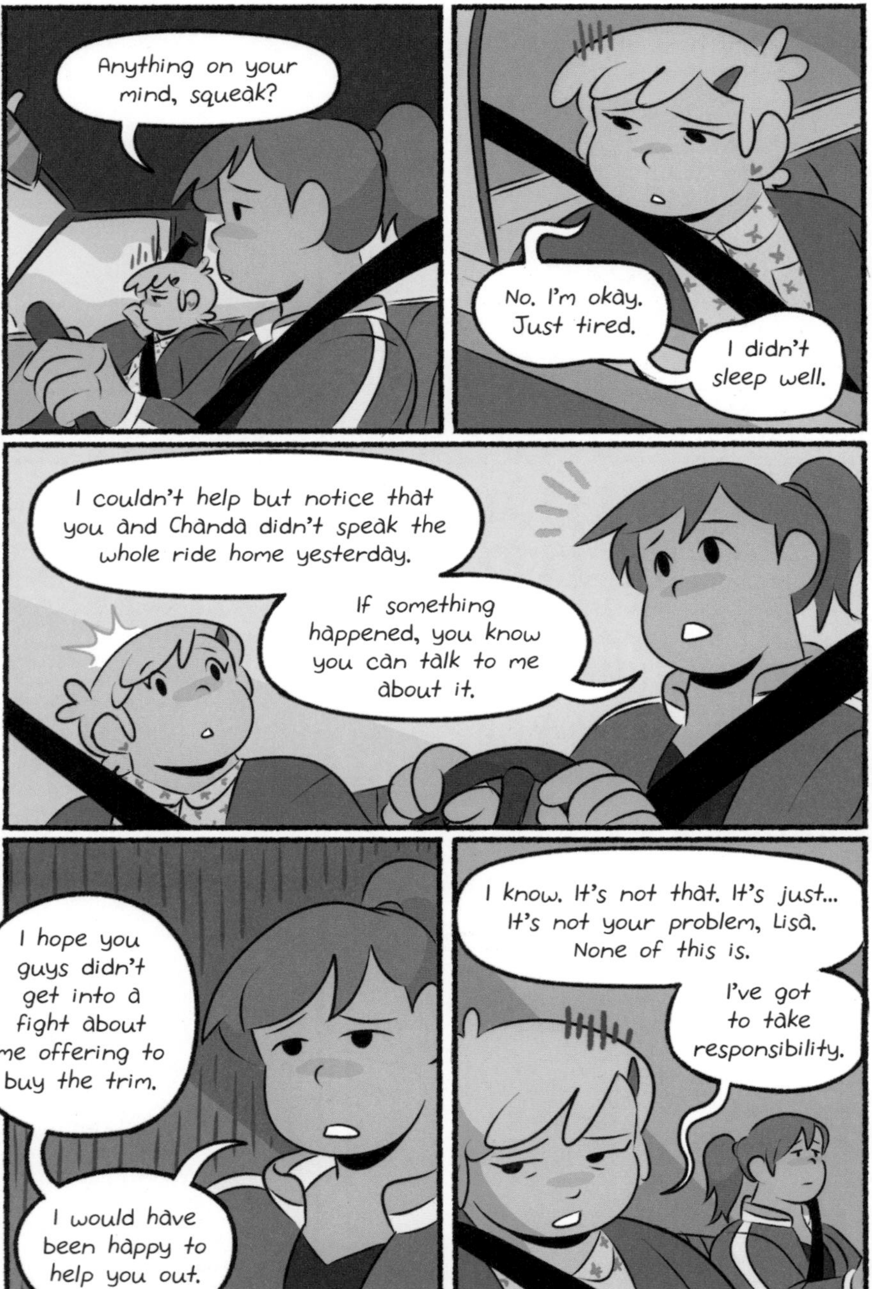
Anything on your mind, squeak?
No. I'm okay. Just tired.
I didn't sleep well.
I couldn't help but notice that you and Chanda didn't speak the whole ride home yesterday.
If something happened, you know you can talk to me about it.
I hope you guys didn't get into a fight about me offering to buy the trim.
I would have been happy to help you out.
I know. It's not that. It's just... It's not your problem, Lisa. None of this is.
I've got to take responsibility.

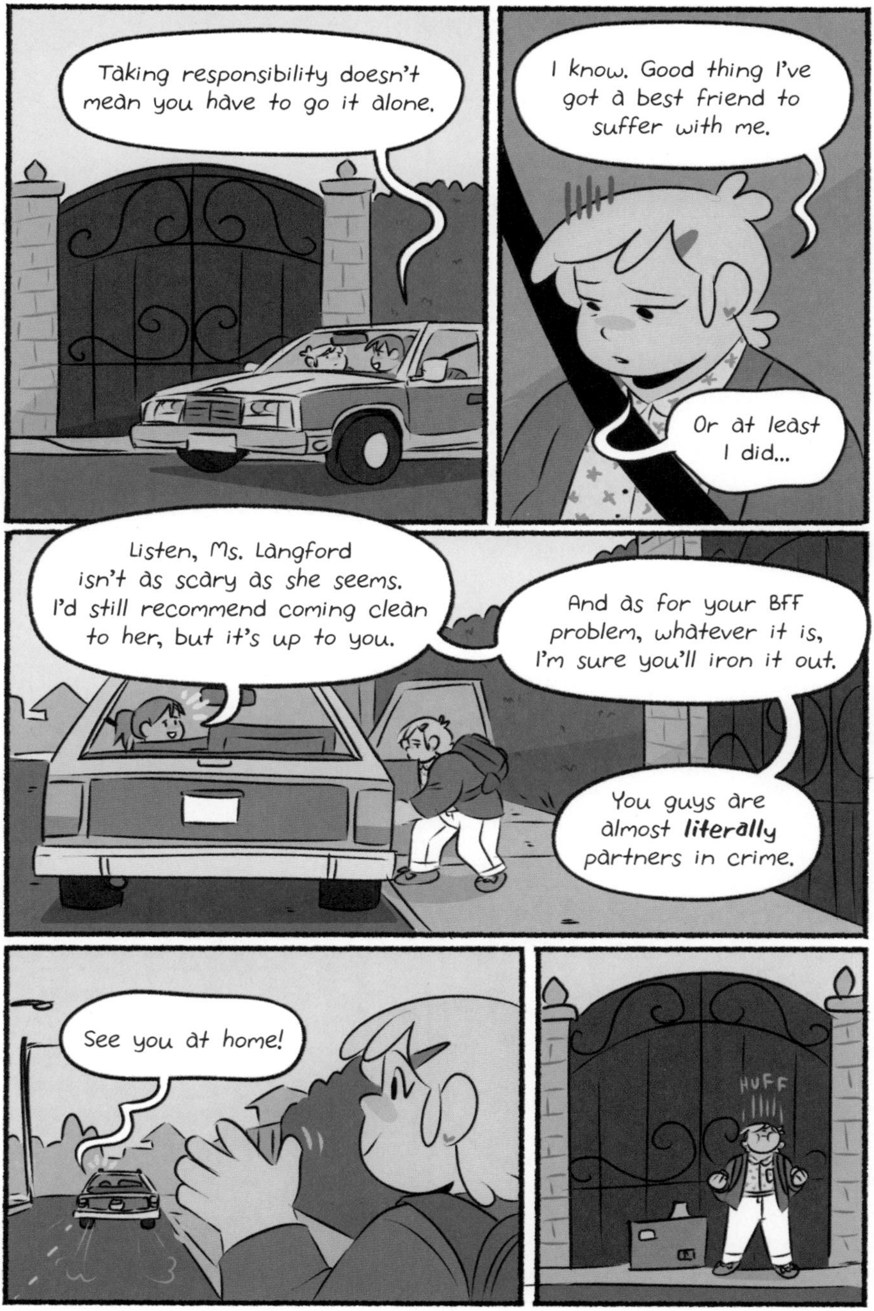
Taking responsibility doesn't mean you have to go it alone.
I know. Good thing I've got a best friend to suffer with me.
Or at least I did...
Listen, Ms. Langford isn't as scary as she seems. I'd still recommend coming clean to her, but it's up to you.
And as for your BFF problem, whatever it is, I'm sure you'll iron it out.
You guys are almost **literally** partners in crime.
See you at home!
HUFF

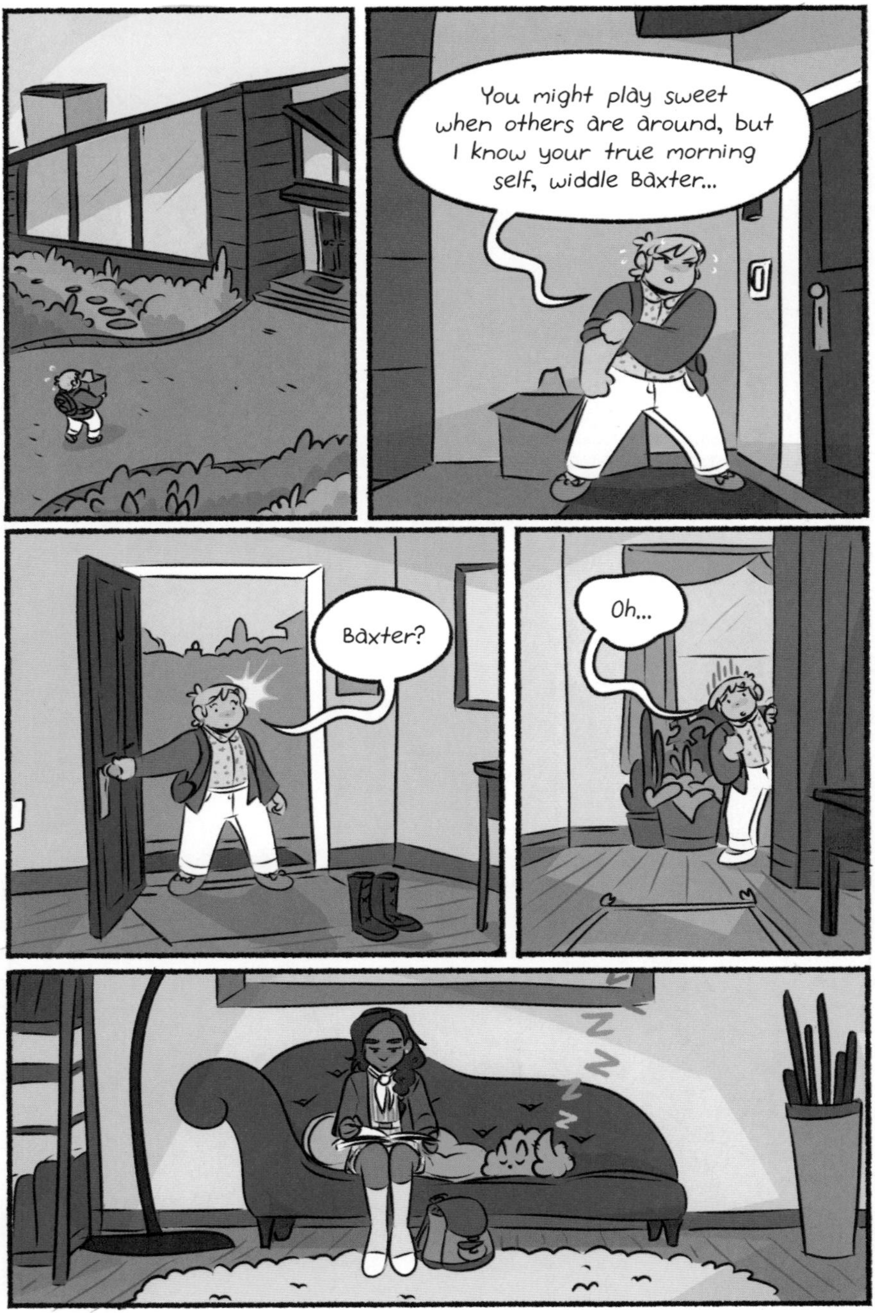
You might play sweet when others are around, but I know your true morning self, widdle Baxter...
Baxter?
Oh...

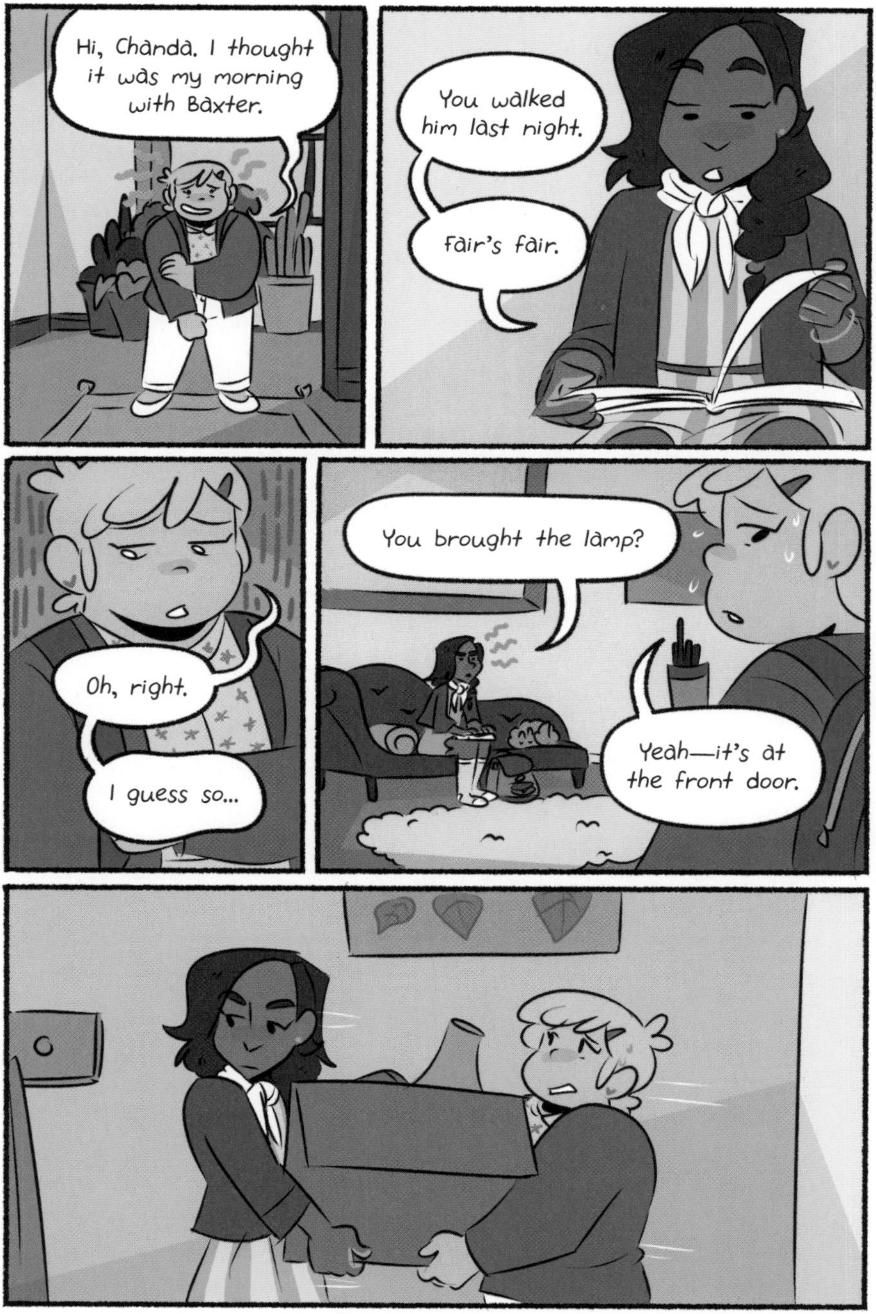
Hi, Chanda. I thought it was my morning with Baxter.
You walked him last night.
Fair's fair.
Oh, right.
I guess so...
You brought the lamp?
Yeah—it's at the front door.

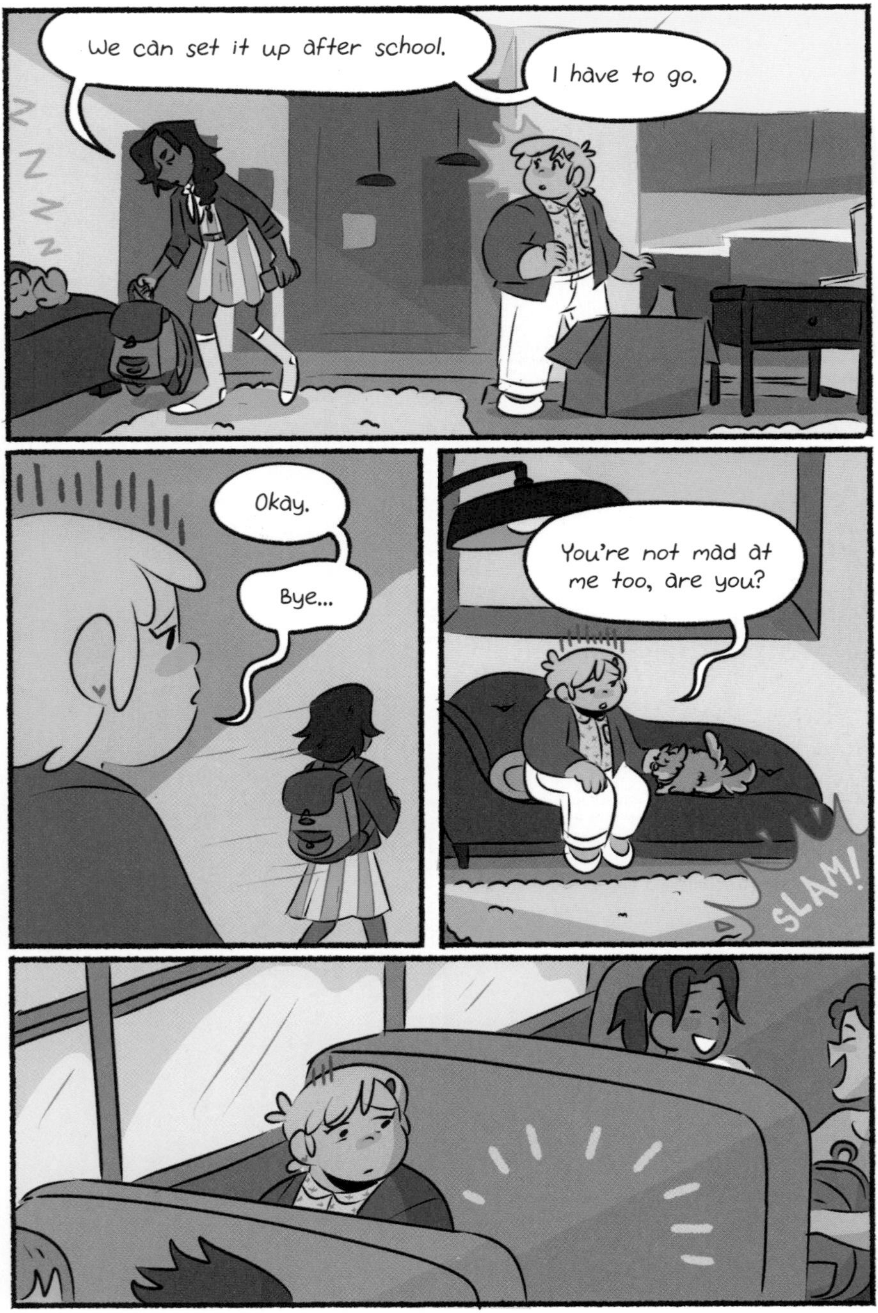

We can set it up after school.
I have to go.
Okay.
Bye...
You're not mad at me too, are you?
SLAM!

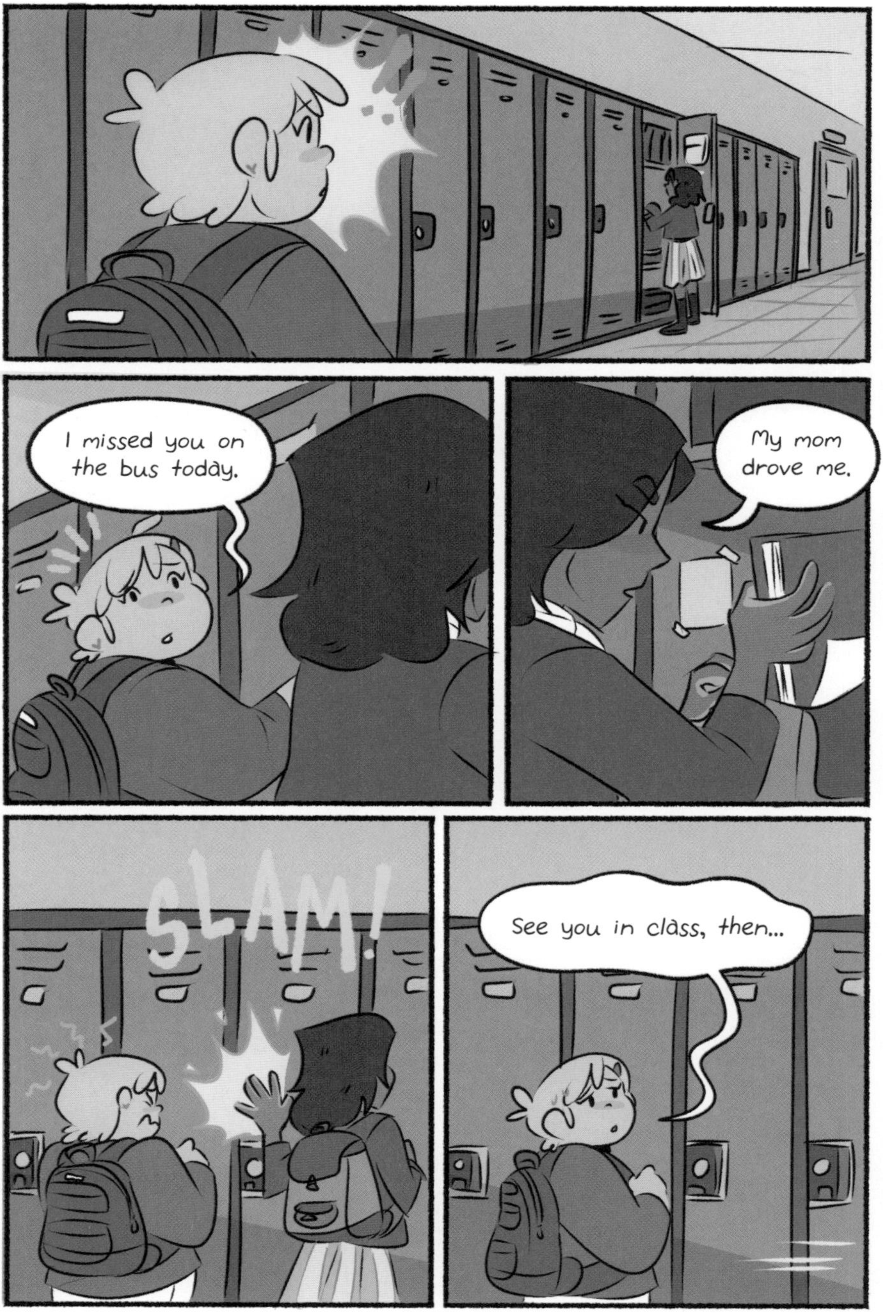
I missed you on the bus today.
My mom drove me.
SLAM!
See you in class, then...

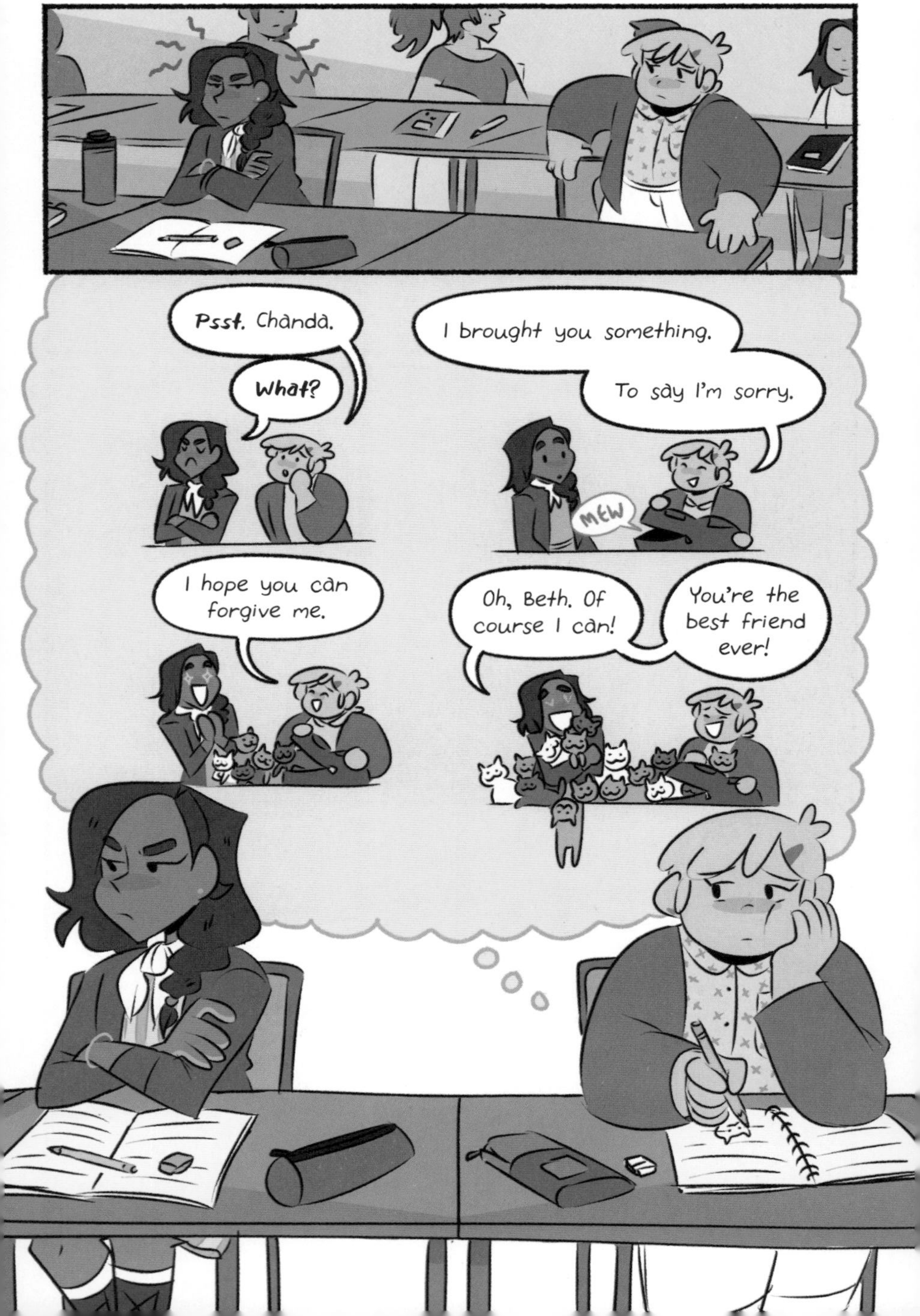

Psst. Chanda.
What?
I brought you something.
To say I'm sorry.
MEW
I hope you can forgive me.
Oh, Beth. Of course I can!
You're the best friend ever!

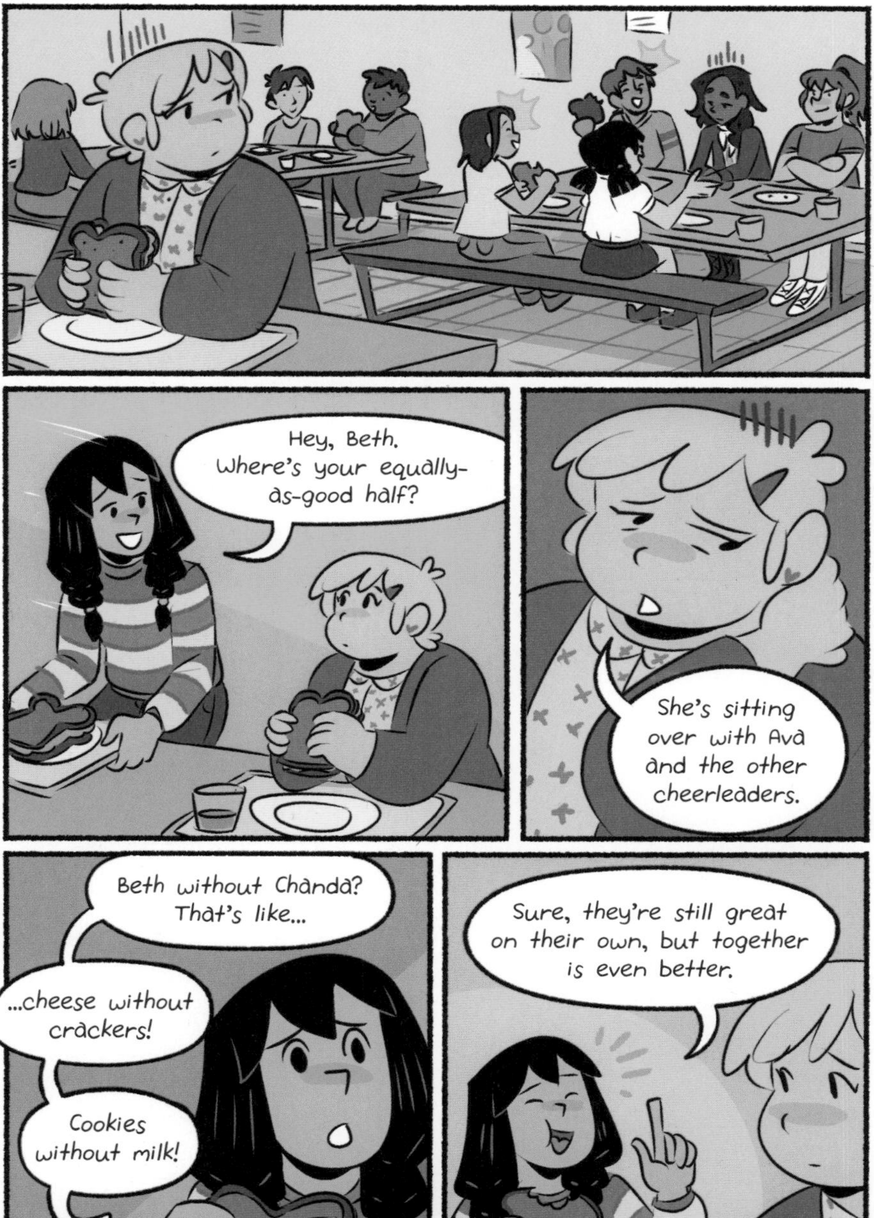
Hey, Beth.
Where's your equally-as-good half?
She's sitting over with Ava and the other cheerleaders.
Beth without Chanda? That's like...
...cheese without crackers!
Cookies without milk!
Sure, they're still great on their own, but together is even better.

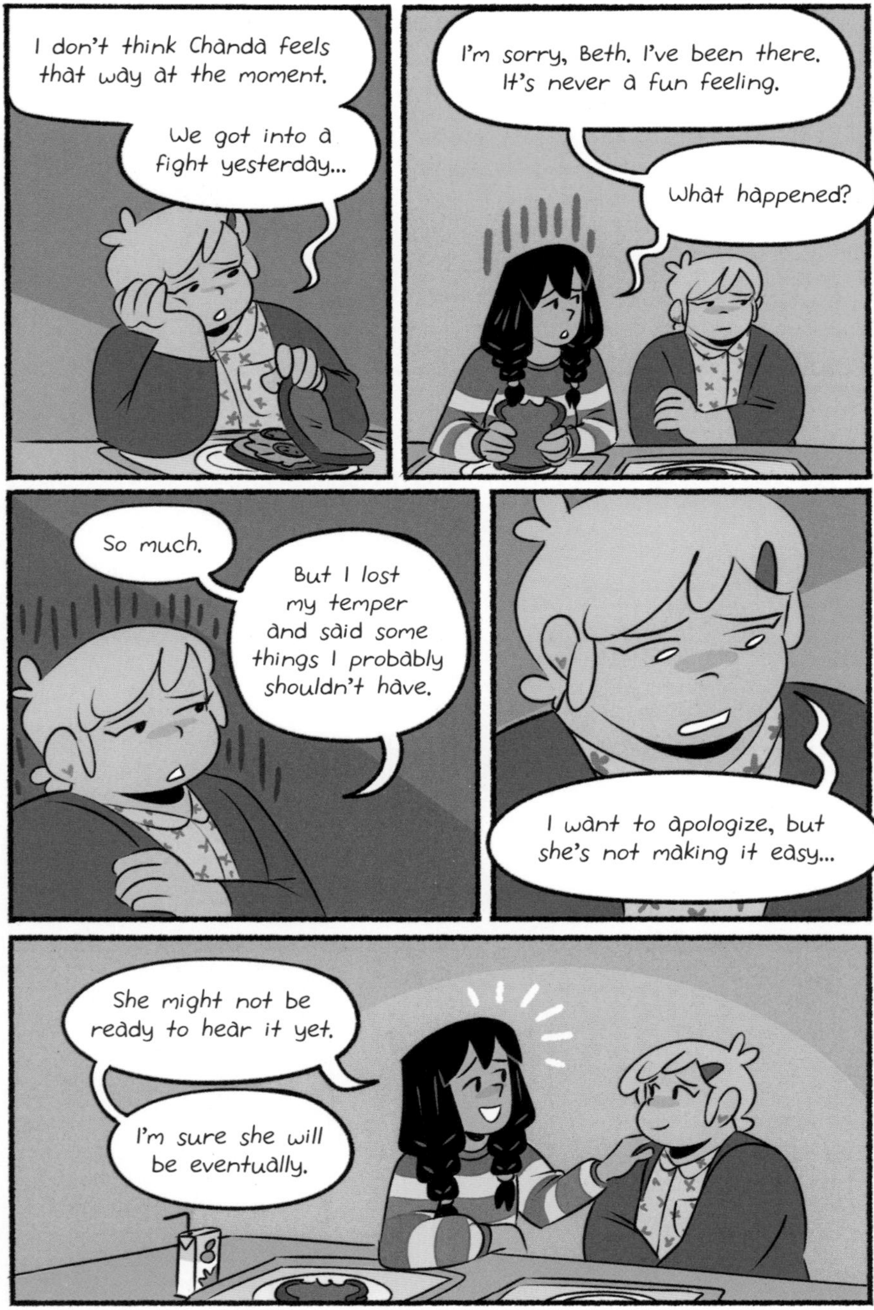
I don't think Chanda feels that way at the moment.
We got into a fight yesterday...
I'm sorry, Beth. I've been there. It's never a fun feeling.
What happened?
So much.
But I lost my temper and said some things I probably shouldn't have.
I want to apologize, but she's not making it easy...
She might not be ready to hear it yet.
I'm sure she will be eventually.

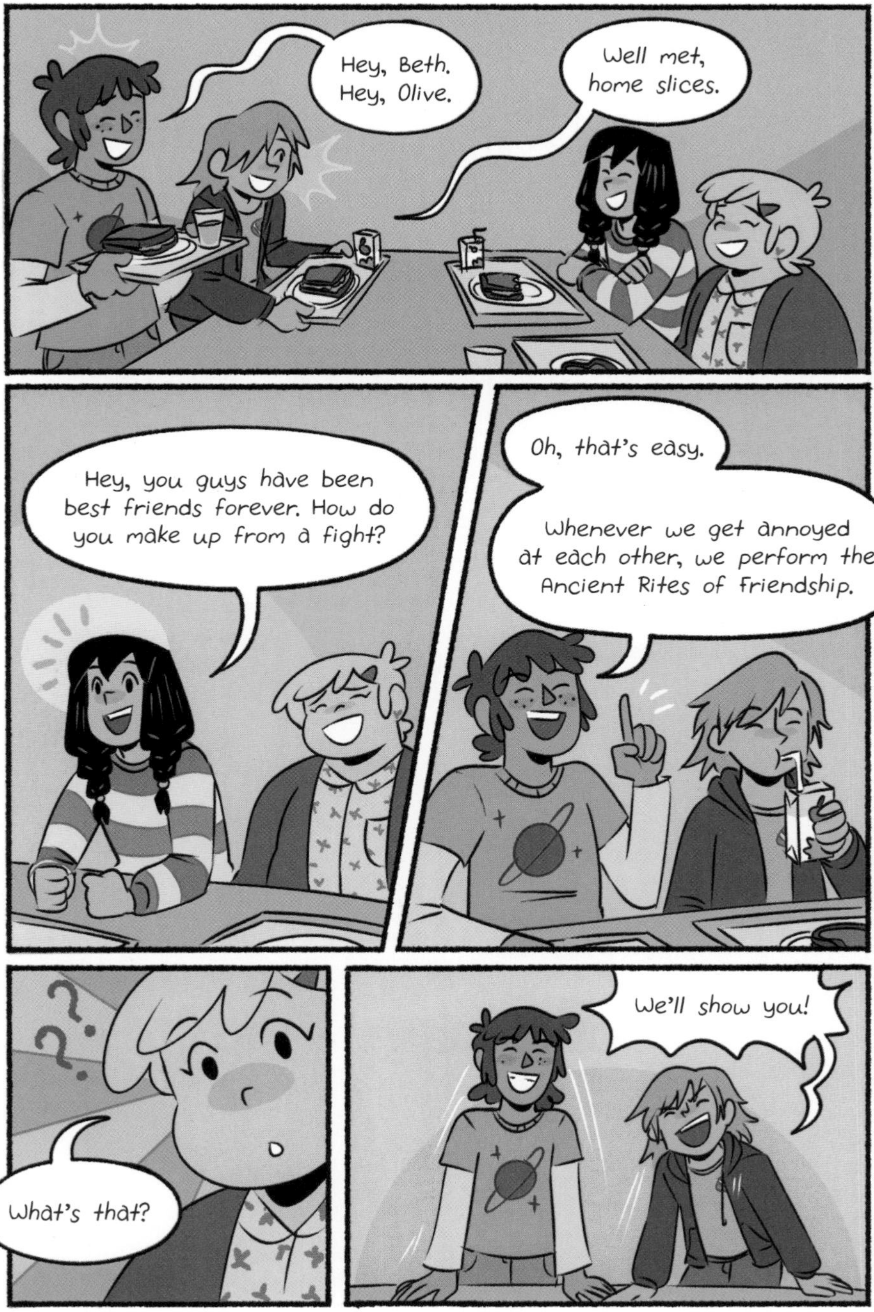
Hey, Beth.
Hey, Olive.
Well met, home slices.
Hey, you guys have been best friends forever. How do you make up from a fight?
Oh, that's easy.
Whenever we get annoyed at each other, we perform the Ancient Rites of Friendship.
What's that?
We'll show you!

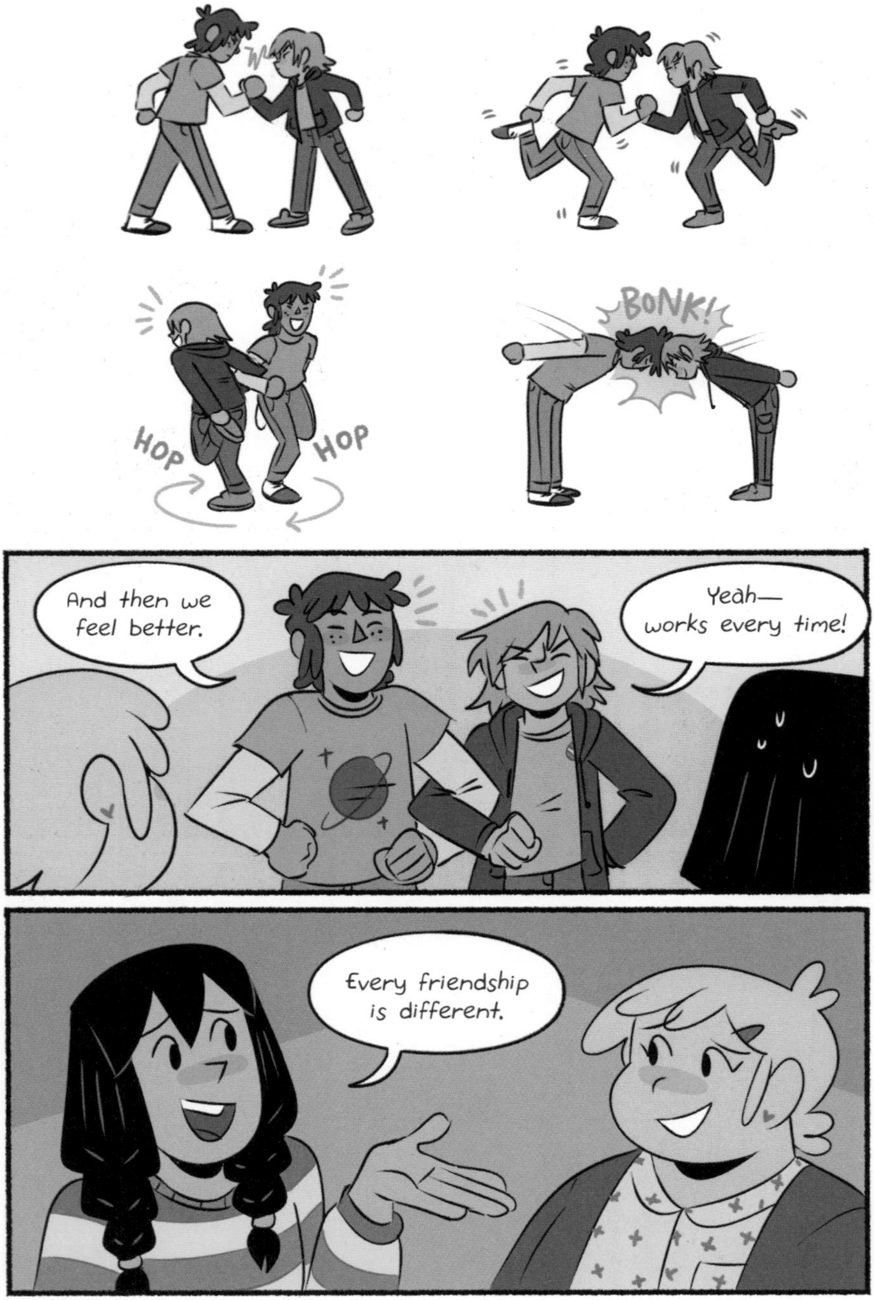
HOP
HOP
BONK!
And then we feel better.
Yeah— works every time!
Every friendship is different.

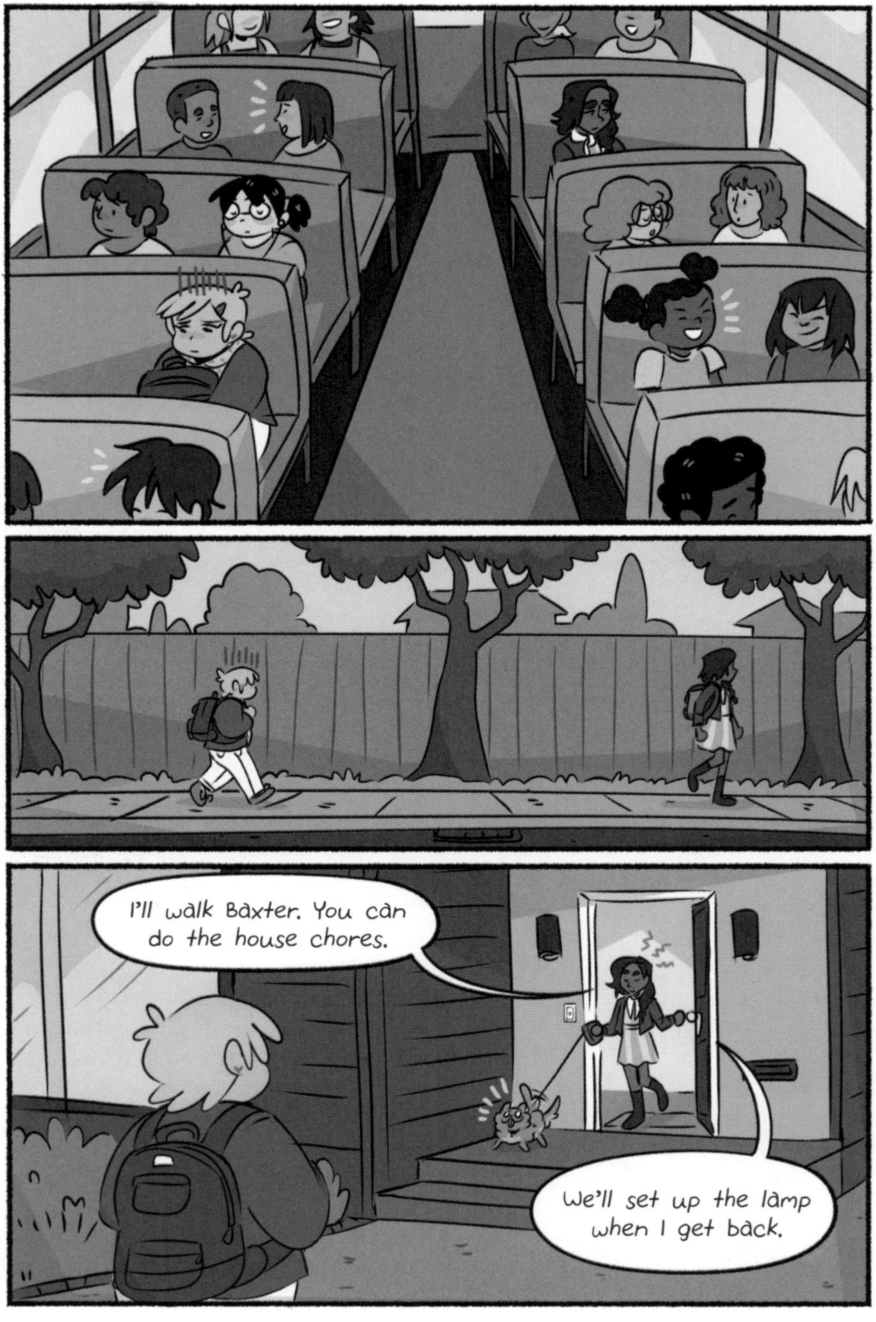
I'll walk Baxter. You can do the house chores.
We'll set up the lamp when I get back.

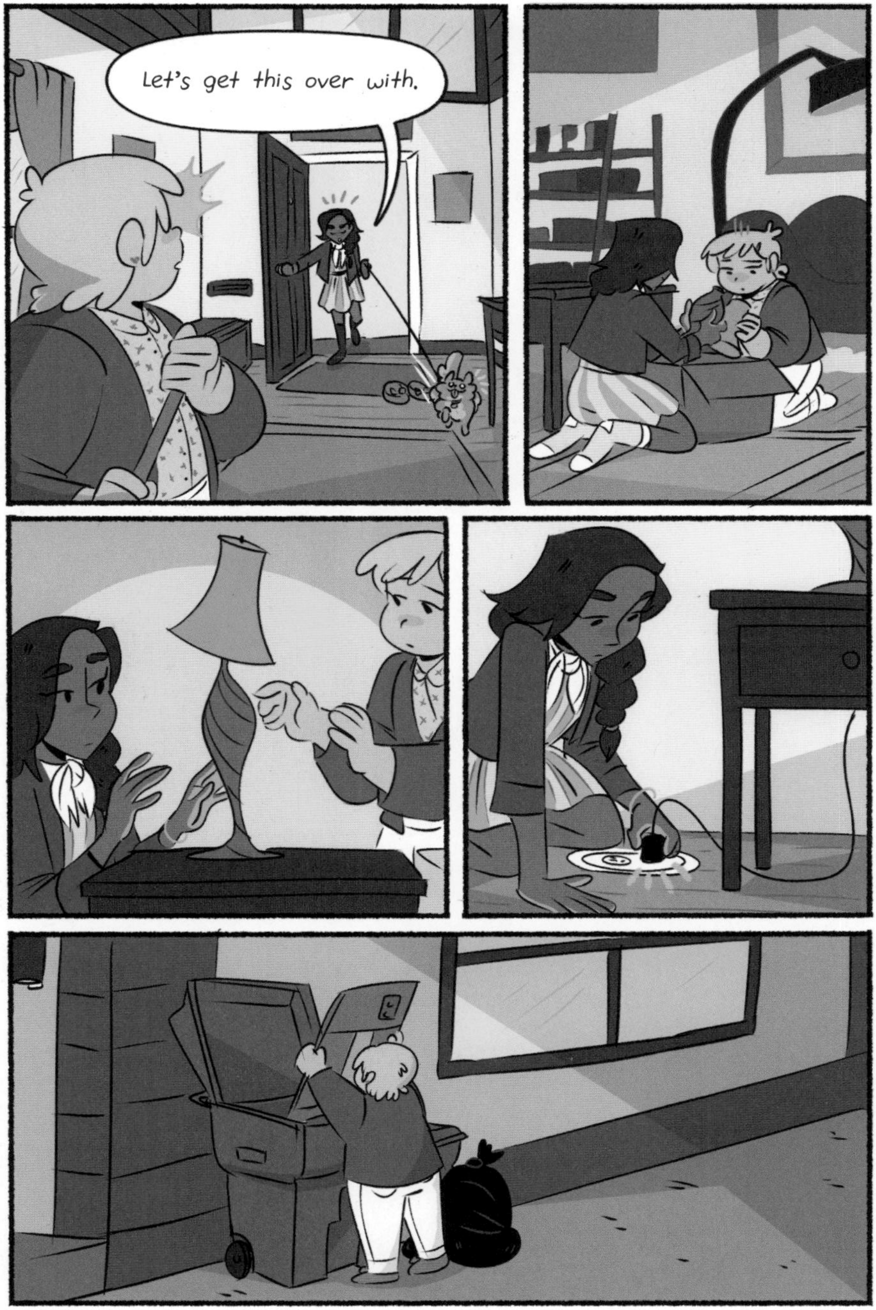
Let's get this over with.

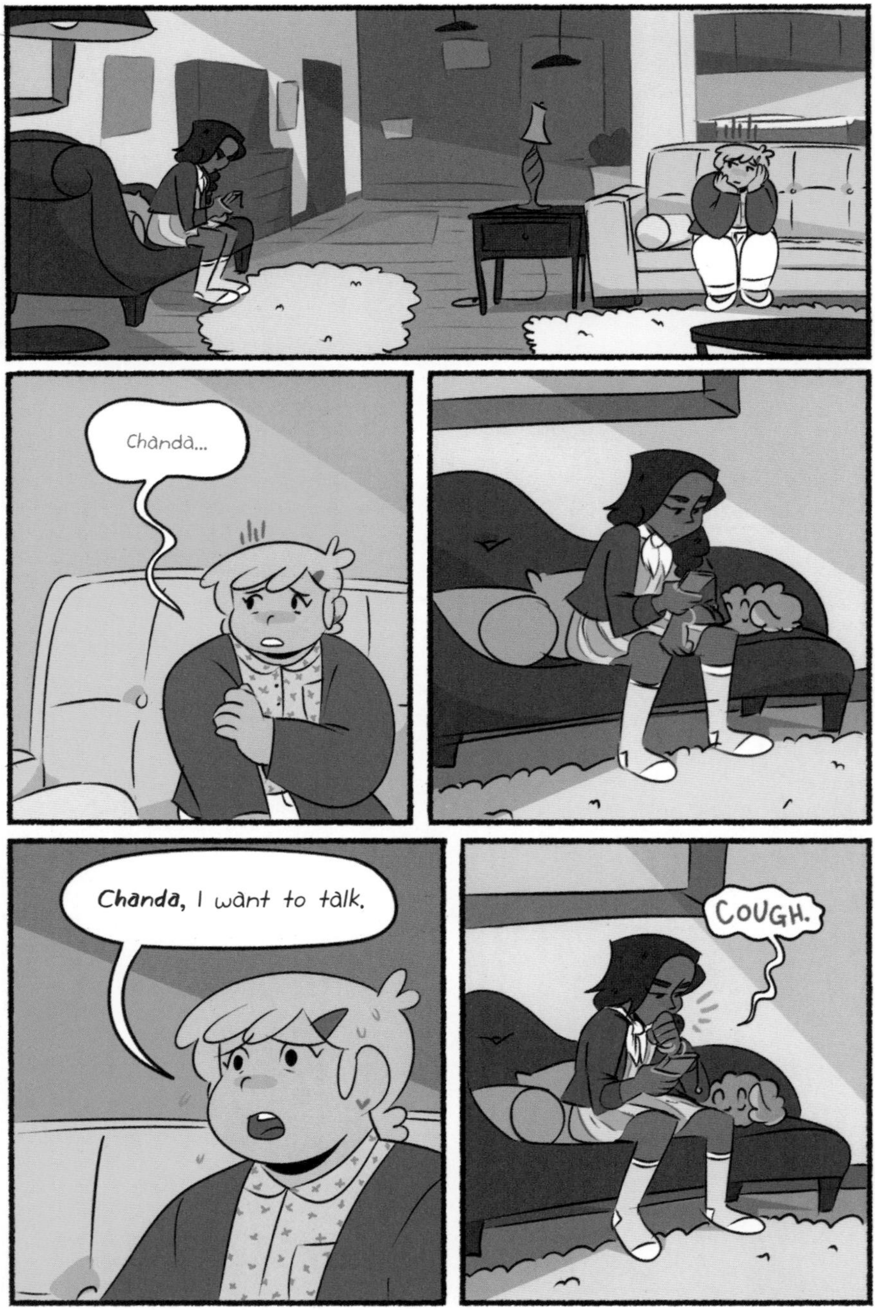
Chanda...
Chanda, I want to talk.
COUGH.

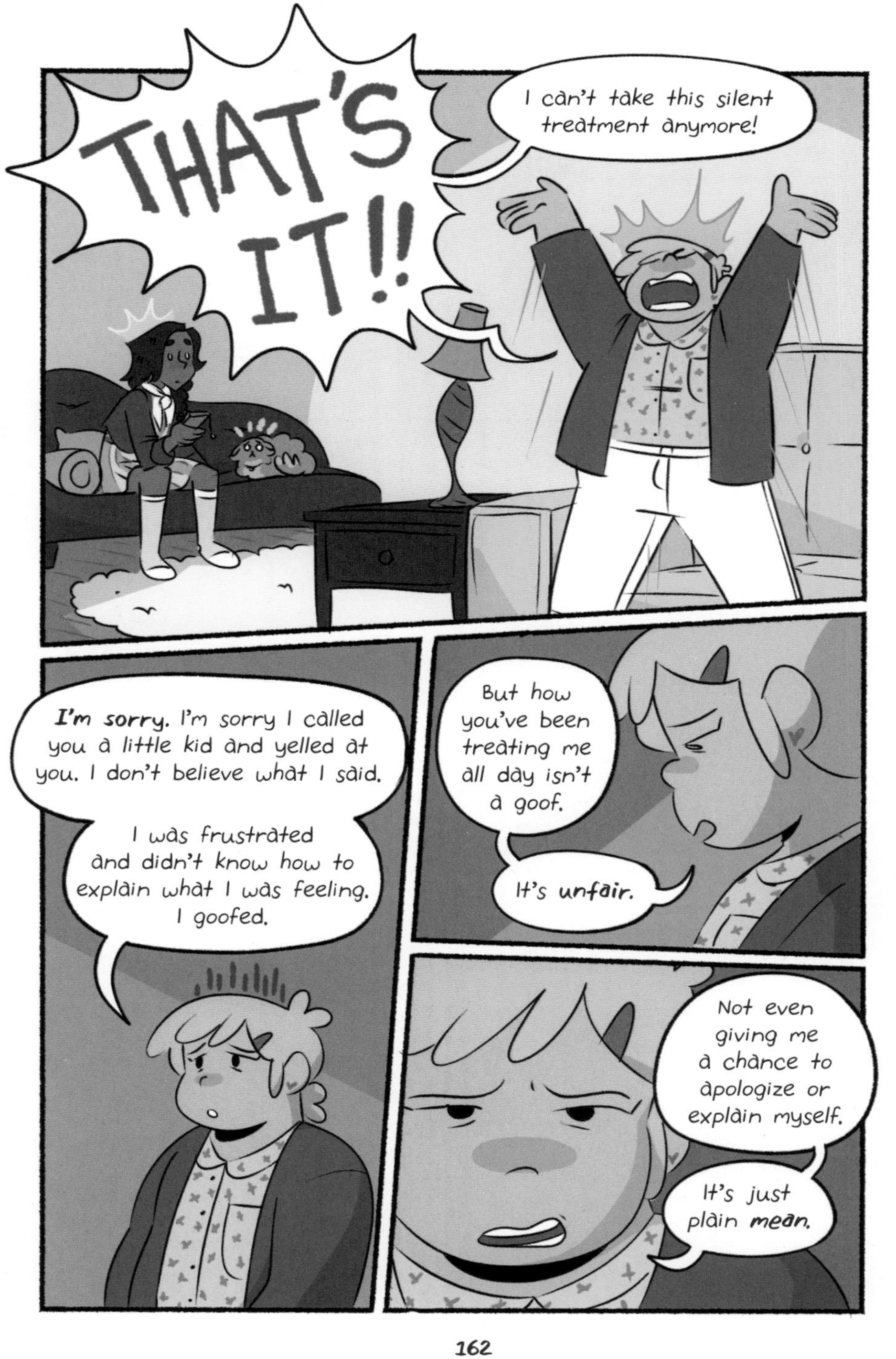
THAT'S IT!!
I can't take this silent treatment anymore!
I'm sorry. I'm sorry I called you a little kid and yelled at you. I don't believe what I said.
I was frustrated and didn't know how to explain what I was feeling. I goofed.
But how you've been treating me all day isn't a goof.
It's unfair.
Not even giving me a chance to apologize or explain myself.
It's just plain mean.

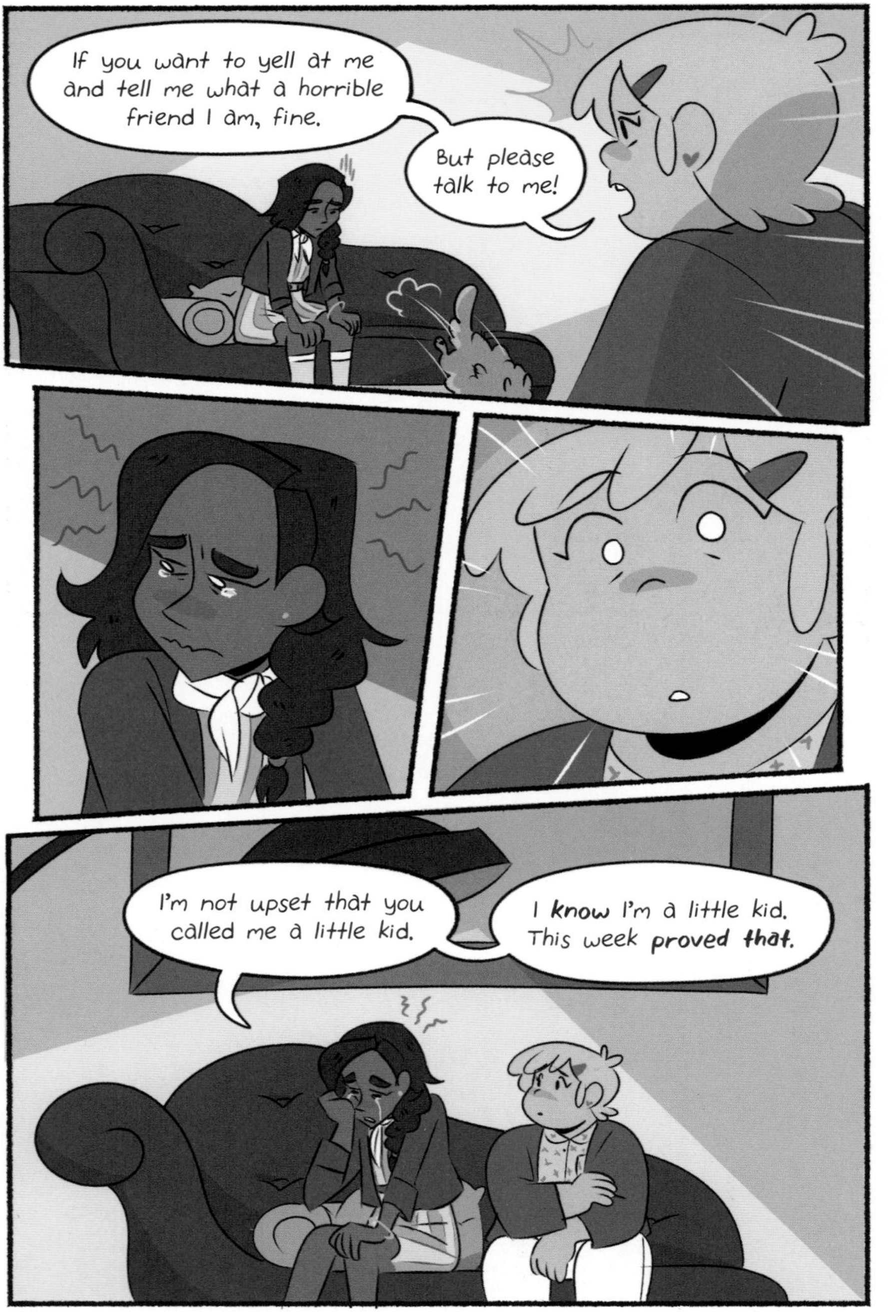
If you want to yell at me and tell me what a horrible friend I am, fine.
But please talk to me!
I'm not upset that you called me a little kid.
I **know** I'm a little kid. This week **proved that.**

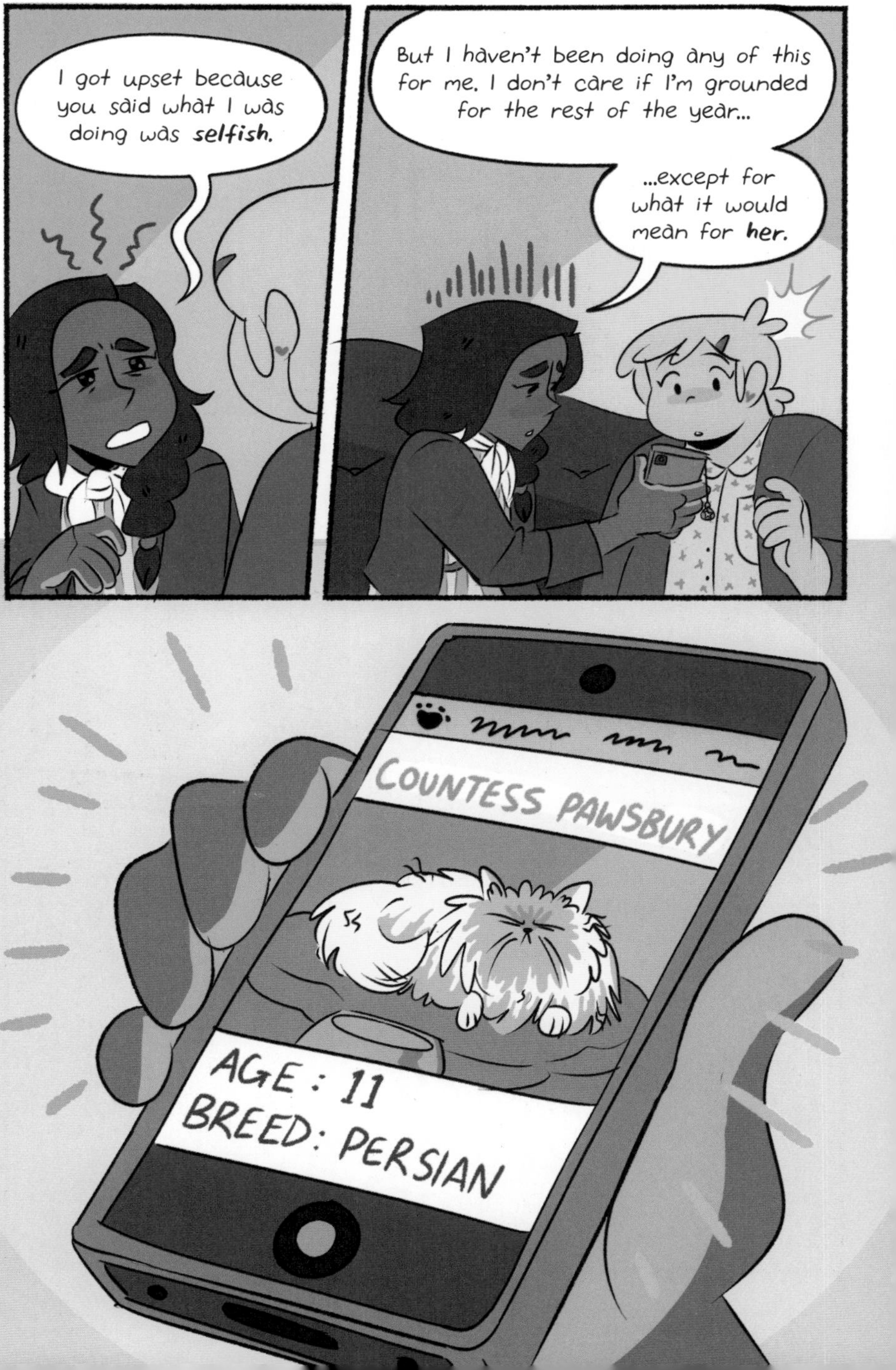

I got upset because you said what I was doing was **selfish.**
But I haven't been doing any of this for me. I don't care if I'm grounded for the rest of the year...
...except for what it would mean for **her.**
COUNTESS PAWSBURY
AGE: 11
BREED: PERSIAN

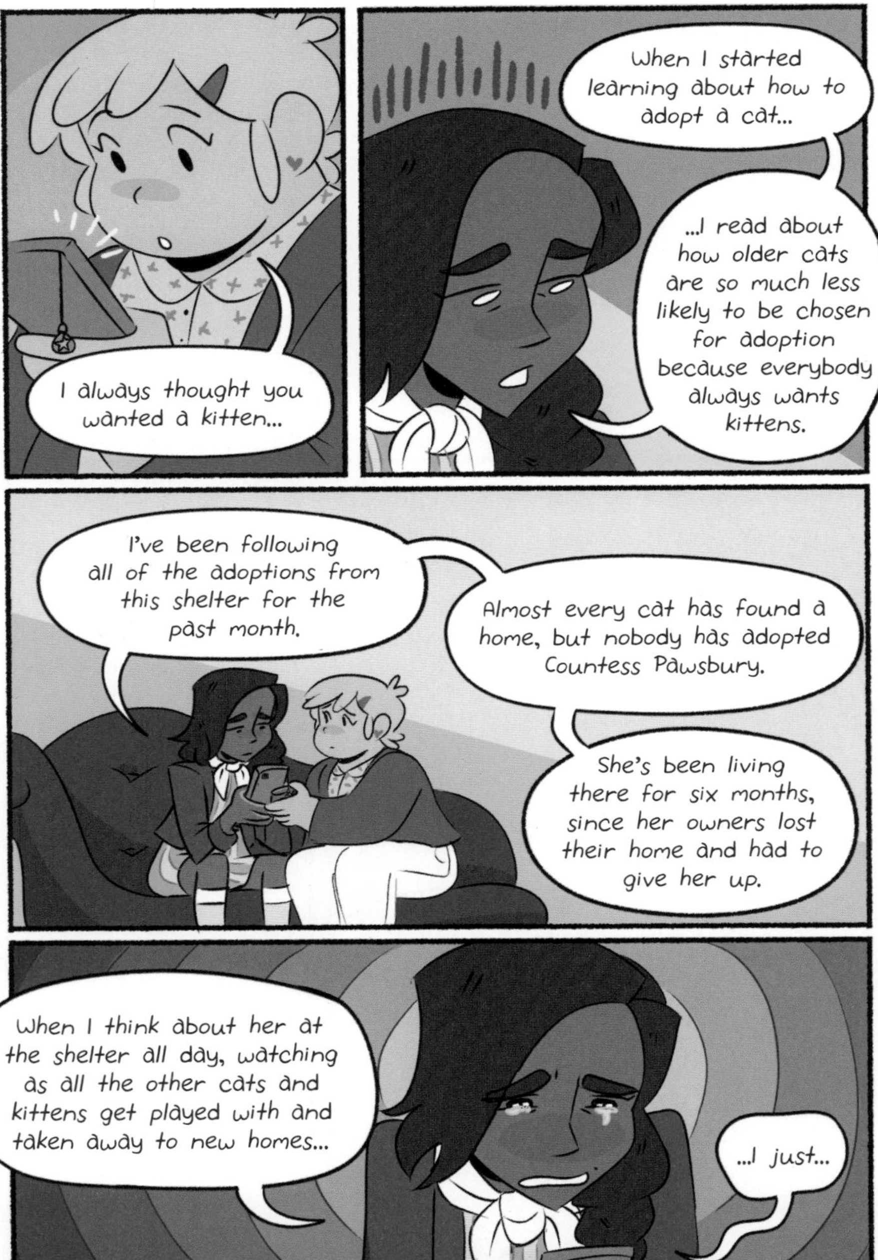
I always thought you wanted a kitten...
When I started learning about how to adopt a cat...
...I read about how older cats are so much less likely to be chosen for adoption because everybody always wants kittens.
I've been following all of the adoptions from this shelter for the past month.
Almost every cat has found a home, but nobody has adopted Countess Pawsbury.
She's been living there for six months, since her owners lost their home and had to give her up.
When I think about her at the shelter all day, watching as all the other cats and kittens get played with and taken away to new homes...
...I just...

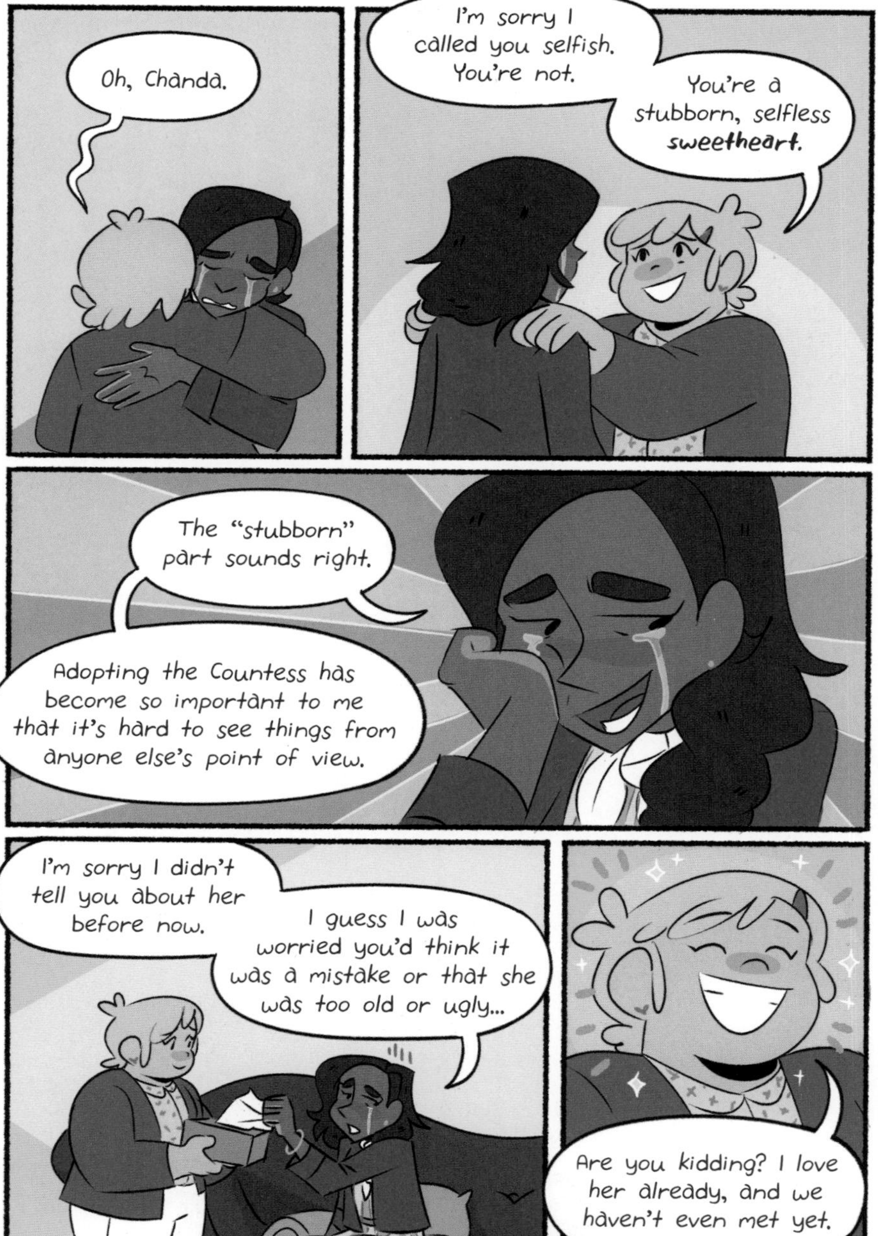
Oh, Chanda.
I'm sorry I called you selfish. You're not.
You're a stubborn, selfless **sweetheart.**
The "stubborn" part sounds right.
Adopting the Countess has become so important to me that it's hard to see things from anyone else's point of view.
I'm sorry I didn't tell you about her before now.
I guess I was worried you'd think it was a mistake or that she was too old or ugly...
Are you kidding? I love her already, and we haven't even met yet.

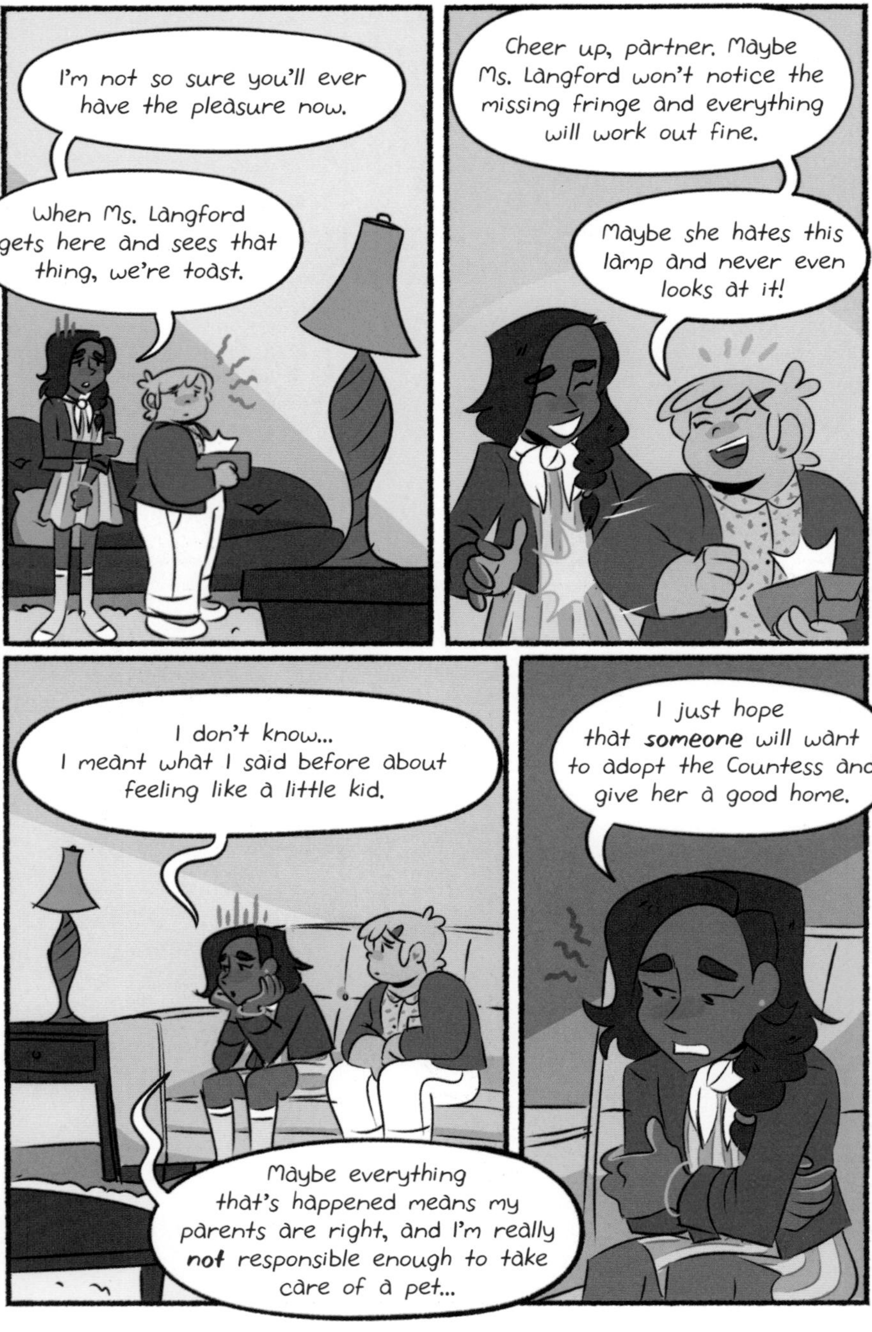
I'm not so sure you'll ever have the pleasure now.
When Ms. Langford gets here and sees that thing, we're toast.
Cheer up, partner. Maybe Ms. Langford won't notice the missing fringe and everything will work out fine.
Maybe she hates this lamp and never even looks at it!
I don't know... I meant what I said before about feeling like a little kid.
Maybe everything that's happened means my parents are right, and I'm really **not** responsible enough to take care of a pet...
I just hope that **someone** will want to adopt the Countess and give her a good home.

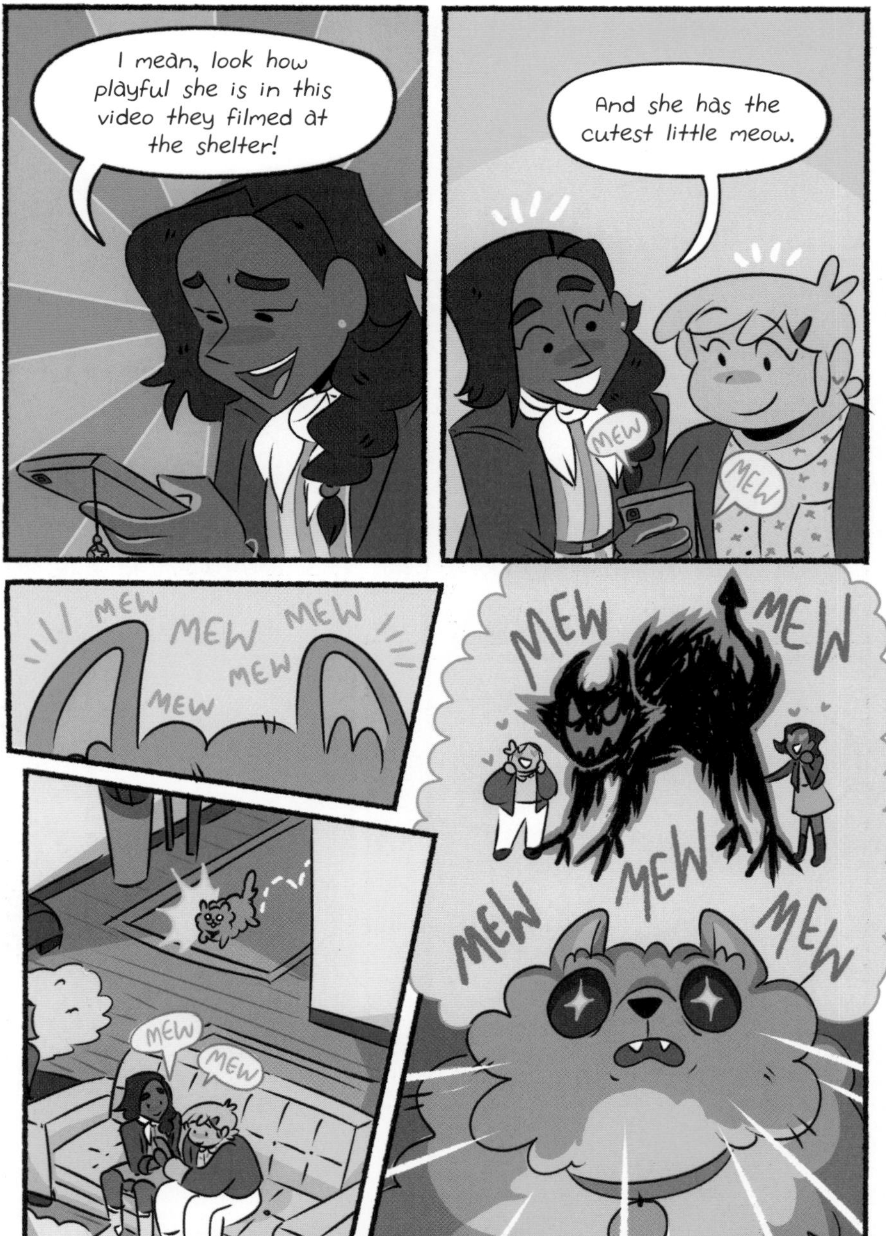
I mean, look how playful she is in this video they filmed at the shelter!
And she has the cutest little meow.
MEW
MEW
MEW MEW MEW MEW MEW
MEW
MEW
MEW MEW
MEW
MEW MEW MEW

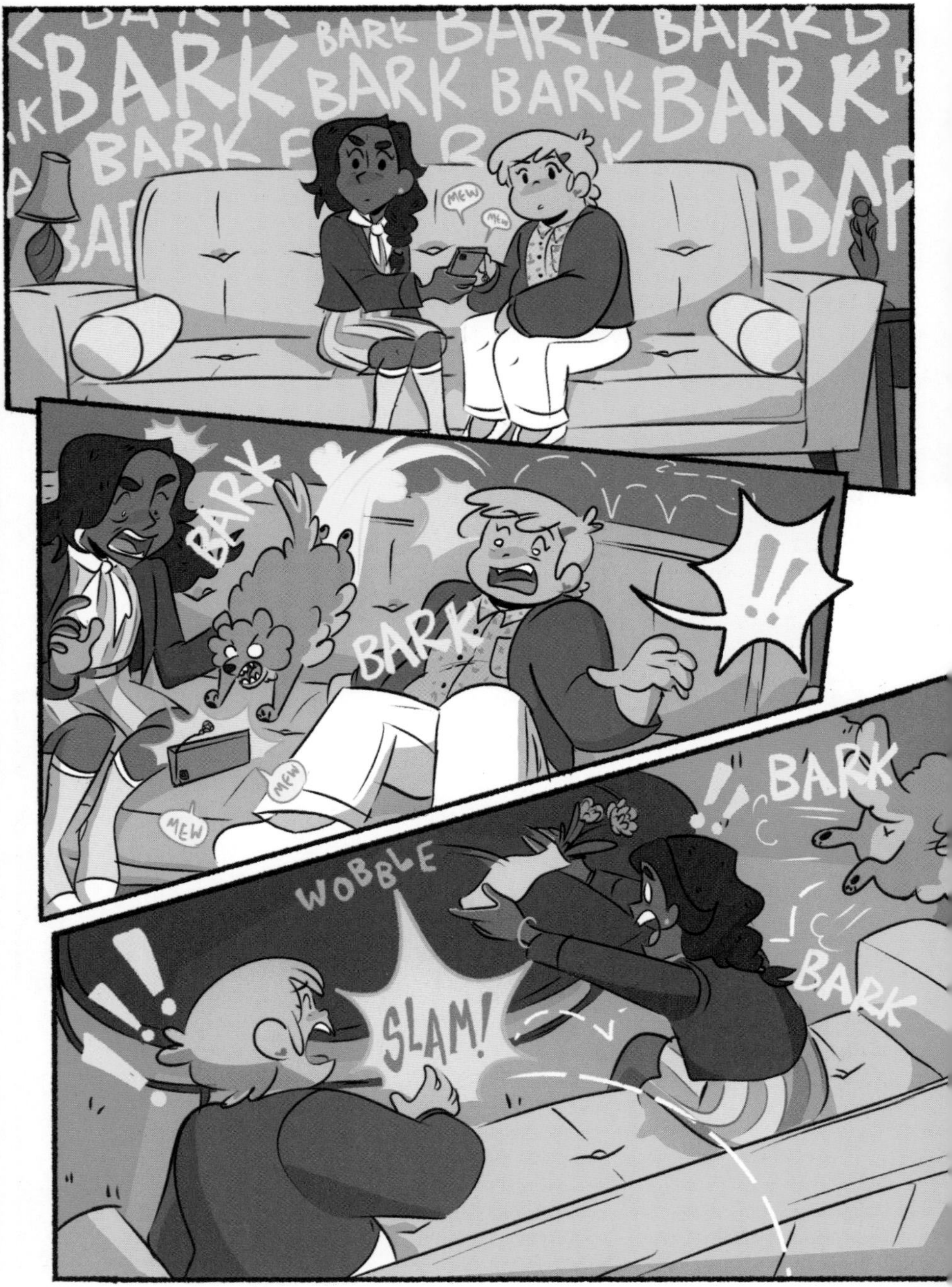

BARK
BARK
BARK
BARK
BARK
BARK
BARK
BARK
MEW
MEW
BARK
BARK
!!
MEW
MEW
!!
BARK
WOBBLE
BARK
!!
SLAM!

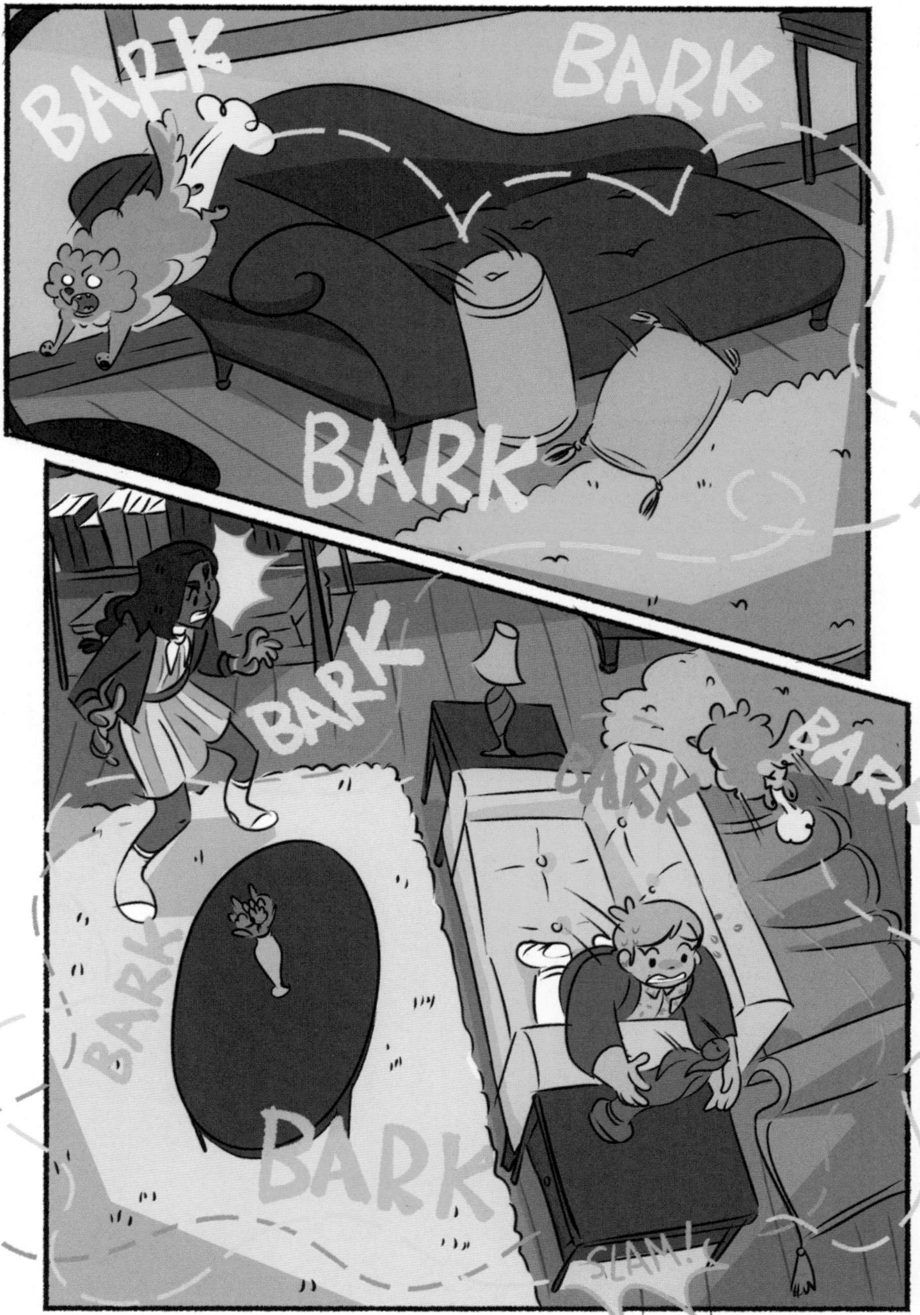
BARK
BARK
BARK
BARK
BARK
BARK
BARK
BARK
SLAM!

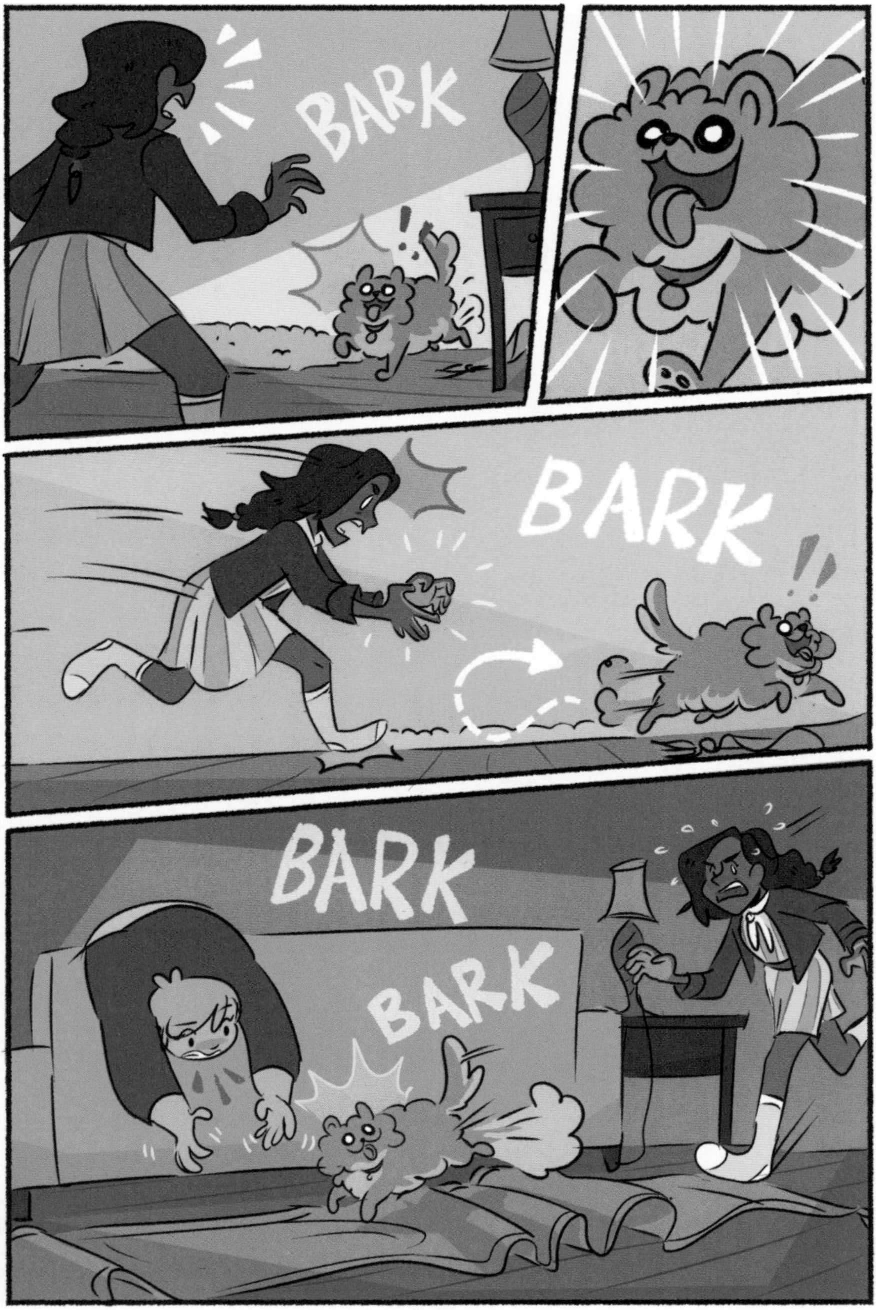
BARK
!
!
BARK
!!
BARK
BARK

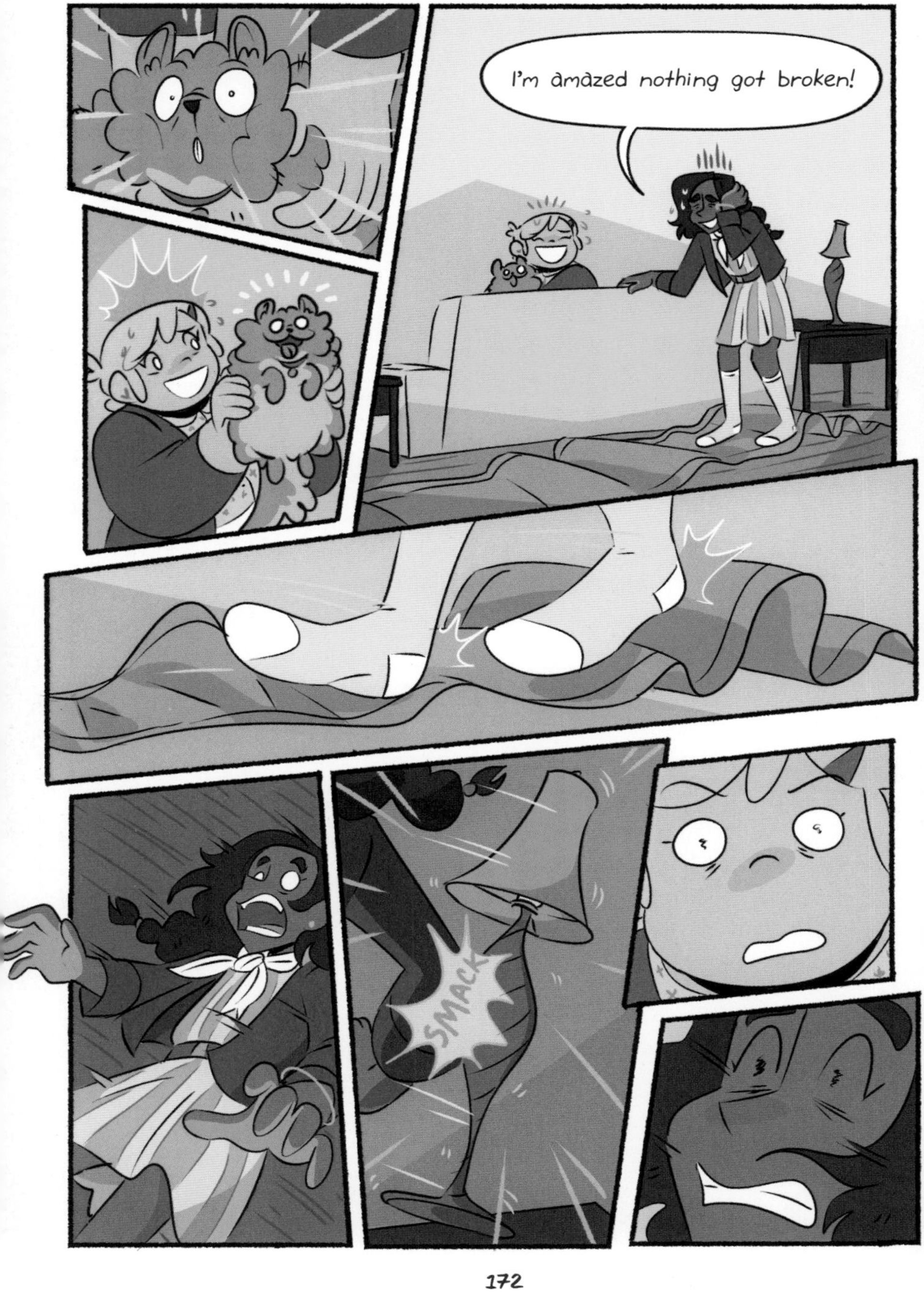
I'm amazed nothing got broken!
SMACK

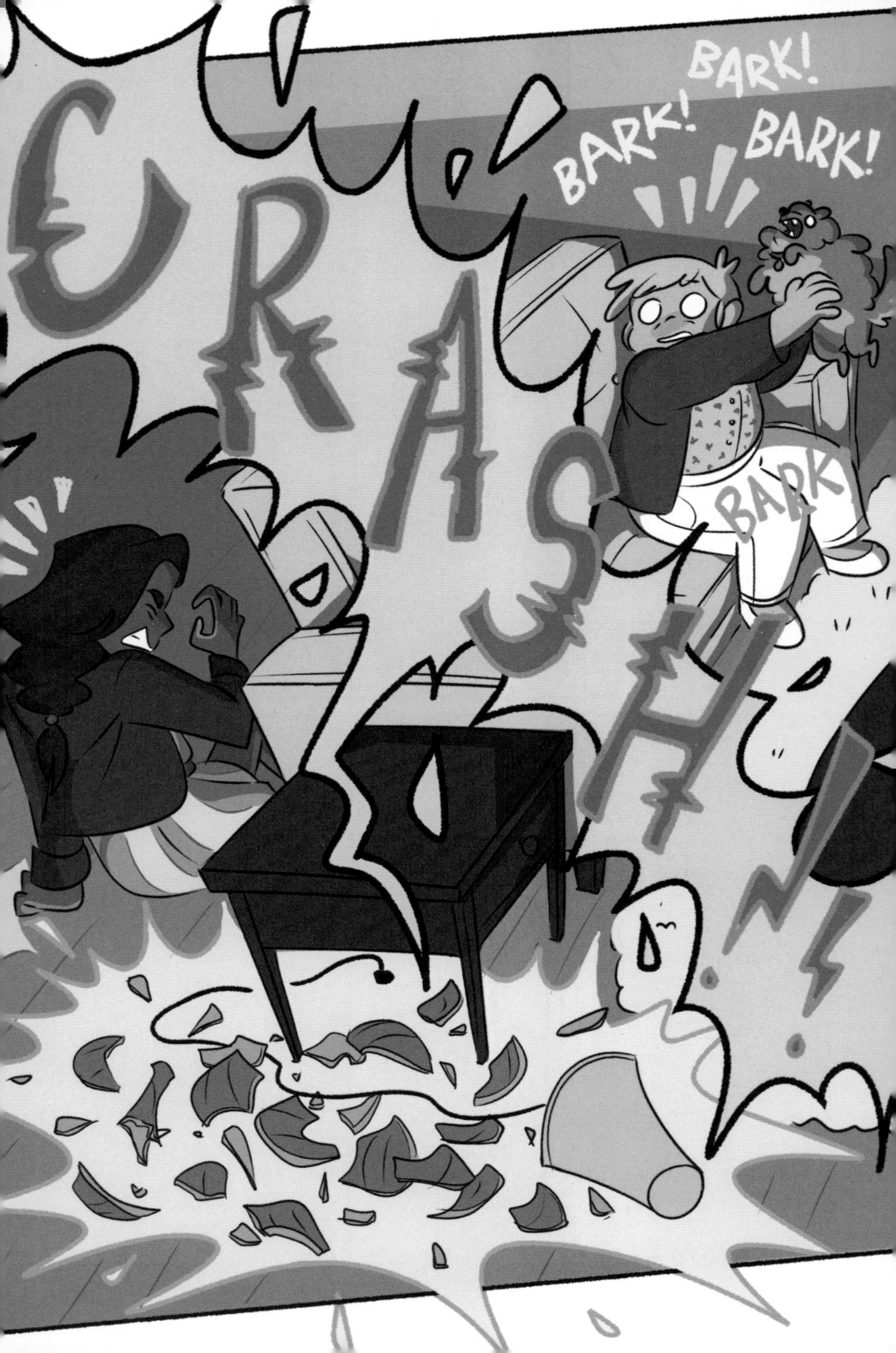
CRASH!
BARK!
BARK!
BARK!
BARK
BARK

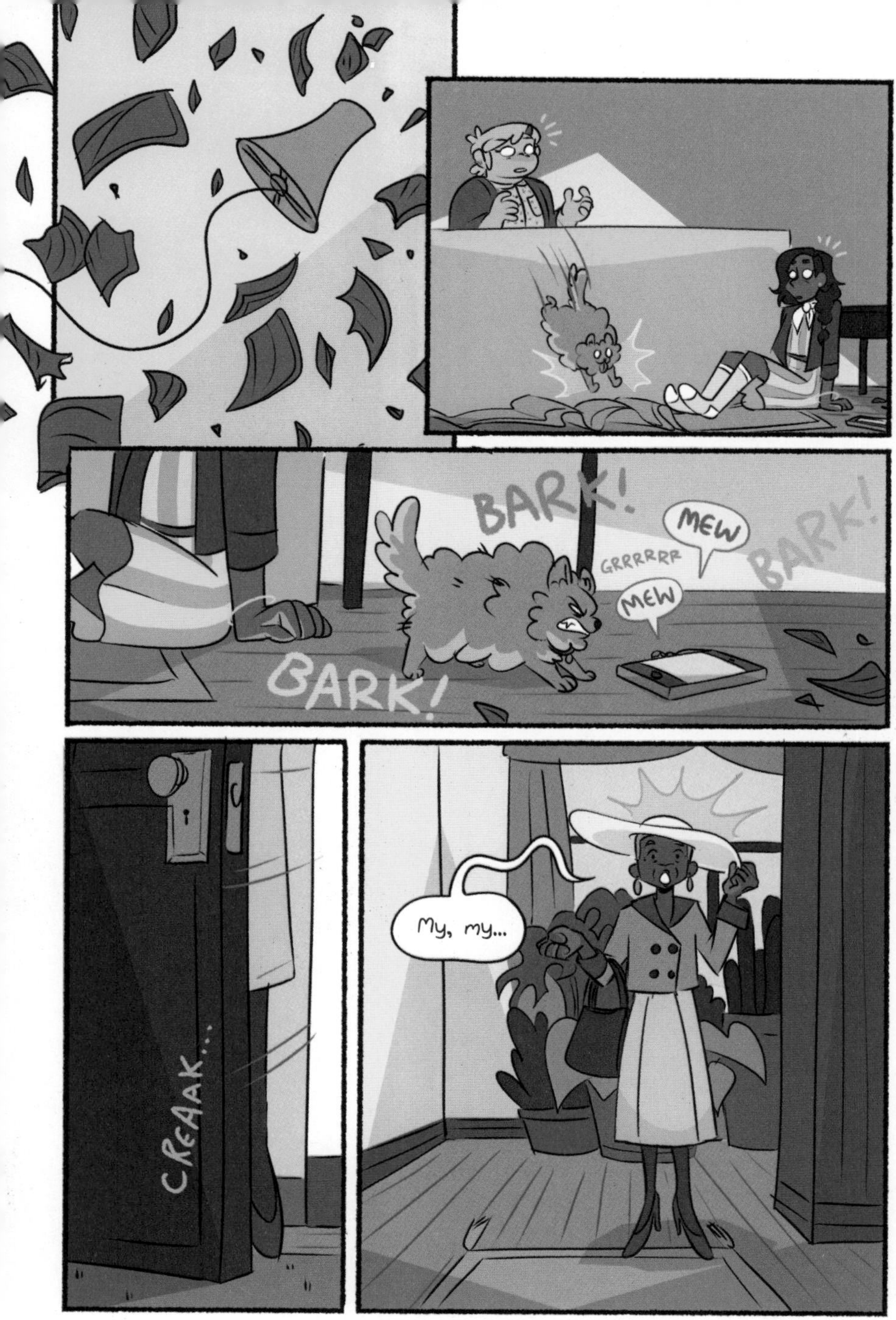
BARK!
GRRRRRR
MEW
BARK!
MEW
BARK!
CREAAK...
My, my...

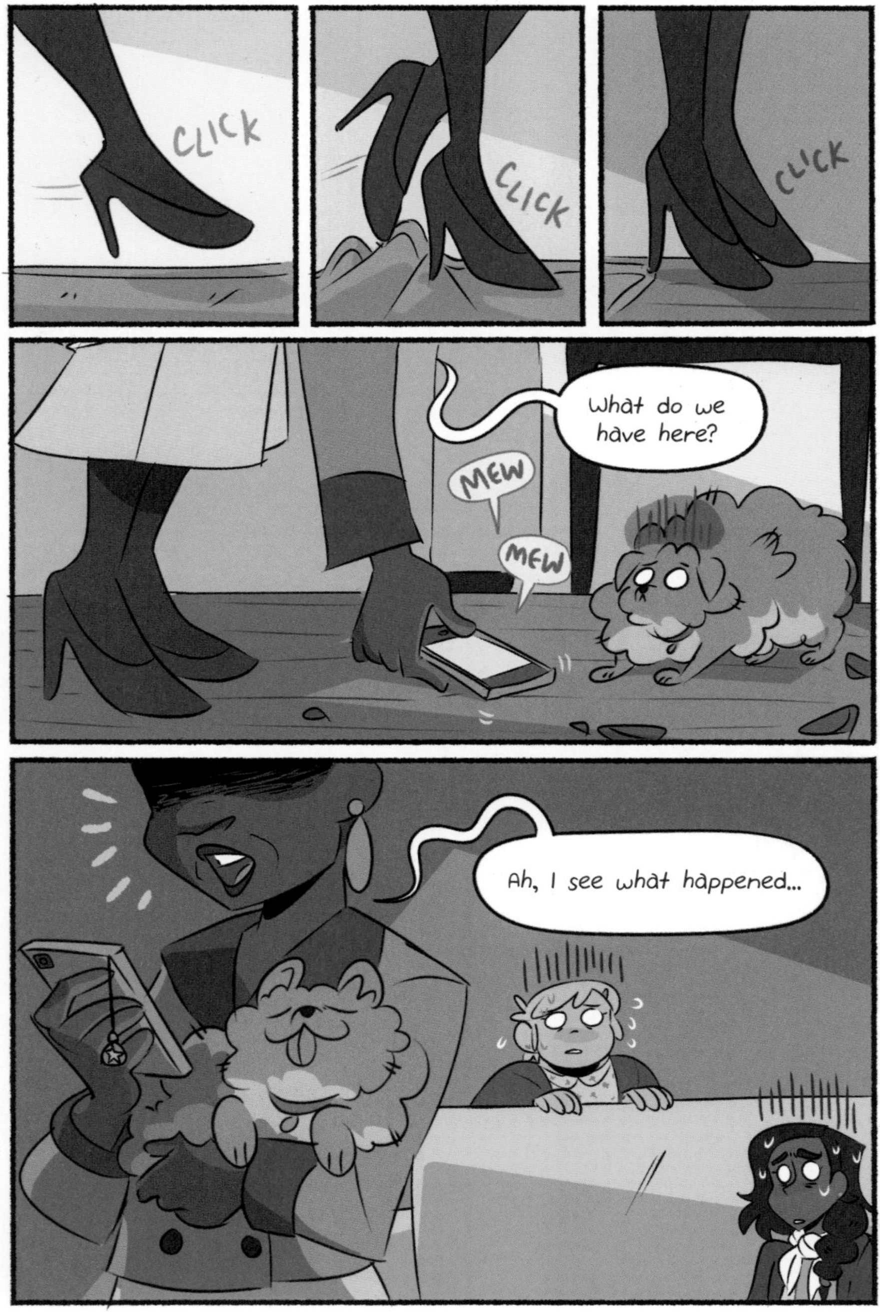
CLICK
CLICK
CLICK
What do we have here?
MEW
MEW
Ah, I see what happened...

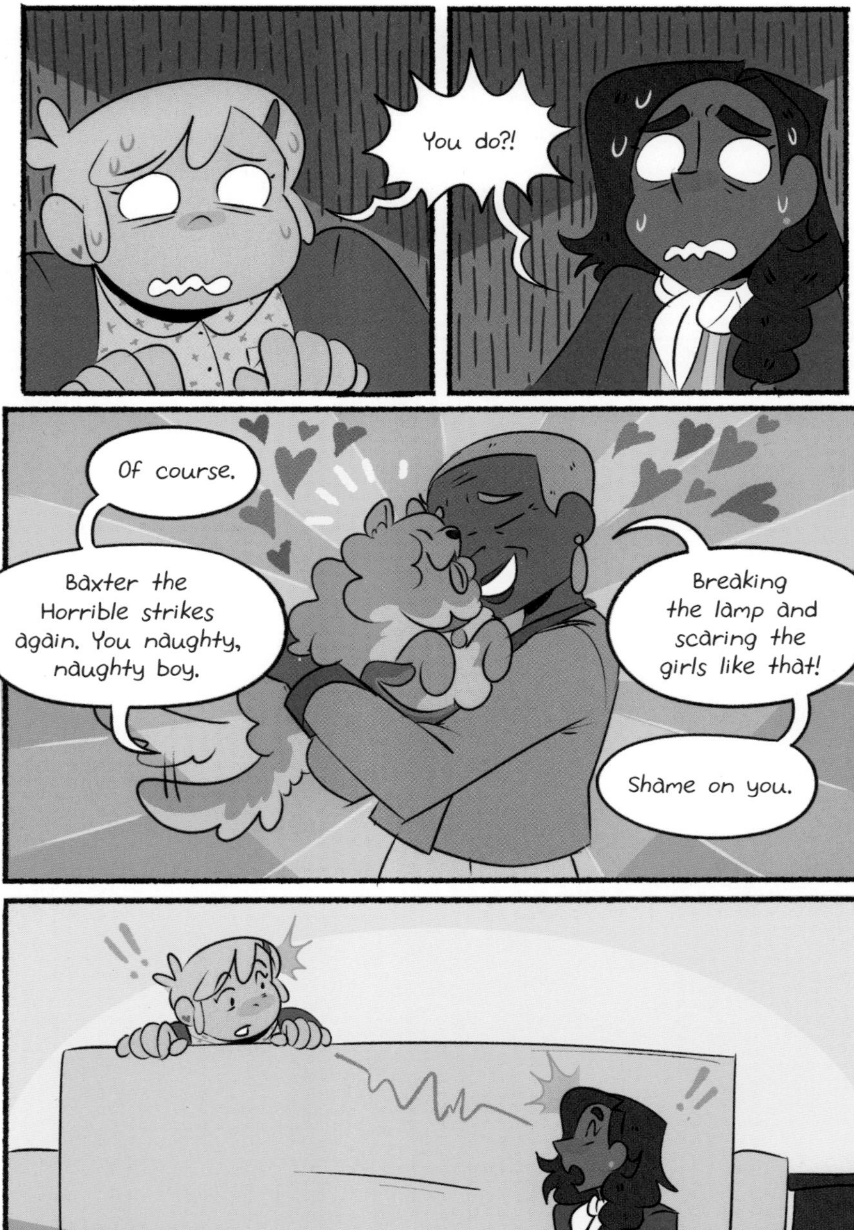

You do?!
Of course.
Baxter the Horrible strikes again. You naughty, naughty boy.
Breaking the lamp and scaring the girls like that!
Shame on you.

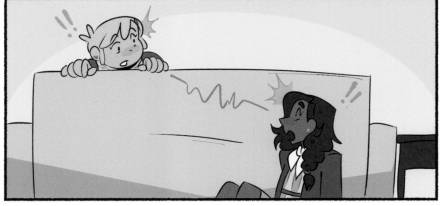

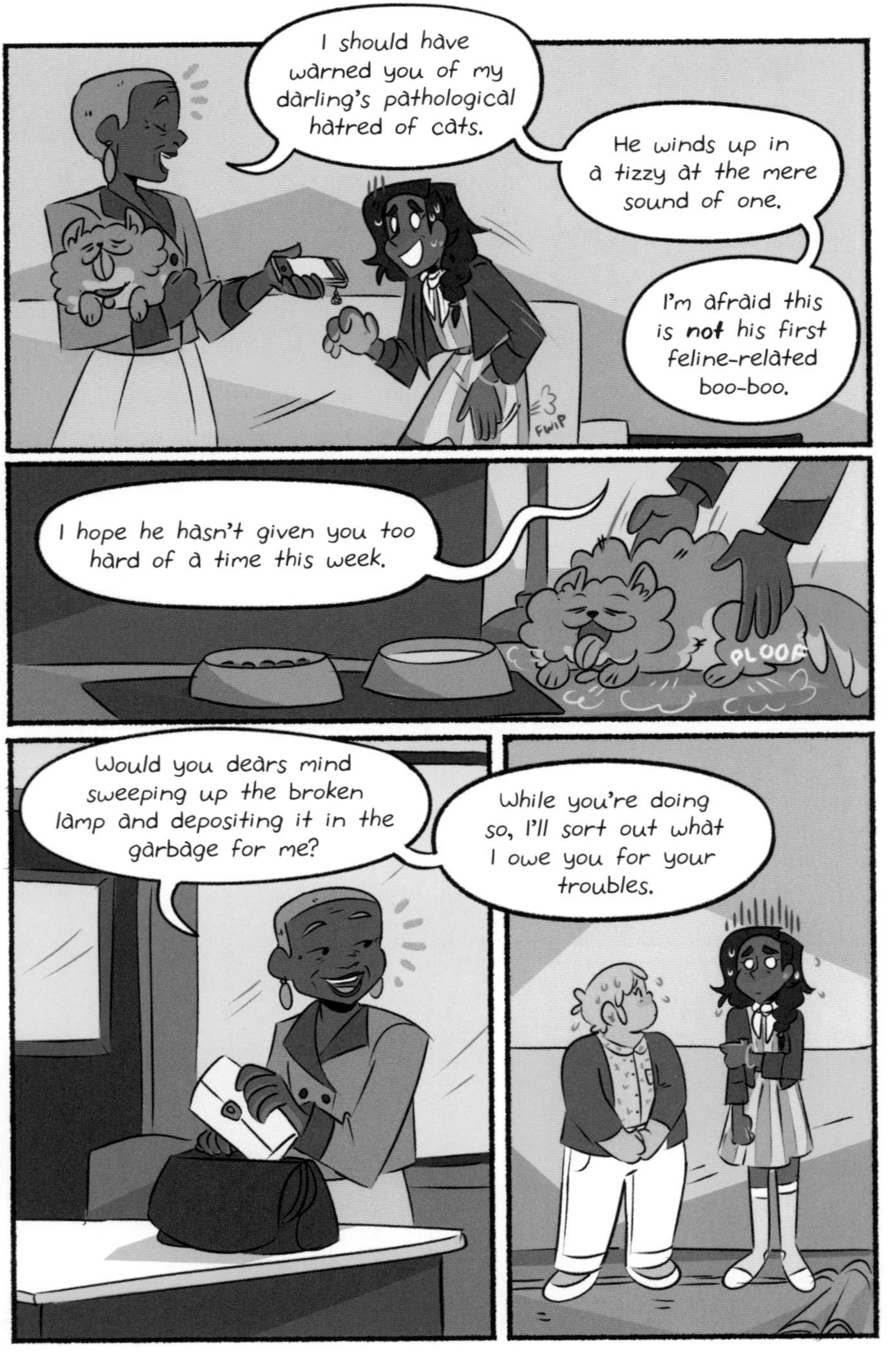
I should have warned you of my darling's pathological hatred of cats.
He winds up in a tizzy at the mere sound of one.
I'm afraid this is **not** his first feline-related boo-boo.
FWIP
I hope he hasn't given you too hard of a time this week.
PLOOF
Would you dears mind sweeping up the broken lamp and depositing it in the garbage for me?
While you're doing so, I'll sort out what I owe you for your troubles.

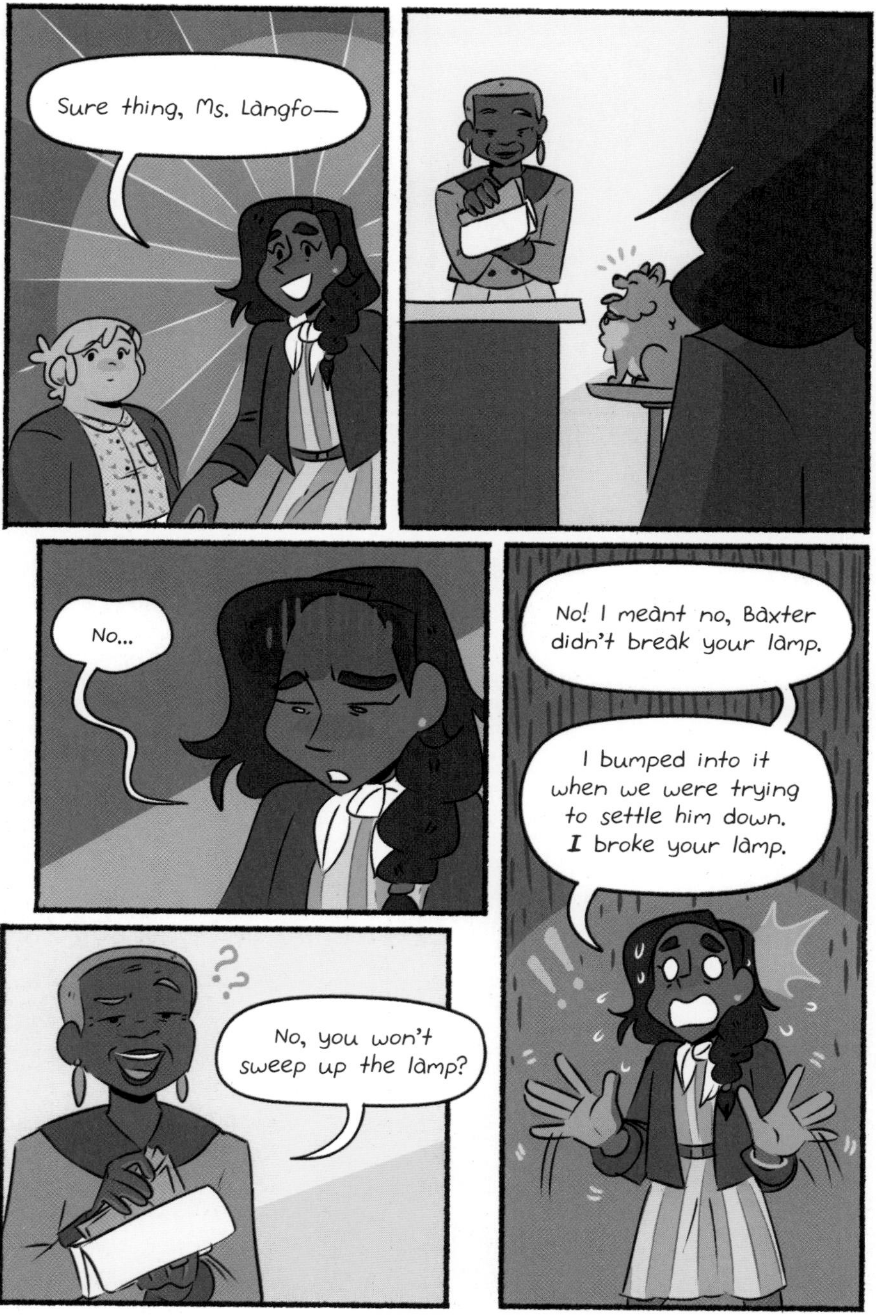
Sure thing, Ms. Langfo—
No...
No, you won't sweep up the lamp?
No! I meant no, Baxter didn't break your lamp.
I bumped into it when we were trying to settle him down. **I** broke your lamp.

Well, **we** did... That lamp on the ground isn't even yours.

We broke the original last week when we invited some friends over to look at all of your great plants and décor and Baxter got too excited.

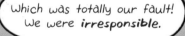

Which was totally our fault! We were *irresponsible*.

We shouldn't have had anyone over here for Baxter to get excited about.

And we're so, so, so, so sorry that we took advantage of your trust.

We bought the new lamp to try to make everything ***better***...

...but I guess we just made it all **worse**.

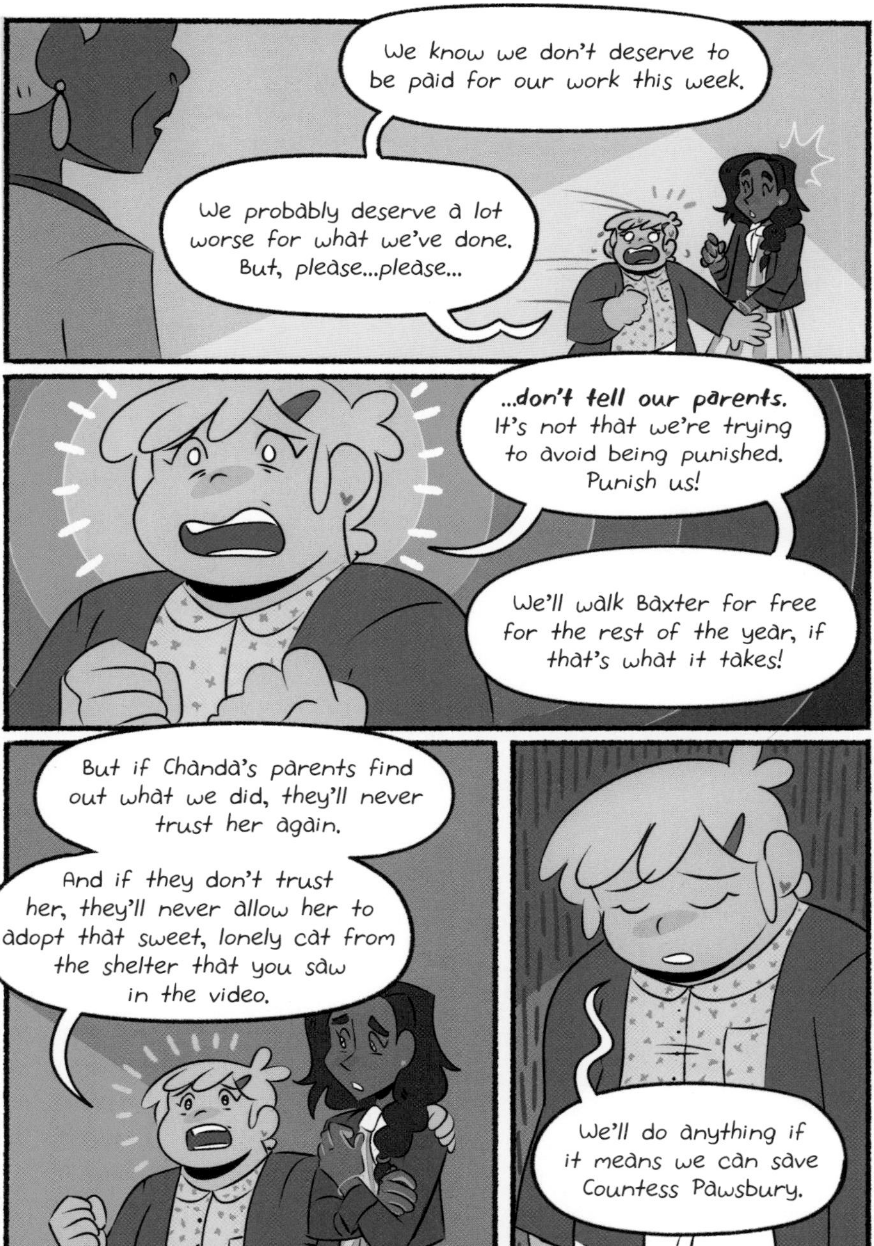
We know we don't deserve to be paid for our work this week.
We probably deserve a lot worse for what we've done. But, please...please...
...don't tell our parents. It's not that we're trying to avoid being punished. Punish us!
We'll walk Baxter for free for the rest of the year, if that's what it takes!
But if Chanda's parents find out what we did, they'll never trust her again.
And if they don't trust her, they'll never allow her to adopt that sweet, lonely cat from the shelter that you saw in the video.
We'll do anything if it means we can save Countess Pawsbury.

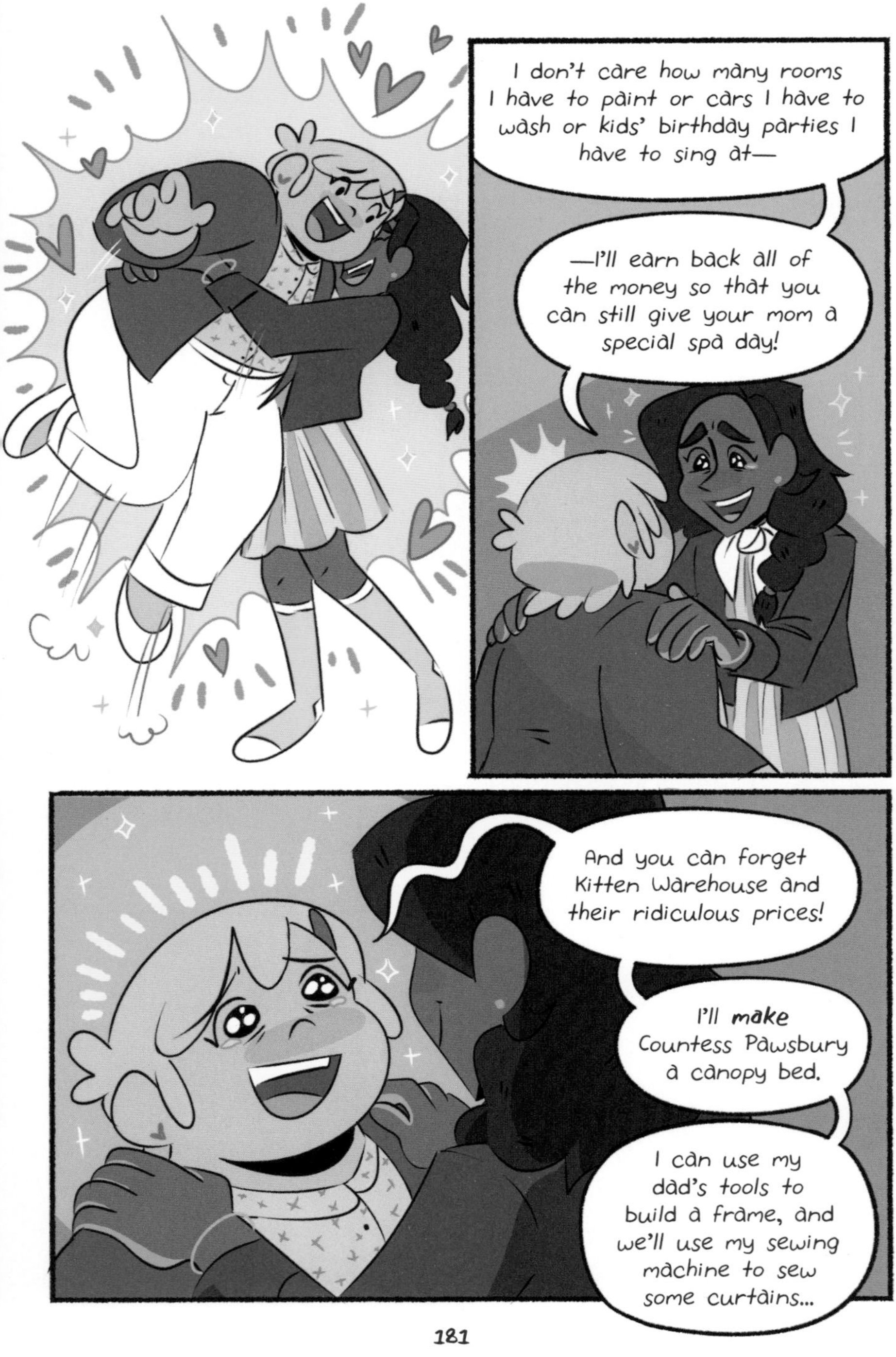

I don't care how many rooms I have to paint or cars I have to wash or kids' birthday parties I have to sing at—
—I'll earn back all of the money so that you can still give your mom a special spa day!
And you can forget Kitten Warehouse and their ridiculous prices!
I'll **make** Countess Pawsbury a canopy bed.
I can use my dad's tools to build a frame, and we'll use my sewing machine to sew some curtains...

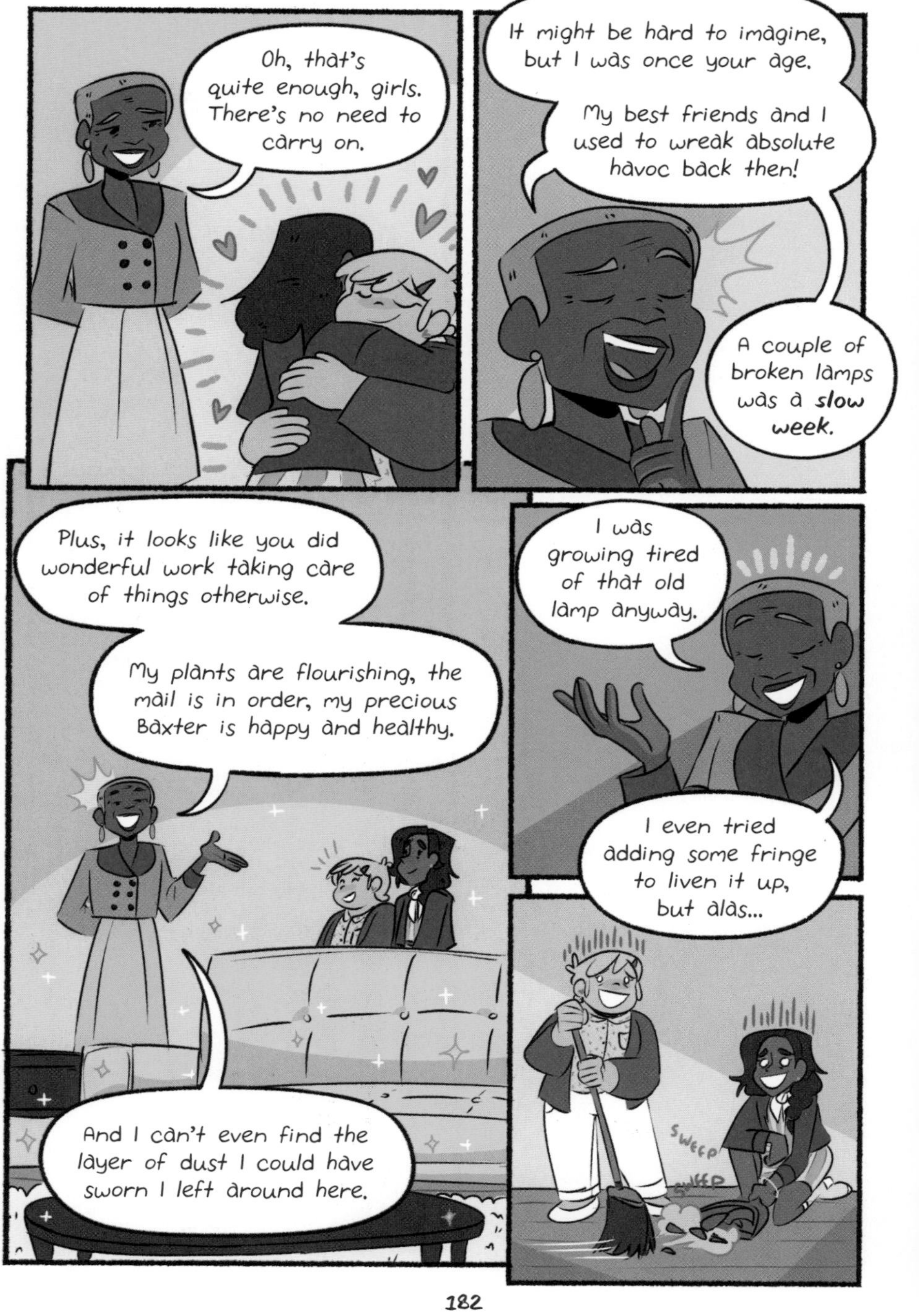
Oh, that's quite enough, girls. There's no need to carry on.
It might be hard to imagine, but I was once your age.
My best friends and I used to wreak absolute havoc back then!
A couple of broken lamps was a **slow week.**
Plus, it looks like you did wonderful work taking care of things otherwise.
My plants are flourishing, the mail is in order, my precious Baxter is happy and healthy.
And I can't even find the layer of dust I could have sworn I left around here.
I was growing tired of that old lamp anyway.
I even tried adding some fringe to liven it up, but alas...
SWEEP
SWEEP

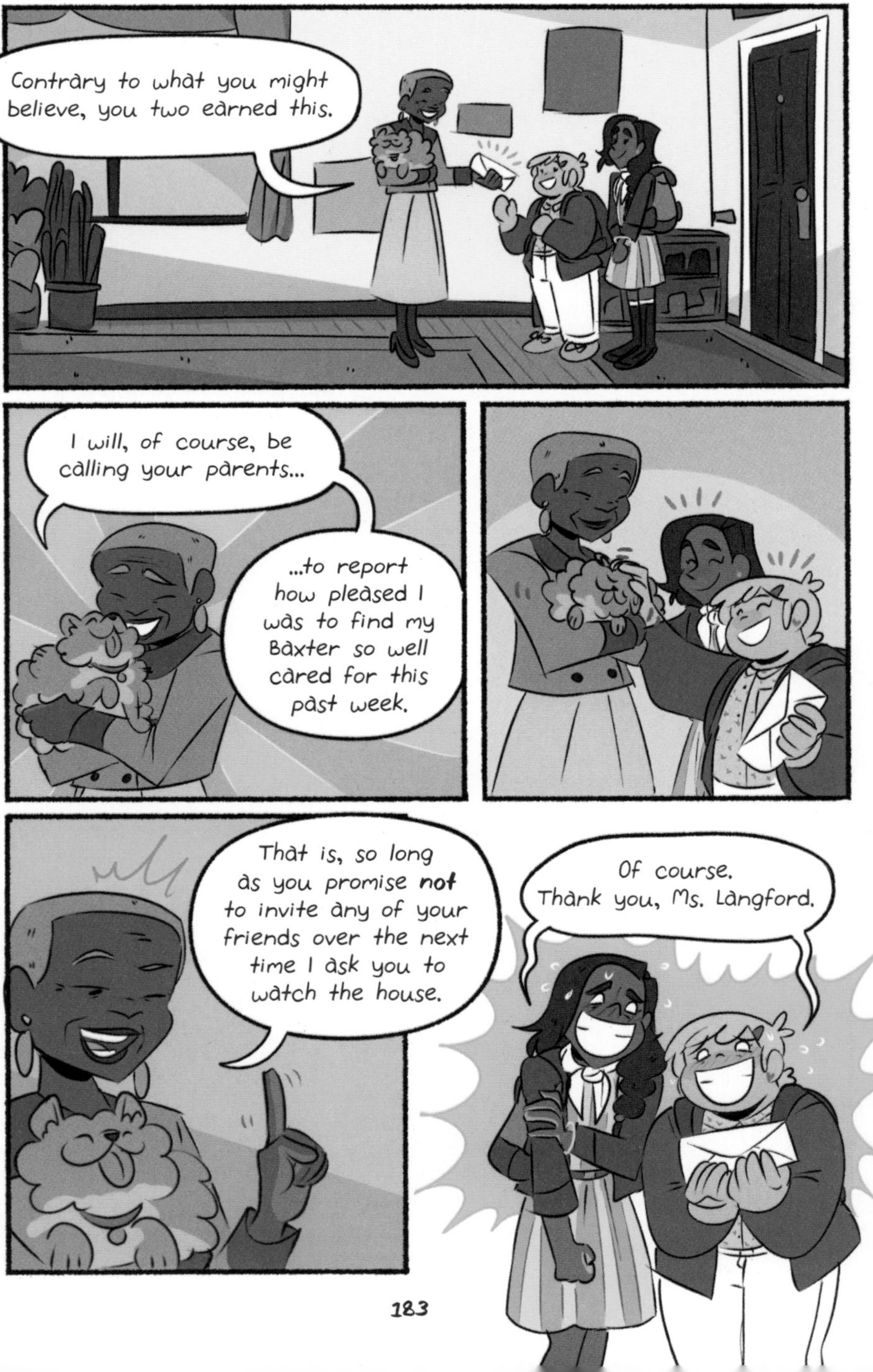
Contrary to what you might believe, you two earned this.
I will, of course, be calling your parents...
...to report how pleased I was to find my Baxter so well cared for this past week.
That is, so long as you promise **not** to invite any of your friends over the next time I ask you to watch the house.
Of course. Thank you, Ms. Langford.

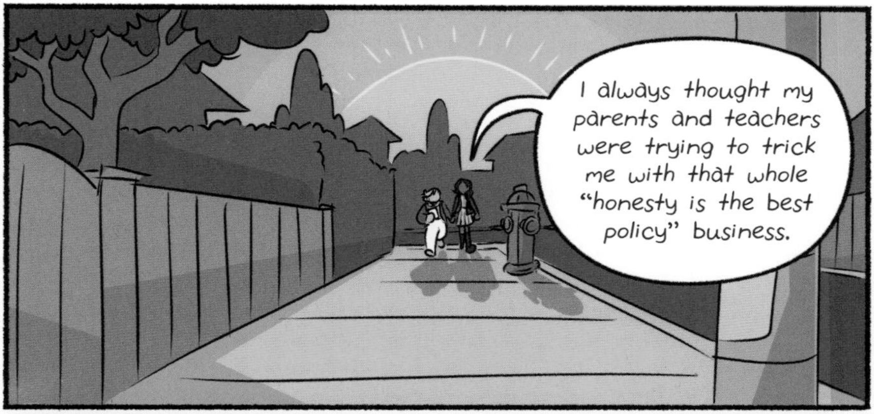
I always thought my parents and teachers were trying to trick me with that whole "honesty is the best policy" business.
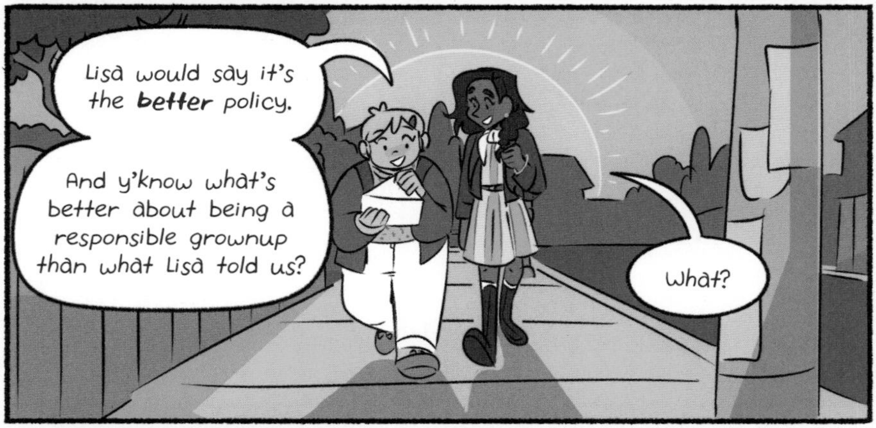
Lisa would say it's the **better** policy.
And y'know what's better about being a responsible grownup than what Lisa told us?
What?
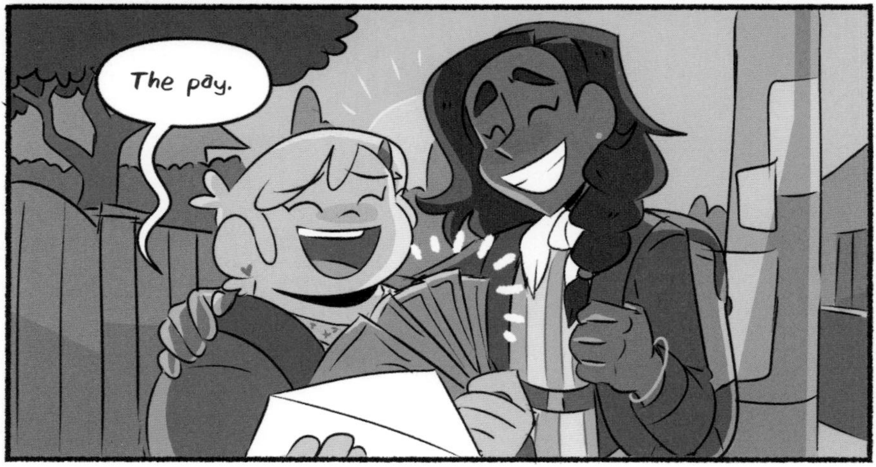
The pay.

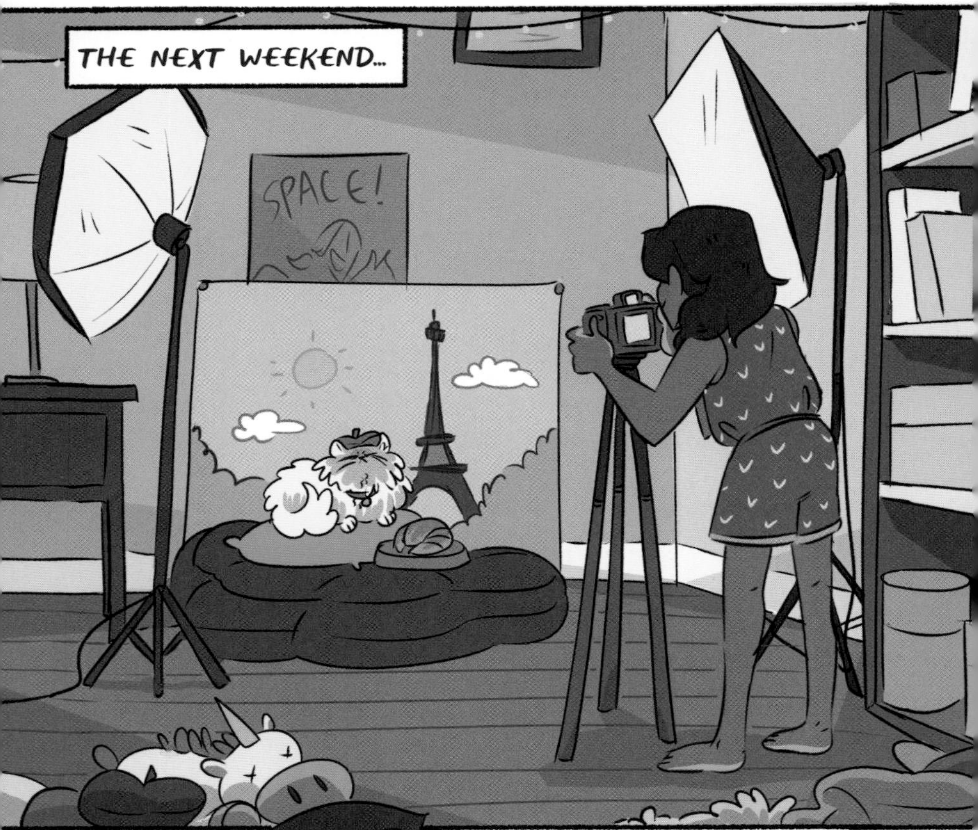
THE NEXT WEEKEND...
SPACE!
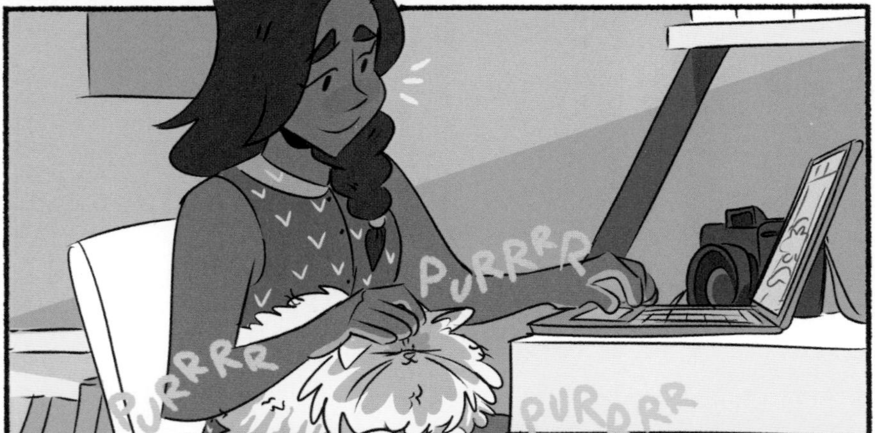
PURRRR
PURRRR
PURRRRR

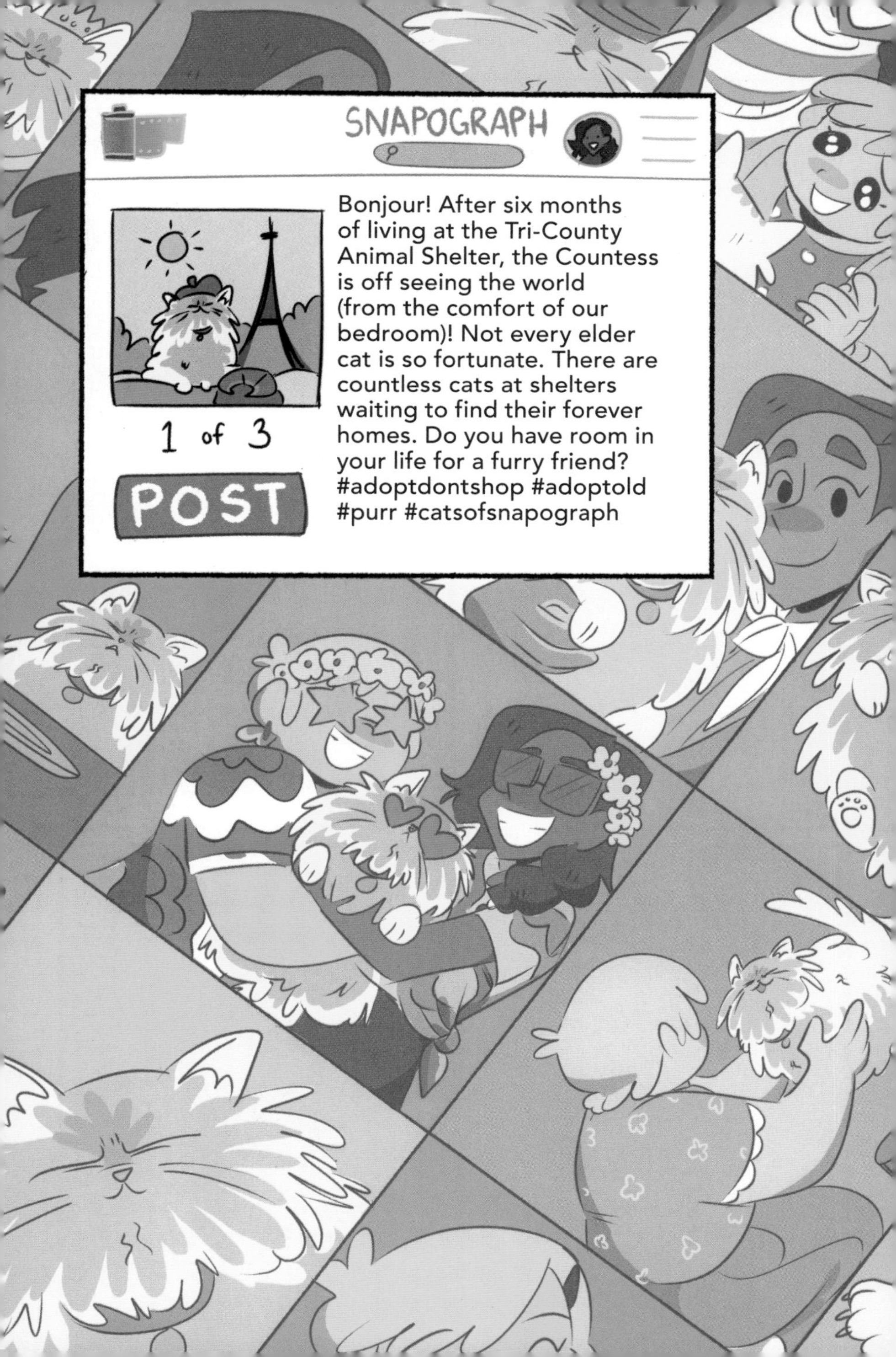
SNAPOGRAPH
1 of 3
POST
Bonjour! After six months of living at the Tri-County Animal Shelter, the Countess is off seeing the world (from the comfort of our bedroom)! Not every elder cat is so fortunate. There are countless cats at shelters waiting to find their forever homes. Do you have room in your life for a furry friend? #adoptdontshop #adoptold #purr #catsofsnapograph

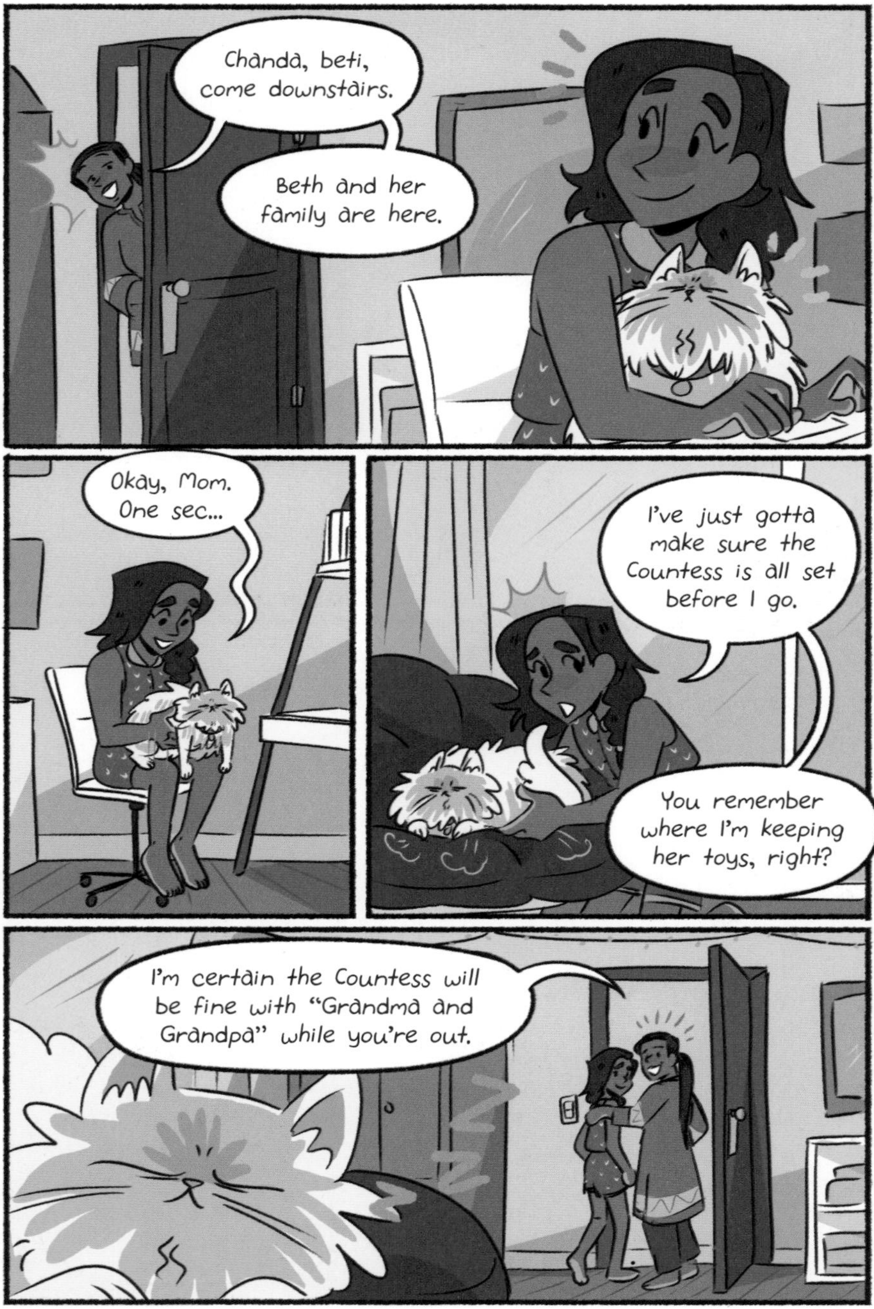
Chanda, beti, come downstairs.
Beth and her family are here.
Okay, Mom. One sec...
I've just gotta make sure the Countess is all set before I go.
You remember where I'm keeping her toys, right?
I'm certain the Countess will be fine with "Grandma and Grandpa" while you're out.

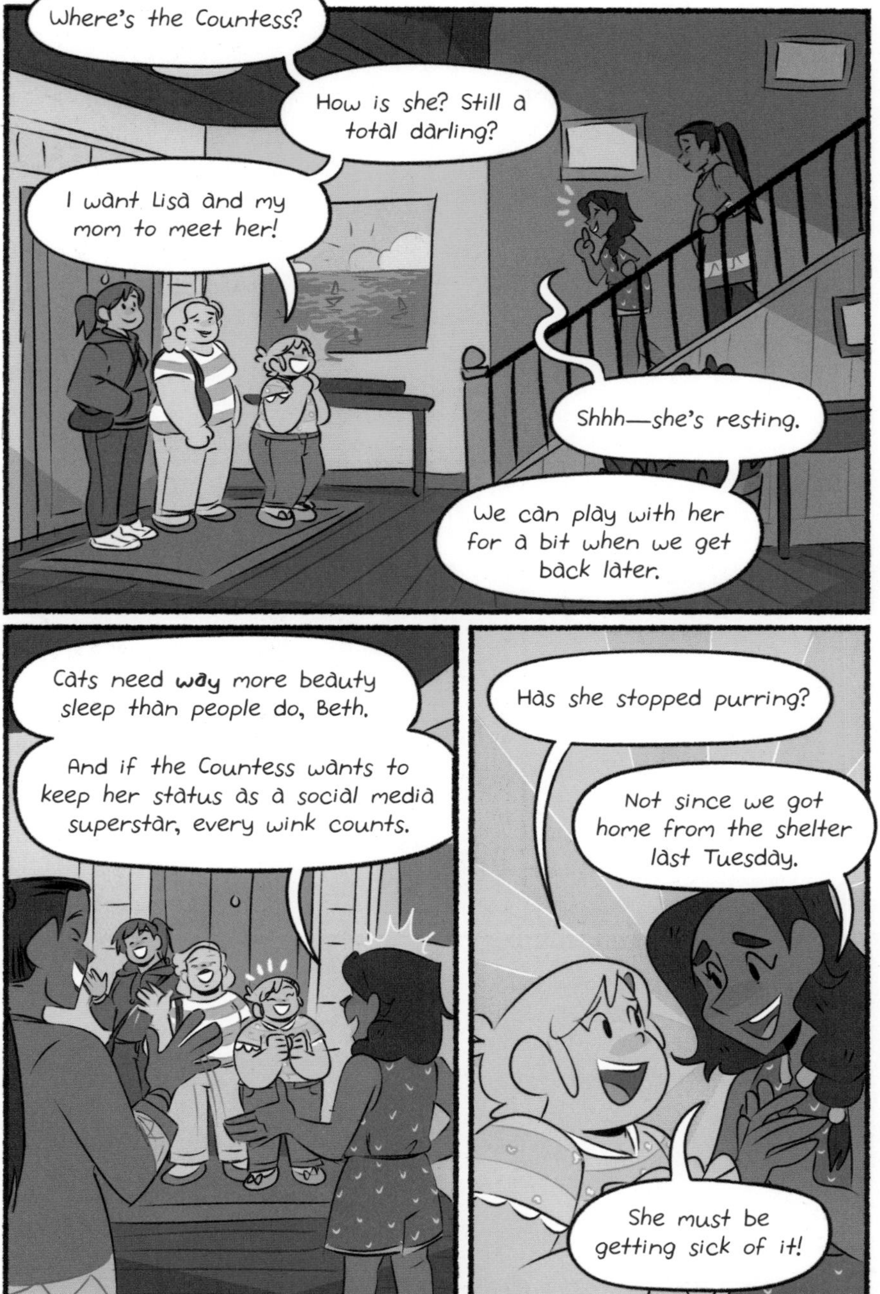
Where's the Countess?
How is she? Still a total darling?
I want Lisa and my mom to meet her!
Shhh—she's resting.
We can play with her for a bit when we get back later.
Cats need **way** more beauty sleep than people do, Beth.
And if the Countess wants to keep her status as a social media superstar, every wink counts.
Has she stopped purring?
Not since we got home from the shelter last Tuesday.
She must be getting sick of it!

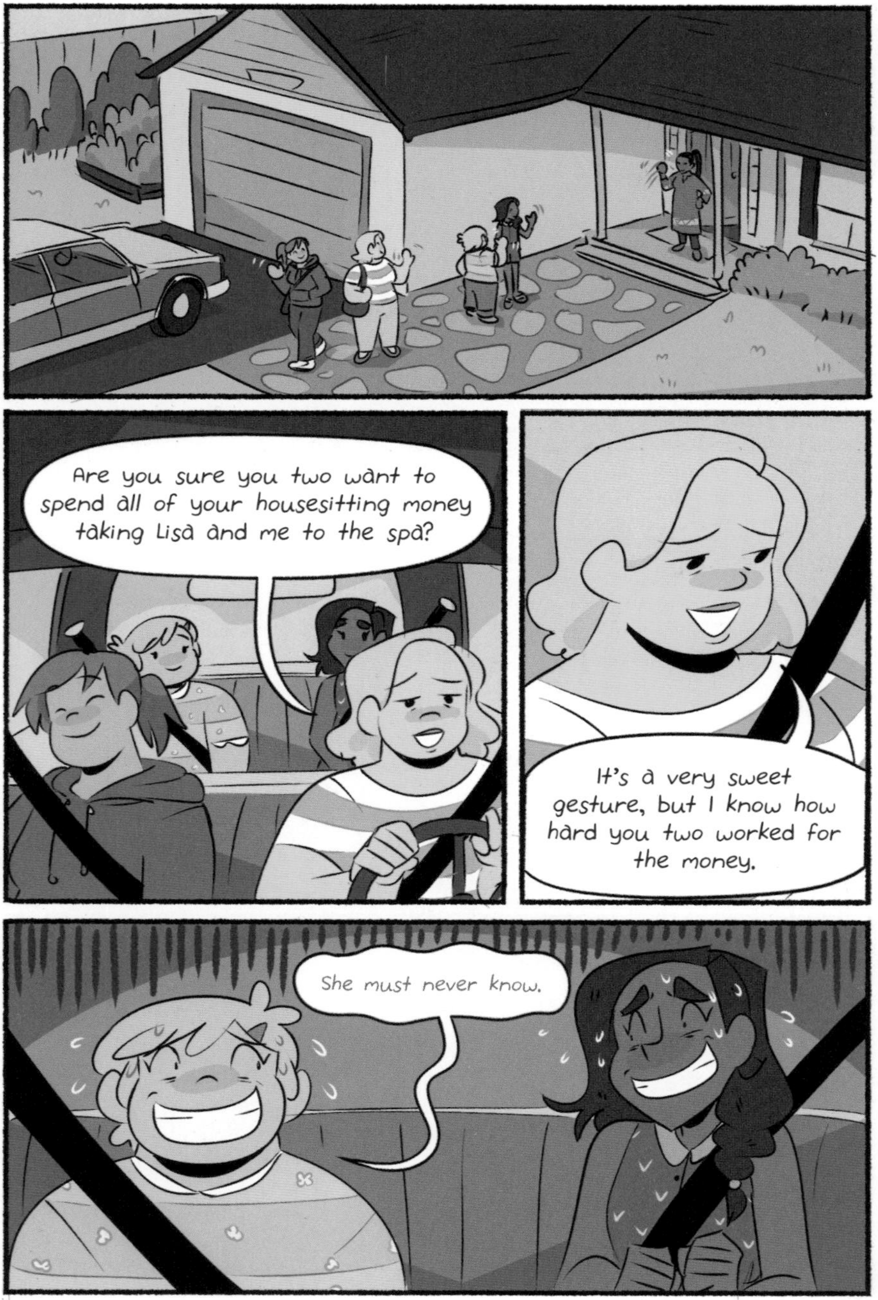
Are you sure you two want to spend all of your housesitting money taking Lisa and me to the spa?
It's a very sweet gesture, but I know how hard you two worked for the money.
She must never know.

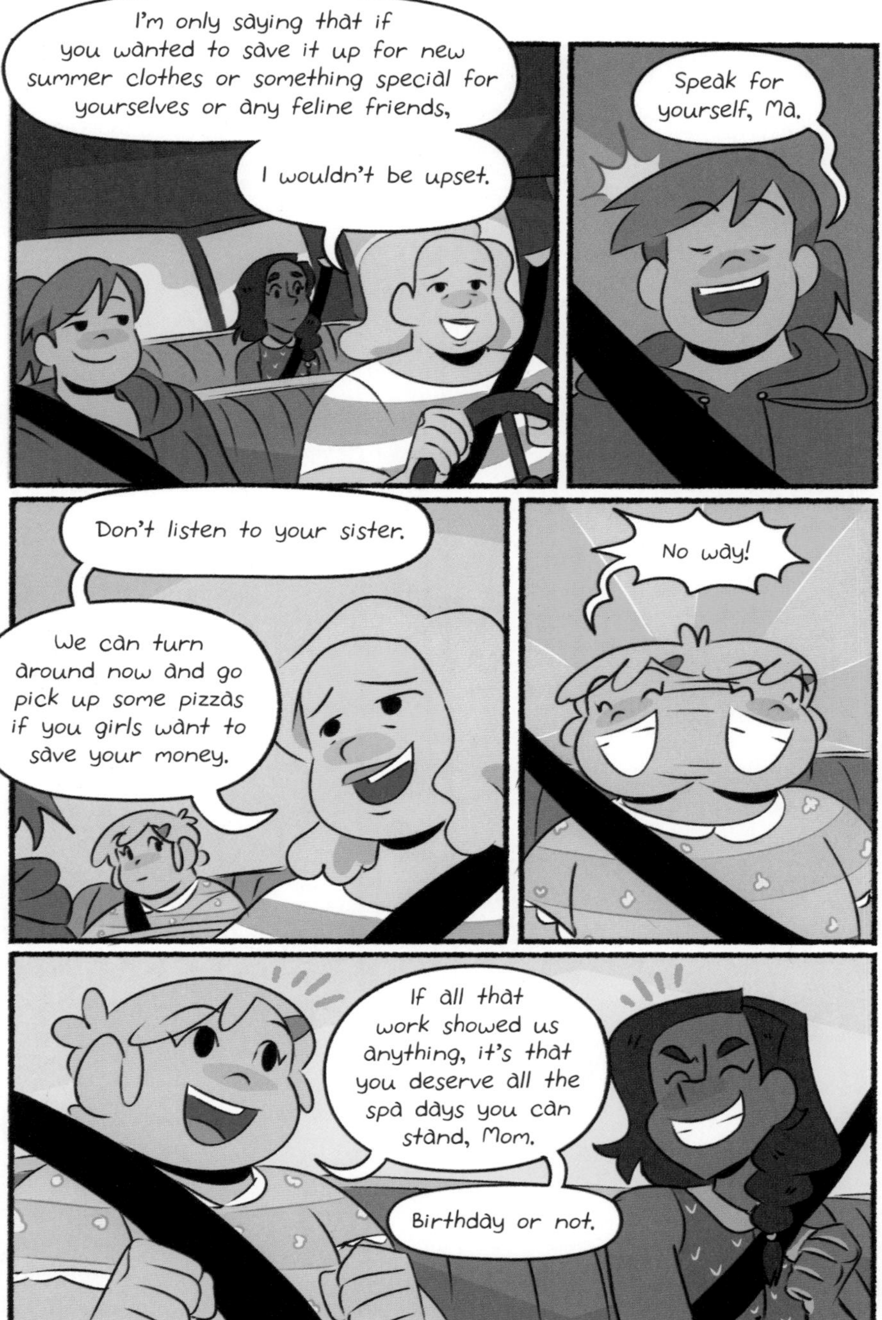
I'm only saying that if you wanted to save it up for new summer clothes or something special for yourselves or any feline friends,
I wouldn't be upset.
Speak for yourself, Ma.
Don't listen to your sister.
We can turn around now and go pick up some pizzas if you girls want to save your money.
No way!
If all that work showed us anything, it's that you deserve all the spa days you can stand, Mom.
Birthday or not.

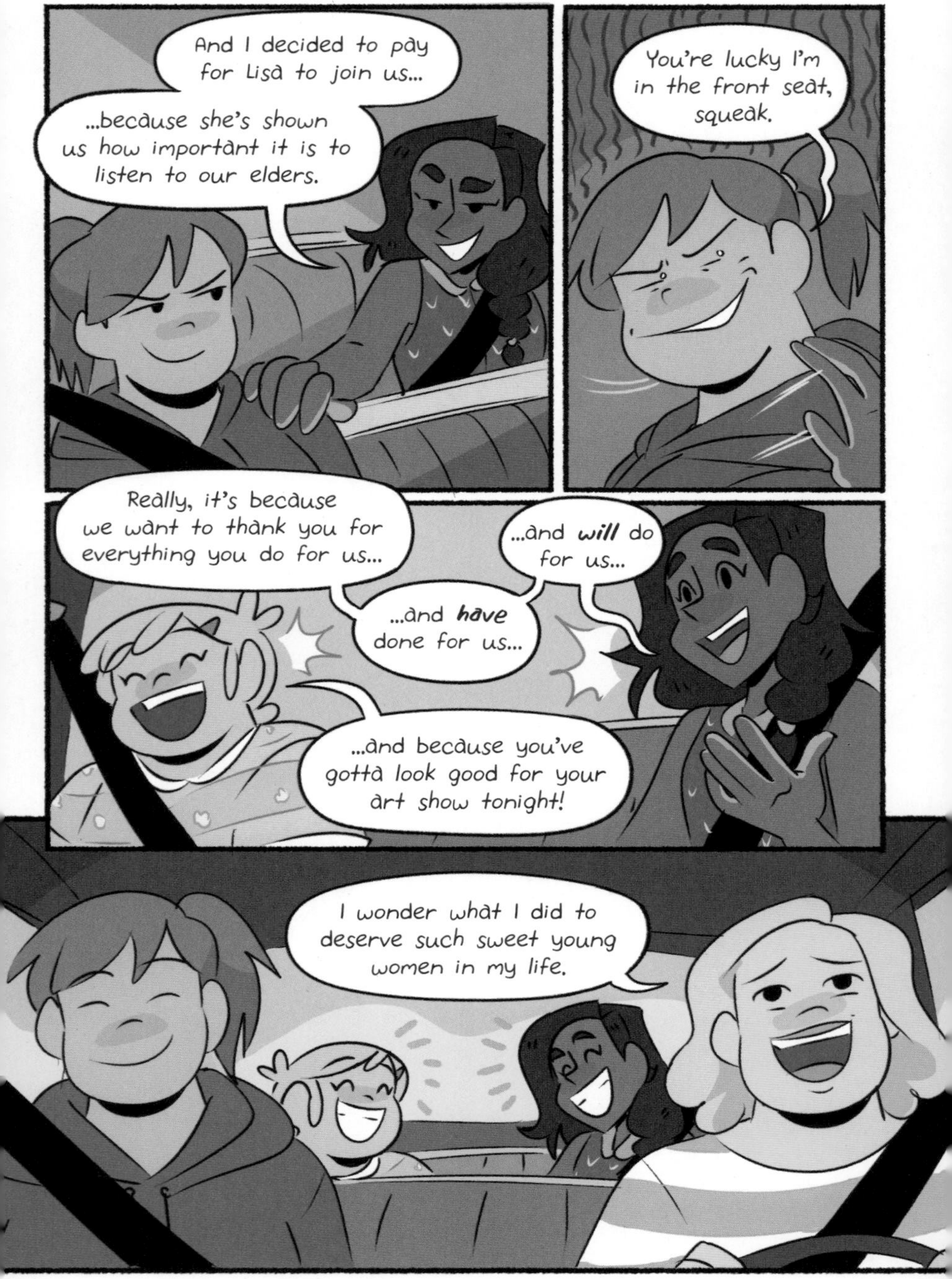
And I decided to pay for Lisa to join us...
...because she's shown us how important it is to listen to our elders.
You're lucky I'm in the front seat, squeak.
Really, it's because we want to thank you for everything you do for us...
...and **have** done for us...
...and **will** do for us...
...and because you've gotta look good for your art show tonight!
I wonder what I did to deserve such sweet young women in my life.

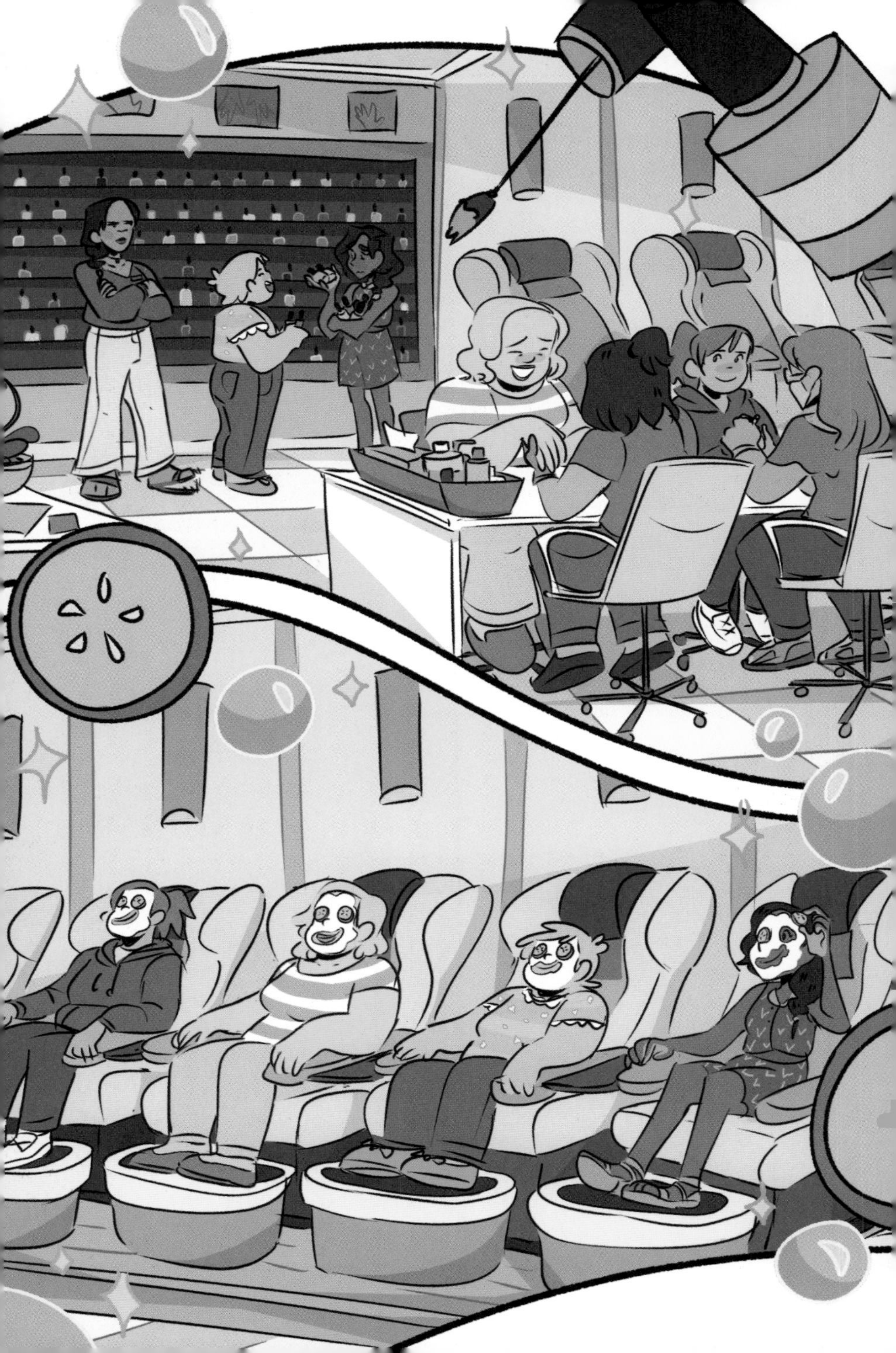

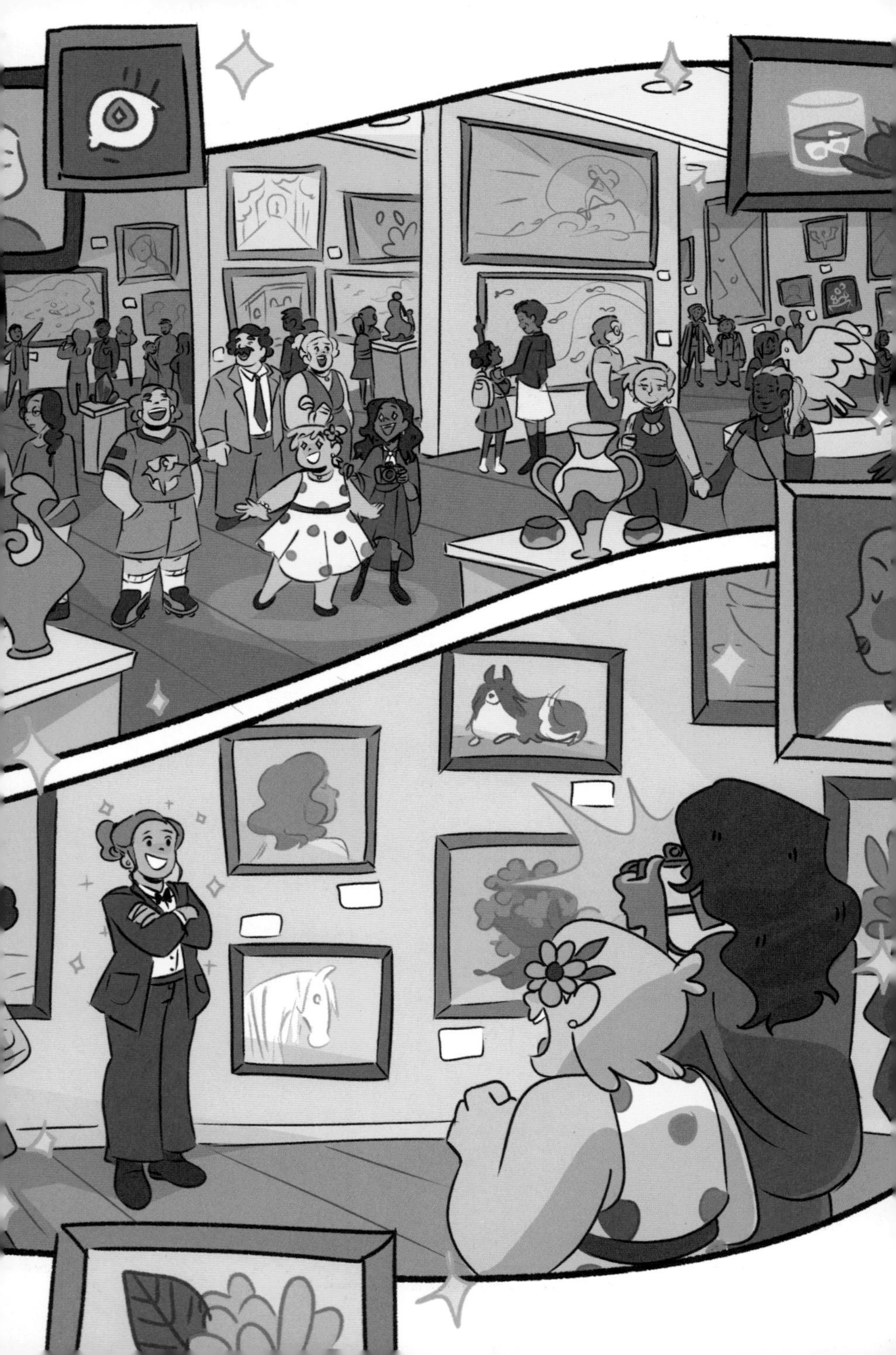

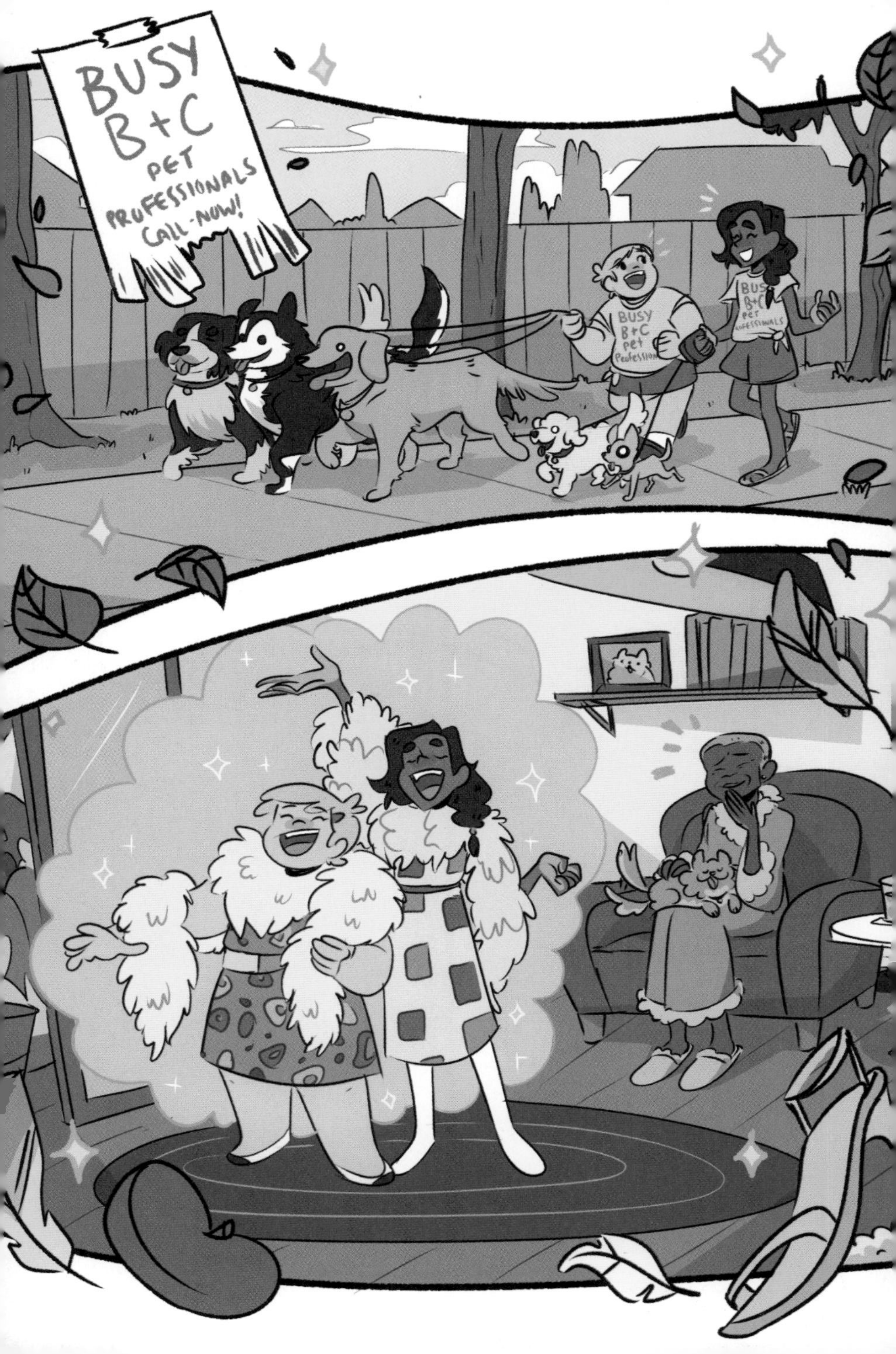
BUSY B+C PET PROFESSIONALS CALL-NOW!
BUSY B+C pet Profession
BUSY B+C pet PROFESSIONALS

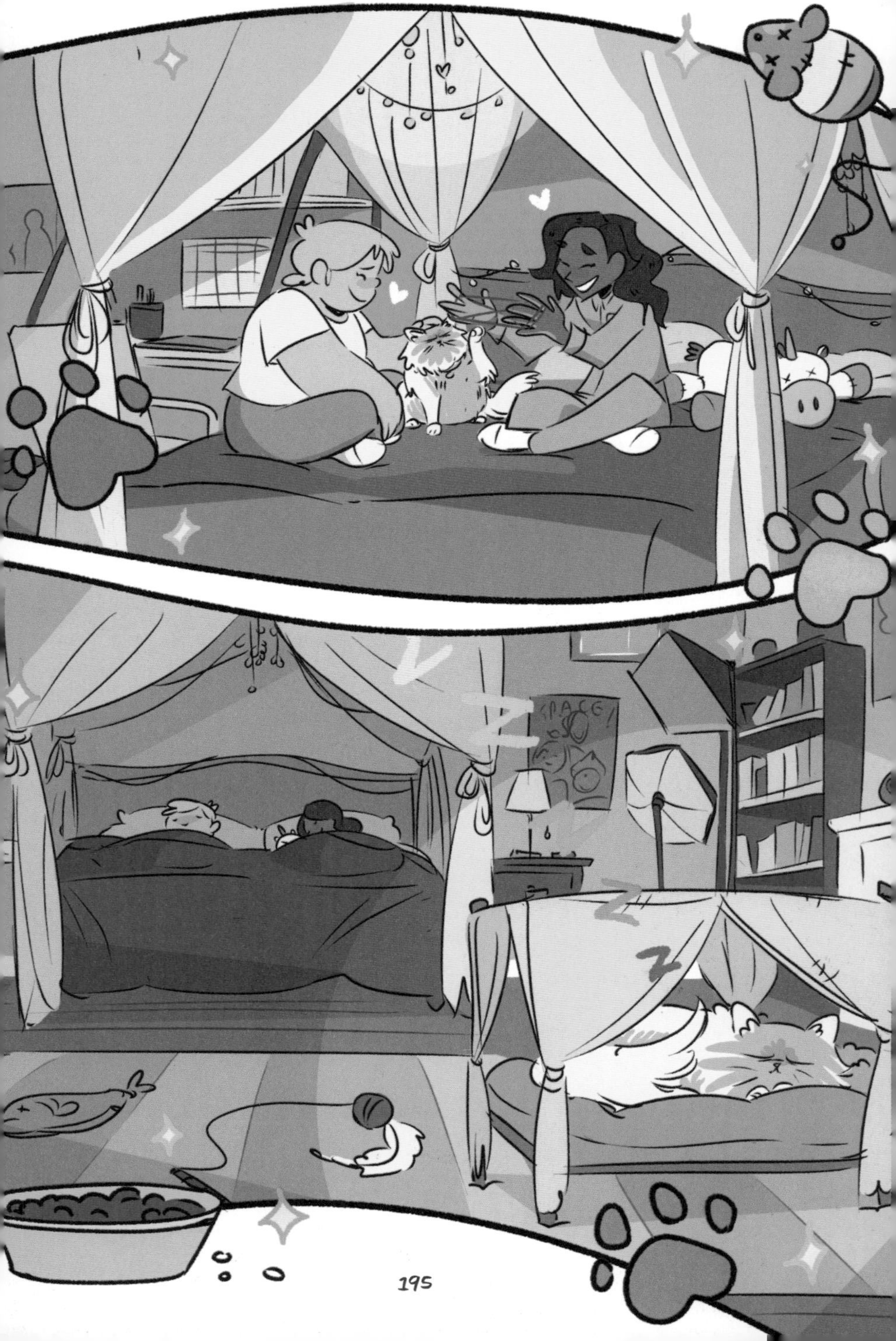
Z
Z
SPACE!
Z
Z

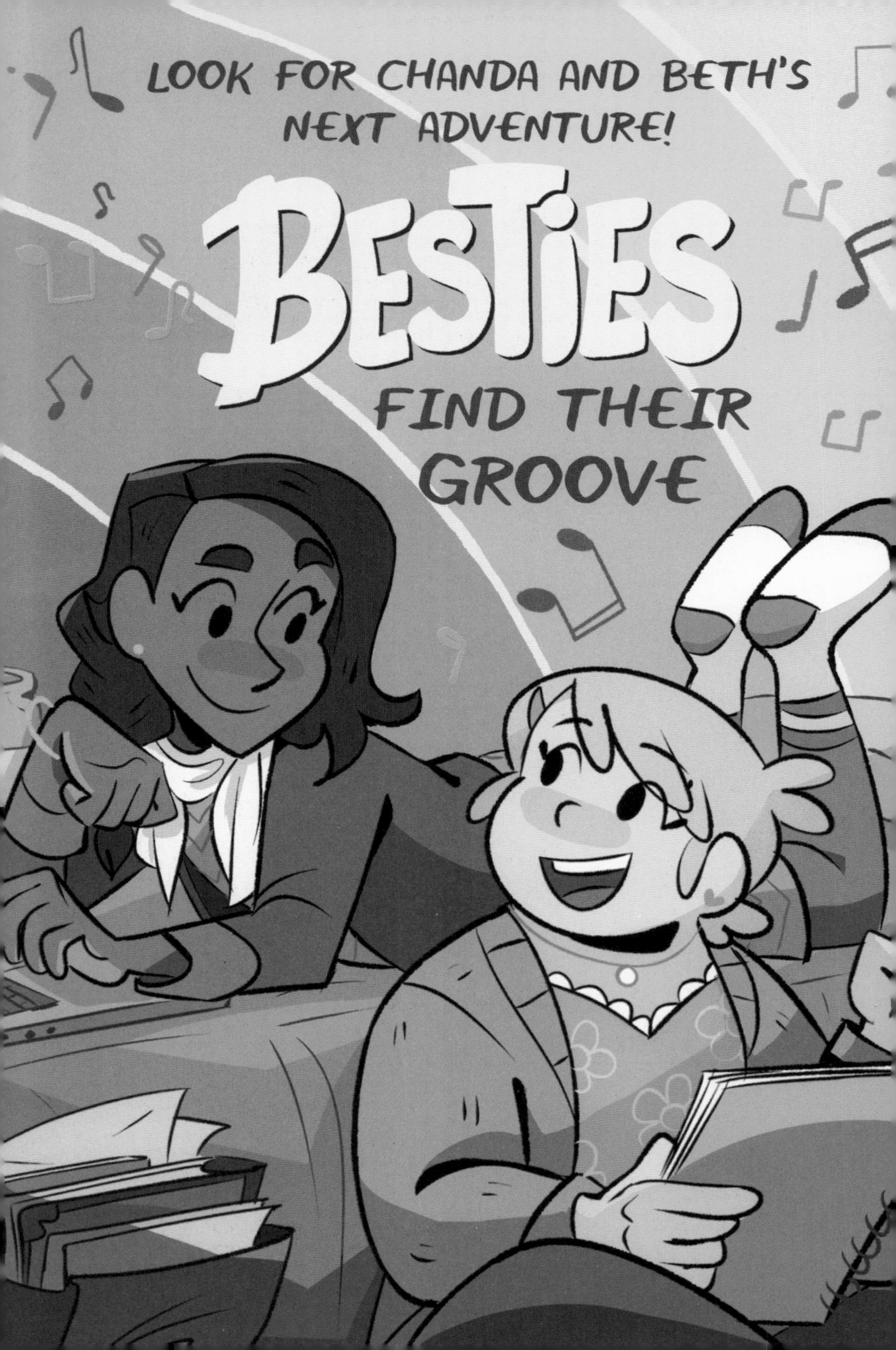
LOOK FOR CHANDA AND BETH'S
NEXT ADVENTURE!
BESTIES
FIND THEIR
GROOVE

Read the *New York Times* best-selling series from

Kayla Miller

A Q&A WITH THE BESTIES TEAM

Q: Could everyone speak to what their role in **Besties** is?

KAYLA: I'm one of the authors, and after a lot of planning with Jeffrey, I write the outline for the story and come back at the end of the process to help tighten up the dialogue and jokes.

JEFFREY: As a coauthor, I develop the story with Kayla and then write the full script.

KRISTINA: I am the main illustrator, so I'm inking and drawing—essentially taking the script and bringing it to life.

DAMALI: I'm the colorist, and it's my job to take all the locals and flesh out the scenes that Kristina draws. Locals, or local colors, are the standard hues you would assign to each object.

Q: Kayla, **Besties** reflects an expansion of the world that you've established in Click. What did you most respond to about directions that Jeffrey took?

KAYLA: I really liked the humor and energy that Jeffrey brought to the story. We wanted the book to have that feeling of when you're a kid or a tween and you're with your best friend and the crazy antics that you get up to. Like a never-ending sleepover! I also enjoyed how Jeffrey took the characters and developed their voices through the dialogue and expanded their personalities.

Jeffrey & Kayla, brainstorming!

Q: What did you most respond to about the direction Kristina took?

KAYLA: How expressive the art is! The facial expressions are big and fun and lively. The attention to detail makes the world of Besties feel really full and lived in.

Q: Jeffrey, were there themes in **Besties** you especially wanted to explore?

JEFFREY: I was most interested in exploring how Beth and Chanda were going to deal with the new concerns in their lives. Money, family, or status can be abstract to younger kids, but when you hit that tween or teenage stage, they become important in your life . . . to the extent that you're concerned with them and your actions start to matter in a new way. Seeing how the girls were going to deal with those new pressures—how they were going to figure out what mattered to them and make the right choices from there—was very fun to explore.

Q: What did you want to bring forward from the Click storytelling?

JEFFREY: The things I like most about Kayla's books are the heart and kindness of them. They're extremely optimistic. They show growth between friends and people. There's not a desire to write people off or give up. So I wanted to bring that here. These girls are not averse to getting into trouble, but there's this core of love that I think is really important.

Q: Jeffrey, can you share some insights into fine-tuning the dialogue?

JEFFREY: It took about half of the first book to figure out what their voices were. There was definitely a lot of going back and revising. It dawned on me that they're kind of like an old comedy duo. They're both funny but in different ways. Beth is more self-effacing. She has a huge heart that I think is her most defining quality, whereas Chanda has somewhat wild schemes that can get them into trouble. They bounce off each other well so that it doesn't seem like they have the same voice, but they have an established dynamic between them.

Q: Kristina, what about *Besties* did you connect with most?

KRISTINA: The thing that touches me about *Besties* and Kayla's books in general is that I can picture myself in my youth or in these exact situations that these girls are in. I feel like I'm channeling the inner twelve-year-old me while I'm working on these books!

Q: How has working on a team been different than working on your webcomic?

KRISTINA: I'm much more used to taking the reins, but in this case there's back and forth. It's nice to have someone to count on to provide another perspective that I haven't considered. For example, how Damali sometimes takes my work in a different direction with colors and it's so much better. I love the cooperative aspect of this because everyone provides the best of what they specialize in, and it becomes something better than what I could have done on my own.

Kristina, inking a page!

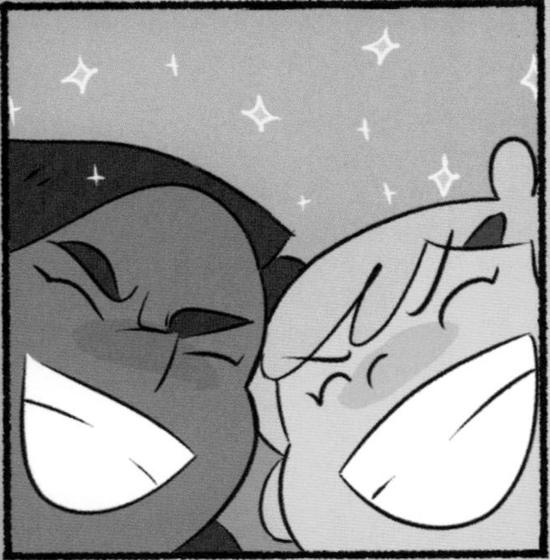

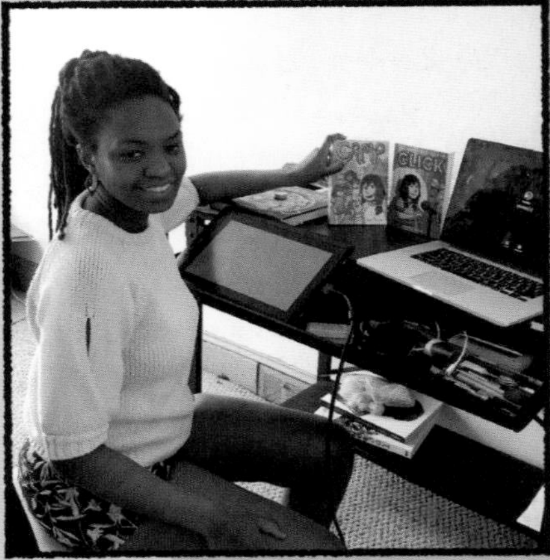
CLICK

Damali, ready to color!

Q: *Damali, could you describe your collaborative process with Kristina?*

DAMALI: The way we've been working so far is that every two weeks I'll get a big batch of pages, somewhere between 16 and 20 pages, and we've come up with a system that breaks down how we do the pages so that it's easiest to edit in a collaborative way. We've made layers, so that if one of us needs to correct a color on a character, it's really easy to pinpoint where that problem area is and correct it. I typically do all the flats at once, which is when you put down the colors of each object, then I come back later on and do things like shading, rounding things out, and tweaking color details, like adding sparkles.

Q: *Damali, can you speak to ways you and Kristina use color to add to the story?*

DAMALI: Color is a really big part of the story. I think a lot in color. I think that the color of ***Besties*** speaks to the vibe that we're giving off in the story. It's very much, you're a tween, it's you and your best friend. Every day your whole world is so lush and full of so many possibilities. I really get that when I read through the story. It reminds me of my own childhood and my own bestie! So the way that we play with color, the way that we make everything bright, the way that we make things pop—especially when it comes to outdoor spaces, Ms. Langford's house, the outfits that the girls get to wear—it's all a reflection of the vibrancy and the excitement with which they approach their world, just like their relationships.

Q: Do you have a favorite scene in the book?

KAYLA: I have two favorite scenes. I really like the second lamp break where Baxter is running in circles around the room and jumping on everything. I haven't had a lot of chances with the Click books to write physical comedy, so it was fun figuring out each thing that needed to happen for that lamp to smash. That was the only scene Jeffrey and I wrote together, and it involved me running around the house and showing how Baxter would do this, and then Beth would lean like that, so it was just a really fun experience of writing that scene. As far as my favorite scene in the finished book . . . I really like the dressing up in Ms. Langford's closet scene. It reminds me of all the dressing room montages in movies from the 1990s and early 2000s. It's just so fun and brings me back to my childhood.

JEFFREY: My favorite scene is their final odd job being entertainers at the birthday party. I enjoyed writing the song, for one. The costumes—everything about it was a joy to squeeze in there at the end.

KRISTINA: My favorite scene is actually one of the sadder parts of the book, when the girls are fighting and they go to school. There's something about that part that really got me like, wow, I know exactly what this feeling is, because we've all been there. We've all had a fight with our sibling, or our best friend at school, or one of our classmates. And you feel that almost-physical woe, especially when you're young. It becomes so tangible. You guys did a really good job of writing that down, so making that part in the book was super fun, but also touching in a way. I'm having fun the whole time, so it was just kind of a switch when I got to this part. It was like, *whoa!*

DAMALI: I like the scenes with Lisa in them. I'm also an older sister and I find her relatable. After the girls confess about what happened at Ms. Langford's house and she was like, "OK, you can't do that. You can't break people's stuff and you can't wear their clothes when they're not around"—that was my thought when I saw that dress-up montage. *That's fun, but those aren't your clothes!*

Q: Do you have something you're hoping readers will take away from the book?

KAYLA: I always come back to how I want my readers to communicate with other people. So many of the problems that we face are misunderstandings that come about because we're not expressing ourselves clearly. So I think sharing your problems with others, talking with other people, and communicating clearly could help a lot of situations.

JEFFREY: I want to add on to what Kayla said, because that's true even in a best friend relationship. This book is very much about how you need to nourish that relationship. We can fall into thinking that your best friend is your best friend—you don't necessarily need to worry about them, they're always going to be there— but that might not be the case, especially if you don't make the effort to figure out where your best friend is at. There are these little moments of miscommunication or omitted communication between Beth and Chanda that they learn to work through. It makes their friendship stronger.

KRISTINA: I think the main lesson is that, overall, friendship takes work, and just because something gets bad doesn't mean it's always going to stay bad. The most wonderful relationships and friendships you have may face big conflict or have some problems that aren't always easy to navigate. But working through it is so worth it. Even when things feel really tough or uncomfortable, making the effort to figure things out can only make your friendships stronger.

A PAGE FROM START TO FINISH

A look at the first thumbnails from the authors

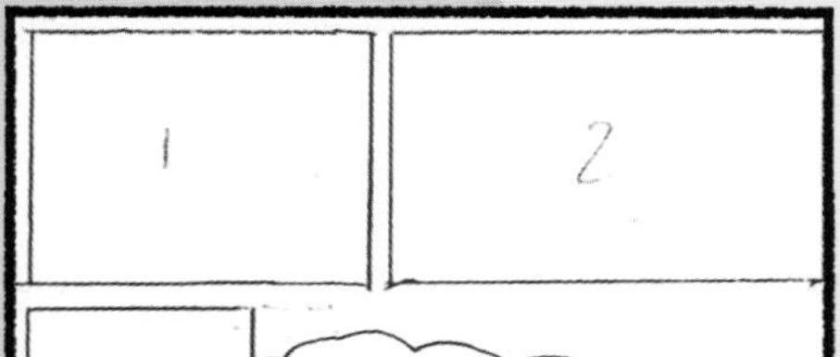
1
2
3

Then over to Kristina!

Sketches

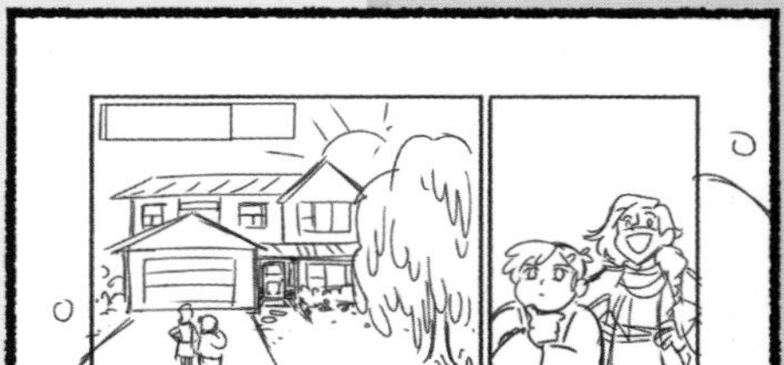
Limón
LiMON

Inks

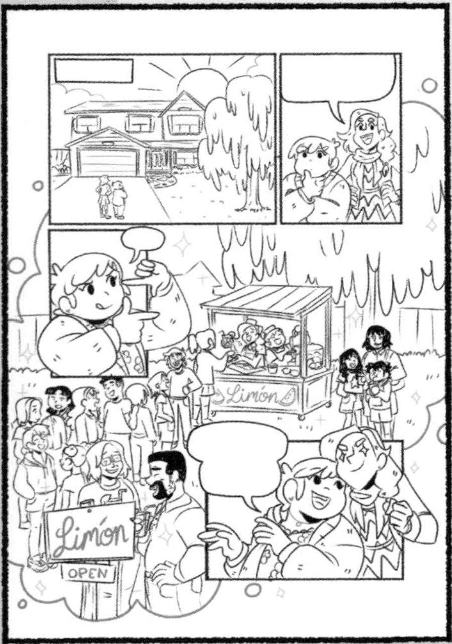
Limón
Limón
OPEN

Finished color

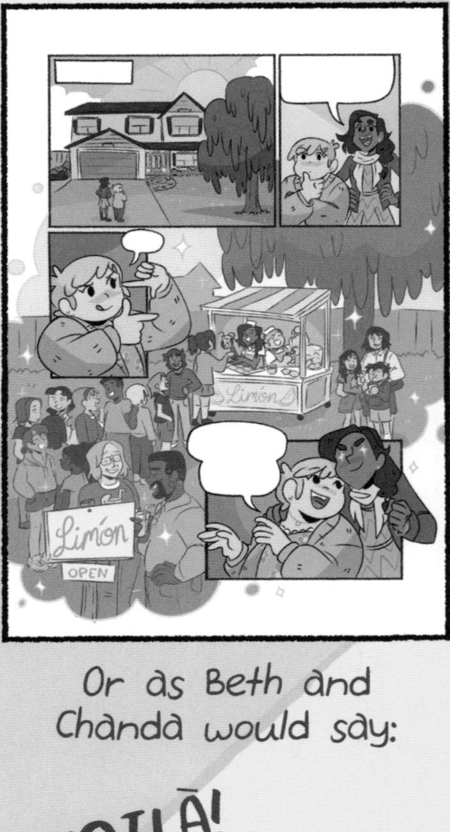
Limón
Limón
OPEN

Or as Beth and Chanda would say:

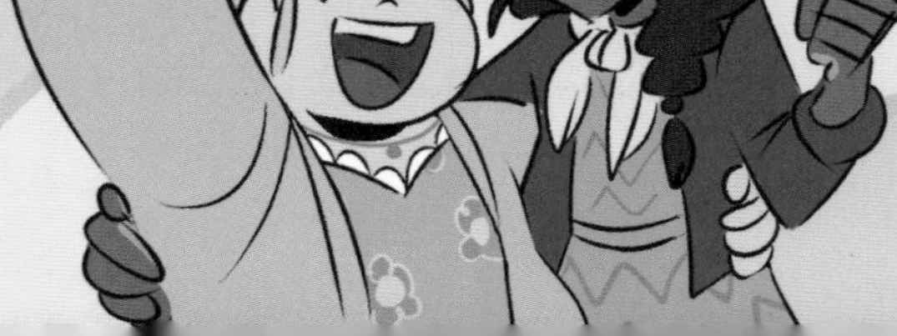
VOILÀ!

DESIGNING BETH & CHANDA

Kristina's initial drawings. She upped the stylish duo's fashion game as she developed the characters.

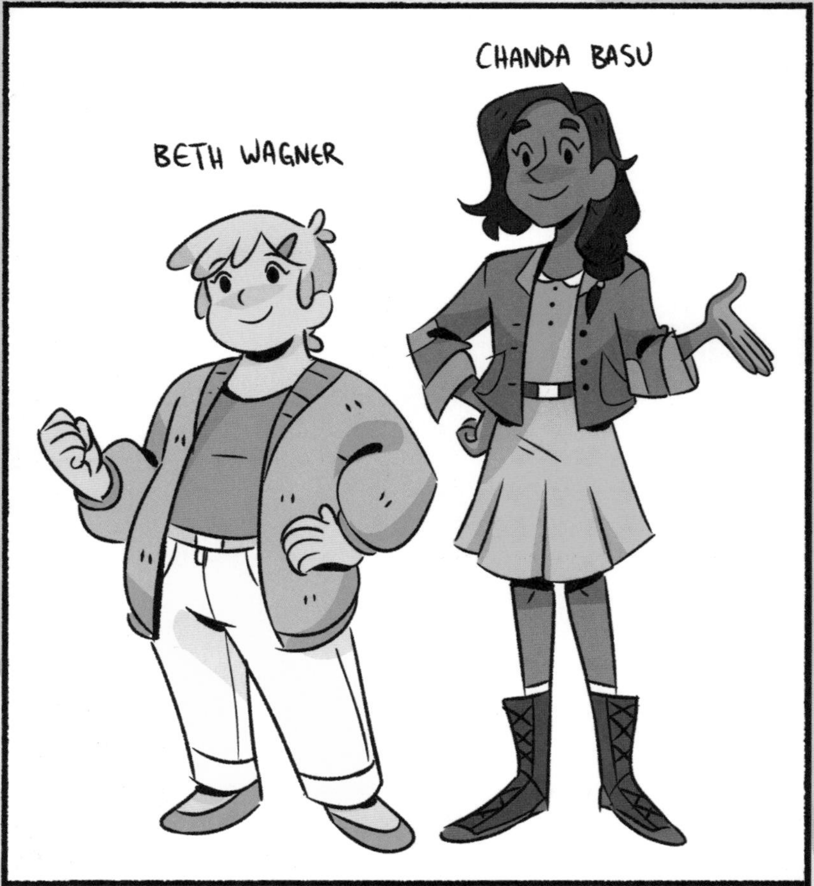
CHANDA BASU
BETH WAGNER

Kristina's initial character
lineup of Beth and her family

Kristina's initial character lineup of
Chanda, her family, Ms. Langford, and Baxter

ACKNOWLEDGMENTS

We would like to thank everyone at HMH for giving us the opportunity to expand the world of Click. Particular thanks go to our editor, Mary, whose enthusiasm and helpful guidance have been invaluable while exploring the lives of these vibrant besties.

We'd also like to thank our agent, Elizabeth, for always having our backs.

And of course, all the thanks in the universe to our stellar creative team: designers Andy and Stephanie, letterer Lor, colorist Damali, and absolute superstar/illustrator Kristina. Your hard work and creativity have made *Besties* into the sparkling, sleepover-filled, dance party–infused celebration of friendship we dreamed of.

Lastly, we would like to thank our family and friends for their constant support. Kayla would like to thank Mom, Dad, Grandpa, K, William, and Tyler. Jeffrey would like to thank Karen and Brad.

—*Kayla & Jeffrey*

I'd like to thank the amazing team behind *Besties* for all the love, patience, and support they've poured into this book. *Besties* is my published comics debut, so I am honoured to be trusted with this wonderful series. I couldn't be more proud of what we've accomplished, and I hope you all feel the same way too. A huge thank-you to Kayla and Jeffrey for being an incredible duo to work alongside. You've been both an inspiration and the ultimate cheerleaders from the first page to the last brushstroke. Also, a big thank-you to Damali for just being utterly fantastic. Your colours make the world feel so lush and vibrant and take my drawings to a whole new level. I'd also like to send a thank-you to my agent, Britt Siess, for helping me every step of the way and just being a star. Everyone's collective efforts have made this book into something truly special, and I'll treasure it forever.

And finally, I'd like to thank all my wonderful friends and family who inspire me every day, keep me going, and are simply incredible people. Thank you, Mom, Dad, and Bryan, for always believing in me and giving me phở when I needed it most. And lastly, a huge thank-you to my friends, at home, online, and across the globe. Your support and faith in me over the years have carried me from my humble webcomic beginnings to my first book on the shelf. So gosh, thank you for believing in this little worm after all these years!

—*Kristina*

GRAPHIC NOVELS FOR EVERY READER!

CLASH
by
KAYLA MILLER

SHERLOCK BONES
AND THE SEA-CREATURE FEATURE
RENÉE TREML

PARANORTHERN
AND THE CHAOS BUNNY A-HOP-CALYPSE
WRITTEN BY STEPHANIE COOKE
ART BY MARI COSTA

Timo the Adventurer
JONATHAN GARNIER • YOHAN SACRÉ

OH MY GODS!
BY Stephanie Cooke AND Insha Fitzpatrick
ART BY Juliana Moon

DINO MIGHTY!
BY DOUG PALEO
ILLUSTRATED BY AARON BLECHA

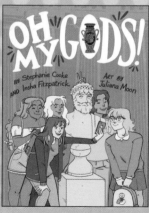